I0802942

The Merril Theory of Lit'ry Criticism

Published by Aqueduct Press
PO Box 95787
Seattle, WA 98145-2787
www.aqueductpress.com

The essay "What Do You Mean: Science? Fiction?" (Parts 1 and 2) published by permission of *Extrapolation*. The essay was originally published as two parts in the Liverpool University Press Journal *Extrapolation* – Volume 7 (May, 1966) and Volume 8 (December, 1966).

9 8 7 6 5 4 3 2 1

ISBN: 978-1-61976-093-6
Library of Congress Control Number: 2015952444

Cover Illustration by Anna Tambour
Book Design by Kathryn Wilham

Printed in the USA by Thomson-Shore Inc.

About the Aqueduct Press Heirloom Books

Aqueduct Press's series of Heirloom Books aims to bring back into print and preserve work that has helped make feminist science fiction what it is today—work that though clearly of its time is still pleasurable to read, work that is thought-provoking, work that can still speak powerfully to readers. The series takes its name from the seeds of older strains of vegetables, so valuable and in danger of being lost. Our hope is to keep these books from being lost, as works that do not make it into the canon so often are.

~L. Timmel Duchamp

Acknowledgments: Original Publications

The Year's Greatest Science Fiction and Fantasy, First Annual Edition. New *York:* Dell, *1956.*

The Year's Greatest Science Fiction and Fantasy, Second Annual Edition. New York: Dell, 1957.

The Year's Greatest Science Fiction and Fantasy, Third Annual Edition. New York: Dell, 1958.

The Year's Greatest Science Fiction and Fantasy, Fourth Annual Edition. New York: Dell, 1959.

The Year's Best S-F, Fifth Annual Edition. New York: Dell, 1960.

The Year's Best S-F, Sixth Annual Edition. New York: Dell, 1961.

The Year's Best S-F, Seventh Annual Edition New York: Dell, 1962.

The Year's Best S-F, Eighth Annual Edition. New York: Dell, 1963.

The Year's Best S-F, Ninth Annual Edition. New York: Dell, 1964.

The Year's Best S-F, Tenth Annual Edition. New York: Dell, 1965.

The Year's Best S-F, Eleventh Annual Edition. New York: Dell, 1966.

SF 12. New York: Dell, 1968.

"Theodore Sturgeon," *Fantasy and Science Fiction*, September 1962: 46-55.

"Fritz Leiber," *The Magazine of Fantasy and Science Fiction* (July 1969): 44-61.

"What Do You Mean: Science? Fiction?" *Extrapolation: Journal of Science Fiction and Fantasy Studies*, Part I, 7 (May 1966): 30-46, and Part II, 8 (December 1966): 2-19.

"Books" Columns. *The Magazine of Fantasy and Science Fiction* (March 1965 – February 1969).

Heirloom Series

Number 4

The Merril Theory of Lit'ry Criticism: Judith Merril's Nonfiction

Judith Merril

edited and with an introduction by

Ritch Calvin

Expanded E-book Free with Purchase

Thank you for purchasing this volume. A copy of the expanded e-book version is included in your purchase.

For your complimentary copy, write to info@aqueductpress.com, with the subject header "The Merril Theory of Lit'ry Criticism," and in the body of the email, one of the following codes:

- MerrilMOBI (for a mobi edition)
- MerrilEPUB (for the epub edition)
- MerrilPDF (for a pdf edition).

Short descriptions of the essays that are only in the e-book are included in this print book.

Contents

1 Introduction: The SF Aesthetics of Judith Merril
Ritch Calvin

17 *S-F: The Year's Greatest Science-Fiction and Fantasy,* First Annual Edition (1956)

23 *S-F: The Year's Greatest Science-Fiction and Fantasy,* Second Annual Edition (1957)

26 *SF: The Year's Greatest Science-Fiction and Fantasy,* Third Annual Edition (1958)

28 *SF: The Year's Greatest Science-Fiction and Fantasy,* Fourth Annual Edition (1959)

32 *The Year's Best S-F,* Fifth Annual Edition (1960)

37 *The Year's Best S-F,* Sixth Annual Edition (1961)

40 Theodore Sturgeon (September 1962)†

41 *The Year's Best S-F,* Seventh Annual Edition (1962)

46 *The Year's Best S-F,* Eighth Annual Edition (1963)

52 *The Year's Best S-F,* Ninth Annual Edition (1964)

59 Books (March 1965)

65 Books (April 1965)

69 Books (May 1965)

75 *The Year's Best S-F,* Tenth Annual Edition (1965)

88 Books (June 1965)

92 Books (July 1965)

98 Books (August 1965)†

99 Books (September 1965)

† Full text in the E-book version.

103 Books (October 1965)
109 Books (November 1965)
115 Books (January 1966)
122 Books (February 1966)
127 Books (March 1966)
137 Books (April 1966)
143 What Do You Mean? Science? Fiction? Part I (May 1966)
161 Books (May 1966)
166 *The Year's Best S-F,* Eleventh Annual Edition (1966)
173 Books (June 1966)
178 Books (July 1966)
182 What Do You Mean? Science? Fiction? Part II (August 1966)
203 Books (August 1966)
216 Books (September 1966)
221 Books (November 1966)
226 Books (December 1966)
232 Books (January 1967)
237 Books (February 1967)
242 Books (March 1967)
248 Books (May 1967)
254 Books (June 1967)†
255 Books (August 1967)†
256 Books (September 1967)
262 Books (November 1967)
270 Books (December 1967)
276 Books (February 1968)
281 Books (March 1968)†

282 Books (May 1968)
287 Books (June 1968)
294 *SF 12* (1968 hb, 1969 pb)
297 Books (August 1968)
305 Books (September 1968)
311 Books (November 1968)
318 Books (January 1969)
328 Books (February 1969)
332 Fritz Leiber (July 1969)

Introduction: The SF Aesthetics of Judith Merril
Ritch Calvin

Most of the science-fiction-labeled novels I see are either unreadable or totally forgettable, and even the small balance remaining—the books I feel are worth at least mentioning here—can claim nothing more than competence in execution combined with a clever concept somewhere or a colorful image somewhere else, or maybe even both together. I can understand why people want to read them, but not at all why anyone wants to write them.

(Judith Merril, "Books," May 1968)

Maybe what s-f really stands for is Space Fish?

(Judith Merril, *Twelfth Annual Edition*, 1968)

Biography of Judith Merril

The writer Judith Merril was born Josephine Juliet Grossman in Boston, Massachusetts, in January of 1923. She was born to the son of a renowned rabbi and avid Zionist, and Judith shared her grandfather's Zionist beliefs until age 16. After her father committed suicide, she and her mother relocated to the Bronx, NY. By Merril's own account, she came to literature (mainstream and SF) late in life, but she threw herself into it. In her "autobiography," *Better to Have Loved*, she writes that "My mother had raised me to be a man.... She never trained me to hide my light. I was encouraged to argue analytically, to assert my opinions, to demonstrate in every possible way how smart I was."

Her first daughter, Merril Zissman, was born in 1942. Four years later, Judith was encouraged by Ted Sturgeon to take a pen name, and she decided to use her daughter's name (though it took some convincing before she did—including a Petrarchan sonnet entitled, "On the Birth of Judith Merril!").

Merril was always politically engaged, and her book reviews and Year's-best summations often reflected the political issues of the day. But the

Vietnam war and the events in Chicago at the Democratic National Convention in the summer of 1968 profoundly disturbed her. In one of her final "Books" columns (January 1969), she laments that so many of the books seem far removed from the pressing realities of the day. Shortly thereafter, she and her daughter Ann moved to Canada. Two years later, in 1970, she donated her extensive science fiction collection to the Toronto Public Library and founded the Spaced Out Library, which was renamed the Judith Merril Collection of Science Fiction, Speculation, and Fantasy in 1991. In 1996, at the age of 73, she was a Guest of Honor at the annual WisCon conference in Madison, Wisconsin. (For more on Judith Merril and her life, see *Better to Have Loved*, the "autobiography" that was written in collaboration with her granddaughter, Emily Pohl-Weary.)

Judy Merril died in Canada in September 1997.

Works/Career

In comparison with some of the other standout writers within the science fiction pantheon, Merril produced a limited number of texts. Her first novel, *Shadow on the Hearth,* was published in 1950, and her second novel, *The Tomorrow People*, in 1960. In between, she wrote and published several novels with C. M. Kornbluth under the collective pseudonym of Cyril Judd, including *Gunner Cade* (1952) and *Outpost Mars* (1952).

She produced more short fiction than novels, publishing thirty stories between her first publication, "That Only a Mother" (1948), and her last, "The Future of Happiness" (1979). These stories include such well known and often-anthologized stories as "Survival Ship" (1951), "Daughters of Earth" (1952), and "The Deep Down Dragon" (1961).

In total, nearly all of Merril's *fiction* was written and published between 1952 and 1963. In 1956, she began to shift her focus from writing to editing and to reviewing. By 1963, nearly all of her writing was nonfiction. One could approach the literary aesthetics of Judith Merril from the vantage point of her fiction (e.g., see Newell and Lamont's *Judith Merril: A Critical Study*); however, I suggest that Merril explicitly developed her literary aesthetic within her nonfiction. In her book reviews, anthology introductions, and critical essays, Merril worked through and developed over time a theory of what constitutes "science fiction," and good science fiction, at that. In this Introduction, then, I would like to focus on Merril's nonfiction in order to tease out and articulate Merril's definition of the SF genre (and I use that abbreviation purposefully), her criteria for the works within the genre, and her standards of enjoyment and pleasure for the genre. In addition, I will focus on Merril's review work because not only was she one of the few female reviewers, editors, and anthologizers at the time (think of Boucher, Carnell, Moorcock, Knight, Pohl, etc.) but also she was enormously influential. Indeed, some saw Merril as the champion and leader of the New Wave (or, as she called it, "The New Thing") in the United States.

I will draw largely on three sources of material: the thirty-eight (semi) monthly "Books" columns that she wrote for *The Magazine of Fantasy & Science Fiction* between March of 1965 and February of 1969; the "Introductions" and "Summations" from her twelve Year's Best S-F anthology series that ran from 1956 to 1968 (the anthology series was a continuous series, even though the name changed slightly over time); and a number of other essays that she wrote in which she addresses the question of science fiction writing, including tributes to Fritz Leiber (1969)and Ted Sturgeon (1962) and an essay entitled, "What Do You Mean: Science? Fiction?" that appeared as two parts in *Extrapolation* in May and August 1966.

Definitions of SF

Defining SF is a can of worms. Hundreds of different definitions have been offered—and a hundred and one refutations. Indeed, Istvan Csicsery-Ronay calls SF "notoriously difficult to define" (3), and Carl Freedman notes that "No definitional consensus exists" (13). Nevertheless, a number of well-known and oft-employed definitions are in circulation. For example, in *Pilgrims through Space and Time* (1947), J. O. Bailey writes that "The touchstone for scientific fiction, then, is that it describes an imaginary invention or discovery in the natural sciences. The most serious pieces of this fiction arise from speculation about what may happen if science makes an extraordinary discovery." Similarly, in "The Future of Science Fiction" (1953), Reginald Bretnor offers three definitions of SF, including works that demonstrate the author's awareness of the scientific method as a "human function," those works that demonstrate this awareness only in "plot and circumstance," and those in which the author is "aware only of certain potential *products* of the scientific method" (273). Several years later, Kingsley Amis defines SF in *New Maps of Hell* (1960) as "that class of prose narrative treating of a situation that could not arise in the world we know, but which is hypothesized on the basis of some innovation in science or technology, or pseudo-technology, whether human or extra-terrestrial in origin" (18). Finally, in his *Metamorphoses of Science Fiction* (1979), Darko Suvin calls science fiction the "literature of cognitive estrangement" and focuses, in part, on the ways in which the constructed world of the fiction differs from the world of the author and reader. (While I'm fully aware of more recent works that discuss genre as methods of reading, as processes, as sets of expectations, these were definitions in circulation while Merril was writing and against which Merril was working.)

Merril read widely in literature, science, SF, and SF criticism, and she was excited by the critical work on science fiction then emerging. She read Scholes and Amis (though she railed against much of what the latter said). She took note of the special topics panel held at a Modern Language Association (MLA) conference in 1962, and she read—and was published in—*Extrapolation*, a journal of SF criticism that grew out of that panel. She had certainly read both Reginald Bretnor, and his thinking influenced hers greatly, as she freely acknowledged. Writer, editor, and critic Anthony Boucher sometimes defined science fiction as "the literature of disciplined imagination" (quoted in Merril and Pohl-Weary 14), and Merril herself used this definition in her Eighth Annual best-of anthology (1963) and her "Books" column of April 1965—though she very quickly abandoned it as unsatisfactory. Instead, her working definition became ever broader in its inclusiveness. Like Bretnor, she came to see SF as "universal" (Bretnor 273).

Indeed, according to Carl Freedman in *Critical Theory and Science Fiction* (2000), science fiction defined broadly could be taken to include all travel literature, modern and postmodern utopian writing, and the epics poets Dante and Milton (15). He further suggests that "all fiction is...science fiction"; further, he writes, "Fiction is a subcategory of science fiction" (16)—an idea that Merril directly rejects. So, in many ways, Merril's working definition of the genre was in line with the thinking of the day.

However, in his *Seven Beauties of Science Fiction* (2008), Csicsery-Ronay shifts the definition from one of object to one of method; Merril often suggests a similar idea. For example, in her "Books" column from April 1965, she writes: "The most basic ingredient of all is a way of thinking. *Science* is not technology, or laboratories, or thick books of data tables; it is a *method.* The trappings of technology do not make science fiction; neither does the traditionally supernatural make a fantasy." She continues in the same column: "The specific for science fiction is the application of the logic *to* the imagination." So, we will see that she, like so many others, struggles with the definition of SF as an object of inquiry. She eventually comes to argue that SF is a way of thinking and writing about the world; it is a *mode* of approaching an object, not the object itself.

Merril's Working Definition of SF

As noted above, attempting to pin down a definition of SF from Judith Merril is also a bit of a fool's errand. As Elizabeth Cummings points out in her essay in *Extrapolation* (1994), Merril redefined SF nearly every month in her "Books" column as she thought and rethought about the previous month's definition. Her definition was always in flux. Merril herself notes in her introductory comments to the (in?)famous anthology *England Swings SF* (1968) that the collection of works by the these writers is "an action-photo, a record of process-in-change," and, consequently, her definition of SF varied along with the writers' practices. And, yet, in order for Merril to offer her monthly and annual evaluations of books and stories, she had to have had a working definition of the genre. As Merril concludes in her *Eleventh Annual Edition* (1966), "It gets a little more difficult each year to decide which ones are *really* science fiction—and frankly I don't much try any more" (9).

First off, Merril played fast and loose with the term she employed. Although she sometimes used the term "science fiction," she was more likely to use the term "science fantasy." This was another term that she learned and borrowed from Tony Boucher, and using "science fantasy" offered, in her view, a bit more latitude in the kinds of texts that she could include. For Merril, a "science fiction" text needed to be logical and predicated upon science—at least as it was understood at the time. She was fascinated by scientific development, and she reviewed many science books in her regular columns. [Unfortunately, this volume leaves out all of her science writing.] Whereas the SF writers of the Golden Age may well have drawn on chemistry or physics, the writers of the '50s and '60s had begun to shift their focus and foundation. In her *Sixth Annual Edition* (1961), she notes: "Until a few years ago, 'pure science fiction' confined itself, with rare exceptions, to speculation about space, the atom, and possible inventions or discoveries in the physical sciences." In the *Third Annual Edition* (1958), for example, she writes that "the interest of the better *s-f* writers has shifted steadily since the war years toward the field of human behavior. You will find rocket ships and alien planets in these pages, as well as robots, mutated monsters, and strange inventions; but the *science* under examination here is not primarily physics or chemistry. It is biology, psychology, anthropology, sociology, politics, economics—*people*." Note that Merril concludes by suggesting that SF studies "people," a formulation that coincides with Reginald Bretnor's notion that the object of SF is man—though Merril offers it in a gender-neutral formation.

So, she believed that SF should be rooted in science of one kind or another. As she wrote in the same collection:

> A few years back, the physical possibility of space flight was still enough in doubt to make space travel a favorite subject for science-fiction, which after all, is *speculative* fiction: meaning a story that answers the question, 'What if?' But in order to be *science*-fiction, the answer must not only be imaginative, but logically reasoned from the accepted knowledge of the day.

Merril contended that the primary purpose of fiction is to engage the intellect of the reader and to respond to the social, scientific, and political changes of the day. As I noted above, she despaired when she thought that SF had ceased to engage in the real world. Indeed, she once stated that she was drawn to SF for its "realism." Despite her belief that science fiction should both respond to the events of the day *and* engage the reader's intellect in a profound way, Merril echoes Virginia Woolf in preferring work that is not explicitly ideologically driven. Woolf notes in *A Room of One's Own* that the best literature should rise above personal grievances and transcend politics; it should reflect a mind that has "consumed all impediments" (59). In June 1968, no less, Merril writes that

> art and propaganda are poor bedfellows at best, and even in the books closest to my own convictions, I have found none so far that merit high praise for their purely literary virtues: the best one can say of some is that they contrive to be entertaining while instructive, and of others that they are provocative enough in content to compensate for novelistic ineptitude.

And yet, in one of her final "Books" columns for *The Magazine of Fantasy and Science Fiction* (January 1969), Merril begins by reporting the events of the Democratic National Convention in Chicago. She notes that she is juggling her time and energy between political issues and book reviewing. In her view, the political concerns of the late '60s outweighed the need to review fiction. Furthermore, in this column filled with her angst and frustration, Merril notes that the fiction she is reviewing is just too removed from the real, political concerns of the day. Not long after that, she left the United States for good and relocated in Toronto.

Merril's Aesthetics

So, according to Judith Merril, for a book or story to be called "science fiction," it had to be predicated upon "actual science" (though she wants to broaden the range of sciences—*including* "sexology") and must maintain an internal logical consistency based on that science. Once she had selected a book for review or analysis, she then relied upon a number of criteria in her judgment of the book. For a book or story to be "SF," the criteria are much more expansive. Among the criteria that she judged necessary for a book/story to work are: Character, Language, Novelty, Newness, or Originality, Imagination, Logic, and Unity of form and content.

Character

One of the first minor aesthetic characteristics for Merril is the strength or weakness of the characterization. I have called it "minor" only because Merril seems to place less emphasis on it. An author can offer weak characters and yet still produce a viable novel. For instance, in September 1965, she reviews Chapman Pincher's novel *Not with a Bang* (1965) and notes that "The characters are perceptively visualized and meaningfully inter-related; but one never quite attains that sense of identification without which the best-constructed and most clearly drawn characters remain just that—characters, and not people." For Merril, the negative consequence of Pincher's poor characterization was the inability to become emotionally involved with the characters. In July 1966, she notes that in Charles Harness's collection *The Rose* (1966), "The novelette reads like too much of the high-idea-content work of science-fiction. The characters are there to argue out the theories." On the other hand, she lauds Thomas Disch's handling of character in *The Genocides* (1965) by saying that he gets human behaviors right; the characters are "personalities" and not "characters."

Language

Another minor component of good SF for Merril is the use of language. Indeed, powerful, effective language can outweigh negative factors. In September 1965, she reviews Philip José Farmer's *Dare* (1965); she dislikes the novel but acknowledges "the vivid colors, pungent odors, sensations of sun and grass and wood and metal, awareness of food and drink and sex and pain. And more significantly, we have Farmer symbols." In the same column, she also dismisses John Christopher's *The Possessors* (1964), but notes that although the book is "Beautifully structured, artfully written, thoughtfully and successfully characterized, this still boils down to a story of devils-and-zombies decked out as aliens-and-victims." In December 1966, she praises Roger Zelazny's *This Immortal* (1966) for its "poetry" and "technical skill" (though it fails in other areas). And, in November 1967, she reviews Samuel R. Delany's *The Einstein Intersection* (1967). She lavishes it with praise and yet writes, "If the book has a serious flaw, it is in the over-tight weaving, the too-careful pruning and packing of meaning into deceptively simple and rhythmic language: that is, that it is in large part closer to poetry than prose, without any of the typographical, linguistic, or structural formalities which usually serve as clues to the reader to proceed more attentively than he expects to do with an adventure novel." Finally, in September 1968, she writes of Joanna Russ's *Picnic on Paradise* (1968), "I cannot think when I last enjoyed so much reading anything so unconvincing." She loves the book because "Joanna Russ *writes* so well": "When it all got too much for me, I didn't stop: I just switched over to a (highly necessary) willful 'suspension of disbelief,' and went on reading into the small hours of the night, for the sheer pleasure of the prose, and delight in the imagery, color, and content of one vivid scene after another."

Novelty, Newness, or Originality

Also a minor component, Merril insists upon originality in the narrative, the form, and the ideas. She was a huge fan of H. G. Wells, and notes that, while he was not a "great writer," he was "an original thinker," which puts him above most other SF writers. Indeed, in her June 1967 column she laments that too many of the received titles were the same: "anti-conformity conformity (science-fiction's most overworked formula these days)." In an idea that she borrowed from Anthony Boucher, she writes that "I see now that it is because s-f is a form which, more than almost any other, by its very nature demands creative originality. The detective story and even the more modern psychological crime novel are—like the western, the love story, the historical romance—fixed forms, in which the creative challenge lies largely in seeing what the author can do within established boundaries. S-f is—or perhaps better, should and must be—a literature of stimulus and fresh horizons." And, "A conventional, competent, uninspired murder novel or western is a perfectly reasonable commercial commodity. Conventional, competent, uninspired s-f has no reason for existing."

As an example, in November 1966, she criticizes Keith Roberts's novel *The Furies* (1966) as unoriginal. She writes: "The astonishing thing about

Furies is that it contrives to be so readable while saying nothing at all (informationally, thematically, any other way) that has not been said, and well said, over and over before."

Imagination

As I noted above, for a while Merril argued, following Bretnor, that science fiction was "disciplined imagination." In her introduction to the *Fifth Annual Edition* (1960), she wrote that "Wonder—informed, thoughtful, purposeful wonder—is loose on the Earth again. And this is what 'SF' means, what 'science fiction' is: not gimmicks and gadgets, monsters and supermen, but trained wonderment—educated and disciplined imagination—a marvelous mirror for Modern Man and the world he is only beginning to make." Although she eventually abandoned that definition, she did believe that imagination was an important component of good science fiction. Certainly, imagination has a great deal to do with originality. For example, she wrote of Charles Beaumont's *The Magic Man* (1965) that he always writes with the "extra element of imaginative speculation that constitutes the essence of s-f" ("Books," February 1966). In a comparison between Beaumont and Poul Anderson, she argues that "Beaumont can write an imaginative speculative story with all the essential ingredients of s-f without ever departing from the forms of so-called 'realistic' fiction, Anderson is using the forms of s-f to write thrillers and historicals, and contriving to do so without introducing an element of speculation or fresh invention."

So, for Merril, the use of "imagination" is directly tied to her definition of SF and the centrality of "speculation" (and sometimes extrapolation) as a definitive component.

Logic

As noted above in her definition of SF, Merril consistently argued that logic was a central criterion: "*science*-fiction, the answer must not only be imaginative, but logically reasoned from the accepted knowledge of the day" (*Third Annual Edition*, 1958). In her April 1965 "Books" column, she writes that "The specific for science fiction is the application of the logic *to* the imagination." In her April 1966 review of John Brunner's *The Day of the Star Cities* (1965), she writes, "More than anything else, it is the painstaking application of interior logic that makes this book *work*; and it is applied to the background situation, the interaction between characters, and the thematic material with equal rigor and comprehension." In the same issue, she addresses Mack Reynolds's *Planetary Agent X* (1965) (which she calls both "unexceptionable and unexceptional"). She notes that "Reynolds offers the same kind of speculative integrity, informed logic, and inner consistency [as Brunner]—with much more room for, but less work at, characterization and emotional development."

In "Books," November 1966, she makes a comparison between Fritz Leiber and Robert A. Heinlein and the ways in which they apply logic to their work: "both manage to sustain a conviction of plausibility for the duration of the story, and to leave something of color as well as thought behind."

Unity of form and content

For Merril, what constitutes an excellent SF novel (or story) is one in which all of these components work together. Most frequently, however, she points out the ways in which novels and stories *fail* to do this. In a review (September 1965), she remarks of a collection by Hal Clement that "they contain the same inherent integrity (of puzzle, plot, character, theme, technical background)" and yet suggests that these stories are not well written. In her November 1966 column, she dismisses a Frank Herbert novel (*The Green Brain*, 1966), writing that, while it contains some "brilliant ecological extrapolation," it "falls short because of *plot* incredibilities and stock characters." In December 1966, she similarly discounts the Zelazny novel (*This Immortal*), which uses language well and offers valid psychological insights, but it is "disappointing as a novel, both in its conception and structure." In her September 1968 review of Russ's *Picnic on Paradise* she notes that—although everything in the novel is unbelievable—it contains the "essential unity between theme, plot, and background, situates the most fantastic or unlikely characters and locales in a subjective matrix of 'reality.'"

Merril also argued that the form of writing must be appropriate for the content. For example, in her May 1968 column, she discounts both Clifford Simak and Algis Budrys for electing to employ "the magazine-style category-science-fiction novel as a vehicle for concepts completely outside the form." Conversely, she lauds J. G. Ballard ("Books," August 1966) for electing to use modes of storytelling that fit the content. She writes that "he is an intensely conscious and purposeful speculative writer, and the modes he elects to use are those best suited to his vital interest in the philosophic basis of the contemporary revolutions in both scientific thinking and artistic expression."

But the novel to which she offers the most praise, that she suggests is the "first true science fiction novel," is John Brunner's *Stand on Zanzibar* (1968). She writes

> ...he has taken a true novel plot, developed it in proper novelistic style, and at the same time extrapolated fully, in accordance with all the basic science fiction rules, a future environment whose initial assumptions provide not only the background for the story but an essential component of its central conflicts. The "classic" science fiction novels of the past have ordinarily achieved their fame by doing (either) one of these jobs *so* successfully that any simply passable performance of the other was acceptable. (February 1969)

Literature

The reviews of Ballard and Brunner point to Merril's attitude toward science fiction as Literature. As we all know, SF has long been considered a marginal form of literature (as has all genre literature). One of the impetuses of science fiction criticism is the attempt to recuperate or elevate genre fiction to the status of Literature. One of the aims of The New Wave was to incorporate the forms of Literature into SF. In the previous section, we begin to see how Merril connects "good" and "true" science fiction with capital-L Literature. In her January 1966 column, Merril remarks on the emergence of New Wave (or, "New Thing") writers Aldiss, Ballard, and Brunner, and notes that they are "more literary" than other SF writers. She lauds Brunner's *Squares of the City* (1965), noting that, with just a *bit* more work, "what is now a first-rate science fiction novel and a good book by any standards, might have been a first-rate novel, with no qualifications." In other words, the book could be "Literature" and not the marked term "genre literature."

However, she argues that given the shifts in culture, in literature, and within genre literature, science fiction is being "re-absorbed [back] into mainstream literature" ("Summation, S-F, 1961"). In other words, she saw the collapse of the distinction between SF and non-SF fiction taking place—a process which has, arguably, continued.

Gender/Feminism

One of the remarkable things about Merril's nonfiction writing is how little attention she paid to gender. For example, she did not comment on the paucity of female writers (even though she reviewed very few of them); did not suggest that female and male authors were published or reviewed differently—

though Merril herself never failed to mention the physical attributes of Carol Emshwiller. She did not relate difficulties that she had as a female writer, anthologist, or critic. She did not comment on the representation of female characters, nor on plots that relegate women to ancillary or decorative roles. However, she did call out a writer if the character seemed logically implausible or unnecessarily flat. In practice, then, Merril seemed to assume a post-feminist argument (in which commentary on gender roles and limitations is no longer necessary or relevant)—which is all the more remarkable considering the role gender plays in her own fiction.

In the end, Judith Merril exhibited both a relatively conservative definition and aesthetic for science fiction. Her definition of the genre, though in constant flux, was rooted in the extrapolation from the known world based on current scientific knowledge and was consistent with many dominant models of the time—even though she did hint at a move away from an object-based model to a process-based model, she never fully developed it. Nevertheless, I do not think that we should underestimate the significance of a prominent female and feminist critic nor her influence in the development and incorporation of critical and literary analyses into "Space Fish" criticism (*Twelfth Annual Edition*, 1968).

Structure of This Book

This book collects some of Judith Merril's nonfiction. Although Merril edited a great many anthologies and although she wrote many introductions to others' books, I have limited this collection to her twelve Year's Best anthologies, her thirty-eight "Books" columns from *F&SF*, and three particularly important essays.

Judith Merril's style of writing was both idiosyncratic and personal. Reading a review by Merril generally feels as though she is sitting across the table from you. Although the "Introduction," "Summation," and introductions to the stories in the Year's Best books sometimes feel as though they are conversational or improvised, in fact, they are well structured and integrated. Furthermore, in the Annuals, the commentaries in between stories sometimes address the previous story, sometimes address the following story, and sometimes contribute to a larger narrative that she weaves throughout the book. Consequently, the idiosyncratic manner of writing, at times, seems haphazard. It never is. It is all part of her own nonfiction aesthetic. Only in very rare instances have I altered her content or style.[1] For the first ten Annuals, Merril also included a list of Honorable Mentions; these have been excluded from this volume.

Much of Merril's early fiction remains vital and current. Despite the (relative) lack of fictional output, her status as one of the early examplars of feminist science fiction has never been doubted and is frequently acknowledged. I would suggest, however, that her status as a commenter and shaper of SF is rarely acknowledged. In fact, Judith Merril held a vital position within the SF community. She was thoroughly networked and knew nearly everyone in the field (and in non-SF publishing, as well). She edited an influential series of anthologies, at a time when the number of annual anthologies was limited (which she details in her own Annuals). She occupied the reviewer's chair at one of the most widely read and most influential monthly magazines. And she never pulled her punches.

Judith Merril succeeded in a male-dominated field—the editors, authors, and reviewers she mentions are almost all male. While gender was almost always an overt component of her fiction, Merril approached gender in reviewing rather differently. While I am tempted to claim that the fact that a woman held such significant posts was enough, I suggest that Merril did more than that. She held a Woolfian vision of fiction (though she never directly mentions Virginia Woolf, she had almost certainly read her). She believed that SF could and should be literary, that it could and should address the social and political concerns of the day (ideology race, gender, sexuality), and that it should integrate those components fully into the fictional world.

Furthermore, this collection of nonfiction by Merril constitutes a history of SF, SF authors and editors, and SF publishing. In her reviews, introductions, and tributes, she chronicles the lives and work of many prominent and lesser known figures. She details the lives and deaths of a number of writers and editors. And she recounts the developments within the field as they happened. Over a period of twelve years, we get yearly, and sometimes monthly,

1 Merril developed an idiosyncratic style of writing, and that style shifted over time. This style was generally informal and conversational. The mechanics and punctuation of the writing often replicate a conversation. To effect this style, she employed unusual punctuation, using frequent ellipses and dashes. She also employed slang and a number of abbreviated words. For example, she would refer to Madison Avenue—by which she meant the advertising industry of Manhattan—as "Mad Ave." I have chosen to maintain Merril's idiosyncratic style, and I have only corrected spelling and obvious typographical errors.

updates on who is publishing, what is being written, and how the field is changing. Through all these changes, Merril continues to try to make sense of it all for us.

In the print version of this book, I have edited out most of the introductions to individual stories in the Year's Best anthologies, excepting in a few instances when she most directly addresses the question of SF aesthetics. I have also edited the "Books" columns to include only the sections that directly address fiction, definitions, and aesthetics. Several columns that dealt solely with nonfiction texts were dropped. Finally, in the interest of space, I have eliminated one of her essays.

In the electronic version of this book, however, I have included *all* of Merril's content from the twelve Year's Best anthologies, *all* of the "Books" columns, and added her tribute to Ted Sturgeon. Although the anthologies and "Books" columns sometimes overlap, the inclusion of everything allows for the fullest record of Merril's work, and the fullest understanding of her SF aesthetics.

Special thanks to Emily Pohl-Weary for her support of this project.

Works Cited

Bailey, J. O. *Pilgrims through Space and Time: Trends and Patterns in Scientific and Utopian Fiction*. New York: Argus, 1947.

Bretnor, Reginald. "The Future of Science Fiction." *Modern Science Fiction: Its Meaning and Its Future*. Ed. Reginald Bretnor. New York: Coward-McCann, 1953. 265-94.

Csicsery-Ronay, Jr., Istvan. *The Seven Beauties of Science Fiction*. Middletown, CT: Wesleyan UP, 2008.

Cummins, Elizabeth. "Judith Merril: A Link with the New Wave—Then and Now." *Extrapolation* 36.3 (1995): 198-209.

——. "Judith Merril: Scouting SF." *Extrapolation* 35.1 (1994): 5-14.

Freedman, Carl. *Critical Theory and Science Fiction*. Hanover, NH: Wesleyan UP, 2000.

Merril, Judith. "Books." *The Magazine of Fantasy and Science Fiction* (April 1965).

——. "Books." *The Magazine of Fantasy and Science Fiction* (September 1965).

——. "Books." *The Magazine of Fantasy and Science Fiction* (February 1966).

——. "Books." *The Magazine of Fantasy and Science Fiction* (August 1966).

——. "Books." *The Magazine of Fantasy and Science Fiction* (November 1966).

——. "Books." *The Magazine of Fantasy and Science Fiction* (September 1968).

——. "Books." *The Magazine of Fantasy and Science Fiction* (January 1969).

——. "Books." *The Magazine of Fantasy and Science Fiction* (February 1969).

——. "Introduction." *The Best of the Best, Part 1*. Ed. Judith Merril. New York: Dell, 1970. 1-7.

——. "Author's Notes." *Daughters of Earth and Other Stories*. Ed. Judith Merril. Toronto: McClelland and Stewart, 1985. 1-3.

——. "Introduction." *England Swings SF*. Ed. Judith Merril. New York: Doubleday, 1968. 9-11.

——. "Fritz Leiber." *The Magazine of Fantasy and Science Fiction* (July 1969): 44-61.

——. "Introduction: The Ghosts We Share." *The Work of Reginald Bretnor*. Ed. Scott Alan Burgess. New York: Borgo, 1989. 5-12.

——. "Foreword." *Tesseracts*. Ed. Judith Merril. Toronto: Porcépic, 1985. 1-3.

——. "Theodore Sturgeon" *Fantasy and Science Fiction* (September 1962): pp. 46-55.

——. "What Do You Mean: Science? Fiction?" *Extrapolation*: Journal of Science Fiction and Fantasy Studies 7 (May 1966): 30-46, and 8 (Dec. 1966): 2-19. Reprinted in Thomas D. Clareson, ed., *The Other Side of Realism: Essays on Modern Fantasy and Science Fiction* (Bowling Green, OH: Bowling Green UP, 1971): 53-95.

——, ed. *The Year's Greatest Science Fiction and Fantasy, Third Annual Edition*. New York: Dell, 1958.

——, ed. *The Year's Best S-F, Fifth Annual Edition*. New York: Dell, 1960.

——, ed. *The Year's Best S-F, Sixth Annual Edition*. New York: Dell, 1961.

——, ed. *The Year's Best S-F, Eighth Annual Edition*. New York: Dell, 1963.

——, ed. *The Year's Best S-F, Eleventh Annual Edition*. New York: Dell, 1966.

—— and Emily Pohl-Weary. *Better to Have Loved: The Life of Judith Merril*. Toronto: Between the Lines, 2002.

Newell, Dianne and Victoria Lamont. *Judith Merril: A Critical Study*. Jefferson, NC: McFarland, 2012.

Suvin, Darko. *Metamorphoses of Science Fiction: On the Poetics and History of a Literary Genre*. New Haven, CT: Yale UP, 1979.

Woolf, Virginia. *A Room of One's Own*. New York: Harcourt Brace Jovanovich, 1989.

S-F: The Year's Greatest Science-Fiction and Fantasy, First Annual Edition (1956)

Preface

The stories in this book, says Mr. Orson Welles [who wrote the Introduction to this first *Year's Greatest* volume], are fables of our time. I think this is a good way to describe them since, like older fables, science-fantasy makes use of the imaginative background and unusual circumstance to add emotional urgency and dramatic power to what are basically problems in philosophy and morality.

Unlike Aesop, the writers of these stories seldom conclude with a clear-cut moral. In a century whose most impressive accomplishments (atom bombs, orlon, rockets, radar, cancer cures, what-have-you-?) are built upon "scientific" concepts with such names as *relativity* and *the uncertainty principle,* the inquiring artist does well merely to formulate a coherent question.

The questions you will find most often put in here might be compressed in one composite query:—

> *How can we learn to live at peace with ourselves and with each other in the complexities of the world we are rebuilding with our new machines?*

Fortunately, the stories are not so compressed. A *good* story must inevitably be unique and individual as the man or woman who wrote it. Unfortunately, if it's answers that you want, you will not find them here—except occasionally, prefaced with *what if?*, *I wonder*, or *supposing that…*

The serious-minded reader will also have to forgive our authors if they resort to the frivolities of space-ships and flying bath-mats, robots and talking rats, to make their points. Even in s-f, a writer is only secondarily a philosopher; his first big job is entertainment…and *that* hasn't changed since Aesop's time at all.

[…]

The Year's S-F: A Summation

This was the year the house collapsed. The house of cards, I mean, otherwise known as the Science Fiction Boom. It's been rough all over, and I *don't* mean only since the pieces began to blow off the top, a couple-three years back; I mean almost from the beginning, since five years ago, when the structure first began to climb precariously higher than its foundations could support.

There were plenty of reasons for the collapse, but none that couldn't have been predicted—none that weren't inherent in the build-up. *Part* of what happened was that science-fantasy got caught in the post-war publishing mushroom (two kinds of mushroom: the kind that grows up overnight, and the kind that makes a big noise—"Boom!"—and blows away in the air). As it happened, just when paper-supplies were loosening up, and people were finding time to read again, the public was discovering some irritating complexities and confusions in the Wonderful Postwar World. Seeking both explanation and escape, readers bought a record number of "How To" books, and scientific popularizations; and at the same time sought the solace of an old companion of hard times and inner turmoil—fantasy. And the experiences of the war itself, five years full of Marvelous Inventions and Heroes of Science, had prepared the reading public to accept—or at least be introduced to—the bastard infant of the union of these forms: science-fiction. (Now that the wedding has been officially sanctioned, there is another, legitimate, offspring of popular science and literary mysticism, the "How to Have Happier Dreams," school, regularly appearing on all bestseller lists.)

The *Boom!,* both in s-f and in publishing generally, was most noticeable in paperback books and in magazines. New companies blossomed like dandelions; new titles covered the news-stands and smothered the drugstores, until the quantity of sheer trash and the bewildering variety of choice, inevitably, made a weeding-out period necessary.

The s-f *Boom!* started later, and lasted longer, than was generally true for the industry. It was 1953 when the bottom fell out of publishing, but for some time after that, s-f continued (comparatively speaking) to flourish—not as it had in the peak year, but still holding better than its own.

There was a reason. In all the excitement, science-fantasy actually *had* grown from an esoteric specialty field to a small, but solid, "category," of interest to a significant portion of the general reading public. It didn't, as some of its prophets had loudly proclaimed, put mysteries and westerns out of the running; it *did* establish a small shelf for itself, beside them.

In the summer of 1955, the *Saturday Review of Literature,* which had been (as I recall it) the first of the serious critical journals to accord recognition to science-fantasy, apparently decided it had a corpse on its hands. Somewhat embarrassed, they engaged a pair of literary undertakers to dispose of the matter for them. These two gentlemen, Siegfried Mandel, an English instructor at Brooklyn Polytechnic, and Peter Fingesten, a sculptor and authority on "world symbolism," produced an article entitled, "The Myth of Science Fiction." In it (as is frequent in funeral addresses) they chose to ignore the erratic behavior of the last few years of the subject's life, and confined their comments largely to the period of infancy. (This extreme is less customary.)

In any event, the co-authors of this higher criticism managed to produce an admirable analysis of what-was-wrong with s-f twenty years ago, and explained adequately why it could never have become a popular fiction-form at that time, addressed as it was to a limited group of intellectual frustrates with technocratic political leanings, and no social leanings whatsoever.

They buried the wrong corpse; but perhaps we should thank them for doing it. Science-fantasy has long outgrown both its worship of machines and its fear of emotion. Where emphasis once was on the mechanical sciences, it has shifted now to the psychological; where Scientific Progress was once the unquestioned goal, the more usual objective now is *to question* just what *sort* of progress might offer the most satisfaction for human needs.

S-f, today, has found a valid and permanent place for itself on the contemporary literary scene. Just *what* that place may be has been the subject of considerable debate. For me, the location was pointed out most clearly in the introductory comments made by the editors of an eminently readable recent collection (no relation to science-fiction), *New Campus Writing* (Bantam, 1955).

Messrs. Nolan Miller and Judson Jerome noted that the submissions they received for consideration were both plentiful and varied—with one exception: "There would seem to be little probing by campus writers into the relation of man to machine, man to society, man to the universe of the atom." And a little later: "We are puzzled that the issues of our times—science, technology, politics, starvation of the mind and body—figure only slightly, if at all...we find people in twos and threes; we examine individuals in the process of discovering themselves—finding the terms by which they can live in the world without changing it."

I believe this is true of a very large part of the best modern literature. And it is *this* gap that science-fantasy fills. This is precisely what the authors in this book *have* done. And that there is a place for it, readers looking for it, is clearly evidenced by the position of the field today—after the *Boom*!

Seven years ago, just before it all started, there were only two regular monthly magazines in this country publishing original (not reprint) science-fiction: *Astounding*, which was then, as earlier, (and still) a first-rate magazine; and *Amazing Stories*, which was then a "pulp" devoted almost exclusively to exploring Lemuria under the guidance of one Richard Shaver. There were five other magazines then publishing original s-f, all bi-monthlies or quarterlies.

Today, there are thirteen s-f magazines appearing in this country: five regular monthlies, four each of quarterlies and bi-monthlies. Eight of these, at least, are good magazines, that may confidently be expected to remain in good health.

Amazing Stories, as of the beginning of 1956, has become a monthly again; this one is for fast action, plot, and pace—though not profundity.

Astounding, which has never faltered in schedule or quality, continues to be directed primarily to the engineer-reader and devotee of the true problem-story.

Fantastic Universe; also monthly. If the science-fiction in here is sometimes weak, the fantasy can almost always be relied upon to be first-rate.

Fantasy & Science Fiction; monthly. The unquestioned leader in the field for literary quality, for innovations in form, and for intelligent humor.

Galaxy is the s-f "slick" (as *F&SF* might be called the "little magazine" of the field). A number of first-rate authors who are too seldom seen elsewhere appear here regularly. Monthly.

If offers a very satisfying selection of solid well-written "genuine science-fiction." Seldom spectacular; always good; no specialized emphasis. Bi-monthly.

Infinity is too new to have acquired a "personality" of its own—but it shows promise of becoming one of the better magazines. Bi-monthly—but only for the time being, I expect.

Science Fiction Stories, a bi-monthly, is published in conjunction with *Science Fiction Quarterly;* they are different in size and price; otherwise, they may be considered as one magazine, with ten issues the year. Notable primarily for the excellent feature material; quality of the fiction is erratic, but its content is often gratifyingly off-trail.

The bulk of the stories included in this collection, and in the Honorable Mentions list, were selected from these and other s-f specialty magazines. In addition, I had three main sources of material:—

1) Magazines outside the specialty field: In 1955, *Blue-book*, *Esquire*, *Good Housekeeping*, *Collier's*, *Playboy*, *Ellery Queen's Mystery Magazine*, and *The Saturday Evening Post* (in approximate order of the quantity published) contained between them perhaps thirty or forty

s-f stories (depending on where you draw the line between science-fantasy and just-plain fantasy). Half again that number were scattered among such an unlikely combination as *The Reporter*, *PEN* (*The Public Employees' News*), *The American Magazine*, *Cats* (for cat-lovers), and others.

2) Books: There is comparatively little original short-story material appearing in book-form, but this year there were two hard-cover collections of more-than-ordinary interest: J. B. Priestley's *The Other Place* (Harper's), and Bertrand Russell's *Nightmares of Eminent Persons* (Simon & Schuster). In paperbacks, there was the annual Star collection from Ballantine; one volume of regrettable originals published by Signet; and at least one new story per book in Ballantine's collections of Chad Oliver, Kuttner-Moore, and Sturgeon.
3) British magazines. There are four of these now regularly appearing. I liked the bi-monthly *Science-Fantasy* the best, but all are surprisingly good, with a much higher average quality than is to be found in the American magazines. *New Worlds* and *Authentic* are both monthlies; *Nebula* is bi-monthly.

I have not attempted to cover any foreign-language magazines, but it is of interest to note that there *are* s-f publications now appearing in a good many other countries. Among them, to my limited knowledge, are Sweden, France, Germany, Italy, and Japan.

One further source of material, not represented in this book, but surveyed for it, were the "fan" magazines, published by readers and aspiring writers of s-f. Fiction and essays of unexpectedly high caliber are printed in several of these, most notably in one offset and rather arty item called *Inside*.

All stories under 20,000 words in length originally published for the first time in 1955 were eligible for consideration—that is, if *either* the copyright date or magazine issue-date was 1955. Ideally, we'd have preferred to be guided entirely by copyright date; but it is not always possible to obtain copies of forthcoming January and February issues early enough. As a result, this volume and the one for 1956 will overlap on certain issues. No story was excluded from consideration on account of previous condition of reprint—but I am afraid they *were* discriminated against.

Stories were selected for a combination of idea-content (and development) and literary virtue...but also with the awareness that, put together in a book, they had to provide some variety and contrast for the reader. Thus, some pieces had to be regretfully excluded, because there was a better example *of the same type* available. Others that might have been included were dropped if anything of similar quality and kind could be had that had *not* been previously reprinted. A very few that I might have liked to use were unavailable due to previous publishing commitments. For the most part, editors and publishers were marvelously kind about releasing rights, in view of the special nature of this collection.

S-F: The Year's Greatest Science-Fiction and Fantasy, Second Annual Edition (1957)

[No Introduction to this volume]

[...]

The Year's S-F: A Summation by the Editor

It surprises me every time.

For months I read stories, weed out the better ones, re-read, re-weed, and read and weed again; at the last minute, there is always a dreadful jumble of twice as much as I can use; and all but the *very* best of it already gone over so often that all powers of discrimination are exhausted. I stew and worry and groan; and somewhere along the way I discover the *shape* of a book.

That's the part that always surprises me. It is clear from the start (my contract *insists* on it) that there will be a book; but right up to the end it seems it will be merely a book full of stories—good ones, perhaps, but without that increment in virtue that appropriate grouping ought to produce. When one and one add up to only two, the combination is sterile.

It was particularly interesting this time, when the pattern of the collection began to emerge, to see how different it was from just a year ago.

Last year the major preoccupation of the better writers in science-fantasy was with the relationship between man and his environment, and especially between people and their machines. This year the emphasis is on interpersonal relationships, and particularly on the problems of communication.

More than half the final selections for this volume deal thematically with some aspect of communication. Again and again the statement emerges: *We do not know each other. We do not understand each other.* And from there they go off in all different directions. Would it really help if we did? How can we find out? Is there a better way than words? *What* better way? Or can we *make* words do the job?

Of the remaining stories, half again are concerned with *self*-understanding, and should perhaps be included therefore in the tally above. Communication is a process commencing within the mind of one person, and terminating inside the mind of another; it is only the means—the *technology*—of communication that bridges the gap between organisms.

[...]

Oddly in keeping with this trend, the year was in many ways one of reappraisal and self-examination within the professional ranks. Writers and publishers alike shifted cautiously from the bottom-of-the-trough gloom of 1955 toward a wary, but determined, optimism. A year ago, a good many editors were flatly refusing even to consider s-f submissions; and some of the best writers were leaving the field for greener (and more edible) grasses. Today the general attitude appears to be rather: *We made mistakes before. If we do it right this time, perhaps we can sell it after all.*

Certainly the year's literary history established that there is a reading public, and a big one, for the subject-matter of science-fantasy. Bridey Murphy alone would have been enough to prove that. (And a good thing, too; the poor girl had to prove *something*!) In any case, as 1957 starts, there are six new s-f magazines on the stands (though most of them appeared too late to be included in my reading for this book); and among those I have seen so far, I'd guess that three at least—*Satellite*, *Science Fiction Adventures*, and, most notably, *Venture*—will probably survive. In addition, I know of at least three book publishers who have once again started looking actively for science-fiction novels.

It was a critical year, in the sense that the field as a commercial whole hit the bottom of the pit and started scraping its way up the sides again. But it was also a critical year in at least two other senses of the word.

Story content was one. With the increasing pressure of the socio-political environment for conformity in all things, fantasy has begun to resume its traditional importance as a medium for expression of social criticism and individualist views. Writers are returning to the field, and new writers are being attracted to it because it provides an outlet for much that cannot now be said (except to perhaps fifty or a hundred readers at a time, in the *littlest* magazines) in other areas of fiction writing. Meanwhile, a big new market has been opened up for s-f (and especially for satirical s-f) by *Playboy* and by the many other men's-interest magazines that have sprung up in the wake of the *Playboy* success.

Finally, 1956 was a year of criticism, in the best possible sense. With all due respect to publications that have from time to time offered up evaluations and analyses of the science-fiction "phenomenon," this year was marked, in my opinion, by the emergence of the most serious and competent literary criticism the field has known.

Two separate (or almost separate) events contributed to this achievement. One was the publication of a book devoted exclusively to serious criticism of the s-f field, written by a man who, as author, TV script-writer, illustrator, agent, editor, *and* critic, has been professionally engaged in science-fantasy for more than fifteen years. The book, *In Search of Wonder* (Advent), by Damon Knight, covers ten years, roughly, of active book publishing, and is as keenly and constructively critical as anything ever written about the field. Knight knows *what* is good and bad, and *why.*

The other big accomplishment of the year, from the writers' viewpoint, was the establishment of the Milford Science Fiction Writers' Conference. This was the first fully professional conference ever held among s-f writers, and the enthusiasm it generated even in advance was perhaps also associated with the feeling expressed so strongly in the new stories—the urgent need for communication. Its effects will show up at longer range, and will be sustained, I think, by a new critical journal now being published as a by-product of those discussions.

On the surface, 1956 was a poor year in many ways. To come back to the communication definition: the year gave clear evidence of a waiting readership on the receiving end; it was nothing less than spectacular for its accomplishments in self-examination and clarification of objectives on the creative end; but the gap between the two is yet to be adequately bridged. The commercial publishing market, while showing signs of improved interest, has not yet discovered the most successful techniques for conveying this highly specialized kind of communication from writer to reader (with profit to all). Perhaps the accomplishment of this goal will be the substance of next year's report.

Inevitably, in compiling a book of this sort, one is left with a stack of stories that *would* have made it *if*—if they were shorter, if they were less like something already included, if rights had been available, etc.

SF: The Year's Greatest Science-Fiction and Fantasy, Third Annual Edition (1958)

Introduction

Someone was always looking at the stars.

Now it appears the stars may shortly have their chance to look at us.

Only a half century has passed since the first workable aircraft gave men the freedom, figuratively, of their own back yard. Now, this past year, we have succeeded in loosening the gate-latch on the back yard fence. Tomorrow, or next year, or ten years from now—but *soon*—the gate will swing open. Men of Earth will, for the first time, leave their native habitat.

Here on our home world we can, and do, behave in ways the universe around us will not tolerate. Here gravity, like Mom and Pop, can be depended on to catch us when we climb too high. And when we fall, the friendly forces of the atmosphere will always give sound to our yells for help.

In space, a temper tantrum may be fatal. If a man does not know his own strength—or his own weaknesses—he is unlikely to survive. What sort of welcome we make for ourselves in the great world outside our world will depend in large part on our capacity for learning caution, and certain basic courtesies as well, for use among ourselves and toward what—or whomever we may meet out there.

A few years back, the physical possibility of space flight was still enough in doubt to make space travel a favorite subject for science-fiction, which after all, is *speculative* fiction: meaning a story that answers the question, "What if…?" But in order to be *science*-fiction, the answer must not only be imaginative, but logically reasoned from the accepted knowledge of the day.

Right now, the unknown quantities, the "What ifs?" of space flight, are mostly either technical details (requiring at the least an engineer to know enough facts to reason or imagine *from*), or they arise in areas where basic scientific research has not yet broken enough ground to provide the minimum of factual knowledge (faster-than-light flight, for example).

But it seems that the closer we come to the certainty of space travel, the more uncertain are our qualifications for the job. Accordingly, the interest of the better *s-f* writers has shifted steadily since the war years toward the field of human behavior. You will find rocket ships and alien planets in these pages, as well as robots, mutated monsters, and strange inventions; but the *science* under examination here is not primarily physics or chemistry. It is biology, psychology, anthropology, sociology, politics, economics—*people*. [...]

The Year's S-F: A Summary

In 1957, the most noticeable trend in science-fantasy was toward a focus on problems of conformism vs. individualism, security vs. freedom, mechanization vs. creativity. A minor trend appeared to be in the direction of the anthropological, or at least sociological, viewpoint, away from the intensely inward, psychiatric vogue of the last two years.

Stories this year were selected from twenty science-fantasy periodicals and twelve short story collections, plus material from non-specialty publications.

[...]

SF: The Year's Greatest Science-Fiction and Fantasy, Fourth Annual Edition (1959)

Introduction

You've heard the one about the old egghead (slightly cracked, but not quite addled yet) who's got this gorgeous girl assistant, and this formula (or Frankenstein, or maybe a giant ant). Anyhow, the old boy means well, but he just can't stop himself. (*One more experiment*! he says each time, *and then I'll quit.*) And he would have sure enough destroyed the world if the young reporter (or engineer, or Marine lieutenant) didn't bust in the door and marry the poor girl *just* in time.

Well, maybe I got it a little mixed up, but you know the one I mean. What I wanted to say was…you won't find it here.

The name of this book is *SF.*

SF is an abbreviation for Science Fiction (or Science Fantasy). Science Fantasy (or Science Fiction) is really an abbreviation, too. Here are *some* of the things it stands for….

S is for Science, Space, Satellites, Starships, and Solar exploring; also for Semantics and Sociology, Satire, Spoofing, Suspense, *and* good old Serendipity. (But *not* Spelling, without which I could have added Psychology, Civilizations, and *Psi* without parentheses.)

F is for Fantasy, Fiction and Fable, Folklore, Fairy-tale and Farce; also for Fission and Fusion; for Firmament, Fireball, Future and Forecast; for Fate and Free-will; Figuring, Fact-seeking, and Fancy-free.

Mix well. The result *is SF*, or *Speculative Fun….*

Happy reading.

[…]

The Year's SF: A Summary

If you do manage to lift yourself by your own bootstraps, do the boots come along? It seems to me they would! It's a "closed system," isn't it?

In which case, perhaps the analogy of a multiple-stage rocket would be more suitable to describe the present paradoxically successful plight of science fiction....

"The trouble is, the whole world seems to have gone '*science-fictional*,'" Isaac Asimov wrote me, while preparing his article on "The Thunder-Thieves." "All sorts of mad ideas (or so they would have seemed a few years ago) are under serious investigation by scientists and—wonder of wonders—are reported in the press without either jokes or sneers."

What's more, the press (still somewhat ill-at-ease with the far-out notions "sober scientists" turn out to have) frequently refers to s-f to bridge the gap between the commonsense facts of a few years ago and the startling new scientific achievements—achievements "that only yesterday were science fiction."

It's not just the newspapers, either. The general magazines are printing more (and *better*) s-f all the time. Public libraries have special displays of new s-f. Several new s-f programs were announced for television at the start of the '58-'59 season.

And while all this was going on, the number of specialty s-f magazines on the newsstands plummeted from twenty-one, at the start of 1958, to ten at year's end.

These trends are not so contradictory as they may at first appear. Science fantasy is simply hoisting itself out of its own bootstraps—or leaving its booster tanks behind, as it levels into a new trajectory.

In a review of last year's *S-F*, Anthony Boucher commented on the new non-fiction section, saying, "Much of the disciplined imagination we used to associate with science fiction now appears without fictional coating." And Asimov, in the same letter quoted before, said, "No matter how fast science progresses, it does not and cannot encroach upon science fiction—though between you and me it can encroach on s-f readers, by saturating them with science-advance, and depriving them of the need for s-f magazines."

I think Dr. Asimov is very right. It is worth noting in this connection that two of the magazines that suspended publication last year were replaced by "space" titles; and that John W. Campbell, Jr., who has edited the field's leading magazine, *Astounding*, for more than twenty years, called upon his readers last summer to subscribe to membership in a new "Society of Gentleman Amateurs"; the Society is to have its own journal, devoted exclusively to speculative science and engineering. (The rules would bar any working scientist from writing in his own field.)

Or consider these bits from a piece published last year on the possible future uses of parapsychology.

"The real idea…is to employ the waves or impulses for long-range transmission of messages, and even for the near-fantastic purpose of moving or influencing inanimate objects at great distances…. One group…has advanced the idea that the brain wave amplification concept offers a possible means of communication between space ships…." And the theory is proposed "that the measurable electrical impulses given off by the human brain are products of a body chemical reaction much in the same way that noise is a product of a combustion engine, and that the true brain waves making possible extra-sensory perception are something else again and not yet understood…"

The article also claims that many "scientists of the highest repute" have come to believe "that there definitely is a special group of humans having the power or gift of transferring thought from mind to mind, and influencing consistently the dice in a game of chance." Now there would be nothing of special note in all this, except that the scientists referred to are not the hand-picked group of known "crackpots" who would have been quoted in an article of the same sort in a science-fantasy magazine ten, five, or just two years ago. They are working engineers and research men at Westinghouse's laboratory in Friendship, MD, at the famous Rand Development Corporation in Cleveland, and at the Army's Redstone, Alabama, missile development center.

The article, which appeared in the Sunday *N. Y. Herald Tribune* on July 13, 1958, was written by that paper's military and aviation editor, Ansel E. Talbert. It starts out: "An amazing series of projects…are receiving serious study in the research branches of the United States armed forces." It closes with a paragraph quoting Col. William Bowers, director of biological sciences in the Air Force Office of Scientific Research, as being "tremendously interested" in finding out "whether messages and even energy emanating from the human brain can be transmitted over thousands of miles…"

"Science-advance" and "disciplined imagination" are no longer the esoteric intellectual entertainment of a specialized cult; it is to be expected that the literature of logical speculation will not for long retain its discrete identity. And if any further evidence were needed, it could be found in the ranks of s-f authors: both in the fast-growing roster of new names attracted to science fantasy, and in the attitudes expressed by older writers in the field.

For the past three years, an annual Science-Fiction Writers' Conference has been held at Milford, PA. Discussions at these meetings cover every facet of the writer's craft, with special reference to science fantasy: markets, agents, editors, critics, research sources, and the basic subjective problems of writing itself. During the 1958 sessions, one point of view emerged repeatedly: the writers who had been in s-f for any length of time, almost to a man wanted to get out—but to take it with them as they went. Some wanted the greater literary freedom of the book form; some wanted to get away from "gimmicks"; others wanted editors without established s-f conventions.

"I want to say the same kind of thing, but I'm tired of saying it to the same people," some of them summed it up. But one way or another, almost all wanted to write "a sort of s-f" or "something in between s-f and mainline fiction," for a wider market.

S-f (the category) is, if not dead, moribund; then long live s-f (the literature, and way of thinking)!

In a year of disquieting news all round in the s-f marketplace, the saddest single item—after the untimely deaths of Henry Kuttner and C. M. Kornbluth—was the retirement of Anthony Boucher from the editorial chair of *Fantasy and Science Fiction.* From its first issue in 1949, through five years of co-editorship by Boucher and J. Francis McComas, and five more of Mr. Boucher's solo guidance, *F&SF* reflected his distinctive editorial personality and exercised a potent influence on science fantasy as a whole, by supplying a sorely needed critical standard to a field which had grown up with pulp traditions and which was often marked by careless prose and stock characterizations.

Wide erudition and keen intelligence are professional requirements for the science-fiction editor, but Tony Boucher was the first to add a discerning sensitivity to good writing.

The Year's Best S-F, Fifth Annual Edition (1960)

Introduction

In the beginning there was Wonder. Early Man lived in a world of alternating light and dark, where wind faded to calm and sun succeeded storm, all without cause—where summer heat and winter's ice were equally marvelous—where the fruit of the soil or the prize of the hunt might, unpredictably, either fill or kill a man.

Ancient Man learned about cause and effect. He sowed, and reaped; trapped the lightning for winter warmth; caught rain in pools against summer's drought. He flew an arrow with the feathers of a bird; smelted ore for a sharper stone to tip the arrow; modeled a wheel from a rolling stone. The natural miracles he could control ceased to astonish him; those outside his grasp were, perhaps, supernatural? He wondered—about giants, gods, and demons.

Historic Man, guided by the recorded increment of wonders noted (resolved or unsolved), harnessed the energies of wind and water, grouped with his kin to raise up walls of stone, to stop the enemy before the battle; lived longer and more leisurely; learned to think in abstractions; devised mental tools—logic, morality, philosophy; made new tools with which to peer through at the macro- and micro-cosmic realms of the gods and devils. He saw the magnificent orderliness of the universe; banished wonder and base superstition together; rejoiced, and proclaimed the Age of Reason.

Rational Man inhabited a law-abiding world controlled absolutely by Cold Facts and Logic, Physical Laws and Mechanical Principles. He himself was the inevitable sum of Mendelian Laws, Chemistry, Conditioning, and Reflexes. A minimum of marveling was contained in a Rational Deity—a Great Architect who had (with compass, protractor, and Euclid's Axioms) laid out the universe. The new verities were classified, catalogued, and cross-indexed for eternity. The new technique of observing, testing, and labeling, was called *the scientific method*.

Modern Man used the new tool of experimentation, and learned: to unleash the lightning; make water from air, cloth from coal, food from metals; to create whirlwinds and earthquakes, brew storms and dispel them; defy distance and gravity; outstrip his own noise; cause a sunburst on Earth; and (now, newly) to animate matter.

Wonder—informed, thoughtful, purposeful wonder—is loose on the Earth again. And this is what "SF" means, what "science fiction" is: not gimmicks and gadgets, monsters and supermen, but *trained wonderment*—educated and disciplined imagination—a marvelous mirror for Modern Man and the world he is only beginning to make.

[...]

The Year's S-F: A Summary

I should not like to have it thought, from my earlier comments, that I take exception to *everything* Kingsley Amis says. On one point at least I am very much in agreement with him, and that is the urgent need for a new name for this field.

Not to carry the sweetness and light too far—his feeling that "'*Science* fiction' is every day losing some of its appropriateness as a name for science fiction," seems to me typical of his failure to understand what science fiction *is*—but for quite different reasons, I do share his conclusions.

The *Sunday Herald Tribune*, a few weeks ago, published a longish and most favorable review which began:

"This is a curious and original and very serious book, and it will be so satisfactory to the right reader that I think a warning is in order: though the action takes place in the future, and though a space ship takes off on the final page, this should not be confused with what is usually called science fiction. What he has really written is a highly imaginative, and basically joyous, celebration of humankind's instinct to keep going."

The book under discussion was Walter M. Miller, Jr.'s *A Canticle for Leibowitz* (Lippincott, 1959), the work of a skilled, experienced, popular s-f author, first published as a series of long novelettes in *Fantasy and Science Fiction.*

Now "science-fiction" books *by science-fiction authors* are simply not reviewed seriously in the major critical outlets. (These days, they are rarely reviewed, at all.) But the canny jacketeers at Lippincott have gotten around this taboo several times now by the simple expedient of not *labeling* their books as s-f. In this case they went a step further: the jacket flap biography explains that Mr. Miller "compromised between art and engineering by writing science-fiction, *until* this, his first novel" (my italics—J. M.).

Then they took care to plaster the jacket with quotes from "respectable literary" names—all clearly "non-science-fiction" people, except the acceptable exception, Bradbury—saying, "It falls into no genre, certainly not science fiction," and "It is not, really, a 'futuristic' novel." (Plus one from old friend Amis, who says, "...a serious and imaginative novel....")

Thus freed of the Curse of the Tag, an excellent novel became eligible for consideration on the level on which it was written—instead of the usual fast paragraph at the space-opera stand.

Well, if this is what it takes to persuade "literary" folk to read a good book and enjoy it—down with "science fiction," sez I. Let's have a new label. Or none, at all. Who knows? That way, Sturgeon might outsell Pat Frank.

I should confess here, also, that I owe a debt of gratitude to Mr. Amis. The wildly improbable circulation figures he quotes in his book led me to get down to a long-postponed job of research on the cross-the-counter condition of health of what we still *do* call science fiction—and I emerged unexpectedly reassured.

Last year I reported here that the number of magazine titles in the combined fantasy and s-f fields had dropped from twenty-one to ten. As of the start of 1960, we are down two more, to eight titles—less than at any time since before the big boom of the early fifties—since 1946, to be exact. *But*—

Of these eight titles, six are monthlies, and two bimonthly. In 1945-46, with eight titles, there was an average of four magazines a month issued; now there are seven. In 1949, when there were also seven magazines a month on the stands, they comprised *17* titles. In the peak year for s-f magazine publishing, 1953, there were four times as many titles as now—but only *twice* as many magazines.

It would be easy—and gratifying—to adduce from this that the publications surviving today are the solid, sound, worthy ones: to some degree it must even be true. But to generalize from that to the notion that "science fiction is maturing" (which I keep hearing, hopefully) would be inaccurate. The reason for all these healthy-looking regular monthly magazines has virtually nothing to do with either publishers or buyers; it is the work of the distributors, who last year began putting pressure on the publishers to go monthly or quit. Two who tried to make twelve books a year pay off, failed; two others "suspended" indefinitely without trying.

There is then less cause for alarm than one might think, but small cause for joy either, in the condition of the specialty magazines. In two other fields, however, s-f is thriving: paperback books, and general fiction magazines.

For the past five years the number of paperback books in the combined fantasy and science-fiction fields has held to a remarkably steady all-time high of 70 to 80 per year. From the looks of things, it will rise sharply this year. In short, we may expect more individual paperback books than issues of magazines this year—but the fact is that for the past two or three years, p-bs *have been* outselling magazines in total quantity. [Sixty thousand] copies is an exceptionally good circulation for an s-f magazine these days, I understand; but very few book publishers will issue a p-b without being able to sell at *least* that many. The average paperback sale is probably somewhere between 90 and 100 thousand.

In the first volume of *S-F*, reporting on 1955, I pointed out with some pride that as many as 50 or 60 s-f stories had appeared in "slick," quality, and other non-s-f magazines. Last year more than that number was accounted for in the "*Playboy*-type" magazines alone. With what appeared in the slick and quality magazines, there were, I should estimate, upward of 200 stories (fantasy and s-f) published in non-s-f periodicals in 1959—equal to the contents of at least three more full digest-size magazines, but with circulations (in many cases) in the hundreds, instead of tens, of thousands.

Granted that most of this non-specialty material is of low quality—so far. So was most of the stuff in *Amazing* and *Wonder* in the early 'thirties. It's being bought by editors who don't know the field, and often as not from writers not much better informed. (As witness: Jack Kerouac's pretentious "City," in *Nugget*.)

But it is being bought and printed. S-f—or whatever we *don't* call it—is being read and enjoyed more widely than ever before.

The new popular interest in what is still best described as "science-fiction thinking" is evidenced, again, in the really enormous quantity of speculative *non*-fiction appearing on all sides. As with the fiction in the unfamiliar media, much of this wordage is only by courtesy of subject matter "speculative," and when a generally thoughtful or imaginative piece does appear, it is immediately rehashed in a dozen other publications till the last drop of new-think has been squeezed out of it. But the titles alone indicate the latent interest on the part of the mass readership:

"This Is Living in 2000," appeared in *Newsweek* a few months ago. The title approximates Gernsback's old series in the *Air Wonder* of the 'twenties, and the subject matter (subheadings—"Ersatz Coffee," "Climate Control," and "Mining the Ocean Floor") was not much fresher to hardened old readers of s-f. To *Newsweek* readers it was ahead of the news. About the same time (the turn of the decade) *The New York Times Magazine* published "Brave World of the Year 2000," and *This Week* produced a pushbutton-happy two pages called "Get Set for the Happy New Decade." And *Esquire*, in its fat gold Christmas issue for 1959, included an article by David Schoenbrun called "1960: Birth of a Century," which was as thoughtful and comprehensive a piece of extrapolative writing as one would wish to see these days.

Then there were the "Adventures of the Mind" series in *The Saturday Evening Post*; the series of articles on ESP, space travel, and chemical warfare, in *Harper's*; and the increasingly fruitful "SR/Research—Science and Humanity" monthly section in the *Saturday Review*.

People—the general public—are getting used to the idea that hurt so hard when the first Sputnik blew the roof off: that there is precious little we know, and precious much to be learned; and that science is a method—not an authority.

Because the academicians, politicians, and spokesmen in general always learn more slowly (being already so stuffed with knowledge), it may seem that this kind of "s-f thinking" is making slow headway; but watch the cartoons in your newspaper or weekly magazine—listen to the new gags—check the number of fantasy or s-f themes in TV shows—in pop songs.

That mass readership is going to be ready for *good* (but don't call it) science fiction sooner than most of us have believed.

The Year's Best S-F, Sixth Annual Edition (1961)

Introduction

Science, they keep telling us, is "catching up" with science fiction. This is happily (at long last) true—precisely as it *must* be true that on any new frontier (space, surface, political, or academic) surveyors will replace the early scouts, and settlers may tread heavily on the surveyors' heels.

This succession is, indeed, the only sure way to determine the validity of the new frontier. And the more swift and certain the waves of succession, the better it speaks for the work of the scouts—and for the alertness and adventurous spirit of man's society. The rhythm of progress has a fixed pattern, but its tempo is variable in the extreme. Not all frontiers are still new when they are explored.

It was almost 2,000 years from the speculations of Aristarchus of Samos to the mathematically verifiable hypotheses of Johannes Kepler; three hundred more before Goddard and Tsiolkovsky (half the world round from each other) began to apply the principles of physical reaction (first observed in China in Aristarchus's time, and mathematically formulated by Newton in the century after Kepler) so that men could and would, a scant half century later, build vessels to carry them into space to test, with physical exploration, the "proven" theories of Kepler.

In any field of new knowledge, on all frontiers, concrete or physical, the fools must first rush out to see what the accepted angels of the day do not credit even enough to fear. The quixotic ass may be a "Somnium" or a glider at Kitty Hawk, a "Rights of Man," a burning bush, a dream of passage to India, a Unified Field of Theory, or a story of space. Whatever its form, it must take shape first in the imagination of some, somehow, less fettered mind, and pass, through the speculations of philosophers, onto the lathe of logic; if it turns true (however slowly or swiftly), it has become Accepted Theory.

With Theory, the cycle begins anew: someone must "dream up" (literally, just about) a completely new way to test a new theory. Better disciplined, less dreaming, men must refine the techniques; mathematical symbols must be found to describe in precise language the verified experiment. And—

With a new technique in hand, a new idea in the mind's storehouse, some new dreamer will first *imagine* the next step, and (barring final warfare) so on, and on, and—

[...]

Summation: The Year in S-F

When I determined to include in this collection the excerpts from Harry Stine's as yet (at this writing) unpublished article, I was motivated by several things.

First, and most evident, was the paucity of *good science fiction.* There was an abundance of high-quality speculative and imaginative fiction of various kinds, published in every conceivable medium, during 1960; there was very little "real science fiction" anywhere—in or out of the specialty publications—and of that little, most was mediocre to poor.

At the same time, I did not, and do not, believe that the genre is disappearing. It is, certainly, diffusing—spreading out from a limited-circulation group of fiction magazines and a select grouping of hardcover book titles, to the mass markets: paperback novels, radio and TV, comic books, newspapers, and large-circulation general magazines.

In another sense, too, it is diffusing. Until a few years ago, "pure science fiction" confined itself, with rare exceptions, to speculation about space, the atom, and possible inventions or discoveries in the physical sciences.

The very technological advances that have swallowed up the old subjects almost entirely have, meantime, opened up whole new frontiers. And in the same way, the new media of communication now open to science fiction provide it with a new function as well.

Science fiction did not invent speculative thinking; it was quite the other way round. For whatever reasons of historical happenstance, the special kind of thinking that lies between outright fantasy and scientific hypothesis was focused for a while largely in the s-f magazines. Now, some of the best story plots are going into reports by research and development men for the government, the armed services, the big corporations, and such novelties in our scheme of things as the Rand Corporation. What part of this thinking is not channeled into governmental or industrial secrecy is as likely to appear in essay form in a serious journal as in adventure trappings in the magazines.

Mr. Stine has pointed out several areas not currently being examined in this way by industry or government, and has provided a tool for the job. Meantime, there is another job for s-f to do—and one it is doing effectively.

The switch to initials just above was intentional. I am talking now about the whole field of science-fantasy, of speculative literature. And the job I refer to is roughly equivalent to that performed by the Encyclopedists before the French revolution: PR, essentially, public relations.

I have stressed throughout the book the underlying theme of communication. Perhaps writers in the field are so concerned with the one subject just now because the motivation of the writers themselves has shifted somewhat from extrapolation to explanation?

The modern scientist cannot possibly even attempt to keep up with progress in specialties outside his own; publications come too fast and frequently. But the modern citizen *must* keep up with at least the broadest outlines of new developments—and must be prepared, continually, for the most radical of new departures. The best of academic educations have not prepared even the most willing laymen to think in terms of tomorrow's strange new world; and few citizens have either the studiousness or the background to keep up with the accelerating rate of change.

TV has proved, or re-proved (the advertising agencies did it first) the relative impact of pictures and words; there is the same distinction to be made between word-pictures and word-studies. To the specialist, the study is more informative; to almost all others, the word-picture is more so—not only because it informs more quickly, but because it does it more graphically.

Theodore Sturgeon (September 1962)†

Merril begins her homage to Theodore Sturgeon by describing him as a series of paradoxes and contradictions. He appears to be a different person to everyone he meets, and yet, says Merril, it is never due to deception or dishonesty. She describes him as an "eternally sincere poseur." She also describes Sturgeon's writing process, which contrary to other areas of his life, lacks structure and "tidiness." Because he does not see himself as a writer, as someone compelled to write, he writes only to justify his other choices. Therefore, he tends to write sporadically and at the deadline. And yet, he turns out magnificently styled prose.

Merril then turns to the ways in which Sturgeon affected her own writing. Finally, Merril recalls that she is Sturgeon's "invention." For one, Sturgeon was instrumental in the creation and publication of her first professional science fiction story, "That Only a Mother," a story that would put her on the SF map. For another, he helped her develop her pen name and identity. He suggested that she should use her daughter's name, "Merril," but when Judith balked at the idea of losing her Jewish surname, Sturgeon wrote a sonnet entitled "On the Birth of Judith Merril." He notes that her given name, Judith, means "Jewess," so her identity would remain intact. More importantly, he worked on the poem even though he desperately needed to meet his own writing deadline for a much-needed paycheck. Ultimately, she describes Ted Sturgeon as a man of style: as a person and as a writer—a style she could never match.

† Full text in the E-book version.

The Year's Best S-F, Seventh Annual Edition (1962)

[No Introduction for this Volume]

[...]

"Among the Dangs" by George P. Elliott

But that's not science fiction...!

Even my best friends (to invert a paraphrase) keep telling me: That's not science fiction!?

Sometimes they mean it couldn't be s-f, because it's good. Sometimes it couldn't be because it's not about spaceships or time machines. (Religion or politics or psychology isn't science fiction—is it?) Sometimes (because some of my best friends are s-f fans) they mean it's not really science fiction—just fantasy or satire or something like that.

On the whole, I think I am very patient. I generally manage to explain, again, just a *little* wearily, what the "S-F" in the title of this book means, and what science fiction is, and why the one contains the other, without being constrained by it. But it does strain my patience when the exclamation is compounded to mean: "Surely you don't mean to use that in *S-F*? That's not science fiction!"—about a first-rate piece of the honest thing.

For some reason, this comes most often from other editors—and most irritatingly from the editor who first bought and published the story in question, and does not want to think that he printed *that* kind of story. But the ultimate in frustration is to hear the same thing from the editor who is publishing me....

"Among the Dangs" first appeared in *Esquire* in 1958; in 1959 it was reprinted in *Fantasy and Science Fiction*, and in the O. Henry Awards. And in both years, my editors said with dismay (you guessed it!)—"*That's* not science fiction!"

Last year, it became eligible for inclusion in this volume once more by appearing as the title story in a collection of Mr. Elliott's short stories. It is a multiple pleasure to be able to reprint it at last—partly because I too am a *real*-science-fiction fan and, in a year when there was precious little of the pure product published anywhere, "Among the Dangs" remains a first-rate sample of what science fiction really is.

[...]

"The Quaker Cannon" by Frederik Pohl and C. M. Kornbluth

"Social science fiction" is too often thought of as limited either to angry satire or to ponderous Utopian novels. Certainly the Pohl-Kornbluth combination has been noted primarily for a highly specialized kind of satirical novel set in a stiflingly overpopulated, advertising-drenched, cold-war-like future.

This kind of novel, whose objective is to pinpoint some of the more flagrant of our cultural absurdities, must of necessity assume the continuation of some sort of peace on Earth, however uneasy or precarious (just as the last group of stories here have done). The novelette that follows is unusual in several respects:

First, it is an atom-war story which is neither about the onset of the war nor its aftermath, but the war itself.

Second, it is a straightforward, serious, subjectively sympathetic Pohl-Kornbluth collaboration (completed by Mr. Pohl after Mr. Kornbluth's sudden death).

Third, it is concerned less with the effects on our society of another war, than with those of our culture on such a war.

[...]

"The Beat Cluster" by Fritz Leiber

The latest thing in subnuclear theory (I learned from an article in *The Saturday Evening Post*) is that the sub-particles have subparticles—and those subparticles have...*ad infinitum*. That is, it may be impossible to reach the ultimate submicroscopic unit of the atom.

A similar likelihood has been evident for some time in the case of scholarly-literary distinctions. For instance: science fiction is a subform of science fantasy, which is a subform of fantasy, which is a subform of fiction—and still, within s-f, the aficionado subdivides repeatedly.

The subspecies most widely identified with the field as a whole is, of course, the space story: this is what is commonly considered the "science fiction" that "science has caught up with." Science fiction (meaning: the space story) is dead—they say—because it has become true-adventure; and they would be right, if science fiction (or even the space story) were limited to speculation about rockets and orbits. But when we consider the *people* in those now so-nearly-true-adventure orbits....

"In Tomorrow's Little Black Bag" by James Blish

An observer of the s-f scene once commented that science fiction-writing was less a means of livelihood than a way of life. It could as easily be said that s-f is not so much a kind of reading as a way of thinking.

Reginald Bretnor and Robert Heinlein (notably, in *The Science Fiction Novel*) have advanced the proposition that this identifying fundamental of science fiction is not the specific science content, but the writer's awareness of science, and in particular of the scientific method.

To utilize this discipline—(observation, hypothesis, experimentation)—in fiction it is necessary, first, to get the best reliable information whether on weather, whales, witches, or whatever; then, to relate data and drama in such a way as to obtain a story line; finally, to devise the most useful environmental situation against which to play out the drama.

One might approach the same area of definition from another viewpoint, and say that the identifying factor in s-f is the interaction between man and his environment. "Mainstream" writing ordinarily confines itself to situations resulting from man's reaction to only one phase of environment: his fellow-men. "Straight fantasy," by definition, deals with unreal—fantastic—environmental factors. S-f, specifically, considers the effect on/of a human being of/on a realistically modern or logically predictable future environment (physical, technical, natural, or manmade).

Part of that physical environment for each man is the body his subjective self inhabits. Mr. Blish, who writes science fiction by night (as a way of life), is by day (for a livelihood) a public relations man specializing in the highly esoteric field of institutional drug promotion. Out of this combined background, he considers some of the possibilities inherent in our persistent efforts to modify, amend, and improve our own fleshly surroundings.

[...]

"The Asteroids, 2194" by John Wyndham

The "space story" (the one science caught up with) was originally concerned with the techniques of space travel—with our ability to manufacture and control what we now call "the hardware" of space flight. The "planet story" has traditionally been rollicking-romance-adventure (prototypically, Burroughs's *A Princess of Mars*). Both of these varieties dealt primarily with man's effect on the environments of space. A third type, and indeed the earliest one, has been the philosophic novel, in which the space (or, most usually, Moon, setting) was essentially a stage for a passion play; in these there was no real interaction; the voyageur was primarily an observer.

Now, more and more, writers confronted by the imminence of space travel, are considering the effects of the trip into the unknown on mankind. One hears the old phrase, the "conquest of space," less frequently now. That there will be immediate and perhaps profound effects on us, physiologically and culturally, is clear; equally obvious, but much less clearcut, are the potential effects on our psychology, philosophy, religion, and mystique.

[...]

Summation: S-F, 1961

For some years now, those of us working in what even we still quaintly call "the science-fiction field" have been increasingly aware of the floating-island nature of that "field." And if it seemed at times that we were simply drifting out to sea, it is now becoming sharply evident that the direction of drift, all along, was into the "mainstream." The specialized cult of science fiction (for which many of us still, and I expect will, feel a lingering nostalgia) is rapidly disappearing, as the essential quality is absorbed into the main body of literature.

More properly, I should say, reabsorbed. S-f had its beginnings in mainstream writing. The literary-sociological analysis of the compartmentalizing of this kind of fiction during the first half of the twentieth century will undoubtedly provide scholastic adventure for innumerable future thesis-writers. For those of us actively interested in the (flooded) field at the present time, it is enough to understand that the reabsorption has not been one-sided. For any prodigal to effect his return, it is necessary not only that the parent body be prepared to offer welcome, but that the wanderer has found cause to come home.

These causes have been varied and complex, ridiculous and sublime: they have included such things as the influence of "the syndicate" on magazine distribution, the International Geophysical Year, Kingsley Amis's book of lectures, and Willy Ley's lectures on books. (The rest of the list I leave to those scholars of tomorrow.) But whatever the causes, the results are obvious.

At the beginning of 1956, when the *First Annual* of this series was being readied for the press, I counted thirteen science-fiction magazines in this country, and four more in England. (Most of them were quarterlies or bimonthlies; it averaged out to about ten altogether each month.) That *First Annual* contained, proudly, three (out of eighteen) stories from sources outside the specialty magazines; the Honorable Mentions listed seven more. And the Summation pointed with a sort of ghetto pride to the fact that thirty or forty of Our Kind of Stories had crossed the line in '55, and found respectable lodging in literary and "slick" magazines.

This year, sixteen of the thirty fiction and verse selections are from general fiction magazines, or books. There are five s-f magazines published here, and two in England—five and a half a month average, with the three bimonthlies.

In '56, I was able to include three "name" writers from outside the specialty field. This year, there are only thirteen stories by writers known *in* the field. Most striking is the number of writers from non-fiction fields who have made their first story efforts in s-f; most gratifying is the growing number of serious young writers who are devoting themselves equally to s-f and "quality" media.

This is the internal evidence. From outside come such items as the previously mentioned seminar of the Modern Language Association (or the word from my scout in Sausalito that s-f is the top seller in the beatniks' favorite bookstore). There is *The Twilight Zone* on TV, which no one (except us Old School Ties) thinks of as s-f. There is *The Saturday Evening Post*, printing without special comment an average of one fantasy or s-f story per issue....

Which brings up a point. The welcome offered to s-f is warm, as only a homecoming can be. But by the same token, the critics, editors, reviewers, publishers, who are uncle and aunt, elder brother, sister, and cousins, who all stayed correctly at home while we went wandering in lurid pulp-paper lands, are not prepared to meet us on the grounds of our own choosing——and certainly not to recognize us by the identity we assumed "outside."

Thus, much of the best science fiction published today is under wrappers and headings that either angrily disclaim the "science-fiction" label, or ignore it completely. As for the broader field defined in this book as "S-F," the most special labeling it's likely to get is "unusual" or "offbeat."

The cult is dead, or at the least, moribund. But one may hope it has infused new life into the culture.

The Year's Best S-F, Eighth Annual Edition (1963)

[No Introduction to the volume.]

"The Unsafe Deposit Box" by Gerald Kersh

Fable and Fantasy—imaginative fiction in general, from earliest myths and early moon voyages to *1984* and the *Eighth Annual SF*—have always served as vehicles for social criticism and for speculation on new ideas in science and philosophy. The most startling, heretical, extreme, or radical new notions could always be explored in fairy tales when risk to personal reputation, or danger of public repression, made "serious" expositions seem unwise; or a hypothesis, as yet unproven, could be pre-tested, as it were, by building a story structure—an imaginary, but logical, "reality"—on the assumption of its validity.

The specialized variety of fantasy that we call "modern science fiction" had its beginnings in the first half of the nineteenth century with the literary discovery (by Mary Shelley, Poe, Hawthorne, and Balzac, most notably) of the Wonderful Invention. It was a time of effervescent technological excitement: the beginning of man's consciousness of his capacity to create his own environment—to remake the actual physical world closer to his own desires. The Wonderful Invention (ordinarily, at the start, a machine or a formula) opened a whole new area of the imagination, with the basic question: *if* we can effect this change (mechanical, biological, etc.) in our world, what will the changed world be like for us?

It is this inquiry that constitutes the essence of "science fiction." And this volume begins, as it were, at the beginning of s-f, with an almost classically pure example of the Wonderful Imagination—complete with a secret formula, an at least moderately mad scientist, a tricky intellectual puzzle, a clutch of comically inept civil authorities, and even the traditional, if somewhat cheeky-tongued, formalized style of first-person narrative.

[...]

"The Face in the Photo" by Jack Finney

Here again are the pure classic elements: the professor, the secret experiments, the frustrated police—and this time the Invention is that perennial favorite, a time machine. Here again is the first-person narration—but it owes rather more in style to Dashiell Hammett than to Conan Doyle. The treatment is subjective rather than impersonal; the basic problem is not so much intellectual as ethical; the theme is concerned with the inventor's responsibility to other people, rather than to science; and insofar as it is *science* fiction at all the science involved is sociology rather than mathematics.

This is, in short, a rendering of the classic components of s-f (meaning science fantasy), in the completely contemporary style of s-f (meaning, speculative fiction).

"The Circuit Riders" by R. C. FitzPatrick

This is FitzPatrick's first published story, and appropriately enough, it is almost a prototype of contemporary s-f (speculative/science fiction/fantasy), in subject matter as well as treatment.

The Wonderful Invention is still with us; but it is neither a secret formula nor a mysterious black box. Actually, it is a mechanism that would once have been considered usable only in the most Gothic of pseudo-scientific horror fiction: a "psychic" machine, an emotion-reader. Today, the concept seems less remote than space travel appeared to most people a scant ten years ago; and the handling of the idea is so quietly naturalistic that the reader almost feels the instruction manual for the gadget must be lying just out of sight.

And out of sight is where it stays. The author's concern is not with the inventor or the invention, as such, but with the functioning relationships of (comparatively) ordinary people adapting themselves to yet one more change in the physical and social environment.

"Such Stuff" by John Brunner

The more we know, the less we know for sure. The once-glorious certainties of "natural law" have dimmed to shaky "statistical probabilities." Modern medicine continues to retrieve new scientific "miracle" from the old pharmacopoeia of witchcraft. Men build machines to think for themselves, and "human engineering" institutes design electronic-linguistic-visual circuits for the mechanical manipulation of men's minds.

And now, across a broad frontier in which the most sophisticated "hardware" and "know-how" is urgently employed (from cybernetics and electronics, through bio-chemistry, over to semantics), the latest, greatest explorations and discoveries are being made *into* the mind of man, seeking to separate, define, and analyze the entire spectrum of the purely "subjective." (One visualizes an examination paper in some future university with such questions as: "Give the respective electro-chemical equivalents for the following concepts: [1] falsehood, [2] fiction, [3] fantasy, [4] creative, visualization, [5] dream.")

This is the research frontier to which, more and more, the most thoughtful and through-provoking writers of s(science? speculation?)-f are turning now.

[...]

"All the Sounds of Fear" by Harlan Ellison

If the distinction between (some kinds of) "fantasy" and "science fiction" is often elusive, this is in part because of the peculiar function of speculative fiction in general.

S-f, by definition, operates just outside the border of "known" facts. It is most valid and usually most successful when it conducts its explorations in those same areas where advance outposts of scientific research are being established. The proper-science encampment, burdened of necessity with all the heavy equipment of experimental evidence and scholastic proof (not to mention the weight of reputation and respectability), is obviously less mobile than the lone-wolf writer-philosopher, who carries no more baggage than his own perceptions, logic, intuition, and imagination. In turn, the usefulness of the scout's early reports will depend as much on the light supplied him by the scattered outposts, as on his own personal equipment. And the farther out he wanders, the more likely will his message to be no more than a report of a new wonder glimpsed. This we call fantasy.

[...]

"The Day Rembrandt Went Public" by Arnold M. Auerbach

...And if you are one who feels his grip on "reality" is firm and clear, then how about the gradations of the "non-real?"

Between the extremes of the most solid science fiction and the sheerest fantasy lies a wide range of potential: the probable, the plausible, the possible, and the purely poetic. On yet another literary line (somewhere, askew, intersecting fact, fable, *and* fiction) lies a whole other set of undetermined points and limits. "Unreal," "surreal," "satiric," "silly"—the label depends, I expect, on whether you incline to *Harper's* or to *Mad*, or both. In any case, it is a joy to experience the renascence of the imaginative essay.

[...]

Summation: SF, 1962

What hath God wrought?

It was, of course, the telegraph. And the sentiment, in 1844, was probably the only predictable (perhaps the only permissible) available response.

Yet, what was significant about the telegraph was precisely the fact that God had not wrought it. It was not—like fire, the wheel, the arch, or even the telescope—a new way to use, understand, or control some "natural" phenomenon. It was, specifically, a human creation: a synthesis—a pulling together—of already-known facts about the God-given (natural) world, to form a new thing, visualized and constructed by natural (God-given) human intelligence.

This was the glittering dawn of the Age of Synthesis, the beginning of man's technological self-consciousness. In two short, fabulous generations, the founders of modern engineering and applied science (Faraday, Henry, Morse, Bessemer, Pasteur, Mendel, Perkin, for instance) took hold of the great discoveries of the past two centuries (the great Age of Analysis—Galileo, Harvey, Leeuwenhoek, Newton, Lavoisier, to name a few) and pointed the way for mankind to remake his own world to suit his own images.

What hath man wrought?

This was the true marvel of Mr. Morse's demonstration of "instantaneous" long-distance communication. And it was this kind of miracle, man-made, that generated in imaginative writers the new kind of exploratory fantasy that became "science fiction."

The Wonderful Invention (literary), in its earliest phase, was almost always a machine or a formula, and it functioned in one of the precisely defined areas of natural science: physics, chemistry, medicine or biology. It was not until the Darwinian explosion (or, more broadly, the philosophic eruption that included Marx-Engels, Darwin-Wallace and Freud) that the concept of process really developed: the Idea that a new way of doing things, or even of looking at things, might change the world as readily as a new machine; and the corollary, that any successful innovation is not merely physical, but social, as well.

What hath the machine wrought?

This was the wonder that brought about what is generally called "modern science fiction"—the school that started with Wells and Verne, Chesterton, Kipling and Forster. And, of course, implicit in their approach (as in the whole notion of process) was the kind of speculative work that constitutes most of the best of s-f today, where the Invention, as such, is often dropped from the middle, and the field of exploration becomes man himself.

What have man's inventiveness, man's civilization, man's knowledge and technology done to man? What *is* man, to have done these things? What roads may lead to what Norbert Wiener calls "the human use of human beings"?

I have before me two statements on contemporary s-f, from the past year's crop of critical writings. One is from *Time* magazine's first essay at reviewing this anthology. The other is from an introduction by Frederik Pohl to Theodore R. Cogswell's short story collection, *The Wall around the World.*

Time discusses the *Seventh Annual SF* under the heading, "Outpaced by Space," in a tone of sanctimonious mourning that represents a dubiously pleasant change from that publication's usual snide, sniping altitude toward s-f in general. This time, *Time* seemed almost to approve of the stories—as stories. It was the lack of "science fiction" that disturbed the reviewer. "Science fiction," he concludes unhappily, will have to take a breather until neutrinos, wave mechanics and information theory grow familiar enough to be clothed in human terms."

I do not choose to quibble with anyone's definition of this most ambiguous of labels. If what the folks at *Time* want is human stories about neutrinos and wave mechanics, they may well have to hold their breaths for a bit (although with a bit more academic knowledge of information theory on their part, they might have recognized the information-theory stories in the *Seventh Annual*). It is not, basically, unreasonable to equate "science fiction" with the man-in-the-street's idea of "science"; it is only inaccurate. Mr. Pohl's semantics are somewhat closer to today's intellectual realities:

> "Science" is, after all, knowledge. The term for any given science is a "discipline"—what distinguishes science from non-science is an attitude. The gadgets, the cybernetic brains and space-drives, are only hardware that transmute into practice the knowledge obtained by methodical investigation.... It is the *study* that is science (or isn't science), not the subject matter. So with science fic-

> tion, it is not the subject matter that determines whether or not it qualifies, but the manner in which it is written. You can write a science-fiction story about ghosts as well as you can write one about rockets...."

And the specifying quality, for Mr. Pohl, of a work handled "as science fiction" is "by the application of brainpower, by investigating the causes and the consequences.

I find the Pohl approach a good deal more useful than that of *Time*; it still leaves, to my mind, an area of the literature unclassified. Obviously, "A Miracle of Rare Device" is fantasy; as clearly, "The Circuit Riders" is science fiction. But what about "Seven-Day Terror" or "Such Stuff" or "The Unfortunate Mr. Morky"? The "attitude" of science is clearly implicit in them all, the detail-work is absent, in each case, to varying degrees; the seriously speculative (studying) approach is present in all.

For my part, I do not care whether you, or he, or the editor in that corner, or the reviewer in the other, call them "science fiction" or not. They are—like all the material considered for inclusion in this *Annual*—examples of the broad field of S (for speculative) F (for fantasy, fiction, or fact), SF: the literature of the disciplined imagination.

[...]

The Year's Best S-F, Ninth Annual Edition (1964)

Introduction

[Nineteen sixty-three] was the year of the first rocket probe to Venus and the year in which Medgar Evers and John F. Kennedy [were] shot to death in the streets of American cities. A complex new electronic brain began translating Chinese, and the proud new atomic submarine, *Thresher*, sank with more than two hundred men on board.

By the time you read this, the record on 1964 will be almost or altogether complete—and we may confidently expect even more contradictions and internal frictions: not in any one country, or in any one field of endeavor, or on any particular economic or social level, religious or political grouping, but within almost all such groups, and between many of them.

There has probably never been so much disagreement among respectable people about morals; among educators about schooling and parents about child rearing; among scientists about basic theories or engineers about specific applications, or doctors about the courses, treatment, or diagnosis of anything from the common cold to terminal cancer.

And it will not get more settled before it is more upset.

Imaginative literature today is preoccupied—necessarily—with the same stirrings, the same conflicts, visions of greatness and of doom that are acting on the imaginations of philosophers, scientists, teachers, industrial and political leaders, throughout the world.

On the brink of more dramatic physical explorations and discoveries than ever before, we find ourselves facing, first and most urgently, a different kind of great unknown: the nature of cultural man; the odds (no less than life and death) on his ability to coexist with cultures other than his own; of the likelihood that natural man can or will learn to adapt to his own technological culture.

In a forum published last year in *Playboy*, "1984 and Beyond," a dozen top writers of science fantasy argued the probable future of man. William Tenn concluded a discussion on future social trends by saying:

> Thoreau wrote over a hundred years ago that "the mass of men lead lives of quiet desperation." Well, the world has changed fantastically since then, but the mass of men still do. History always repeats itself, but on another step of the spiral. We are a wildly imaginative, inordinately idealistic, incredibly persistent, hopelessly naïve, incurably corrupt species, and no matter what we do we always seem to wind up somehow or other in the same position on the tree, except that occasionally it's a different tree. Tomorrow we'll be looking for the mechanical bananas in a nickel-plated jungle.

[...]

Summation: SF, 1963

Never before have so many been threatened with so much.

If the fallout doesn't get you, the fault slip will. The next ice age, we are shiveringly reminded, is practically upon us. It may be a matter of only thousands, or hundreds, of generations before our sun goes nova. And if neither natural nor man-made Doomsday befalls us, it will be not hundreds, but ten or less generations before we must cope with the prospects of starvation—or suffocation—in the foul-aired plankton-fed single supermegapolis of Earth's sardine-can-packed population.

It is not that the dangers are new: just that we are newly aware of them.

Never has so much been promised to so many.

The wealth of our technological civilization, today, is beyond the wildest fantasies of earlier times: wealth measured not in such abstractions as "capital goods" or "national incomes," but in the actualities of physical comfort, health, leisure, longevity, and even that most vital (and most alienable) of "natural rights," the freedom-and-capacity to pursue individual happiness.

That wealth, like technology, is unevenly distributed, we know. But even the most horrifying (to us) conditions of life on Earth today were only the norm for the human condition until a few scant centuries ago. (Neither Plato nor Lao-tse would have paused long in their dialogues on politics or morality, to be shocked at the deaths of four children in a rebellion-quelling like Birmingham's bombing. Apartheid standards of living would have seemed slave-coddling to Cheops or Genghis Khan. The civil rights available to a Red Chinese peasant today would have dazzled a serf in the kitchens of Louis XIV of France.) And the increment in knowledge and productivity continues to accelerate while it spreads. The real-wealth potential is constantly greater both in total quantity and in wide availability.

The resources of our world are not new; we have just started to make use of them.

Never has so much uncertainty been felt by so many.

In our relations with the physical environment, we first learned simple skills to use it, then acquired some understanding of it; only then could we start to remake it to our advantage. The accumulation of observations by countless naturalists and discoverers provided a basis for analytical science; the scientist's hypothesis-and-experiment is the base on which the inventor and engineer stand.

As far back as any history goes, human beings have observed each other; primitive techniques for controlling and utilizing human intelligence and personality were discovered in the age of myths. But the first systematic, analytic, scientific studies of mankind by man began barely a century ago—five hundred years behind physical science. If the rate of progress has been swifter, it is because we had already learned something of the techniques of scientific investigation, and because we now have the products of earlier sciences to use as tools and mirrors for self-study. (Electroencephalography probes and measures the functions of the brain; a cybernetic machine mirrors it.)

We are now rapidly approaching the kind of understanding of our own thoughts, emotions, capacities, and behavior which will, abruptly (next year? next decade?), break through to the level of application and invention. The true science of *humanics*, when it emerges, will of necessity convey the power to remake our intellects and personalities to our advantage...or to our final doom.

The concept of self-determination is not new; but we are now about to acquire the capacity for it.

Science fantasy is not so new now, either; it has apparently just reached the level of self-consciousness. That is: never before has so much been published by or about writers and writing of speculative fiction.

There was the usual scattering of individual items:

Fredric Brown had a page of poetic definition in *Fantasy and Science Fiction*. Isaac Asimov had two pages in *The Bulletin of the Atomic Scientists*, urging the use of an early taste for good science fiction as a selection test for creative scientific potential more effective than any combination of intelligence, aptitude, and personality tests now in use in our schools.

Walt Kelly had four pages in the *Atlantic*: "Ka-Platz! The Delight in the Unexpected." Robert Bloch devoted his column in one issue of *Rogue* to the annual World Science Fiction Convention. At least two pieces by Soviet authors appeared here: one by Arkadi Strugatsky, in USSR, about Soviet science fiction; and "A Soviet View of American Science Fiction," by Alexander Karantsev, in *Amazing*.

The first series of Sam Moskowitz's bibliographic biographies of leading writers in the genre appeared in book form as *Explorers of the Infinite* (World Publishing Company, 1963). Michael Moorcock began a series which has since completed a scholarly analysis of fantasy fiction, in *Science Fantasy*. *Life* had a lengthy photo-biographic essay on Hugo Gernsback and "scientifiction."

In addition to these individual statements, some fifty-two writers of s-f, and nine assorted editors, agents, reviewers, producers, publishers, etc. (A list of the participants will be found at the end of the "Summation.") were involved in three separate publishing ventures: the *Playboy* symposium, the *Double Bill* survey, and a series of guest editorials in *New Worlds*.

The opinions expressed in the editorials would take too much space to summarize individually; as a group, they fall largely within the range of attitudes more concisely formulated in the *Double Bill* survey.

The questionnaire, compiled by Lloyd Biggle, Jr., asked eleven questions, most of which concentrated on advice to new writers. The three that evoked the most widely interesting responses were the *raison d'être* question quoted earlier, and these two: "For what reason or reasons do you write (or edit) science fiction in preference to other forms of literature?" and "What is your appraisal of the relationship of science fiction to the 'mainstream' of literature?"

Among forty-three participants, there were at least six or seven distinct notions of what "mainstream" meant—and even more differences about the relationship between mainstream and s-f. Some felt the first was a subdivision of the second; some that the second was a subdivision of the first; and some said there was no real distinction between the two, except that imposed by artificial labels. A large and vigorous minority felt the two forms are radically different and probably will not—certainly should not—merge and lose their separate identities. And cutting across all other differences (except among those who saw none) was a roughly half-and-half split on which is "better" literature.

In view of all these permutations of disagreement, the clear-cut response on the other two questions is startling. Discounting the several authors who gave as reason for personal preference, "easier to write and sell" or "entertainment" as the major significance (since these are applicable to any field in which a writer happens to work), the overwhelming majority gave as their main answer to both these questions the freedom offered in s-f, as compared with other contemporary forms: freedom to express any and all opinions, to explore unconventional and unpopular ideas, to examine human problems and relationships, and to experiment with style and technique. ("It stretches the imagination." "I am a surrealist at heart." "The most iconoclastic form of literature." Or John Campbell's, "There's room to think and move.")

Next most important, and mentioned by at least half the authors, was the use of s-f (in this case primarily science fiction) as a learning medium. For some, this meant simply a vehicle for teaching (or preaching); others—and rather more—were interested in what they themselves learned, both as readers and writers; the largest number referred to the sheer intellectual exercise involved. ("Mind-stretching." "Exhilaration." "Kicks." "Creative challenge.")

The *Playboy* discussion was a showcase for this kind of thought-kick. The twelve participants were invited, not to discuss their work, but to demonstrate it. Although the published version did not appear until the summer of 1963, the project was initiated almost a year earlier, at a taped midnight discussion during the World Science Fiction Convention in Chicago in 1962.

Seven of the final panel members were present at that first session, and it was the only actual "session." Many tapes and mailings later, much-revised and re-exchanged, the symposium emerged as a wide-ranging, colorful résumé of science-fiction thinking over the past twenty-five years. If there was a certain lack of freshness of idea, at least for the case-hardened s-f reader, in most of the subjects covered (space race, aliens, nuclear war, population explosion, genetic control, ocean farming, automation, robots, transportation, and communication), it was a different matter when the discussion turned to the prospects for what I have called here *humanics*.

This is, of course, the true frontier of science in our day. When we have crossed it, we may come to new perceptions which will require a genuine re-evaluation of our understanding of the physical world. But for now, outside the most esoteric work in cosmology and, on the other end, subnucleonics, the largest part of our physical science is in the engineering stage. And by definition, it is where the breakthroughs are just about to come, that speculative fiction becomes exciting and fruitful.

Among the subjects covered were psychochemicals, as specifics for mental disease, as education conditioners, as sleep substitutes, and as pleasure enhancers; current work in mapping the brain with psycho-electronics, and the possibilities of its application in all the areas mentioned above; progress in medicine, surgery, and cybernetics, toward the total elimination of physical disease—and for a dramatic increase in the ordinary lifespan; the use of cryogenics to preserve bodies until new biochemical or surgical techniques are available; and of course the effects of these developments, and of other-aspects of technology already in hand, on the sexual, domestic, intellectual, ethical, religious, and social behavior of human beings.

Lightly touched on, here and there, were the upheavals in economics, politics, religion, and education, which are already irrevocably under way, as a result of automation and communications advances—but which are still due for much more radical changes as psychological and physiological innovations occur, and as the more adventurous engineering research projects begin to bear fruit: broadcast power (solar or atomic), domestic automation, exploration of the solar system; or, less immediate, antigravity and perhaps the matter duplicator.

Noticeably absent from the discussion were two major themes of the last generation of science fiction: time travel and ESP. In the case of time travel, one might feel the vein has been thoroughly worked; pending new information, there is nothing much more to be said. But ESP, or "*psionics*," has been one of the most active areas of inquiry in the past decade, and still is. Presumably, *Playboy* is happy to be unconventional and iconoclastic, and willing to give space to eccentric or even possibly subversive ideas, but not quite prepared to be called "crackpot."

This distinction—and I mean "honor"—belongs to the specialty science-fiction magazines. (Remember—it was crackpot, not long ago, to believe in the future of rocketry or space travel; and that "crackpots" was security-guard slang for Manhattan District scientists.) It was precisely this extra dimension of freedom of thought that the writers were talking about in the *Double Bill* survey. It was in terms of this much latitude that Campbell said, "There's room to think and move."

The increasing pressures for conformity and homogeneity in today's culture are unfortunately not limited to suburban housing developments, clothing styles, or automobile shapes; nor even to the more rigid areas of religion, politics, and education. They work on science, art, and philosophy as well.

These pressures are not new. In the past they have operated against rationalism and scientific inquiry, even as today they inveigh against what institutionalized science finds irrational. At the height of the Inquisition, Johannes Kepler could publish his theories only as science fiction in Journeys to the Moon [*Somnium*, 1608, 1634]. In our present-day commonsensical philosophic atmosphere, imaginative literature still gives scope to inquiry in those areas of human experience not recognized by any currently sanctified systems of classification.

When the vast body of phenomena now stigmatized by association with "magic" and "mysticism" are finally incorporated into a more inclusive view of nature and cosmology, some of the credit, one hopes, will go to the freewheeling thinkers who are now busily prying the lid off Pandora's *psi* box, and to the magazines and editors who are providing the outlet for "crackpot" ideas.

[...]

Books (March 1965)

The Rest of the Robots, Isaac Asimov, Doubleday, $5.95
A Pail of Air, Fritz Leiber, Ballantine, 50¢
Doctor to the Stars, Murray Leinster, Pyramid, 40¢
Shock II, Richard Matheson, Dell, 50¢.
Sturgeon in Orbit, Theodore Sturgeon, Pyramid, 40¢

There is a fantasy of fantasies cherished alike by friends and foes of science fiction: the self-image of s-f as an *enfant terrible* of literature, glittering in space-mail against the metallic sheen of sharp-angled twirly-knobbed technocrats.

The fact is, s-f has a past. I am not speaking of heroic ancestries the classical and medieval voyages to the Moon. I mean the immediate line of descent common to all contemporary fiction forms, starting in the early-mid-nineteenth century with Hawthorne, Shelley, Poe, Verne, Swift, and Butler, and taking contemporary forms with Kipling, Doyle, Twain, Bierce, Wells, and London around the turn of the century.

Not even the specialty field of popular magazine science fiction can still honestly be either faulted or favored as juvenile. It is almost forty years now since Hugo Gernsback's first "scientifiction" magazines established a vehicle for his pre-Time linguistricks; almost thirty since Howard Phillips Lovecraft's death consolidated his Stranger-seeking cult. It is a full quarter-century since the combined readership of these overlapping circles formed the dedicated audience that underlay the "Golden Age" of the early Campbell *Astounding* and *Unknown*....

It was in these magazines that the first science fantasies by Leiber, Sturgeon, and Asimov first appeared (all three, as it happened, in 1939). Leinster was writing in the genre before Gernsback invented the label. The youngest writer in this current crop of short story collections is Matheson, with only fifteen years behind him—the same fifteen years in which s-f has firmly established itself as a book publishing "category."

Clearly, neither critic, author, or publisher may any longer responsibly either ignore the field, or overlook its failures, because of its supposed youth or lack of background.

Unhappily, neither the Sturgeon nor Asimov volumes are representative of the authors' current work. The most recent of the robot stories dates from 1957; the Sturgeon selections were all written in the early fifties. The fact is, neither writer has done more than a handful of s-f stories in the last five or six years. Asimov turned to science fact writing in '57; since then he seems to do just about one piece of science fiction a year. Sturgeon—since his story in the special issue of *F&SF* honoring him in 1962—seems to have done everything *but.* I keep coming across movie novelizations, suspense stories, articles, columns, and reviews in everything from *The Realist* to the *National Review*....

Both authors have, also, been extensively collected and anthologized; the present collections are, then, barrel-scrapings—and as such they come off surprisingly well.

The Rest of the Robots is just what it says: all the positronic robot stories not previously reprinted in *I, Robot.* There is no need to report here on the two novels included in this giant package, *The Caves of Steel* and *The Naked Sun*, beyond saying that they are there; both have been too much reprinted and reviewed to need further comment. The eight short stories that make up the first third of the book run a clear, but close, second to the group in *I, Robot*—and they do include such memorable items as "Victory Unintentional," "Let's Get Together," and "Lenny."

At this size (556 pp.) and price and in view of the availability of much of the material elsewhere, this is primarily a volume for collectors and gift-givers; but it *is* a must for collectors and completists, enhanced as it is by revealing author's notes between the stories; and for anyone to whom even half the stories are new, it's still worth the price.

The Sturgeon collection is less even-textured. Three things for/about/against it must be said immediately:

1) If, like me, you missed "Extrapolation" when it appeared in magazine form in 1953 (as "Beware the Fury"), run—do not walk—to your nearest newsstand; all you need is forty cents.
2) Reading instructions: When you finish that first story, put the book down for a bit, before you start downhill on the others. And, if you *must* read the author's intro notes—leave them till last.
3) So far as I know, none of the five selections have ever appeared in book form before.

There is, I am afraid, some cause for this last item. "The Wages of Synergy," for instance, has one of the most compelling openings you have ever read; I wish I could say half as much for its end. "Make Room for Me" will, I think, fascinate other Sturgeon fans as it did me; it seems to have been a sort of first-take on the ideas that grew, shortly afterwards, into "More Than Human" (the *gestalt*, *bleshing*, et al.). Here the concepts are undefined, the terminology still undeveloped, the characters arrested halfway between lifelike realism and artistic truth in one of the hoariest old s-f plots on the books. But the germ is there.

The last two stories in the book are there, I assume, only because no one else has reprinted them. I approve the motive, in general; but with such items as "Fear Is a Business," "The Perfect Host," and "Tandy's Story" (to name just the most obvious few) still not available in any Sturgeon collection—well, it seems odd, at least, that no hardcover publisher has realized that there is still enough prime Sturgeon uncollected to fill just such a giant volume as the Asimov.

The Leinster book picks up chronologically where Asimov left off, with a 1957 novella, "The Grandfathers' War"; this and the other two shorter, but still hefty, novelettes (both 1963), "Med Ship Man" and "Tallien Three," are all part of the Interstellar Medical Service series.

I have never read a bad story by Murray Leinster, and do not expect to. At his standard level, he is a superb craftsman; occasionally he rises far above it, but never sinks below. These are typical Leinster standards: tightly woven, solidly structured, absorbing, credible space-science adventures. Nothing spectacular; very good reading.

If Richard Matheson had Murray Leister's structural strength and story-telling technique—but he doesn't. *Shock II* is, typically, full of brilliant conceptions and incomplete executions. Well, not quite full—I keep reading Matheson because about one time in ten he does what he sets out to do. That is doing a great deal, and in this book he does it once, and perhaps twice, in thirteen tries.

Seven of these are primarily horror stories. One, "Graveyard Shift," actually horrified me and "Crickets" contained one scene of possibly unforgettable horror. The problem here, I think, is that though Matheson's characters ring true, it is more the ring of a coin on a counter than of a struck gong: the overtones are missing. We see the people, even recognize them, as we might familiar faces on the street; we do not *know* them, as we come to know even the most bizarre and unlikely beings, for instance, in Sturgeon's work. (This can be a matter of style. Leinster, for example, seldom takes us inside his people—but neither does he rely for effects on the kind of emotional shock which requires strong empathy.)

Of the other six entries, one is an amusing-enough *Playboy*-joke story "A Flourish of Strumpets," and five are psychological or philosophical s-f. "From Shadowed Places" has a profound theme, inventively plotted, and superficially written. "Mute" is the kind of story that keeps me reading Matheson hopefully; this one works—and by itself would make the book worthwhile.

The Leiber collection, like Matheson's, ranges from 1950 through 1962. Like Matheson and Sturgeon, Leiber is an uneven writer. Unlike Sturgeon, he is still active in s-f; unlike Matheson (or, hopefully, just ahead of him) he has mastered his craft to the point where even the least of the stories hit a good average. Like both of the others, Leiber is colorful, inventive, emotional, sometimes shocking—more the pyrotechnician than the cookbook cook. And his versatility includes a pronounced flair for satire, well displayed here.

Between the warmth and optimism of the opening and closing stories ("A Pail of Air" and "The Nice Girl with Five Husbands," both statements of the endurance and power of personal love in two very different future worlds) are a scattering of soft-satires, affectionate needle-jabs at a wide variety of human experience: art-and-culture, advertising and marketing, chess, beatniks, s-f fans, science, business, religion, politics....

These are gay stories, laughing at our follies more than mocking at us. (*F&SF* readers will remember "Rump-Titty-Titty-Tum-Tah-Tee"; SF readers, "The Beat Cluster"; chess addicts, "The 64-Square Madhouse.") But scattered among them are three of the angriest, most effective, true horror stories I have ever read: "The Foxholes of Mars," "The Last Letter," and "Coming Attraction," all searing indictments of the anti-love, anti-laughter, forces at work in the world of today-till-tomorrow.

Leiber's effectiveness is largely due to his knack of suiting style to theme. He knows how to use both a broad canvas and a hairline brush, when to illuminate with moonglow and when with spotlights. His least efforts are, I think just that—least effort. "Bread Overhead," "Time Fighter," "Pipe Dream" (which complete the Table of Contents) are all good entertainment—and as long as editors, critics, and publishers keep their standards (of pay and praise) at the low level considered suitable for science fantasy as a supposed step-child of literature, even our best writers will sometimes settle for providing no more than that minimum, with the too-quick story for the too-quick check.

Magazine editors have the excuse of pages to fill and budgets to fit. Book editors might fulfill their responsibilities to authors, publishers, and readers better by exercising a more demanding selectivity, tossing out the shoddy "category" standards, and setting "mainstream" criteria for quality. I think they would get it—and I think they would sell more books.

The Planet Buyer, Cordwainer Smith, Pyramid, 50¢

Perhaps the most exciting new "name" in s-f this decade has been Cordwainer Smith's. Like most of Heinlein's early work, Smith's stories are written out of a carefully planned future history, with a uniform set of principles of sociology, psychology, and political economy applicable to all. But Smith is much more the poet than the engineer, and the shapes and colors that flare across the horizons of his framework are more reminiscent of Sturgeon and Leiber than Heinlein and Asimov.

The Planet Buyer is not, to my taste, the best of his work, and if you read the magazine version ("The Boy Who Bought the Earth"), you will probably find very little more that matters in this expansion. But I have not yet been able to put down a Cordwainer Smith story unfinished—including this one.

Regan's Planet, Robert Silverberg, Pyramid, 40¢

I cannot say the same for Robert Silverberg, or for his fairly entertaining new novel. Silverberg has been writing only ten years—but because he is one of the most prolific writers ever to hit the s-f field, he has packed half a lifetime of writing experience into that decade. And he has learned; he is one of the few men who might, with respect to them both, be compared to Murray Leinster for honest craftsmanship. He rarely lets a reader down; but it is just as rare to be uplifted—out of yourself, as they say—by a Silverberg story.

The cover blurb calls *Regan's Planet* "a wild and wacky novel of the next World's Fair." The adjectives are a bit strong, but the general impression is correct. The Fair is on the Moon, the protagonist a super-entrepreneur in 1992's Big-big-business network of global finance; the tempo is fast, with no intrusive "message" or complex characters to slow the pace. Moderately funny, occasionally pointed, consistently well plotted and smoothly written. Good commuter reading.

The Great Time Machine Hoax, Keith Laumer, Simon & Schuster, $3.95

One might almost say the same, with a different synopsis, for this novel—but not quite. Keith Laumer's first story was published only five years ago. He is a Captain in the Air Force, and for a part-time writer, has turned out a prodigious amount of material in a short time. Superficially, the similarities between Laumer and Silverberg are considerable: great productivity, continually better craftsmanship, strong plotting, fast action, but—

With the exception of the *Retief* series, Laumer has rarely repeated himself in content or in technique. One feels that with this book he did less than he might have, that he was perhaps trying to write a "purely commercial" novel. Once again, the jacket blurb is close to accurate when it says, "an explosive mixture of danger, excitement, and high good humor." (Read "enjoyable" for "explosive.") More significant: behind the fun and games, the not-yet-expert technician has permitted the reader a glimpse of something vigorous, assertive, and stimulating—presumably the author. If he decides to use the craft he is rapidly acquiring to communicate as well as entertain, if he learns to say more instead of less, Keith Laumer may well become a very good writer.

[...]

Books (April 1965)

The Day New York Went Dry, Charles Einstein, Gold Medal, 40¢
Sweeney's Island, John Christopher, Simon & Schuster, $4.50
The Mind Benders, James Kennaway, Signet (reprint), 60¢
The Worlds of Robert F. Young, Simon & Schuster, $4.50
Short Friday, Isaac Bashevis Singer, Farrar, Straus & Giroux, $4.95
[...]

More and more, authors from the literary "mainstream," or from other specialized "categories" of publishing, have been trying their hands at science fantasy. Some of them have done very well indeed. Certainly their work tends to show more attention to prose techniques and literary polish than that of many of the most-admired Old S-F Hands. But it is unusual for a complete "outsider" to produce a work of good "solid science fiction." It is even more uncommon when the first try is done at full novel length.

Of the books on hand this month, three are novels which meet all the basic requirements of the highly specialized literary discipline called science fiction. This would be moderately surprising all by itself; it is even more so, since only one of the authors—John Christopher—is an established s-f writer. Charles Einstein has, I believe, done an occasional short story in the field before, but the bulk of his work has been in other fields. James Kennaway, to the best of my knowledge, has never written anything resembling science fiction, before this.

No. I am *not* about to define what I mean by "science fiction" as distinct from "fantasy," or from the more inclusive "science fantasy." The *What is it anyhow?* game has been played too long by too many (still-undecided) experts for me to begin it in the space available here. But I can say what I mean when I talk about the "basic requirements of science fiction."

Anthony Boucher has called it "disciplined imagination," and that is as good a place to start as any. The most basic ingredient of all is a way of thinking. *Science* is not technology, or laboratories, or thick books of data tables; it is a *method*. The trappings of technology do not make science fiction; neither does the traditionally supernatural make a fantasy. There has been some first-rate sci-fic about werewolves and gnomes. Ray Bradbury, on the other hand, has written some fine and meaningful space fantasy. And C. P. Snow produces volume upon volume of science-background philosophic fiction. In all three kinds of work, there is logic involved, and imagination; both qualities are vital to fiction of any kind. The specific for science fiction is the application of the logic *to* the imagination.

Properly applied, the result will be a story in which a believable human problem is directly related to a scientific, technological, or other environmental problem, in such a way that the resolution of one must involve the solution of the other. For the writer, this means learning narrative techniques of a highly specialized sort. "Good writing" as such—the techniques of prose, dialogue, characterization, etc.—is not enough to do the job; there is also the matter of *structure*. It is one thing to move characters effectively in relation to each other, against a known background; something else again to have both characters and stage, so to speak, simultaneously in motion. (Some of the things that happen are happening *to* the environment.)

Most writers from other fields of literature tend to fall short in the initial application of logic to their imagined construct; the extrapolation is seldom as thorough as it should be. Those who manage a novel fulfilling the basic conditions, adequately planned and carefully thought through, tend to forget the *people* in the story.

Charles Einstein suffers somewhat from this last problem—but not so badly as to dull his story (nor as badly as many standard s-f writers). *The Day New York Went Dry*, in case you were wondering, is not a book about prohibition, but about water shortage. If there is less depth and conviction in most of the characterizations than one might wish for, that is not a condemnation of this kind of novel. The problem involved concerns millions of people. It might have been handled in terms of individuals; Mr. Einstein chose instead to use the great City itself as his real protagonist, and still work primarily in longshots; the close-ups he does use seem designed to serve as brief magnifications of samplings of an overall statistical reality, rather than individual subjective revelations.

The significant thing is that he does achieve a feeling of reality, and a convincing picture of the emotional, as well as technical, problem of the city-at-large. Portraiture and mural-painting are different techniques. The mural here is effective as well as informative.

Sweeney's Island suffers from a similar lack of treatment-in-depth of its characters—but for the opposite reason. This is essentially a morality play, a study of human values in microcosm, with a cast of characters who seem sometimes to be wearing Greek masks, establishing themselves as prototypes, rather than stereotypes.

The book will inevitably, I expect, be compared to Golding's *Lord of the Flies*—and I also expect it is something like literary heresy to say I thought that one was *also* a good readable sci-fi morality play. It would be as valid to compare either one with *The Swiss Family Robinson.* All three are about a group of civilized people cast away on a deserted island. In *Sweeney*, as in *Swiss Family*, there are some artifacts of civilization to start off with; in *Flies*, as in *Sweeney*, the artifacts prove more durable than the mores.

The distinctive features of Christopher's book are: first, that he includes adult sexual morality in his field of study; and, second, that the conflicts here arise not so much from problems of primitive as from the surviving dangers of the lost civilization. The carefully (contrivedly?) ill-assorted community on the Island is undermined less by physical hardship than by the artifacts and attitudes left over from the macrocosm.

The Mind Benders, by James Kennaway, whose two previous novels have had no connection with science fantasy, is a startlingly sound piece of science fiction, as well as a good job of writing in any category. Both of the other novels are good reading, and both fall within the permissible range of balance of logic/imagination, poetry/philosophy, intellect/emotion, which constitutes "science fiction." This book achieves near-total balance, as a study in depth of the effects on one man, his wife, and his immediate associates, of an experiment in "reduction of sensation"—better known as "brainwashing technique." [...]

The distinctions I have been discussing between science fiction, science-fantasy, and "straight" fantasy, are significant once again in connection with the two volumes of short stories on hand. *The Worlds of Robert F. Young* comes labeled as "science fiction and fantasy." The jacket copy writer for *Short Friday* said simply, "Anything can happen," in a story by Singer, but references afterwards to ghosts and demons convey a sense of "pure," supernatural-type fantasy.

Mr. Young's most successful stories are for the most part his science fantasies: "The Girl Who Made Time Stop," "Hopsoil," "The Dandelion Girl," "The Stars Are Calling, Mr. Keats," and "Goddess in Granite." There are eleven others in this collection, all smoothly written, and most at least entertaining. In his introduction to the book, Avram Davidson says of Robert Young, "He writes with love." This is true—and almost so true as to be exclusive. The weakest stories are the satires; and in one or two of the others, the emotion seems closer to sentimentality than love. But when the stories are of noble feelings, high adventure, and romance, Mr. Young is at his best.

Mr. Singer has a wider range of emotions. He writes with anger, compassion, bitterness, tenderness, horror, delight, and amusement—to name a few. Not more than half of the stories in this collection are even clearly fantasy; some are crime, shock, horror, or what-have-you, but in most of these, there is an element of fantasizing *inside* the characters that makes it difficult to draw a sharp line of division.

Both books, actually, are primarily fantasy collections; the oddity is not so much that those of Mr. Young's stories which concern themselves with space flight and future technology are not quite science fiction, as that Mr. Singer, in portraying a universe peopled with angels, demons, and witches, conveys such a feeling of method in his magic, and makes such expert use of the basic science fiction approach to the substance of superstition. (Please note: the Singer stories are *not* sci-fic, or even science-fantasy—with two or three exceptions—because he does not rationalize them with reality-as-we-know-it. He simply succeeds in convincing us that our reality is perhaps less than conclusive.)

[…]

Books (May 1965)

I sincerely believe that science fiction has been, and continues to be, not a separate flow paralleling the mainstream of modern writing, but a fresh current in it, clearly distinguishable at its point of entry, and eventually so entirely merged with the larger body as to retain existence only in terms of the measurable addition it has made to the content, turbulence, and current speed of the whole.

But ours is not the only freshet feeding the stream, and I think another is currently merging with ours—one that seemed a short time ago, more like a cross current. I mean the *avant garde*, the experimentalists, the little-magaziners, the modern poets, and "beats." Significant of this merging and of the added impact on the mainstream are William S. Burroughs's *Nova Express* and John Hersey's *White Lotus* (received too late for inclusion in this column)—two of the most important of this season's new novels, and both clearly and indisputably science fiction.

Andromeda Breakthrough, Fred Hoyle and John Elliot, Harper & Row, $3.50
Nova Express, William S. Burroughs, Grove Press, $5.00
The Alien Way, Gordon R. Dickson, Bantam Books, 50¢

There are three books by three authors worlds apart from each other in background, training, experience, and even physical distance. (Oceans, anyhow: Dickson lives in Minneapolis; Hoyle and Elliot in England; Burroughs, when he wrote this, in Tangier.) Fred Hoyle, as everyone knows, is one of the world's leading astronomers and cosmologists. Gordon Dickson is the rule-proving exception who decided to be a writer, studied writing in school; started writing; kept doing it; and is today a leading writer of science fiction. William Burroughs is probably the world's most famous living junkie. He has written candidly and vividly about his own experiences with dope addiction and crime; and in fiction at least as autobiographical, and rather more intimate, has dealt with dope, crime, and homosexuality. He is also, within the "beat" movement, what Wells, Bradbury, and Heinlein all rolled into one are to sci-fi—front-runner, godfather, mentor, and current world champ. Jack Kerouac, who is popularly considered Mr. Beat, began as a Burroughs disciple. Norman Mailer, ranking publicist for the group, calls him "the only American novelist living today who may conceivably be possessed by genius." His works have been published by all of the Big Three publishers of erotica, existentialism, and experimentalia: Grove Press in New York, City Lights on the West Coast, Olympia in Paris, and in the new wave of *avant garde* "fanzine" publishing, there is hardly a hectographed, mimeoed, or offset effort that does not contain at least its page or two of Burroughs—original, reprint, or commentary.

Burroughs is a surrealist. Hoyle is a scientific writer, who has recently, wisely, enlisted John Elliot as collaborator for his fiction. Dickson is a straightforward story teller, with a tendency to the sweeping historical-novel type plot, heavy intellectual-philosophic content, and a bit of swordbuckling adventure.

Which book has the most striking scientific concepts? The tightest—and corniest—plot? Burroughs, both times.

Which is the most successful morality play? Why, Dickson, of course.

And which is the real old-fashioned s-f adventure? You guessed it. Hoyle and Elliot.

Nor are they hard to compare in these respects. As diverse as they are in style, mood, and intent, the three novels have so many features of story line, gadgetry, scientific and philosophic content in common, that the overlappings and similarities constitute a science fiction phenomenon of greater interest than any one of the books individually.

All three are stories of a near-future (or present time) attempted conquest of Earth by cosmic aliens. Two of the books can even be reduced to identical library-card-type précis:

> Through the use of a combination of advanced electronic and biochemical techniques, an effectively instantaneous means of communication is established between Earth and a remote planet inhabited by a scientifically sophisticated race. Due to mutual failures in understanding of both the physical and motivational character of the contacts, humanity is almost destroyed. Dedicated research by one unprejudiced non-xenophobic scientist, plus a last-ditch, to-the-death rebellion against frightened and short-sighted military-political leaders by the protagonist, and a last-minute rush of feminine hormone to the aid of sweet reason, stern

science, and the lonely rebel, combine to avert the physical danger, and to initiate true communication between alien species.

(That's *Andromeda* and *Alien Way*.)

Two of the books (*Andromeda* and *Nova Express*) make use of the notion of planned DNA-RNA "imprinting" of molecules to create a life form whose specific function is communication. Hoyle and Elliott do it conventionally: a giant electronic brain, built according to instructions from a distant star, helps an Earth scientist to synthesize living cells and "grow" a biologically complete human being (the girl Andromeda), whose thought processes are linked to the machine's memory banks, so that an almost-equivalent of instantaneous communication across the light years is achieved.

Burroughs uses the "image virus" as a weapon of his Nova Criminals: "We first took our image and put it into code. A technical code developed by the information theorists. This code was written at the molecular level to save space, when it was found that the image material was not dead matter, but exhibited the same life cycle as the virus. This virus released upon the world would infect the entire population and turn them into our replicas." (But don't get me wrong; this is one of the very few coherent paragraphs composed of simple sentences in the book.)

Dickson is different; he does not use a synthetic virus or engineered life form. *His* gimmick is a "virus-sized mechanism" utilizing "recent developments in interpreting, transmitting, receiving, and associating the electrical activities that accompany activity of the brain," which will enter the brain of an alien and "set up a transmission link, embodying no time-loss, between this alien and a volunteer subject." (And just to keep the record straight, this book is not written this way either—at least not all of it. Both quotes are from putative scientific reports.)

This life-making, life-taking, life-simulating variety of ways to transfer information is the most dramatic parallel in the three books, though there are many instances of further overlap between the two.

Alien Way utilizes the mechanical telepathy virus to establish contact between Jason Barchar of Earth and Kator Second-cousin, of the Ruml, a humanoid, but marsupial, race of approximately the same degree of scientific development as Earth at a time perhaps twenty or thirty years from now. From that point on, Dickson works with a double protagonist, actually experiencing the sensations and thoughts of both characters. The resulting detailed subjective study of one rarely xenophiliac human engaged in a near-killing conflict of identification with himself and the alien is fascinating. And would be quite convincing without the equally detailed, to the point of tedium, anthropological-zoological extrapolation (*with* documentation) of the really not-terribly startling thesis that the physiological characteristics of a given species (body structure, infantile nourishment patterns, growth rates, etc.) will inevitably affect the cultural ethos, not just in government and economy, but in areas often considered survival or moral absolutes: procreative behavior, the concept of good-and-evil, the meaning of honor, courage, love, etc.

Andromeda touches this theme twice—in the gradual influence of her human body on the loyalty of the synthetic girl, Andromeda, to "her own" physically and physiologically remote people—and again in the one glimpse given to the scientist-hero, John Fleming (via the machine-and-Andromeda) of the strange creatures he has been alternately, ambivalently, fighting and helping throughout the two novels. (The present book is more like a second installment to *A for Andromeda* than like a sequel.) Lines of scientific development in the two books are devoted to the problems of communication (built up excitingly in the first book, summed up here), and then to the ecological effects and biochemical nature of a bacterium created in the early experiments with molecule-building, under the direction of the machine; the bacterium is infesting earth's oceans, multiplying at incredible speed, and sucking the oxygen out of the atmosphere.

The book suffers from routine writing, stereotyped characters, and an apparent belief in the Ian Fleming (one wonders if there is a relationship) school of international intrigue (ex-Nazi cowards, slinky near-East lady agents, etc.). These dispensables, however, provide a reasonably amusing background to a genuinely intriguing scientific puzzle. More importantly, the scientific cast of characters are anything but stereotyped. Neither Saviors nor Crackpots, they are a fair cross section of the kinds of people who are attracted to scientific work, and they are revealed here in intimate and informative detail. In the hero especially, all the conflicts and two-culture anxieties about which C. P. Snow writes so endlessly, emerge sharply, comprehensively, and even empathetically. (Although I did find Dickson's final disposition of his Reluctant Rebel was more realistic than Hoyle and Elliot's conclusion for Fleming.)

In *Nova Express*, Burroughs makes use of just about all the devices and concepts of the other two books—and *lots* more—to create his Nova Mob and describe their terrible weapons. He conceives cosmic cops and robbers: Crab Nebula creatures, Death Dwarfs, Venusian green people, the blue metal men of Uranus, shape-changers, flesh-stealers, image-virii [sic], oxygen-suckers, etc. (*ad ult*, but never quite *absurdum*), as well as the intrepid Inspector J. Lee of the Nova Police and his cosmic cohorts in the Biologic Courts. All these are, always, and obviously, figments of *your* imagination (and mine) as much as Burroughs's. The planet they inhabit is Earth, because he *is* talking about our culture and civilization; but it is also (both separately and jointly—simultaneously and interdependently) the universe of an—of any—individual human awareness.

I am not at all sure that I either like or approve of Burroughs's (anti-) novel technique. But it is his technique, and I will not amend it by describing the plot. What is of interest is that there is one. After fifty pages or so, the repetitions and accidentals and re-twistings begin to add up—a little.

There is much in this book I do not understand. It may be that there are parts of it no one but Burroughs *could* understand. From what little I know of his chosen technique (and it *is* chosen; I have read an article of his written in excellent English prose), the first "take" is set down exactly as it wells up from (presumably) the subconscious. This material is then processed through such mysteries as the "fold in" or "cut up," which are—I gather—just about what they sound like. Some similar method of redistribution seems to be used for purposes of retelling certain incidents—or possibly these are just cases where the same action was written by the hand of the author (*not* by the conscious mind) in different sets of words as part of the basic narrative. In any case, the characters, throughout the book, regroup in different combinations; the Nova crimes recur as deeds of different members of the Mob; the Police ploys are formulated similarly under different circumstances, and differently in the recurrent cases; pieces of the action reform themselves with different casts in different times and places; and within this constant realignment, inside any part of the narrative, the paragraphs, speeches, sentences, phrases, words, are continually realigned and re-patterned.

The result should be sheer nonsense. It is not. It is, instead, startlingly like the surreality of certain dreams, or the intense fascination of a confusion of new impressions in real life. The colors, after a time, are all brighter, the people more alive, the smells stronger, deaths deadlier, fears more terrible, rare moments of rest or pleasure more delicious, than most of us experience at any time after the clearest perceptions of childhood have begun to fade into the learned-and-known-and-formularized kind of seeing-the-expected and finding-the-predicted of normal adult life.

I cannot recommend this book. You probably won't like it. I don't know yet whether I do. I have to read it again, and find out.

The Year's Best S-F, Tenth Annual Edition (1965)

[No Introduction for this volume]

[...]

"Descending" by Thomas M. Disch

"When Darwin and Wallace propounded the theory of evolution in the middle of the last century, it was explicitly stated that man is no longer subject to evolutionary processes.... I do not think that we control the future at all, and I do not think that we are in any way free from, the evolutionary process."

The quotation is from *Of Men and Galaxies* by cosmologist (and SF writer) Fred Hoyle, who argues that human evolution is no longer determined by the physical environment, but by "the things we know and the things we believe.... We cannot think outside the patterns that our brains are conditioned to, or to be more accurate, we can think only a little outside, and then only if we are very original." And, "New concepts are like genetic mutations...most of them turn out badly. But without mutations there can be no evolution."

If there is a Significance to science fiction—a capital-S sort of thing—I think it lies in this area. Not only does it provide a platform for speculation and prophecy, but by giving voice to what Hoyle calls the "very original," it attracts other original minds—both as readers and writers.

The "mutant concepts" then fall on the most favorable soil; if they are viable, they will grow and multiply. More important, perhaps, is the chain-reaction effect that sets in (to create a sort of environment within the environment) as the new concepts of original minds become a part of the "conditioning" of others—who are thus freed a bit more for more original thinking.

The first generation of what might be called the "science-fiction community" (beginning in the twenties) did much of the "mutant" thinking that energized the development of atomic power and space flight. The present generation is dealing with concepts in very different areas—and one clue to the "mutation" process is the identity of the new writers.

[...]

"It Could Be You" by Frank Roberts

Frankly, the Great Evolution Upset has made me nervous, and I hesitate to say, in print, anything so problematic as "scientific opinion is…" or "biologists agree…" Chances are by now the biologists are in radical disagreement, but the last time I noticed, most of them seemed to think that what killed the dodo and the dinosaur—what causes the devolution of any species—is overspecialization.

It is an appealing concept—if only because it is a concept, and provides at last something like an informative synonym for "decadence." (Perhaps even closer is Theodore Sturgeon's definition of "perversion": anything you do to the exclusion of everything else.)

Art, music, literature, then, become decadent when they lose contact with the living body of work, by overspecializing to an extreme degree. Is this, perhaps, the basis for our subjective evaluation? When the emphasis on any one value or set of values (in the arts, the scientific disciplines, public morality, or anything else) becomes so intense as to lose contact with the frame of reference provided by other values customary to the form, we react immediately with, "Decadence!"

(And of course, in any highly experimental or path-breaking effort, the connection with the frame of reference may be so tenuous, or so subtle—but still so significant—that only another adept in the same discipline will recognize it—thus providing the frequent distinction between critical and popular success.)

If this is a true measuring stick, it should be applicable to all areas of human behavior: not only to the comparatively well-understood rules of the "disciplines" (in art, science, etiquette, communications, for instance), but to those "games" we are least conscious of "playing," and which evoke the greatest emotional stress—nation, family, religion, property rights, for example; or the even deeper-rooted codes and moralities related to those "inalienable" rights—life, liberty, the pursuit of happiness.

I think it is of particular significance that "It Could Be You" was written by an Australian newsman, and that it first appeared in the United States in the pages of *Short Story International.*

I had somehow thought (or hoped?) that the terrifying—and terrifyingly recognizable—trends projected here were an exclusively American version of the world's agony. I don't know if I find more reassurance or despair in the author's account of the sources of his story:

> "(1) An Australian television show in which people's misfortunes were paraded before audiences of grim, grey old ladies.... (2) The fact that eleven million Australians support no less than twenty-five Government-run lotteries a week, tickets costing from a half dollar to about seven dollars each, with prizes from $12,000 to $200,000.... (3) People whose disregard for a death or two a day has long been conditioned by the road accident toll, which was around 2,000 dead and 60,000 injured in the early 1960s."

Well, then, our sins are not exclusively our own; but neither is our sense of sin—nor our awareness of danger. And increasingly, there is evidence that neither "they" nor "we" any longer expect to resolve our problems inside the cultural or political isolation of those national sovereignties which have become ruinously overspecialized in today's world—not because the outlook or behavior of national governments is narrower or more provincial than it used to be (quite the opposite) but because technology and communications have so altered global realities that the very concept of "national sovereignty" is now too narrow, localized, overspecialized.

I think there is a growing awareness of the true decadence of, not just political, but social, cultural, and (rather more obviously) literary, artistic, and scientific customs and usages as well. If our awareness of decadence itself is subjective (and perhaps intuitive), it is reassuring to find indications that we reach just as instinctively for what is viable and (in the purest sense of the word) virtuous.

Among the most congenial of these portents has been the appearance of a magazine like *Short Story International.* I find myself equally pleased that the publishers of this new venture have put it in the hands of an editor of fine literary discernment and that they have put on the cover, by way of a symbol, a picture of Telstar.

"A Benefactor of Humanity" by James T. Farrell

...And speaking of overspecialization, I have not yet made reference to The Categories.

"Science fiction" has about the same utility as a label, by now, as "beatnik" does. To the majority of readers, both words describe something exotic, ultramodern, oddball, egghead, and probably unwashed. To the respective and only slightly overlapping in-groups, the labels have a proud, bold, modern feel, full of truth, beauty, and the Keatsian assurance of "all ye know, and all ye need to know."

Certainly, to the "outsider" majority, and sometimes even to the "ins," both words are definable more in terms of costume than anything else...unless the something else is status. No one calls Picasso a "beatnik," and it is not just the absence of beard that sets him apart from other wearers of sandals and turtlenecks.

Most publishers use "categories" to determine costume—or "packaging," as the trade calls it. Science fiction, like fantasy, crime, suspense, Westerns, doctor and nurse stories, sex, love, war, is a "category." And then there are "novels"—the non-category category, where subject does not matter, because either the book or the author is considered serious or literary or popular. (*1984* and *The Disappearance* were serious books; *The Lord of the Flies* and *Brave New World* were literary; *Fail Safe* and *Earth Abides* popular; *More Than Human* and *A Canticle for Leibowitz* were science fiction: the latter in spite—or perhaps because?—of the publisher's overfervent denials.)

I don't mean it is impossible for an author to step out of his "category." Just almost impossible. And sometimes it is as hard to break into the ghetto as out of it—

[...]

"Synchromocracy" by Hap Cawood

Hap Cawood is a graduate student at Ohio State University. Has published satires and poetry in University publications and in *motive*. Spent two years teaching with the Peace Corps in Sierra Leone. Is now completing work for his Master's in—you guessed it—journalism.

He says what he wrote is a satire. I agree, the style is satirical. But what bothers me is, while everybody's talking about how "science is catching up with science fiction," nobody seems to notice how IBM is catching up with satire.

There is an IBM down in Florida that writes love poems. Like:

Darkly the peaceful trees crashed
In the serene sun
While the heart heard
The swift moon stopped silently.

What really hurts is, the 709 had a vocabulary of exactly 78 words when that was written. Presumably it knows more now. At the time that Russell

Baker reported on it (but this one was no joke; it was a straight news article), 709 could only do 30 poems a minute, but it was supposed to work up to 500/per shortly.

And then there was this inspirational photograph in the paper the other day—a happy schoolgirl looking up at the beaming broad panel of the teacher. I mean, that one was no joke, either.

Sometime between the spring when I write this, and the winter when it is published, Peter Redgrove (who was represented in the *Ninth Annual* with a prose-poem short story, "Mr. Waterman") will have initiated a series of programs on the BBC to show, he hopes, that "poetry and SF are trying to digest the same things."

"Machines are so much in our lives," he says. "Why have so few poets tackled this? Is it that they don't know enough? Is it that they're so afraid of the machine that all they can make of it is satire…?

"Hart Crane saw that one way of making a complete living world-picture was to treat machines as a kind of comrade in evolutionary advance—if you treat them as mere instruments, when of course they're images of the mind, then you deaden yourself and them….

"We don't want satire," he concludes, "we want synthesis."

[...]

"The Terminal Beach" by J. G. Ballard

I know very little about Roger Zelazny, because he claims to get amnesia when asked to write about himself. Among the few things I do know are that he can fill a page with fine, funny copy describing a writer having amnesia when asked, etc.; that he fairly recently acquired a Master's degree at Columbia in some particularly esoteric field of literature; and that he is an (or perhaps the) outstanding example of the influx of literate young writers into the SF field during the last three or four years.

Perhaps it would be even more valid to say that Zelazny—and Ballard, who follows here—are the kind of writers working in and out of SF, who are making the idea of a separate "field" disappear.

Writers outside SF have begun to discover the uses of extrapolative and speculative writing. Inside SF the best people—like Zelazny, like Ballard—are reaching toward poetry, metaphysics, religion, psychiatry, symbolism, and myth as systems through which to explore the nature of man; and reaching, too, for the new techniques of expression being explored in the experimental and *avant garde* fringes of the "mainstream."

James Ballard has, I think, been more successful in this effort than anyone else writing "inside SF" today—comparable perhaps to Jorge Luis Borges on the "outside." Ballard says of this story:

> "'Terminal Beach' represents the most extreme expression to date of what I have called 'inner space'—that area where the outer world of reality and the inner world of the psyche meet and fuse. Only in this area can one find the true subject matter for a mature science fiction."

"Problem Child" by Arthur Porges

> "Eliot stayed contritely sober for two days after that, then disappeared for a week. Among other things, he crashed a convention of science-fiction writers in a motel in Milford, Pennsylvania....
>
> "'I love you sons of bitches,' Eliot said in Milford. 'You're all I read any more. You're the only ones who'll talk all about the really terrific changes going on, the only ones crazy enough to know that life is a space voyage, and not a short one, either, but one that'll last for billions of years. You're the only ones with guts enough to really care about the future, who really notice what machines do to us, what wars do to us, what cities do to us, what big, simple ideas do to us, what tremendous misunderstandings, mistakes, accidents and catastrophes do to us. You're the only ones zany enough to agonize over time and distances without limit, over mysteries that will never die, over the fact that we are right now determining whether the space voyage for the next billion years or so is going to be Heaven or Hell.'
>
> "Eliot admitted later on that science-fiction writers couldn't write for sour apples, but he declared that it didn't matter. He said they were poets just the same, since they were more sensitive to important changes than anybody who was writing well. 'The hell with the talented sparrowfarts who write delicately of one small piece of one small lifetime, when the issues are galaxies, eons, and trillions of souls yet to be born.'"

from *God Bless You, Mr. Rosewater* by Kurt Vonnegut, Jr.
(Holt, Rinehart and Winston, 1965)

"The Wonderful Dog Suit" by Donald Hall

A short time ago, I attended a dinner meeting of the literary society, PEN, at which the subject of the evening was "The Two Cultures." Arthur Clarke, as one of the speakers, delivered an eloquent argument to the (mostly) editors and publishers assembled, on the status of science fiction as a bridge across the gap.

I think this is largely true. But listening, that evening and since, to scientists and science writers, and to literary-academic people, I have come to feel even more strongly, with Max Beerbohm, that, "There are not two cultures, only half-cultured individuals." Happily, I have also seen an increasing number of individuals reaching out from their culture-halves to complete themselves. I think I should prefer to say that SF is an area where such people often meet—and more and more often, contrive to communicate.

Arthur Porges and Donald Hall, juxtaposed here, come from opposite ends of the academic range. Porges is a retired college teacher of mathematics; in literature, an admirer of Kipling, London, Mundy, Edgar Wallace, T. H. Huxley. Hall is a member of the faculty of the Department of English Language and Literature at the University of Michigan, and a former editor of the *Paris Review*.

What they both have to say, each one says very differently.

[...]

"A Living Doll" by Robert Wallace

I have been conscious for some years of the gradual merging of SF with the "mainstream." The trend is dramatically noticeable this year; but my own big discovery in the work on this *Annual* was the extent to which SF and the *avant garde* had already merged, and begun to overlap.

For some time, Reginald Bretnor and David Bunch had been murmuring about the reviews and quarterlies and "little magazines"; they still seemed unlikely sources to me, until Carol Emshwiller called my attention to the Redgrove story in *Paris Review* last year.

About the same time, James Ballard wrote me the first of several angry letters of praise for William Burroughs. During the year, I had occasion to review Burroughs's strange, brilliant surreal-science-fantastic *Nova Express*, and found myself impressed and fascinated by a book whose confusing (and perhaps pretentious) style might otherwise have prevented me from reading it at all. Meanwhile, *Short Story International* had begun demonstrating, with reprints, that the magazines I had thought of as "anti-story" were not necessarily to be so considered.

There were the letters from Redgrove, and more from Ballard and Bunch. And somewhere in there, I met Seymour Krim, then editor of *Nugget* (and of *The Beats*, an anthology of same), who set about undercutting my preconceptions mercilessly.

[...]

"The Last Lonely Man" by John Brunner

[...]

It is in the nature of speculation that it cannot dwell continuously on one subject: there is just so much that one man's knowledge and imagination can do with a theme; then he needs either fresh information or a fresh topic. Perhaps because writers inside the field stimulate each other, perhaps under the impact of outside events, the same kind of topical drift seems to occur in SF as a whole. Each *Annual*, at least, has proved to have some distinct emphasis of its own; each one is different from the others.

To some degree, these pattern shifts are predictable—or at least recognizably expectable, when they occur. I have mentioned the new writers entering the field, and the closing gaps between "culture camps." These changes, I believe, are part of a much wider and more important phenomenon.

I think there is a desperate and determined—if often intuitive and unconscious—effort on behalf of thinking, imaginative people, from all backgrounds, in all intellectual and social microcosms, to place themselves in a "whole culture," to "despecialize," while there is still time; to widen, by whatever efforts they can make, the intellectual environment that limits our evolution toward sapience and sanity.

Certainly, the direction of the broad SF field these past ten years has been continuously and (one cannot but feel) meaningfully toward areas most likely to attract just these newcomers: the examination of human behavior, both individually and in groups; an investigation into the nature of interpersonal communication; an attempt to formulate a relationship between man and the technological environment he has created, and is continuing to create, for himself; and the study of man in his most immediate natural environment—that is to say, the mind-body relationship.

It is in, or out of, this last trend that the big qualitative change occurred this year. I expected to find a large number of automation stories, learning-process stories, political-sociological-anthropological stories—perhaps a few psychiatry and/or religion stories. I was not prepared for a broad-spectrum probing of the essential nature of life and death; the meaning and mechanics of mortality; the significance of procreation and of child-rearing; the metaphysics and biophysics of death.

[...]

Summation

"There have been more changes in the past 65 years than in all other centuries put together. No longer do most people believe in the orderly progression of cause and effect; no longer do they believe in the natural goodness of man and the inevitability of progress. Stability is gone. This is an era of quibble, doubt, and qualm. Science, technology, art, architecture, music, literature have all acquired new values, and revolutionary conflicts rage."

Call that one #1. (Here's your chance to see if you can tell the writers from the scientists, or the mainstream from SF.)

#2: "I am going to make one big hypothesis—a religious hypothesis—that the emergence of intelligent life is not a meaningless accident. But I am not going to follow orthodox religions by presuming that I know what the meaning is.... Let us see how much of the plan we can discover."

#3: "The next great breakthrough in science—the breakthrough that will have the kind of impact on us all that the Hiroshima bomb had—will be in the area of psychophysiology: mind and brain. And the man who will bring it about walks the earth today."

#4: "Today, science stands fair to join Religion, Motherhood, and the Flag as a domain so sacrosanct and so sanctimonious, that leg-pulling isn't allowed, levity is forbidden, and smiling is scowled at."

(Three of these nine quotes are by tried-and-true science-fiction writers; three are by scientists; three by serious writers.)

#5: "At any given time recording devices fix the nature of absolute need and dictate the use of total weapons—like this: Take two opposed pressure groups. Record the most violent and threatening statements of group one with regard to group two. Record the answer and take it back to group one—back and forth between opposed pressure groups. This process is known as feed back. You can see it operating in any barroom quarrel—in any quarrel for that matter. Manipulated on a global scale feeds back nuclear war...."

#6: "Each of us wants what Ponce de Leon wanted, and unless the road maps are all wrong, we are well on our way to finding it.... It is, in fact, a good betting probability that some of us, and perhaps a great many of us, may never have to die at all."

(Well, perhaps I made it sound a little less complex than it is; at least one of these authors spreads over all three categories, and three of those in the "scientist" and "serious" groups have written some science fiction.)

#7: "I believe it is realistic to say that the manned lunar program will be carried to a successful conclusion in spite of the wasted time and cost; but let's be clear. This isn't science. It's adventure and propaganda."

(For purposes of the Concept Guessing Game, I am considering Arthur C. Clarke a science-fiction writer, along with Frederik Pohl and Theodore Sturgeon,)

#8: "We need very urgently to know that we are not strangers and aliens in the physical universe.... We did not arrive like birds on barren branches; we grew out of this world, like leaves and fruit. Our universe 'humans' just as a rosebush 'flowers.' We are living in a world where men all over the planet are linked by an immense network of communications, and where science has made us theoretically aware of our interdependence with the entire domain of organic and inorganic nature."

(The three scientists: Philip Abelson, editor of *Science*; Fred Hoyle, cosmologist; James V. McConnell, comparative psychologist.)

#9: "The most controversial, and widely criticized of all space experiments took place in mid-Pacific on July 8, 1963, when...the AEC and the Department of Defense detonated a megaton bomb 200 miles above Johnston Island. (Sociological note: In the press releases, it's always a 'nuclear device.' I say it's a bomb, but I say the hell with it.)"

(And seriously three more: William S. Burroughs, of *Naked Lunch*, etc.; John Gunther, *Inside* author; Alan Watts, Zen philosopher-theologian.)

The answers are here; you'll get to them. But if you make an honest try at matching them up first for yourself, you may get my point better. SF has become more sophisticated, as well as more literate. We can no longer rely on flashing-panel gadgets or mad scientists, any more than on poor prose or flamboyant illustrations, to set it apart from other literature. Nor can we determine the nature from the source: there are comparatively few specialty magazines, and any publication is likely to carry some SF. Presumably, the distinctive quality is in the concepts; and if the SF writer's ideas are different from other people's, it ought to show up in such vigorous statements as those above.

(Burroughs, Hoyle, and McConnell are the three who have written some SF; does that help?)

Throughout this volume, I have been pointing out the meeting places on the literary scene where the once-sequestered science-fictionist now mingles freely with the journalist, the experimentalist, the poet and philosopher, and an occasional visitor from the academic or international world of letters. I have mentioned the journalists, and the newsmen in particular, who have made their way onto the SF scene—as well as the students and *avant-gardistes*. But there is another change in the author statistics that is more significant.

Most of the people included in this *Tenth Annual* are mostly-writers: that is, writing is the occupation by which they earn their living, and with which they would have to fill in tax returns and credit applications: Fully half of them this year are full-time free-lancers—and half of the balance have writing jobs.

Ten years ago, when I began editing this series, the number of people writing SF who did not have other jobs was very small (and the number of full-time SF-writers smaller yet, by far). The average contributor was either a spare-time science-fictionist—a scientist, technician, teacher, doctor, what-have-you?—who regarded his writing as a second profession, and probably wrote only SF, or a would-be freelancer who took his writing seriously enough, but still had to have an outside job to eat on.

Nine of the authors in this book have non-writing jobs (and "non-writing" includes the PR men and English professor).

Let me hasten to make clear that the change has not occurred because science-fiction writing has become a lucrative business. It is quite as miserably underpaid as it used to be. The difference is, simply, and once again, that the distinction between the specialty writer and the writer-in-general has almost vanished. For instance—

The Big Names of SF—the names everybody knows—Sturgeon, Heinlein, Asimov, Bradbury, Clarke—how many of them are actually "SF writers" today? Only Heinlein still writes primarily in the genre.

Conversely, the best new names in the field, this last decade, are almost all either young writers of serious literary intentions, who regard SF as one of their preferred modes of expression (Aandahl, Aldiss, Davidson, Ellison, Sheckley, Wilhelm, to name a few who do not happen to be represented this year); or already established writers just discovering the uses of the speculative and imaginative techniques (George P. Elliott, "Cordwainer Smith," John Hersey, Charles Einstein, Graham Greene, for instance).

(All right, you can start eliminating. Numbers 1, 2, and 3 are, respectively, John Gunther, in *Look* magazine's special "Inside the Twentieth Century" issue, January 12, 1965; Fred Hoyle, in *Of Men and Galaxies*, University of Washington Press, 1964; Theodore Sturgeon, in *If* magazine, March 1964. Try again on the other six.)

Or look at the new books.

[...]

Of course, everything on the various publishers' "science-fiction category" lists comes in (including re-re-re-reprints of Edgar Rice Burroughs). Almost any other fiction has to be asked for specifically: for instance, Simon & Schuster publishes John Christopher, but not on their "science-fiction list," for some reason; we had to ask for a copy of *Sweeney's Island*, just as we did for Hersey's *White Lotus* (Knopf, 1965) and Burroughs's *Nova Express* (Grove, 1965)—and was glad I had asked, with Christopher and Burroughs. Hersey was sadly disappointing, after *The Child Buyer* the year before.

(*Nova Express* is the source for Quote #5; and I must admit I cheated slightly on this one, and changed Burroughs's unmistakable punctuation to a more conventional system, to make it less obvious.)

We got Singer's *Short Friday* (Farrar, 1964) and McConnell's *The Worm Re-Turns* (Prentice-Hall, 1965), but not Gironella's *Phantoms and Fugitives* (Sheed and Ward, 1964), or Gary's *Hissing Tales*, although Harper & Row did send Fred Hoyle and John Elliot's *Andromeda Breakthrough*.

(#4, by the way, is from McConnell's "Compulsory Preface" in *The Worm Re-Turns*.)

Holt sent Kurt Vonnegut's *God Bless You, Mr. Rosewater* (a non-SF novel, full of references to science fiction, by an author associated with the genre—and God bless Holt for publishing it!) but New Directions did not send their enlarged 1965 reissue of Jorge Luis Borges's remarkable *Labyrinths*, nor did Viking send R. K. Narayan's fine collection of Indian legends, *Gods, Demons, and Others* (1964).

Snobbishness or confusion? It is hard to say; but easy enough to see that someone, somewhere, needs to take a long, fresh look at this mixed-up business of literary "categories."

In some ways, the nonfiction submissions are even more curious: we got Sullivan's superb *We Are Not Alone* (McGraw-Hill, 1964), and Bonestell-Ley's *Beyond the Solar System* (Viking, 1964), but not Arthur C. Clarke's *Man in Space* (Life Library, 1964); we were sent Rosalind Heywood's *ESP: A Personal Memoir* (Dutton, 1964)—one of the most sensible, as well as best-written, books on the subject I've ever seen, but not David Solomon's fascinating anthology of articles, *LSD: The Consciousness-Expanding Drug* (Putnam, 1964).

(Alan Watts's selection in *LSD* was the source for #8.)

If I seem to be saying that the situation is just as confused one place as another—why, it's only because that is what I mean to say. With the final criterion of authorship slipping out from under them, publishers, general reviewers, and the poor book salesmen have no way to tell their friends from SF.

(And how much better did you do? The last three mix-matches: #6 is by Frederik Pohl, from "Intimations of Immortality," in *Playboy*, June 1964. #7 is by Philip Abelson, quoted in an article, "$30,000,000,000 Trip to the Moon," in *Cosmopolitan*, October 1964. #9 is from Arthur C. Clarke's "The Meddlers," in *Playboy*, March 1964.)

[...]

Books (June 1965)

[...]

White Lotus, John Hersey, Knopf, $6.95, 683 pp.

I am, in common with a great many other readers, an admirer of John Hersey. Unlike many of the others, I thought *The Child Buyer* by a far cry his best book to date. It is disappointing to have to continue to feel so, after reading *White Lotus*. And since I am much more of a science fiction fan than a Hersey enthusiast, it is downright painful to have to say, of his first all-out science fiction novel, that it is a dull book. Most distressing of all, its faults are typical of the novice in the field, and of the amateur propagandist...yet Mr. Hersey is a writer of stature and experience, who has previously handled a marginally science fictional book magnificently, and who has in his other writings, repeatedly proven himself a highly skilled, effective, and restrained propagandist.

White Lotus is a lengthy parable of slavery and racial conflict, set in an alternate probability timestream where white America has long been subject to slave raids by the dominant yellow race. The story is told, in first person, by a young woman leader in the passive resistance movement of the whites in China. It covers a period of what I'd estimate to be at most twenty years, from the time of the capture of a fourteen-year-old girl in a raid on her Arizona village, through the confrontation of the Chinese authorities by White Lotus, symbol of the white civil rights movement. In the course of the book, the girl, White Lotus, lives through the experience of slavery, the impact of the abolitionist movement, the trading of slavery for freedom-in-prejudice, the beginning of egalitarianism, and the struggle in the white underground movement between the militant activists and the proponents of passive resistance.

The background of all this is China of (I infer) about the 1920s. I assume the Chinese background is entirely authentic—and suggest this is one of the serious flaws in the novel. World supremacy would surely have affected the Chinese personality and way of life as profoundly in another direction as (and this Mr. Hersey *did* understand) American subjugation changed the personality and culture of the White Lotus herself.

Perhaps the greatest problem is just that it is, as I said, a lengthy parable. It is not, in the usual science-fiction sense, a projection, but a simple transformation, East to West, white to yellow, black to white. At 68 pages it might have been great; 683 was far too many. Nor was the choice of narrative technique a wise one; parables are seldom best told from a subjective viewpoint; and a young girl's subjective view does not appear to be Hersey's strong point in any case.

Philip Dick did it better three years ago, in *The Man in the High Castle.*

The Three Stigmata of Palmer Eldritch, Philip K. Dick, Doubleday, $4.95, 278 pp.

I don't mean, this time, that his new book is similar in theme or treatment. Rather, that I wish it were more so, at least in characterizations and structure.

Phil Dick is, one might say, the best writer s-f has produced, on every third Tuesday. In between times, he ranges wildly from unforgiveable carelessness to craftsman-like high competence. In the case of *Palmer Eldritch*, I would guess he did his thinking on those odd Tuesdays, or rather on *one* of them, and the actual writing in every possible minute before another Good Tuesday came on him.

Here is a riotous profusion of ideas, enough for a dozen novels, or one really good one; but the stuff is unsorted, frequently incompleted, seldom even clearly stated. The style is alternately dream-slow-surreal and fast-action-pulp. Thematically, he at least approaches, and sometimes stops to consider, virtually every current crucial issue: drug addiction, sexual mores, overpopulation, the economic structure of society, the nature of the religious experience, parapsychology, the evolution of man—you name it, you'll find it.

The book, with all this, is inevitably colorful, provocative, and (frustratingly) readable. I wish I thought it possible that Dick might some time go back to this one, publication notwithstanding, and finish writing it.

Sunburst, Phyllis Gotlieb; Gold Medal, 40¢, 160 pp.

At thirteen, the only world Shandy Johnson knows is the ingrown, progressively degenerate, society of the walled and guarded town of Sorrel Park. Cut off from the world by an atomic accident in 1994, the city has now been isolated for a full generation, containing a secret the government is determined to keep hidden, and plagued with the atmosphere of fear and superstition emanating from the triply-guarded strong-hold inside the city: the Dump.

In the Dump are the children whose existence must never be known: the mutants whose powerful *psi* talents pose a constant threat to progress-as-usual in the great outside world. And with them, inside, are a cross-section of non-*psis*, guards, teachers, researchers, with a wide range of attitudes toward the mutants.

Shandy has no *psi* powers; she has lived, so far, in the dinginess and poverty of the town proper. Now, suddenly, the Dumper spy comes for her. Inside the Dump, three new worlds open up to her: the civilization of outside, represented by a scientist; the anarchy of the mutants; and her own self, with its unique "talent."

New twists on a very old theme—certainly. So were Wilmar Shiras's *Opening Doors* and Zenna Henderson's *People*. If this book falls short of full comparison with those, it is still a quietly effective, warmly convincing first novel by a writer whose scant handful of published stories has already taught me to watch for her byline.

Mutiny in Space, Avram Davidson, Pyramid, 50¢, 159 pp.

Avram Davidson is a master of the short story form. He has an ear for dialogue and an eye for detail unsurpassed in this field, and not too often equaled outside it. With this, he has a rarer skill—precision: the ability to convey in a brief (sometimes exquisite) phrase, by intonation, connotation, linguistic induction, what wordier less finely attuned writers may need paragraphs or pages of detail and denotation to accomplish. What he has once heard or seen, or even dreamed, he can, it seems, evoke unfailingly in the sharp polished prose of his short stories.

Unfortunately, *Mutiny in Space* is a novel—and worse yet, one of the currently popular swords-and-spacery variety. (The Barbarians of the Spaceways neo-historical thing, full of great oaths and bloody slashings, nubile priestesses and lustful conquerors from the skies.) Davidson does it no worse, I suppose, than many of s-f's enduring hacks (and some at least of its now-brightest names) used to do in the old *Planet* and *Amazing*. But space-sailors' swearings and sweatings and lecherous lootings are not among the things he has seen or heard—or, it would seem, even dreamed. I doubt if anyone has—not like this.

They might better have called it *Ayesha Goes to the Stars*.

The Reassembled Man, Herbert D. Kastle, Gold Medal, 45¢, 192 pp.

A Walter Mitty type hero is rebuilt to superior physical specs by meddling experimental extraterrestrial observers, and given strength, endurance, appearance, sexuality, beyond his wildest dreams.

A powerful concept is reduced to a plot gimmick by pedestrian handling, and given an underdeveloped, oversexed, pulp-paced, slick-glib treatment, well inside the author's proven capabilities.

It also seems to have a moral: it is best to be only a little bit better; being the best is too much. On the way to this conclusion, however, there are any number of interesting concepts and intriguing notions tossed out (and away)—as for instance, that super-energy entails super-hunger. A good book for commuters and tired-night reading—you can drift off and finish the thoughts for yourself.

[…]

Books (July 1965)

In his latest book-length angry love-letter to the world, Kurt Vonnegut, Jr., who once spent two days at the Milford Science Fiction Writers' Conference, has his hero, Eliot Rosewater, crash "a convention of science fiction writers in a motel in Milford, PA."

Eliot is somewhat soused at the time. He makes a speech:

> "I love you sons of bitches. You're all I read any more.... You're the only ones zany enough to agonize over time and distances without limit, over mysteries that will never die, over the fact that we are right now determining whether the space voyage for the next billion years or so is going to be to Heaven or Hell."[1]

Eliot admitted later on that science fiction writers couldn't write for sour apples, but he declared that it didn't matter. He said they were more sensitive to important changes than anyone who was writing well.... Eliot told the writers that he wished they would learn more about sex and economics and style, but then he supposed that people dealing with really big issues didn't have much time for such things.

The author also explains the essential similarity between pornography and science fiction, inasmuch as both are "fantasies of an impossibly hospitable world."

Now, I don't know if Vonnegut's book is science fiction, or fantasy (of any kind of world), or properly speaking, a novel at all. What it is, is the damnedest plea for human love that I have ever read, written by the tenderest nihilist of them all, with so much viciousness-and-compassion, wit-and-warmth, acid-and-rosewater, that I defy the coolest of detached contemporaries to come away feeling besmirched by noble sentiment.

It starts like this:

> A sum of money is a leading character in this tale about people, just as a sum of honey might properly be a leading character in a tale about bees.

And it ends like this:

> "And tell them," he began again, "to be fruitful and multiply."
>
> "God damn it, you've got to be kind."

If this is the theme of the book, and I *think* it is, the author excepts himself. He is not kind. He is harsh, terrifyingly clear-eyed, and loving. The conniving lawyer, the pompous senator, the confused heir, the jet-set wife, the rich lesbian, the fat insurance salesman, the virgin housekeeper, even the noble fisherman, are shown, every one, in the most pitiless of brilliant light, And every one of them—foolish, greedy, nasty, selfish, prurient, impotent, ugly, false, falsifying—is somehow, in the hands of this most extraordinary of contemporary writers, an object of love: yours as well as his.

As I said, I don't know what "category" a book like this belongs in; one of the best things about Vonnegut is that he never has been taggable. I have a vaguely indignant feeling that he went too far—that he must have infringed something in an anti-trust law, or maybe some part of the Bill of Rights—when he plunked down his critical views on science fiction smack in the middle of a book almost sure to be reviewed by s-f critics. On the other hand, it was precisely this episode (together with an s-f author inside the book, name of Kilgore Trout), which provided the handle to pull the whole thing into this column—and, further, to initiate with it a discussion which will, I trust, put an end to the necessity for categorizing and justifying hereafter.

The fact is, I don't think the outworn label, science fiction, means much of anything any more, except a description of an attitude. My own frequently stated attempt at definition, having to do with interaction between environment and characters, and between emotional and intellectual problems, was thrown, deservedly, in my teeth recently by the *New York Herald Tribune*'s Maurice Dolbier, who pointed out that my formulation would include, for instance, *War and Peace*. Barely a month later, I found myself doing battle with Tex McCrary in a radio interview, because I would not grant that *Mein Kampf*, a predictive and superficially logical fantasy, was science fiction. Another of my favorite phrases was pounded to shreds for me by Seymour Krim, editor of *Nugget* magazine, when he insisted that "disciplined imagination" was a redundancy—that discipline is the component that changes fantasy into imagination.

Now, just a few days ago, I had a letter from James Ballard, whose newest book is reviewed below, describing his story, "The Terminal Beach," as well as the novel, *The Drowned World*,[2] as expressions of what he calls "inner space—that area where the outer world of reality and the inner world of the psyche meet and fuse. Only in this area can one find the true subject matter of a mature science fiction." Now this sounds to me much more like a definition of poetry—but I know beyond a doubt that, to my taste, Ballard is writing some of the finest s-f in the field. And anyhow—

There was this other letter a week or so earlier, from Peter Redgrove, also in England, a scientist-poet now teaching English literature at the University of Leeds, and currently preparing "an anthology with commentary for the BBC, that will show, I hope, that poetry and SF are trying to digest the same things, and that so far SF has done more, but that poetry will win out in the end. I'm talking machines specifically—machines are so much in our lives, but there's been no poetry of the first rank about machines...." And in a scribbled PS, he offers *his* definition: "An SF story is one that shows that matter and spirit are the two sides of the one coin."

There is a certain correlation of intent, if not of denotation, between Redgrove's remarks and Ballard's and Vonnegut's—but let me add quickly, lest anyone feel any part of the confusion dispelled, two further brief items:

A few weeks ago, I found myself in a discussion with Terry Carr, co-editor of an excellent new annual anthology (to be reviewed next month by Ted White). I also edit an annual anthology; Carr's is "pure science fiction," and mine includes science fiction in a much wider total range. Presumably, we both know the difference—whether we can define it or not. Yet, although both of us had *liked* both stories, I denied that "The House by the Crab Apple Tree" (S. S. Johnson, *F&SF*, 2/64) was science fiction: he insisted that "Once a Cop" (Rick Raphael, *Analog*, 5/64) was not; and we were equally flabbergasted.

Finally: I heard a panel discussion on C. P. Snow's "two cultures," and how to bridge them, at a PEN meeting. Arthur Clarke was one of the speakers and *he* said sci-fi is that bridge.

If you find all this as instructive as I did, you will be about ready to accept happily this pronouncement: hereafter, the books reviewed here will be included because I think they are of interest to readers of this magazine. If I speak of this book or that one as "fantasy" or "s-f" or "a novel of science" or "satire" or "a serious novel," or anything else, it will be descriptively, and with no intent to label or categorize. Any reader who wants to play the game of Definitions is welcome to do so, and even to inform me if he so wishes. *I* shall not make the distinctions.

As it happens, this month there are four hooks of unusual interest on hand by four of the sweetest-apple writers in or out of s-f; and all of them, although long associated with the field, have demonstrated more than an awareness of sex and economics, not to mention style: Vonnegut, Ballard, Clarke, and Walter M. Miller, Jr. And if there is one point they all demonstrate, it is Vonnegut's contention about the belief in a "hospitable universe"—whether "impossible" or "fantastic" is harder to judge.

The Ballard book contains two novels, curiously ill-fitted to share a volume. *The Wind from Nowhere* is a good standard s-f magazine-serial novel, well handled and excitingly told, full of ingenious attention to detail, and well-thought-out background. It is quite unrepresentative of the main line of Ballard's work, and stands in relation to *The Drowned World* rather as a first-rate Hercule Poirot novel does to *Crime and Punishment*.

I do not mean to equate the author with either Christie or Dostoyevsky. I think James Ballard is well on his way toward becoming the first truly conscious and controlled literary artist s-f has produced. Certainly he is one of the very few who has tried and succeeded at all with modern literary techniques and experimental styles. But, as with most of the far-out writers, I find myself often uncertain, when I finish reading, just what he was trying to tell me—or whether he himself knew.

I am *quite* certain of the effectiveness of his method of telling it, however. *The Drowned World* is, superficially, a story laid in a future where the temperature of Earth is rising dramatically, the polar caps are melting, and the water level is rising all over the globe. The surface action of the story occurs in an area that was once the city of London, now fast regressing to primitive rain-forest. The more essential drama is an exploration, both fearsome and fearful, of that area of human experience which gives rise to such phrases as "collective unconscious" or "religious experience" or "racial memory," and provides endless room for speculation and research in our dreams.

The technical-scientific aspects of the novel are intriguing and thoughtful. The human aspects are confusing, terrifying, fascinating, and all too often brilliantly credible: too often, because this is not a happy book. (Yet even here, the author can conclude with a phrase like, "the forgotten paradises of the reborn sun." Man may not know how to live with it—but the universe itself is hospitable.)

Perhaps the most effective and striking virtue of this novel is its texture: the very prose has the weight of the waters in it, and its rhythms swell somehow with the slow tempo of the inexorably rising tide. And perhaps it is as well, after all, that the publishers put this one volume with *The Wind from*

Nowhere. When you finish *World*, you can let *Wind* blow away the thick atmosphere—if you want to.

I want to make it clear, to readers unfamiliar with my attitudes, that I am not given to constant hyperbole. It just happens that out of perhaps a dozen (at least potentially) truly *good* writers who have worked extensively in the broad spectrum of speculative and imaginative fiction in the past fifteen years or so, three are represented this month by samplings of some of their best work.

The View from the Stars[3] contains five short stories and four novelettes by the author of *A Canticle for Leibowitz.* The selections in this long-overdue second collection are all from Miller's first few years of magazine work—and they emerge both remarkably memorable and strikingly fresh. Unlike the compassionate laughter of Vonnegut, or the searing subjectivity of Ballard, Miller is vigorously actional, frequently violent—in his prose as well as his plot. Never quite the poet Ballard can be, nor the satirist Vonnegut is, Miller still contains some of both qualities, and with them an almost savage emotional force that pounds through intellect and art with the roar of a bloodpulse.

This is a good collection, varied and representative, and the more valuable for the recent complete absence of any new work by Miller. Many readers remember "Dumb Waiter" and "Blood Bank" best; for me, the outstanding inclusions are "Anybody Else Like Me?" ("Command Performance" in its original magazine publication; a depth-study of a telepath), "Crucifixus Etiam" (the Indian laborer and the Mars terraforming), "You Triflin' Skunk" (originally "Triflin' Man," about the product of alien seed), and above all the story (if it can be called that) that first made *me* sit up and take notice of a then-new young writer, the glory-chant called "The Big Hunger," which begins and ends:

> I am blind, yet I know the road to the stars. Space is my harp, and I touch it lightly with fingers of steel. Space sings. Its music quivers in the flux patterns, comes creeping along the twitch of a positron stream, comes to whisper in glass ears. I hear....
>
> ...I am the spider who walked around space. I, Harpist for a pale proud Master, have seen the big hunger, have tested its red glow reflected in my circuits. Still I cannot understand.

> But I feel there are some who understand. I have seen the pride in their faces. They walk like kings.

I find it difficult to say which is more surprising—or gratifying: that a poetic statement of "The Big Hunger" written a long thirteen years ago (as time is measured in technological advance nowadays) should still be valid and exciting in this Year of the Gemini; or that, a scant thirteen years later (as time is measured in literature), there should he an authoritative factual book of the nature of *Man and Space*,[4] published by such notorious non-dreamers as the Time-Life people. Lavishly illustrated and lucidly written, this big (8 ½ by 11 size) book traces the Space Hunger from ancient myths to future hopes, combining the comprehensiveness, authority, and production excellence of a well-organized Luce team effort with the informed prose and clear insight of one of our time's most effectual dreamers, Arthur Clarke.

If you have only one fact book about space on your shelves, this should probably be it. If you have all the others, add this one; you will find something in it, somewhere, you didn't know. If you are already an expert on space, get it anyhow—for some of the illustrations and photos. (Purchasable only by direct mail from Time-Life Books, Time and Life Building, Chicago, Ill.)

Notes

1. *God Bless You Mr. Rosewater*, or *Pearls before Swine*, Kurt Vonnegut, Jr; Holt, Rinehart and Winston, $4.95, 217 pp.
2. *The Drowned World* and *The Wind from Nowhere* (two novels in one volume), J. G. Ballard; Doubleday, $4.50, 162 pp & 150 pp., resp.
3. *The View from the Stars*, Walter M. Miller, Jr.; Ballantine, 50¢, 192 pp.
4. *Man and Space*, Arthur C. Clarke and the Editors of *Life;* Time-Life Books. $3.95, 191 pp. plus appendices and index.

Books (August 1965)†

In this unusually short "Books" column, Merril turns her lens onto the "half-serious and half-wit" scientists at the Planaria Research Group at the University of Michigan. As she notes, the scientists there conduct serious research on planaria, their ability to run through mazes, and their ability to pass on learned traits. They publish their results, along with "spoofs, satires, fantasies, parodies, verse, cartoons, science-fiction, and surreal-science," in the *Worm Runner's Digest*. They have collected some of the wittier bits from the journal and published them in book format, including "provocative new schools of thought as hydroanalysis, tail envy, the foodian psycholosis, nasal psychosexual development, the cokological projective technique, and lots more."

† Full text in the E-book version.

Quotes from original "Books" column.

Books (September 1965)

[...]

I am rather pleased to report that nothing on this month's list excited me much. (Bad show, you know, for a critic to be uncritical, and I have been bouncing with enthusiasm, it seems to me, for months now.) Mostly standard fare, with three new novels providing an interesting contrast in terms of the number or ways a book can fall short of excellence and yet remain well-readable.

Not with a Bang, Chapman Pincher; NAL-World, 1965, $4.95, 248 pp.

This is a first novel by a British zoologist-turned-journalist, who worked on weapons development for the army during World War Two, and is now, according to the book jacket, "noted especially for his political reporting. He has written seven books on subjects ranging from fish to animal breeding and evolution."

All this is, for once, very much pertinent. Writing about the effects of the discovery of a longevity drug, Pincher clearly demonstrates his knowledge, not only of laboratories, council halls, and city rooms, but of the individuals who inhabit them. Unhappily, his lack of background in fiction is just as much in evidence.

The book moves clumsily, but convincingly. The shift from recognizable authenticity of background to authoritatively extrapolated scenes and events is accomplished particularly effectively. The stream of events, affecting individuals and nations alike, has the feeling of reportage rather than invention.

The only thing the book lacks entirely is emotional involvement. The characters are perceptively visualized and meaningfully inter-related; but one never quite attains that sense of identification without which the best-constructed and most clearly drawn characters remain just that—characters, and not people. In this case, "subjects" might be the better word: the technique is more that of the case-history writer than the storyteller.

The book is well worth reading, and judging by the author's demonstrated keenness as an observer, and from the excellence of those aspects of technique with which he is familiar, I suspect this is the only amateurishly-written novel Mr. Pincher will publish. If there is another, it will probably be very good.

Meantime, a black mark against NAL-World for the common publishers' conceit that has done more to lower the level of s-f than any other cause: the smug assumption that style is superfluous in a "category" book. I cannot help but feel that a more demanding editor would have elicited a much better novel.

Dare, Philip José Farmer; Ballantine, 1965, 50¢, 159 pp.

This time I cannot blame the publisher. Farmer has demonstrated, on too few occasions, what he *can* do (cf. *The Alley Man*, *F&SF*, June 1959), when he elects to provide appropriate care and cultivation for his extraordinary inventiveness, intuition, and imagination. More often, as here, his work is so casual as to be embarrassing in its obviously unnecessary inadequacies. Yet I find that while I rail at the sloppiness on every page, I keep turning the pages—eagerly.

This time we have a plot out of *Planet Stories* by Charles Fort, which might be alright in its way, if it were not abruptly cut off in the middle (well, maybe two-thirds or three-quarters through), and hastily synopsized in the last few pages—peopled by colorful cardboards cut right out of the book club ads for historical novels. But we also have, in scene after scene, Farmer's uniquely sensory scene-setting: the vivid colors, pungent odors, sensations of sun and grass and wood and metal, awareness of food and drink and sex and pain. And more significantly, we have Farmer symbols.

There *are* other writers with the kind of direct-line Phil Farmer seems to have to the collective unconscious—but few indeed who can disport themselves so mirthfully with the archetypal shapes. The major stream of symbolism this time has to do with a submerged race (literally, of course; they live underground) whose (literal) sexual superiority is demonstrated (to begin with) in their name, *Horstels*, from horse-tails, from, of course, their (literal) tails. And that's only the beginning....

The Possessors, John Christopher; Simon & Schuster, 1964, $4.50, 252 pp.

The only thing missing here is meaning. Beautifully structured, artfully written, thoughtfully and successfully characterized, this still boils down to a story of devils-and-zombies decked out as aliens-and-victims. (One part of

Who Goes There?, two parts of *Puppet Masters*), with not enough freshness, scientific plausibility, *or* superstitious terror to make it work. Easy reading, for train trips and hammock afternoons.

Galactic Diplomat, Keith Laumer; Doubleday, 1965, $3.95, 227 pp.

Nine of the "Retief" stories from *If* magazine: farce-toned tales of the *Corps Diplomatique Terrestrienne* of the space-expanding future. The CDT, as caricature, rings as wryly true as its counterparts in Lawrence Durrell's present-time fantasy-farce "Antrobus" series. I cannot even say that Durrell's touch is any more deft or delicate with the satiric strokes than (fellow-ex-diplomat) Laumer's: I find the brush a bit broad for my taste, increasingly, in *both* series.

Maybe what jars me most in the Retief yarns is Retief himself—such a fine figure of a fellow, full of moral and intellectual, as well as muscular and social virtues—that I never quite believe that he is *still* with the CDT when the next story starts. Maybe merit does not necessarily imply rejection in the diplomatic employ, but this particular heroic figure has humor *besides*. If the *Corps* didn't cashier him, Retief would long since have cashed in his chips for himself.

And I can't help wishing that Laumer would take his own abilities more seriously. (See *F&SF*, March, on *The Great Time Machine Hoax*.) His rare excursions into non-farcical fiction—or even the misplaced hero, Retief—indicate the likelihood of a heroic writer under the gimcracks. Slapstick is great garnish for the *hors d'oeuvres*, or maybe even the dessert; but a well-done hero is still the meat-and-potatoes of literary fare—and there are simply not enough of them to go around, these anti-novel days.

Natives of Space, Hal Clement; Ballantine, 1965, 50¢, 156 pp.

It is not easy to persuade a commercial publisher to bring out a collection of short stories—and only slightly less difficult to sell a trio or quartet of novelettes. I suppose it should not be surprising, then, that so many of the collections that do get published appear to have been selected by literary historians rather than working editors. The unreconstructed evidence of the quarter-century-ago pulp apprenticeship of a man who has since become a skillful writer has very little place in the general fiction market, and less, I should think, on the overcrowded paperback stacks.

(What really astonishes me is the willingness of the authors themselves to have their early magazine work presented without refinishing to the book-reading public.)

Don't get me wrong. Every one of these three stories ("Impediment," "Technical Error," "Assumption Unjustified," all from *Astounding* 1942-43-46) contains the same inherent integrity (of puzzle, plot, character, theme, technical background) that has sustained Clement at the top of the field from the beginning. The difference is that on the way he also learned to *write.*

As it stands, the book is for solid s-f buffs only.

Sleeping Planet, William R. Burkett, Jr.; Doubleday. 1965, $4.95, 297 pp.

Goodish standard-brand *Analog*-type novel: a double-handful of unaffected Terrestrials beat off the sleeping-gas invasion of Earth by the Llralan Empire, countering overwhelming military force with Yankee ingenuity, rebel stubbornness, bulldog courage, outback unpredictability, and a little bit o' luck for good measure (mostly in the form of the superstitious ancestor-worship prevalent among the cosmic invaders).

The odd thing is, as long as it's at all competently done (and this one is), I keep right on enjoying this story.

[...]

CORRECTION: A missing line at the bottom of the second column on p. 78 of the July issue resulted in a major misquote from Kurt Vonnegut's book, *God Bless You, Mr. Rosewater*. The line, "God damn it, you've got to be kind," appears, as printed, to be the last line in the book. It's actually from the middle of the novel, and should have had a line saying so to precede it. My most sincere apologies. JM

Books (October 1965)

Some months ago, I met a gentleman. His name is Chard Powers Smith, and he is a writer of repute in fields remote from science fiction. He is a New Englander, both by passionate attachment and by intellectual-literary personality, and he has been a New Englander long enough so that he could tell me (and did, at a delightful dinner, the day after I sought out his acquaintance) charming stories of college days at Yale at the time when *every* young gentleman kept a drawer-full of white gloves, to be worn once only and discarded.

I did not know such details as this when I first heard him speak, of course—but his appearance, accent, and rhetoric conveyed a total impression quite in keeping with the image I have tried to present with trifling detail here. The occasion was a rather impressively respectable literary gathering of the sort I seldom attend; this time I had gone to hear Arthur Clarke speak on the putative "two cultures." Mr. Smith's five-minute address to the group occurred during the discussion period following the program, and stemmed from some of Clarke's comments on sci-fi. The burden of the speech was, as nearly as I can paraphrase at this distance in time:

> Man needs myth. We are not able to live with raw truths. The Judaeo-Christian mythology nurtured our civilization, and has sustained it for two millennia; now it appears to be no longer appropriate to the needs of modern man. Science fiction seems to be serving in some ways as a makeshift, patchup mythology to those most conscious of the realities of our burgeoning scientific culture. Is it possible that a new myth of adequate scope and significance will emerge from s-f? And if not, where will it come from?

If I have misinterpreted, or mis-stated his intentions, or perhaps added unconsciously, too much of my own thinking to his actual words, I hope Mr. Smith will correct me; I will in turn pass on the correction. But I believe my paraphrase is reasonably correct; in any case, it is the way I remember the statement, and close enough to the original to make clear my astonishment when I heard it delivered in the unmistakable accents of literary Vermont.

Since then, I have ceased to be startled at the sources of new insights into s-f, *or* new insights through the use of it. This month, not entirely by happenstance, I am in a position to spread out a sampling of the variety of style, and diversity of origin, of some of the best new work being done in the way of modern myth-making. Some of it is what even the hardest-shelled buffs would call "real science fiction;" some is wildly surrealistic fantasy. (Most, I think, contains aspects of both.) Of the six authors involved, only two are "genre writers," whose names would ordinarily be associated with the s-f field: Cordwainer Smith and Ray Bradbury. The others are an Argentinian author well-known in this country primarily in esoteric literary circles, Jorge Luis Borges; a Spanish author, José María Gironella, known here before this time only for his (officially approved, Catholic-award-winning) historical novels of the Spanish Civil War; a Polish-born Frenchman whose faintly fantasy-flavored work had already won a wide readership here, before his current best-seller, *The Ski Bums*—Romain Gary; and Jesse Bier, a young American author, a professor of American literature at Montana State University, with one previous book to his credit, the 1963 novel, *Trial at Bannock*.

Let's start with Cordwainer Smith,[1] because *he* starts with a prologue to his book which speaks, to some extent, for all these writers:

> This is science fiction, yes. But it comes from your own time, your own world, even your own past.
>
> All I can do is work the symbols.
>
> The magic and the beauty will come of our own past, your present, your hope, your experience. This may look alien, but it is really as close to you as your own fingers. Some people will like this very much. Many will not understand it and push it aside. That is their loss, reader, not yours, not mine.
>
> We two have this story between us....

Or more accurately, five stories, all novelettes, four from *Galaxy* ("Mother Hitton's Littul Kittons," "The Dead Lady of Clown Town," "The Ballad of Lost C'mell," "A Planet Named Shayol"), and "Drunkboat," from *Amazing*.

You may have read some of these before, even if you are not a regular reader of either magazine; two have appeared in my own anthologies ("Shayol" and "Drunkboat," in the *Sixth* and *Ninth Annuals*), and I think "C'mell," at least, was reprinted elsewhere (*A Galaxy Reader*?); but it won't matter—they take re-reading very well. And (unless you are one of those who "push it aside"—and there *are* those who do), the chances are that when you have re-read once, you will do so again.

Perhaps it would be more to the point to say that they don't *need* re-reading? Of the five, three came back to me from the depths of memory, as soon as I read the first page again—came back, not as plots or memories of something learned, but with all the color and sensation of personal experience. (Two are obvious: "Clown Town" was the third.) I re-read these, too—as one listens again to well-loved music, or looks again at a favorite painting, for the renewed ritual of the experience, not for refreshment of the mind.

I suppose it is in the nature of myth (or fable, or poetic prophecy—or any other operative "symbol working") that it not only improves on acquaintance, but cannot be fully savored until it has become completely familiar: only when the plot and characters are transparent with use, do the underlying meanings and insights show through clearly.

The publication of *Space Lords* as a Pyramid Science Fiction paperback marks another point in the already high score of editor Don Bensen (who might consider giving a course for other book editors on "How to read science fiction"); but it is even more unfortunate than usual that entrenched mainstream snobbishness will thus deprive the collection of the critical attention it should have, and might attain if it did not have *both* paperback and category strikes against it. The stories, in any case, will outlast the binding, and perhaps they will find their way meantime into more durable covers.

The two Bradbury volumes[2] at hand are reprints, and would not ordinarily be reported on here, since both were reviewed at the time of original publication (*F&SF*, May 1963 and July 1964). But in a discussion of this sort, two freshly available volumes of Bradbury short stories can hardly be ignored.

Ray Bradbury is probably the world's best-known s-f story writer; to many people outside the field, he almost identifies "science fiction"; inside s-f, he is a controversial figure, much admired and much rejected by those of the True Faith.

I myself have very varied reactions to Bradbury—but then he is a varied man. I have at times railed against Bradbury as an anti-science-fiction writer. I find his sentimentality intolerably sticky at times; his nostalgias are not mine; the world of my childhood was so remote from his—or from his fantasies of it—that I am compelled (you see) to question whether that midwestern boyhood ever was or *could* be, except in the world of the American Dream (circa 1900). Bradbury-the-writer seems to step in and out of this own dreamy attic, onto the main street of the world *I* know. But when he does step out onto that street, he does it with style, with integrity, and with the magic of that attic still inside him. (This attic-image, by the way, is not mine, but Bradbury's; I lifted it out of an interview with him in *Show* last year—a remarkably readable and solidly meaningful statement, about himself, his work, and his views on s-f. The "attic," which he spoke of figuratively, was the storage place for the accumulated experiences and enrichments of the past).

It may be, then, precisely *because* he is looking at the world I know through eyes adjusted to the light of his own private world, that Bradbury at his best can show me such startling and sometimes beautiful new aspects of my own "realities." In any event, he is one of the most skillful "symbol workers" in the business—and the business he is in is myth-and-magic making: the application of the quality of wonder in the human mind to the natural wonder of the universe and the mysterious wonder of life itself, and of *man* as a precious, special case of life.

José María Gironella's tripartite collection[3] is a curious and fascinating book, not readily classifiable in any way. The opening 40-page narrative, "Twilight," contains a detailed, powerful, and sometimes sickening account of the author's two-year experience of an acute state of melancholia, accompanied by vivid hallucinations, visions, and "psychic experiences"; the 16-page closing section, "Fugitives," is a sort of scrap-book-compilation of sentences and paragraphs of writing produced during the illness. Between these, are eight short stories comprising the section, "Phantoms," all derived from the same visionary experience.

The other-world reality of the stories is compelling; the closest parallel that comes to mind is Poe. And as with Poe, the symbols on which Gironella hangs his fantasies cover the whole range from religious and supernatural phenomena to the traditional apparatus of science-fiction.

In "The Death of the Sea," he uses the same frightening figure of finality Kurt Vonnegut manipulated so successfully in *Cat's Cradle*—but there is nothing else in common between the two. "The Red Egg" is the adventure story of a cancer cell seeking its nesting place; but it is neither a dramatized essay nor a horror story. "Miracle in the Village" makes use of the familiar idea of a man living backwards in time, to tell a tender love story.

The other stories use devices more familiar to outright fantasy, but in all of them, the use of the symbols is somehow pure—untainted, as it were, by any efforts at rationale or even relevancy to the usual world.

Gironella is, from the evidence of this book, a man of intense intellectual interests, and probing curiosity. He is also a profoundly religious Catholic, and presumably a Franco-patriot. His *real* world is remote enough from mine so that his perceptions of mutual realities might, in any case, bring me new insights. But these stories sprang from a vastly remote interior universe that might as well have been in an entirely different space-time—or, indeed, actually was.

Labyrinths[4] is, by a few hairs (four pages, to be exact), not a reprint, but an "augmented edition" of the 1962 title published in boards by New Directions. (One story, "The God's Script," has been added—as well as some of the end-of-the-book informational material.) Again, there are three sections to the book: "Fictions," "Essays," and "Parables"—and I cannot say in this case which I found most exciting. There is no room, in a "roundup" of this sort, to discuss the variety and significance of Borges's work; I prefer to wait, in any case, till I have in hand his other recent volume, *Dream Tigers.* I do not know whether Borges is as familiar with standard s-f writing as s-f readers have been, mostly, *un*familiar with his work; if not, the man seems to have invented for himself virtually every major concept the field as a whole has produced in half a century—and they are all here, tightly packed, sometimes only outlined, occasionally written in full emotional depth.

But whether he casts the work in the form of short story, parable, or essay, and whether he sketches or paints in full color, the man combines, on every page, so much intellectual ferment and such impactful symbolism, that it is only afterwards one realizes the startling quality of the prose itself. (If this seems a strong statement, it is stronger than you thought: the quality of the language seeps through half a dozen different translators with almost equal effectiveness.)

There will be more on this in a month or two. Meantime, there remain two volumes to discuss, which are not primarily s-f collections, but deserve mention here not only for the handful of genre stories, but for some of the others in each book which are informed by the same spirit, while adhering to a different code of letters.

Romain Gary's work has always displayed a remarkable apprehension of the essential wonder of out times—the constant startlement, fear, awe, magnificence, which are implicit in this Age of Change (to what, we know not, but the change is constant and cumulative). *Hissing Tales*[5] contains two outright s-f stories. "Decadence" might be described as a contemporary Goya etching, portraying a Syndicate Boss caught in the toils of Art, caught in turn in the talons of the Organization People; or you could call it a charming sophisticated farce on Labor, Crime, Art, and assorted hangers-on. "New Frontiers" is a quietly horrible (or perhaps slyly delightful?) end-of-the-world (or beginning?) surreality, having to do with man's return to the seas.

Jesse Bier,[6] whose work I have not read before, emerges as another writer of intense awareness, though (not yet at least) with Gary's sophistication and stylistic skills. Again there are two stories with outright elements of (in this case) fantasy; "Father and Son," and "Migdone." "Father and Son" is a what-if about the end of World War II in Germany; but don't think you've read it before. Its proposition is different and terrifying; its resolution somewhat disappointing—maybe necessarily so? I think there is no answer yet to the ethical questions involved in punishment for genocide. "Migdone" is the story of a man with a mote in his eye; or you can read it as a ghost story, or if you prefer, as a psychiatric study. Its mood was evocative for me of a story I think possibly the best instance of modern-gothic—Leiber's "Smoke Ghost."

And, as with Gary's collection, much of the other work lies only marginally across the borderline between fantastic and realistic literature; the title story, in particular, has all the elements of good s-f—except of course the essential one of extrapolation.

Notes

1. *Space Lords*, Cordwainer Smith; Pyramid, 1965; 50¢, 206 pp.
2. *R Is for Rocket* and *The Machineries of Joy*, Ray Bradbury; Bantam reprints, 1965; 50¢ and 60¢; 184 pp and 213 pp.
3. *Phantoms and Fugitives*, José María Gironella; Sheed & Ward, 1964; $3.95, 177 pp.; translated by Terry Broch Fontsere.
4. *Labyrinths*, Jorge Luis Borges, edited by Donald A. Yates and James E. Irby; New Directions, 1964 (NDP #186); $1.90; 251 pp. plus Chronology, Bibliography, Introduction, & Preface by André Maurois.
5. *Hissing Tales*, Romain Gary; Harper & Row, 1964; $4.95, 186 pp.
6. *A Hole in the Lead Apron*, Jesse Bier; Harcourt, 1964: $4.50, 248 pp.

Books (November 1965)

You read this in October, but I write it in July. The books are mostly June, July, and August publications, and I suppose this is what they mean by "summer reading." The surprising thing is not how unreadable the current batch of novels is, but how serious the bulk of this "light reading" turns out to be.

I rush to clarify. *Serious* is not a word to bandy lightly. I am not talking about the publishers' kind of "serious," interchangeable with "prestige;" nor the critics' "serious," which is somewhere between "worthy" and "impressive;" nor the casual reader's "serious," roughly synonymous with "dull." I have in mind the writer's meaning: "important"—to the writer.

I suppose all the shadings actually relate to "message" or theme. When a writer has something to say that is important (to him), he is serious about the writing of it. The critic takes it seriously if the writer manages to impress him with the worth of the statement. What yardstick the publishers use to measure the merit of any man's message, I have no notion—some occult equation, perhaps, combining in mystical quantities the critical, commercial, and cocktail party-clairvoyants' assessments of a given writer in a given year? But I am quite sure about the casual reader's meaning; when the message obtrudes to the point of obscuring the action, the book is too serious.

It is the writer's kind of "serious" I am using here. Every one of the eight novels stacked in front of me is at least technically "light fiction;" they are action stories, adventures, thrillers. Yet all of them are vehicles for thematic statements and/or ethical explorations of utmost seriousness. One might almost entertain the hope that writers (in s-f, at least) are giving new consideration to the quaint old notion that the best way to instruct is to entertain. And if seven out of eight do not *quite* bring off the double effort—well, perhaps that is *why* they are "summer books;" and none fail entirely; and besides, there is only one John D. McDonald.

The MacDonald entry[1] is not actually one of this summer's crop, but a reissue of *The Girl, The Gold Watch, & Everything*, which somehow missed being reviewed here when it first appeared. I am, frankly, pleased that the chance now falls to me: the opportunity to discuss MacDonald in an s-f column is all too rare.

The first MacDonald story I remember reading was "A Child Is Crying." (If you missed it, try *The Shape of Things*, ed. Damon Knight, Paperback Library.) Since then I have read everything of his I've seen: short stories and perhaps thirty or forty novels: mysteries, suspense, sex thrillers, satires, and, infrequently, fantasy and science fiction. I have never read a bad one; and though I recall only one book that had the trappings of the officially-serious novel I cannot recall more than two or three that seemed to me to have been *written* unseriously.

TGTGW&E is the first full-length MacDonald s-f since *The Planet of the Dreamers*, but he is not only one of the best s-f writers when he does it—he *thinks* like one no matter what he's writing.

MacDonald's characters do not live in the never-never land of most popular fiction. They inhabit the familiar world of machinery and motels, political upheavals and realty scandals, syndicates and supermarkets, conventions and court orders, automobile accidents, road repairs, floods and storms and trees and swamps, urban renewals and rural electrifications. They not only inhabit this world; they live with it: their problems come out of it and they must cope with it somehow to find their solutions. Inevitably, the characters themselves are genuinely contemporary, with mores and morals and methods recognizably similar to yours and mine and the people's next door.

I do not for a moment intend to say that MacDonald is a "realist" of the camera variety, painstakingly, painfully, recording the ordinariness of the ordinary. On the contrary: he is a storyteller in the grand style, a singer of bright romances, bold adventures, deep tragedies, and high humor. He selects the unusual and colorful to write about—but the selection is made from the richness of choice offered by the complexity and excitement of the world we live in. His heroes are almost always muscular and competent, his heroines beautiful and loving—but the masculine competence is technical as well as physiological, and feminine tenderness expresses itself as generously in bed as in the kitchen. He writes fast-moving yarns about situations charged with conflict and suspense—but behind it all is an informed and thoughtful comprehension of the forces (natural, technological, political, economic) actually at work in our society, out of which the drama emerges.

And just every now and then, he also writes a gleefully balloon-busting, pomposity-pricking farce. *TGTGW&E* is one of these—to start with. (The Miami Scene, with settings straight out of musical extravagant: beaches and bikinis, yachts and hotels, conventioneers and arty-parties; *plus* the slinkiest villainess since Caniff stopped doing the Dragon Lady, the sturdiest secretary since Winnie Winkle got married, and the bounciest hillbilly since Daisy Mae.) It is also a solid science-fantasy, with some fine detail-work attached to the Gold Watch Gimmick. And (like it says in the title) it has at least a touch of just about everything McDonald does best: cops-and-robbers, shipboard stuff, financial intrigue, slugfests, suspense-and-pursuit, and several varieties of plain and fancy sex.

Did I mention that under the antics this is a serious book?

Unfortunately, there is only one MacDonald—though I might make Poul Anderson a much closer second, if I could take the presumably serious part more seriously. *The Star Fox*[2] is the book version of the Gunnar Heim stories originally published here ("Marque and Reprisal," "Arsenal Port," and "Admiralty"): a fast-moving future-historical full of song, drink, blood, brawn, and lofty-minded piracy in the high spaces, with even a little bit of sex thrown in this time. If you overlook what may have been intended as Serious Political Significance (the roaring blood of the Vikings physically and morally triumphant over the mealy-mouthed conformist e-t-lovin' peacemongers), and what appears to have been *set* forth as serious economic and tactical theory (the advantages of private enterprise in space-faring, and of privateering in space warfare), it's the usual rip-snortingly readable Anderson adventure, complete with a multi-lingual spaceswinging minstrel, and a lovely interstellar lady spy.

As for Gunnar himself—if only Errol Flynn were still alive!

And while I'm being nostalgic, what ever happened to Poul Anderson—I mean that *other* Poul Anderson: the man who wrote, for instance, "Sam Hall?"

Not up to the same level of good fast summer reading, but short, unpretentious, and adequate, is *The Ballad of Beta-2*[3]—a space-mystery in which an anthropology student of the far future unravels the meaning of a ballad sung by the descendants of the degenerated survivors of an early "universe"-type starflight. If the protagonist had a touch of Gunnar Heim's arrogant charm (or any other kind) in place of his scholarly smugness; or if the style were less noticeably (or more successfully) reminiscent of Cordwainer Smith's distinctive technique, the whole thing would have come off better. As it is, the basic idea is good enough to carry you through the novella length.

Alpha Yes, Terra No!,[3] on the flip side, is a considerably more ambitious effort, in several ways. Its most successful effect is the characterization of the emissary from Alpha to Earth, a complex, credible and likeable extra-terrestrial who unfortunately turns out *not* to be the hero after all. The major device of the novel, equally unfortunately, is the familiar Galactic Council hearing, at which the alternatives of destruction or membership for Terra are considered, and decided, on the testimony of a short handful of earthmen. This situation has defeated some fine authors in the past; Petaja contrives to make the whole thing even weaker than usual by using as Earth's representatives a group of Earthers with some admixture of Alphan blood, and then having his friendly Alphan stage-manage their whole show for them.

In spite of all this, the book holds up tolerably well; Petaja sets his scenes vividly and convincingly—and if his philosophical points tend to be sentimental, his emotional convictions are strongly communicated.

How much the book may have gained for me by being read in close conjunction with three other new novels, each of which attempts a somewhat similar ethical exploration, I'm not sure; certainly, all four books gained interest by contrast and comparison.

I suppose there must be some profound pseudo-literary significance involved when four separate writers of rather different backgrounds (and with four different publishers) all turn at the same time to the same kind of Stapledonian universe-survey to examine metaphysical-and-ethical questions. But there is another multiple coincidence I found even more intriguing: the return, as it were, of the Lone Space-ranger.

Whether through inner motivation or external pressure, the protagonist in each of these books either makes, takes, takes over, or breaks into, a previously unavailable means of swift travel through space-time; then, either alone or with a tiny group of handpicked companions (*not* a crew, *not* an expeditionary force), ventures into the unknown for personal reasons which become subordinated to the urgencies of ethical problems arising out of contact with varied alien races.

(Was it just a month or so ago I was complaining about the lack of proper heroes? Well, it is true that some of this month's batch have heroism rather thrust upon them—but they *accept* it. All these, and Gunnar Heim too!)

Lloyd Biggle,[4] like Petaja, makes use of a comparatively conventional s-f format: the Mysterious Machine from Somewhere—in this case, Somewhen. His hero is an air-force engineer type who seizes semi-control of the strange sphere, involving himself in voyages through time *and* space that result in a sort of reversal of the Galactic Trial problem: Major Karvel has to decide how to apply his own ethics to civilizations with vastly different values.

Although the past and future folk all come off a bit Flash Gordonish, and most of the 20th Century types carry a faint taint of cardboard too, Biggle has created a warmly believable character in the bitter, capable, one-legged Major. He has also taken thoughtful care in both the setting and the solutions of his ethical problems, and—*hallelluja!*—has worked out some of neatest time-travel non-paradoxes I have come across.

Neither *Fury* nor *Alpha* has the richness of texture or complexity of theme to be found in Moudy's *No Man on Earth*[5] or Davidson's *Masters of the Maze*[6]; and if neither of these manages to bring off quite-successful resolutions, it is probably because of the major proportions of the problems they try to explore.

[…]

Like Petaja, Moudy makes use of a human-e-t crossbreed as hero—but this time the device provides credibility for both the super-capabilities and the motivations that enable Thad Stone, single-handed, to invent, finance, build, and operate his own star-ship at a time in the fairly near future when solar space travel is a going thing, but faster-than-light is no closer to terrestrial technology than it is today.

The most successful parts of the book are those concerned with Thad's development and the beginnings of his urgent search for his alien father. I *believed* Moudy's 21st Century Kansas City, and I came about as close as I *do* come, to believing in his young superman—for a while. This was a considerable accomplishment, because I had first to overcome the complete lack of convention of the overdone opening, describing young Thad's birth on a reservation (maintained by callous sociologists to study primitive hill people), and his survival despite his rumored "man-witch" paternity. And then I'm afraid I lost not only credence, but most of my interest, when the search for daddy became by degrees a search for a civilization to satisfy super-Thad. Too many planet-stops with too many superficially created civilizations, perhaps? Or a loss of emotional identification with the maturing superman? I don't know—and it is perhaps unfair to make such comparisons with a first novel, but it may be counted as high credit to the book that I consider the contrasts—but I still remember the impact of such a tour in Stapledon's *Starmaker*; and I never lost touch with Robin in Sturgeon's *Maturity*.

Certainly an encouraging first offering—rather more rewarding than either *Alpha* or *Fury*, and in many ways as successful as Davidson's book.

As for Davidson, he goes far to redeem himself for the travesty of *Mutiny in Space* (*F&SF* "Books," June). (This time, you see, he was *serious*.)

His device is a mystical-metaphysical Maze, accessible (from our world) through entry-points known to, and guarded by, certain selected members of an ultra-secret esoteric order of freemasons; the Maze shortcircuits space-time in some way, so that it provides passageway between an infinite variety of universes and probabilities.

In lesser hands, such a construct could easily have been an amalgam of all that's worst in Lovecraft and *Weird Tales.* Davidson's incredible ear for dialogue, his sharp eye for detail, and his resulting deft touch with a wide range of characterizations (the explorer-writer hero; the very Victorian elderly gentleman; the New England Sheriff; fascist-minded Major Flint; Darius Chauncey, soldier and ardent snake-worshipper; Arrettagorretta, of the Chulpex; Et-dir-Mor of Red Fish Land; and *lots* more) turn the Maze into a curse-and-convenience adjacent to the most matter-of-fact realities. And for three quarters of the book, while the scene is being set, and Nate Gordon is making his first accidental and fumbling, then eager and questing, journeys through the Maze, the quality of the adventure is almost Carrollian in feeling.

And then the whole thing falls apart (as Moudy's did), from the point where the ineffable Masters of the Maze are introduced, and Nate starts dashing through flashing vistas of strange worlds, seeking Ultimates which seem to be far over his head, and perhaps the author's too.

I do not think Davidson can be faulted for failing to accomplish what he essayed here; but one might say mildly that a writer of his experience should possibly have known better than to attempt a Definition of Truth in a short action novel.

[...]

Notes

1. *The Girl, The Gold Watch, & Everything*, John D. MacDonald, Gold Medal, 40¢, 207 pp.
2. *The Star Fox*, Poul Anderson, Doubleday, $4.50, 274 pp.
3. *The Ballad of Beta-2*, Samuel R. Delany, and *Alpha Yes, Terra No!*, Emil Petaja; Ace double, 45¢, 96 pp. & 156 pp.
4. *The Fury out of Time*, Lloyd Biggle, Jr., Doubleday, $4.50, 257 pp.
5. *No Man on Earth*, Walter Moudy, Berkley, 50¢, 176 pp.
6. *Masters of the Maze*, Avram Davidson, Pyramid, 50¢, 158 pp.

[...]

Books (January 1966)

London, September 1965— The climate is different here. It rains more. The houses are colder. Everyone seems to drink a great deal more, and fewer people seem to get drunk. Nothing ever gets done the same day. No one eats lunch before one o'clock, or dinner before eight. The tea is insidious: I no longer drink coffee all day; at four or five in the afternoon, I make a pot of tea.

Rock-'n'-roll sounds better; it has a beat. Publishers discuss books as often as markets. Small children do talk in the clear high sweet voices suggested by Milne and Carroll and Nesbit. Everyone looks younger: rainwashed complexions perhaps? There is much less newness for newness's sake—and rather less sentimentality about oldness too. And the writers I've talked to seem to feel they have some purpose in their work. It is not considered impolite to indulge in serious discussion in public, whether about literature, world politics, the arts and sciences—even one's own work or that of one's colleagues.

Education for its own sake is widely approved, and in intellectual circles at least, the enquiring mind is quite socially acceptable. Intensity of spirit, or conviction, or both, is not necessarily considered a sign of emotional imbalance.

S-f here still suffers somewhat from the same sort of ghetto-consciousness that has afflicted American publishing and reviewing; but its effect here is more on the in-group of writer-reviewers than on the publishers or the reading public. Most important, there is a feeling of excitement, a ferment of interest and creative activity, both within the field and surrounding it, such as has not been felt on the American scene for almost fifteen years.

(1949-52: The first years of *F&SF*, under Boucher and McComas; the beginning of Gold's *Galaxy*; Howard Browne's *Amazing*; new magazines springing up every month; *Collier's* and the *Post* publishing s-f! The new writers: Anderson, Beaumont, Budrys, Clifton, Clingerman, Cogswell, Dick, Dickson, Finney, Henderson, Knight, Maclean, (Merril), Walter Miller, Pohl, Cordwainer Smith, Tenn, Vonnegut, Bernard Wolfe. The return of Bush, del Rey, Kornbluth, Leiber, Sturgeon. The first serious reviews in mainstream sources; the building up of the Big Book Boom.)

The British scene today is different in many respects. There are only two English magazines; book publication is almost more sure than magazine;

reviews are widespread and mostly serious—certainly not supercilious when half of them are being written by Aldiss, Amis, Ballard, and Phillips.

The three biggest differences are the existence of the American field as a second (and often first) market; the comparative absence of an active Old Guard (either of authors or editors); and fifteen years during which it has become unnecessary to prove that science fiction *can* be good—and vital to determine how and where and when it is.

The result is—the climate is very different indeed. A feature article on the recent World Science Fiction Convention here, by *Spectator* writer Bill Butler, began:

> "Burroughs would have been lost...Edgar Rice Burroughs that is. Since the days of his novel, *The Warlord of Mars*, things have changed in outer space. Yet William Burroughs, he of *Naked Lunch* and *Nova Express* fame, would have loved nearly every minute of it."

Another piece, in the *Times Magazine*, described John W. Campbell, Jr., as the field's "acknowledged father-figure.... He provides the continuity, he shaped much of the thought, he made many reputations. SF narrowed from the vastness of space to the greater complexity of 'sociological' SF with him presiding. But now it is narrowing toward the highly-focused, upside-down detail of 'inner space.' The tone is personal and subjective, the quality of expression important. The prophet is J. G. Ballard, author of *The Drowned World*, the bright star William Burroughs...."

Actually, Burroughs is not much more popular with s-f fans here than at home, but he has exercised a significant influence on British writers, both directly and through the much more widely read work of J. G. Ballard.

The three names most in evidence here are Ballard, Brian W. Aldiss, and John Brunner. This is not to say that the older generation of British writers (Clarke, Wyndham, Christopher, Russell, et al.) has lost its following—but that Aldiss, Brunner, and Ballard, as much as they differ in style, technique, and philosophy, are all peculiarly British, and current, in their work; it is these three who constitute the stimulus center for the rather more subjective, perhaps more thoughtful, certainly more literary, direction of British s-f in the mid-sixties.

All three are comparatively young authors; each of them entered s-f less than ten years ago, through the pages of *New Worlds* and *Science Fantasy*, when E. J. Carnell was editing both magazines. Of the three, Brunner is probably the most conservative in terms of literary technique and adherence to the "science fiction conventions" (Ballard's fulminating phrase, which in his usage appears to be a portmanteau containing almost all conventional literary techniques, some social conventions, and all Science Fiction Conventions). Starting in the mid-fifties in America, Brunner might have become a Silverberg, a Garrett, an Anvil—but I do not think he would have written, ten years later, a book like his recent *Telepathist* (*The Whole Man*, in the American edition).

Aldiss might conceivably have developed much as he did here; certainly he is the most versatile of the three, and his work relies more on emotional content, imagery, and style, than on plot or idea content. Yet he is stylistically, literarily, the most typically British one, particularly in his role of critic (literary editor of the *Oxford Mail;* co-editor of the new *S. F. Horizons*).

Ballard, starting in the American market, would probably have left s-f before he entered it; not one in ten of his early stories would have sold in the States in the late fifties. I have heard Ballard's work compared here to Bradbury's and to Burroughs's, and I feel it is a measure of Ballard's accomplishment that no such comparisons are meaningful in his case—unless in the sense that he needed an enclave such as the Nova magazines to start in, just as Bradbury needed *Weird Tales* and Burroughs, Olympia Press. The only thing they have in common is uncommonness. (The only established writers active on the American s-f scene today whose work is in any similar way unique to themselves are Kurt Vonnegut and Cordwainer Smith—both of whom have been from the start in, but not of, science-fiction.)

In this respect, Ballard is again unique: he reviles the inadequacies of science fiction endlessly; but he directs his criticism primarily at other writers, reviewers, and editors inside the field. Stylistically, he allies himself with the *avant garde*, with experimental techniques, and surrealism. But his subject matter, his preoccupation with the metaphysics and biophysics of time and space-time conformations, his "ontological" explorations of psychic and sur-realities, his deep awareness of the inextricable relationship between mind and matter, organism and environment are directly on the main line of speculation in serious science fiction—and particularly current throughout the British field.

Ballard is fond of defining science fiction as "that area where inner space and outer space meet and merge"; it might be as valid to say that his own work represents that area where s-f thinking and surrealist writing meet and marry. That marriage seems to me to be the Big Event of the contemporary literary scene, and its impact on other writers, in both camps, is increasingly evident.

Whether it is more true to say that the vitality and excitement one feels in s-f publishing circles here owes its existence in part to Ballard's influence, or that his literary existence was made possible by the climate here, I should not care to guess. Certainly, the climate *is* different; and in many ways, British s-f writers today can enjoy the best of two worlds.

To begin with, there has been an eager magazine market continually open to new writers here for almost fifteen years, because as soon as a British s-f writer begins to make a name for himself, a sizable proportion of his work starts going to the higher-paying American magazines. There are still only two magazines, now published by Roberts and Vintner, in a new format, and under two new editors with radically different approaches from Carnell's, or each other's.

Kyril Bonfiglioli edits *Science Fantasy* from the office of his art gallery in Oxford—where he also lectures in antiques and mediaeval art. Mike Moorcock, of *New Worlds*, holds virtual open house for his contributors in the living room-office of his London flat, stone's throw from Notting Hill in one direction, and Hyde Park in another—and sometimes still picks up the guitar with which he earned his way around the Continent a few years back, and wails wild stomping blues. What the two men have in common is a great impatience with the artificial limitations of *genre* or "category" if one set of standards is based on the body of English literature, an the other on the advance front of contemporary writing, still they are standards, and both editors expect at least the best of s-f to meet them. In any case, both magazines remain vehicles for the more literary and experimental efforts of the established writers, as well as for the work of the proliferating crop of young potentials.

Again, when the budding writer reaches the level of book publication, the chances are his first one or two efforts will be placed fairly readily with an English publisher in search of original work on which American rights have not been previously sold. Or he may bypass this step, and find his books appearing from the beginning in the US first, with British edition following.

This is the usual pattern, in any case, for the established writers. The basic money comes from the mass-distribution American market—but the basic edition, from the writer's viewpoint, is the English one—and when the time gap between American and British editions is a bit longer than usual, it is not uncommon to find that the text varies considerably.

A number of factors enter into the differences between editions on either side of the ocean, and most of them are rooted in the different marketing and production problems of the two countries. An American paperback publisher, for instance, expects to sell—indeed, *must* sell—anywhere from two to ten times as many copies as a British firm. The mass production and distribution setup in the States makes it vital for the publisher to be able to forecast his sales accurately—and mass sales methods provide him with the techniques for prediction.

The end result is that the sales department tends to dominate the editorial; you cannot determine from the quality of the prose how many copies a book will sell on the newsstands; it is the "package" which has some predictability. Hence, the phenomenon of the "category" book, the importance of the "name" author, and the increasing tendency for the editor to become a sort of liaison man between sales-and-production and the author—functioning primarily as a judge of whether the product is suitable for the predetermined package and production schedule.

At the same time, mass production methods make production schedules less flexible. Companies are larger; print orders must be scheduled well ahead of time; red tape accrues in all directions; everything slows down.

It is hardly surprising, then, that the book editor in the States sometimes sacrifices literary standards in favor of length, content, and date of delivery. He may take a sloppily written book if he can have it in time to fill the hole in his schedule for next September; he may insist on editing out of a book material considered offensive or unsalable to the market for which the book is destined; he may ask for additions to justify a certain kind of cover.

British editors I have talked to, not subject to the same pressures, react with what might seem on Mad Ave, quaint old-fashioned horror, at the notion of unauthorized editing of a writer's work; they find it not at all strange for a writer to delay delivery of a book in order to do a last revision; they assume it is basically the quality of the work that will determine the eventual sales of the book.

As a result of all this, it is not uncommon to find considerable variation in British and American editions of the same book. Sometimes the writer submits his first complete draft to American publishers, while working at comparative leisure on a more satisfactory final draft for publication at home. Sometimes it is the American publisher's rush-completion date which demands an unfinished job, from the writer's viewpoint—but he consoles himself with the American advance, which, again, provides the time to do the polishing job. Sometimes, the differences are due entirely to editorial changes in the publishing house.

The British author's literary standing, in his own mind, rests on British critical reaction, and British sales. It is easy for him to forget—even while he collects the royalties—that three or four times as many copies of his book (or even more) are being sold and read across the ocean in a form unsatisfactory to him. It is his version his friends and local critics are reading. And of course, regardless of how many people read which one, his own version is at least *on the record in print.*

Brian Aldiss's *Greybeard* (see *F&SF*, "Books," Dec. 1964) is a case in point. The Harcourt Brace edition published in the US last year received a much less enthusiastic reception than the Faber edition published in England shortly afterwards. I understand the forthcoming Signet paperback will contain the full British version; and I suggest that American readers who were disappointed in the novel try the paperback again.

Ballard's latest book[1] (*The Drought* in England, *The Burning World* in the US) is perhaps a more typical instance; the differences between the two versions are less drastic and, I suspect, more representative of the whole range of "climatic" variation between the two countries.

I have read the British version, and skimmed through the American. The apparent great difference in length is due primarily to the smaller print and longer page of the Berkley edition, and to the breaking up of the narrative into many short chapters; there is little actual expansion. Yet with work as stylized and intense as Ballard's, even the white-space breaks between chapters are significant, as are the results of a last prose revision.

It is becoming almost impossible to review a new book of Ballard's all by itself. The author is building from book to book, and from story to story, in such a way that although each unit is meaningful on its own terms, it assumes full dimensions only in the context of the whole body of work.

The Drought might be regarded as a companion piece to *The Drowned World* (*F&SF* "Books," July 1965), this time exploring the effects of dryness, instead of deluge, on the human psyche. Once again, the book is populated with exotic, evocative, archetypal characters, moving in curiously intersecting patterns through the dust and flame, salt, soot, and shadows of the desert landscape. Time seems to slow almost to a stop—and in this time-desert, the action and dramatic momentum of the book appear to gather speed.

Some of the concepts here were prefigured in earlier short stories—"The Delta at Sunset," "The Reptile Enclosure," "The Cage of Sand"—but in the novel, the elements and ideas merge into a surprisingly exciting piece of story-telling, even while they fall into perspective in the larger landscape of Ballard's ontological explorations.

I think this is a more easily readable book than *The Drowned World*, and almost certainly a better *novel.* Whether it is a better book—because Ballard does not really write novels anyhow—will take time to determine; the significance seems to keep seeping up to the surface of the mind for a long time after the book is closed.

[...]

Note

1. *The Drought*, J. G. Ballard; Jonathan Cape (London), 1965; 252 pp.; 21/0 ($2.94); first published as *The Burning World*; Berkley, 1964; 160 pp.; 50¢.

Books (February 1966)

Something is radically wrong when, in a stack of two dozen assorted review books, more than half the novels—and all the best of them—are reprints or reissues, and most of the "new" short story collections—those that are not reprints or reissues are either collections or cross-collections from earlier collections, or barrel-bottom scrapings from ten and fifteen years ago.

This month, three books brighten the picture: a satirical novel by a pseudonymous Soviet writer; a new collection of Zenna Henderson's short stories; and one fully justified, warmly welcome cross-collection, culled from Charles Beaumont's three earlier volumes of short stories (*Yonder*, *The Hunger*, *Night Ride*).

Refreshingly enough, the publishers have pulled a switch on the standard disclaimers; the front cover of *The Magic Man*[1] carries the subtitle, "and other science-fantasy stories," although neither the title story, nor most of the rest, was—technically—s-f at all. [...]

Oddly enough, the jacket is right. Twelve of the eighteen stories are set in the here-and-now, with no significant departure from things-as-they-are, on the surface at least. Yet I do not think Beaumont has ever written anything without the extra element of imaginative speculation that constitutes the essence of s-f. You might say he has been more of a writer about fantasies than a writer of them. He makes use of the typical forms of science fiction or conventional fantasy fiction sometimes, to externalize one of his insights into the seeking soul of modern man—or, again, to project (and thus exaggerate to humorous proportions) some aspect of inner fantasy. But he is usually at his best working in the literary borderland of such stories as "The Magic Man," or "Black Country," "A Classic Affair" or "Miss Gentilbelle."

The themes are the themes of science-fantasy; the style and construction are Beaumont's and uniquely his; the characters are sometimes cryingly true to life.

[...]

It's a hard act to follow, but Henderson does it. And until I sat down with the two books in front of me, I'd have sworn there couldn't be two more different writers. Stylistically, this is true—most of the time. But here again, the writer's major interest is in the true inner fantasies of real people. "The Anything Box,"[2] title story of the collection, is characteristic of the best of Zenna Henderson's work. It is fascinating, when the two books have been separately enjoyed, to look at her "Food to All Flesh" next to Beaumont's "Last Rites," or his "Dark Music" next to her "Walking Aunt Daid," or "Turn the Page" and "The Magic Man."

There is no need to compare or contrast, however. One need only remember. "Come on Wagon" has lost nothing since it introduced Zenna Henderson to her first readers in the pages of this magazine almost fifteen years ago. Some of the more recent stories here may well prove as memorable: "Something Bright," "Things," "The Grunder," "Subcommittee," "Hush!"

Abram Tertz is the pseudonym of a writer living in the Soviet Union. Three earlier books (*Fantastic Stories*, *On Socialist Realism*, *The Trial Begins*) have been published here and in England; none of them—including the current volume—in the USSR.[3]

The Makepeace Experiment is the story of a bicycle mechanic who—almost—becomes the Emperor of the world. It is also a great many other things, but most of all it is a true fable; it caricatures the human condition rather than any particular set of mores or ideological labels. Undoubtedly, the fact that the setting is Russian makes it a funnier and more comfortable book for reading this side of the world. But it is not so much a criticism of sovietism as of bureaucracy and governmental mismanagement anywhere, everywhere.

I think the same happenstance of background that makes the book more agreeable to critics here than the same story might be if set in Iowa, for instance, detracts somewhat from the pointedness of the satire for American readers. Just as parody can only be written properly with love and admiration for the source, so political satire is really meaningful only in a framework of sympathy and concern for the political entity involved. The author has this essential sympathy: he smuggles his manuscripts out of his country, and remains there himself to write more. But we who receive the books inevitably miss much of what is being said: we laugh at the right places; we are instructed and informed; we do not, I suspect, cry when we should.

In compensation, perhaps because he uses the bolder strokes of the cartoonist's pen, Tertz's work seems to me to convey a more realistic sense of life-as-it-is in Russia today than most deliberately informational writing.

The same virtue inheres, for quite different reasons, in George Langelaan's French settings. Langelaan's book[4] carries no translation credits. I assume he writes in English; but he is French-born of English parentage, educated in America, and now again a resident of Paris, one of the rare breed of truly trans-Atlantic citizens.

It is just as confusing to attempt to classify Langelaan's work in terms of familiar literary conventions. He says he is writing horror stories—and most of them are. But: "Horror is a form of fear," he says in a brief preface, "therefore of ignorance.... Time is for me one of the best elements of horror, not only because we know so little about it, but because it is nothing and everything.... We are beginning to discover that time is something more than real, something tangible and even solid. In it, scientists can already begin to 'feel' the past and the future; in time and space they are discovering time cells, or time in time. For the insect that lives a few minutes, we are eternal, but for a range of mountains, we flit about so rapidly that we do not really exist...."

It is this attitude that transforms most of these stories from simple horror to intriguing speculation. The story best-known here, "The Fly," (of *Playboy* and movie fame) is to my mind one of the least effective; my favorites are "Past the Time Limit" and "The Lady from Nowhere" (as it happens the two most clear-cut "science-fiction" stories in the book), in both of which Langelaan gives free rein to his curiosity about the nature of time, subjective and objective, and its relation to human mortality.

This seems as good a place as any to pause and explain that I intend (or hope, with the cooperation of British publishers) to include British books in these columns hereafter, whenever there is no American edition planned, or when the two differ significantly. [...]

Three [...] British editions not scheduled for American publication are of interest—one particularly so because it is the first book publication of an American author. Rick Raphael's first novel will appear here this year from Simon & Schuster, but a collection of four of his novelettes was done in London last spring.[5] The title story, "The Thirst Quenchers," is one of the best pieces of solid science fiction—the sort of thing you used to read *Astounding* for in the old days—I have seen in a long time and "Guttersnipe" runs a close second.

Also from Gollancz is a first novel by Leonard Daventry,[6] a book in some ways almost quaintly "scientifictional" in tone—but very new in its examination of this idea of telepathy as a manifestation of the collective unconscious, and in its exploration of the effects of limited supermanhood on the private life of the putative superman.

Now Then,[7] by John Brunner, is a collection of three novelettes: only one of which has been published here. "Thou Good and Faithful," appeared in *Astounding* in 1953 under the pseudonym, John Loxmith; it was, in fact, Brunner's first published story, and he has done considerably better since. Happily, one outstanding instance is included in the collection, the opening story, "Some Lapse of Time," which is worth the purchase price by itself.

While we're on the subject of Brunner, I should like at least to mention in passing his Ballantine novel of last year, which missed review here: *The Whole Man*. If you haven't read it and can still find it on the newsstands, you will find it a good deal more meaningful and more exciting than the usual run of Brunner's carefully constructed novels.

I wish I could say the same for Poul Anderson's new novel. All the best bits [in Poul Anderson's new novel] are vivid passages of early English and Danish history.[8] And in the two new volumes of (not so new) novelettes published by Chilton,[9] what is most interesting are the parallels between Captain Sir Dominic Flandry of Terra's Imperial Naval Intelligence Corps, and one James Bond from (Flandry's) remote past. Let me make clear that I *do* mean parallels. As near as I can see, Fleming and Anderson initiated their characters and laid down the unvarying pattern for their performances, at much the same time, in remote literary fields.

What I *am* saying is the flip side of my opening paragraph. Beaumont can write an imaginative speculative story with all the essential ingredients of s-f without ever departing from the forms of so-called "realistic" fiction. Anderson is using the forms of s-f to write thrillers and historicals, and contriving to do so without introducing an element of speculation or fresh invention.

Why?

[...]

Notes

1. *The Magic Man*, Charles Beaumont; Gold Medal, 1965; 256 pp., 18 stories plus Foreword by Ray Bradbury and Afterword by Richard Matheson; 50¢.
2. *The Anything Box*, Zenna Henderson; Doubleday, 1965; 205 pp., 14 stories; $3.95.
3. *The Makepeace Experiment*, Abram Tertz; Translated by Manya Harani, Pantheon (New York) and Haverhill Press (London), 1965; 195 pp., including a Translator's Note $3.95.
4. *Out of Time*, George Langelaan; Four Square (New English Library paperback), 196; 190 pp., 10 stories; 3/6 (60¢).

5. *The Thirst Quenchers*, Rick Raphael; Gollancz (London) 1965; 175 pp., 4 stories; 15/0 ($2.30).
6. *Man of Double Deed*, Leonard Daventry; Gollancz (London), 1965; 176 pp.; 15/0 ($2.30).
7. *Now Then*, John Brunner; Mayflower-Dell paperback (London), 1965; 143 pp., 3 novelettes plus author's preface; 3/6 (60¢).
8. *The Corridors of Time*, Poul Anderson; Doubleday, 1965; 209 pp.; $3.95.
9. *Agent of the Terran Empire,* Poul Anderson; Chilton, 1965; 198 pp., 4 novelettes; $3.95. *Flandry of Terra*, Poul Anderson; Chilton, 1965; 225 pp., 3 novelettes; $3.95.

[…]

Books (March 1966)

I want to apologize to Poul Anderson. Last month in this column, I criticized him for writing historical novels and spy-thrillers under the guise of science fiction. If I had read this month's batch of books, I might have praised him instead: his historical background had a feeling of authenticity that made for good reading.

Out of ten new novels here, most of them by prominent and experienced s-f writers, four may validly be considered speculative novels (and two of those are good ones: Clifford Simak's *All Flesh Is Grass*, and John Christopher's *The Ragged Edge*—about both of which, more later). The others include a medieval romance (set in an interstellar empire); a colonial-frontier-adventure story (in an interstellar federation); a modified spy-thriller-international-intrigue (mad-scientists-and-psionics) novel; a super-historical combining elements of all of these (interstellar empire again); a clipper-ship adventure (first interstellar exploratory voyage); and for a real change of pace, a doctor-love romance (return of interplanetary exploratory expedition).

Perhaps the most irritating thing about all this is that none of these books can be dismissed as worthless. Every one of them has something to offer: convincing characterizations or well-integrated background, or narrative skill, or a basic idea of interest. Some have more than one: Frank Herbert's *Dune* (the super-historical) has some of everything. Everything, that is, except the essential without which it does not fall into even the broadest definition of "speculative literature." It is not enough to ask: "What if...?" That is, there must be a reasonably thoughtful attempt to answer the question. And if the work is to be considered science fiction (or, to be less demanding, science fantasy), there must also be a direct and significant relationship between the question under consideration and the imaginative or hypothetical element introduced.

When that connection exists only on the other end—between the *answer* and the fantasy—the more usual label is *deus ex machina.* Harry Harrison's new book,[1] for instance, posits the intriguing problem of a viral epidemic for which the human body has no antibody reaction—and spread by birds. How do you lick a thing like that? Apparently by quarantining the boy-doctor and girl-doctor together long enough to explain the problem, and to give them a chance to develop a (genteelly restrained) itch for each other—about one-quarter of the book; then junketing the boy-doc around the countryside with bird-shooting expeditions while the girl-doc stays in the lab doing experiments until she contracts the disease—another quarter. At this point, boy-doc realizes that medical research and public-health methods are inadequate, so he calls in the marines—well, actually, enlists an Army General in a private commando-type attack on the quarantined Jovian exploratory ship which brought back the infection. And what do you know? It turns out not to be treason or piracy but heroism, because sure enough there is an evil alien on board, who can be tortured into releasing the handy phial of cure he brought with him.

All right. If this book had come to me with an unknown name, from a lesser publisher, I would have dismissed it with a sentence and forgotten it. But Harrison knows better, and Doubleday, the biggest hard-cover s-f publisher in this country, ought to know better.

The problem as initially stated was fascinating. As stated, it might have acquired additional significance if, for instance, the plague was the result of a mutated terrestrial virus, and if the combined forces of World Health had had nothing but their best efforts to fall back on, or if the problem had been differently stated (how to persuade an unknown alien to release the antidote to the fatal disease he has deliberately introduced) there might have been a (very different) equally good book in it.

As it is, the only thing that might have helped is a title change: something like "Dr. Kildare and the Jovian Menace."

Gordon Dickson's *Mission to Universe*[2] has only two things in common with *Plague from Space*. One of these is another exploratory spaceship with equally little justification for its existence. The interstellar journey conducted by General Ben Shore and his crew of twenty-four could as well have been to Mars in 1967, to the Antarctic or the Congo in 1927, on a sailing ship in 1887, or work your own way back through periods of exploration and discovery. The actual experiences on board ship, as well as the adventures on alien planets, are all basic, familiar, easily translatable into any other framework. The significant idea here had no connection with the physical environment, but with the social one: Dickson is exploring the personality of a hero-leader, a man who feels himself set apart from others, whose ego-satisfactions have narrowed into the puritan range of "rightness" and "respect," and "responsibility." Shore fakes orders to undertake the journey out of his own conviction that he is right; takes the standby crew with him on his own responsibility; establishes a military form of organization and adheres to it rigorously, out of a sincere belief that the lives of everyone on board depend on their respect for him and willingness to take his orders. His most terrible experience on the voyage is not when he must shoot his only friend, but when he is publicly humiliated by a group of aliens; he is flattered when a reporter says to him that he has ice-water instead of blood flowing through his veins.

It is a good study, as far as it goes, and given a more appropriate setting, might have been a much better one. Since primitive conditions creating individual deaths and personal embarrassment were the stuff Dickson worked with, rather than metaphysical or technological difficulties, he could have concentrated more effectively on his central character's relations with the other crew members had he made use of a less exotic, more familiar, journey for the General's trials. But even that might not have helped, because in terms of the problem set up, he did exactly what Harrison did: at the end, he avoided having to sum up the experiences of his character, or outline any conclusions, simply by having the whole world decide Shore was just as right as he thought he was. Instead of having to face himself, Shore returns eventually to find himself not only a hero, not only universally admired, but *loved* as well.

It makes him happy.

Dickson introduces, mostly by implication, a theme that runs through most of this crop of books—the *All Them Zombies* theme. (Listen: you can hear the movie music!) In *The Altar of Asconel*,[3] one of John Brunner's less noteworthy efforts, the theme is given full rein in a hypnotic-control religion. Brunner also gives us (in just *one* side of an Ace double), a dying interstellar empire, a scholarly monastic order, a rip-snortin' space warrior, a waifish girl telepath, a small band of loyal patriots, and this ugly psychotic alien, who is perhaps the prototype for one of the most popular (by frequency of appearance) characters of the season, the Fat Man (of whom more, much more, later).

Actually, this is a more than adequate adventure yarn—well-told, well-paced, filled with thrills, chills, and spills, and the very model of the modern version of the Pseudoscience Story.

"Pseudoscience" is the heading under which the *Reader's Guide to Periodical Literature* and other similarly respectable reference works, used self-consciously to list what little science fiction they could not avoid mentioning. The term is not precisely applicable these days I suppose, when hardly anyone bothers with scientific gobbledygook any more. "Pseudospace" or "pseudopsych" or even "pseudospec" might be better; *Asconel* could fit under any of those.

Nor am I being sarcastic when I add that Brunner does it almost as well as Rider Haggard. I just don't know why he bothered.

Ted White's first novel,[4] on the flip side, is the first one so far of which I can say that it is at least fully justified in its use of a futuristic setting. The protagonist is an android, and *validly* so: in the conflict between his conscious awareness of himself as a man, and his discovery of his machine origin, White sets up a vivid and highly appropriate symbol of a society in which mankind is struggling between a machine-like (zombie-type) conformism, and "criminal" naturalistic impulses.

Unhappily, once having set up an ideally related theme, background, and personal problem, the author proceeds to abandon the background in a series of dream-like sequences of alternate-life probabilities, and to ignore all the conflicts that stem from the hero's peculiar composition. There is no effort to reconcile even the most obvious technical anomalies, let alone the psychological derivatives. Our android does pause to wonder at one point how he can bleed, regenerate flesh, and heal super-fast, with no marrow in his steel bones; but he never finds out, and never even seems to question his susceptibility under ordinary conditions (which tend to be of the Raymond Chandler-derived school, emphasizing seduction in luxurious surroundings) to hunger, thirst, fatigue, and a variety of other biological compulsions, whereas his "overdrive" performances when under control of The Machine (during which times he has the strength and speed of a steel-boned superman) seem to have him hardly tired, let alone in need of food or drink.

Presumably, he has two complete separate energy systems, both able to operate through both the steel bones and the protoplasmic musculature. All this might be no more than a minor irritation, because there is the book, and because the basic proposition was not a technical one anyhow. But when the author abandons not only his superficial premises, but his own superb symbol-setting, by permitting the story to be resolved in a conflict between the (it turns out) basically beneficent machine and the Small Group of Evil

Men (such as are no longer called Mad scientists) who had attempted to turn it to their own uses—

What we are left with, I am afraid, is what (in a family magazine) I can only refer to as the apocryphal invention of the limerickal young man from Racine. (*And* a Fat Man. Patience, I'll get back to him.)

Nevertheless, score one for White: with whatever inadequacies, this is s-f. At least the God-machine was there from the beginning, and had some function all along.

Michael Moorcock's *Fireclown*[5] comes even closer. Once again, the theme is—on one level—the growing conflict between individualism and conformity in our culture. In this book, the other level of meaning inherent in the Zombie theme emerges more clearly as a sort of inside-out version of s-f's old favorite, the Superman. Apparently we have tired of thinking of ourselves as freaks, no matter how terribly clever; now it's *All Them Zombies*—and the few "normal" people who have not yet become conformist puppets. In any case, Moorcock comes up with a symbolic figure quite as appropriate as White's android, and rather more colorful: the Fireclown, a half-mad hero-villain (and quasi-Fat Man), who uses live fire as propaganda and laughter as a weapon, inflaming the buried instincts and responses of the citizens of a supremely safe-and-sane near-future rationalistic state.

On both the sociological and subconscious levels, the book sustains itself admirably. The zombie populace, roused from complacency, becomes a raging (but just as zombie) mob; the glorious Fireclown is, after all, a freak, and inevitably destroys himself; the viable solution is neither stasis nor psychosis, but the truer sanity of a sustained balance between order and innovation.

Thematically, it's great. If the surface story halfway measured up to the symbolic and subliminal significance, this one might be something to shout about. But the protagonist is hopelessly enmeshed in a complexity of relationships—variously legitimate, illicit, and lustful—inside the politically powerful Powys family (who hold sway in that rational oversane state, you see), and computer-age politicking is conducted much on the model of a high school Student Council election—whereas some of the best bits in the book seem to be displaced scenes from some *other* book—something Moorcock would like to write, perhaps, but hasn't yet. (Chapter Fourteen, for instance, is a *great* scene in a decayed and decadent London; but *why?*)

One careful rewrite might have made all the difference.

Avram Davidson's *Rork!*,[6] on the other hand, owes most of its merit to the skill of the treatment. This is a frontier adventure story (complete with bashful dustkickin' young hero), which on second thought barely qualifies as some sort of s-f, simply by the inclusion of the *rorks*. It would have been gratifying if these fascinating creatures had any integral part to play in the ecology of the planet, or in the relations between the settlers and the natives. As it is, they do turn out to serve a *purpose*, somewhat make-work, but—well, it did have to be an alien planet to have the rorks, and they're worth having, even if they have nothing much to do with the story.

Just to keep the score straight, this one is basically about—you guessed it—conformity vs. individualism. It has three separate and distinct zombie-types, and a small group of Real People (outcasts raised among the rorks) in addition to the half-breed girl (daughter of a Terran and a "Wild Tock," a native not yet contained in the Terran sphere of influence). Plus, of course, Jimmy Stewart—I mean, Ran Lomar, the inexpertly enterprising hero. And then there is one semi-Real character—the Fat Man: this time he's the Colonial Administrator, over-civilized rococo, homosexual, although more blasé than malicious or psychotic.

The truth is, Davidson is in exceptionally good form in this one, and I suppose when the writing is good enough, and some conscientious effort has been made to supply a little extra in the way of exotic background, one needn't insist on intellectual content or speculative values besides.

Fred Pohl's Fat Man is the pure prototype; in fact, *A Plague of Pythons*[7] probably brings both Fat Man and Zombies to their peak, for this batch. The zombies are anybody, everybody, one time or another: people become "possessed," and do anything from senseless rape-murder-arson-etc. to mindless, backbreaking, till-they-drop labor. The Fat Man is so fat he can hardly move: obscene, corrupt, disgusting, and a Mad Scientist to boot. I won't say who the Possessors are, because Pohl actually tells this absurd story so smoothly that you may enjoy two-thirds or three-quarters of it before the foolishness of the whole thing gets to you: but I balk at the notion of a thousand individual minds controlling a population of two billion totally, when each can dominate only one person at a time, and most of their energies seem to be used in private pleasure (?) pursuits.

More seriously, I quibble, nay quarrel, with the assumption on which this whole plot is based, that any invention today can be kept secret by a few assassinations; or that scientific knowledge attained and in use can be retained as the property of a limited group, in an advanced technological civilization.

This quarrel is rather more significant in relation to Frank Herbert's much more serious (and perhaps a bit pretentious) long novel, *Dune*.[8] My feeling about most of the books discussed previously is that they were in all likelihood written too fast and too facilely, for an eagerly expanding market—and published by editors either too unknowing or uncaring to demand the work the authors are capable of. *Dune* is a complex, closely worked book, and a handsome volume besides. There are charts and maps and glossaries and pseudo-historical essays to prove that Herbert did his homework—if proof were needed beyond the skillful construction, close attention to detail, and painstaking narrative edifice of the novel itself. There is no carelessness involved here on the part of either publisher or author—except the most basic lack of care.

I don't think any amount of effort or ability could have made this odd hodgepodge of concepts stick together. I cannot possibly trace the many strands interwoven in the novel, in this space, but the "Bene Gesserit" is sufficient, really. Herbert hypothesizes an esoteric organization which has brought all the cults, mysteries, arts, and quasi-sciences of mind-body control to a peak of practical working accomplishment; he then elects to believe that people who have attained the serenity, wisdom, self-discipline, mental, physical, and emotional powers ascribed to the Bene Gesserit women would allow themselves to become hopelessly involved in court intrigues on the pattern of the Borgias' Italy, dealing wholesale in assassinations and assignations—to what end? Why, to bring together (over many centuries) certain "blood-lines" whose culmination will be in a single birth, a boy who will be known as the *Kwisatz Haderach*, the "Shortener of the Way," whose "organic mental powers would bridge space and time."

In some unknown way, this boy is to be the savior of all—and "all," in this case, means an interstellar Imperium with a technology advanced enough to permit intersystem trips for bickering feudal lordlings' fêtes and festivals—an economy of marvelous abundance in its larger aspects—in which nevertheless there *are* bickering feudal lordlings, and their young sons are raised to knife fights and dueling in exactly the manner of the manor—6th Century Arthurian.

Herbert comments somewhere in the book on the dignity with which a culture treats its dead as a measure of its civilization. A more accurate measure, I think (if only because more obvious—"dignity" is very much in the eye of the beholder), is the value it places on life. Human life is cheap only when the population exceeds its means of subsistence; individual human lives become dearer as the per capita wealth increases. Again, the industrial revolution demolished the social and economic structure of feudalism as ruthlessly and inevitably as the technology, first of mass production, and now of automation, is eradicating the small businessman, the small independent farmer, and the sociology attendant on free competitive enterprise. No matter how many science fiction writers choose to place their far future stories in far past settings, the gladiatorial arena and the *duello* are as inconsistent with energy shields and starships as the divine right of kings with the European Common Market.

Again (and back to my main point), as science and technology advance, as human control over the physical environment and the means of subsistence grows stronger, as the standard of living of the "common man" rises (whether in a family, tribe, nation, or Interstellar Imperium), that man *becomes less common*. He has leisure, and then more leisure; he acquires education.

If there is one lesson the citizens of the Atom Age should have learned by now, it is that beyond a certain level of civilization, there *are no esoteric mysteries*. Knowledge is infectious; it seems to contain its own built-in urgency for communication. If an organization like the Bene Gesserit existed in the Imperium, they would not (and could not if they would) retain the secrets of their wisdom. It is reasonable in Pohl's *Pythons*, in Davidson's *Rork!*, in Christopher's *Ragged Edge*, for groups of people abruptly deprived of a familiar civilization to revert almost as rapidly to tribal and feudal patterns in which the Boss is symbolic of the power to kill—because in time of hunger, man is effectively a cannibal: he may not eat the flesh of his victims, but he will and does slaughter his own kind to feed off them *or* their possessions. At such times, the farsightedness involved in the search for abstract knowledge, or the leisure to pursue it, are so rare as to be suspect; at such times, civilized thinking and metaphysical abstractions do indeed encyst and become "mysteries." But the situation is temporary and "unnatural," it occurs only in times of technological and economic ebb.

That Herbert knows this he demonstrates with skill, with care, with delicacy and precision, in his portrait, inside this wild mural, of the desert society of the "Fremen" on the planet Arrakis. Here he gives us a planetary ecology, and a civilization to suit it, which are as thoughtful, thought-provoking, and fascinating as any I have ever come across. And he is as right to speak of the dignity with which they treat their dead—whom they do, literally, cannibalize, not for flesh, but for essential water—as he is completely correct in describing their avid response to an opportunity to learn.

This is a long book, and in its major premises quite unworthy of the work put into it. But it is worth your while for the story inside the story—not to mention a Fat Man unsurpassed for vicious villainy.

It has been unfair, perhaps, to expend, as I have, almost all my space and words on critical reports, leaving for last (among the novels) the two books I liked best. In effect, I have already bespoken their virtues in opposites.

The Ragged Edge[9] is a "survivor story," describing the effects on a small area of southern England and the Channel Islands, of an almost totally destructive series of earthquakes and planetary upheavals. Christopher is writing here about country and people he knows well; the geography and the artifacts, as well as the needs and fears, hostilities, hopes, suspicions, strengths, cruelties and kindness, of the characters, are compellingly convincing. I hesitate to say this, because the earlier book has lived vividly in my memory for some years now, and I have not reread it recently, but it is *possible* that this one is the equal of George Stewart's *Earth Abides*. Well, I do hesitate to say it; by next year I'll know; meanwhile, suffice it that I couldn't put it down.

This was just as true for Cliff Simak's *All Flesh Is Grass*,[10] which will probably be my personal nomination for the best science fiction novel of 1965. It will perhaps surprise you to learn that the theme—in part, at least—of this one has to do with conformity vs. individualism. And there are—in a way—some zombies, too. But no prancing princes, no fidgeting fat man; no hasty conclusions or unwarranted preconceptions; just believable people confronted with a situation they'd rather *not* believe, backed up with some solid speculative content, and sustained by the oxymorons of insightful objectivity and sturdy tenderness that seem to characterize Simak's work. A book both meaningful and eminently readable.

[...]

Notes

1. *Plague from Space.* Harry Harrison; Doubleday, 1965; 207 pp.; $3.95.
2. *Mission to Universe*, Gordon Dickson; Berkley #F1147, 1965; 175 pp.; 50¢.
3. *The Altar of Asconel*, John Brunner; Ace Double #M-123, 1965; 143 pp.; 45¢.
4. *Android Avenger*, Ted White (113 pp.), and *The Altar of Asconel*, John Brunner (143 pp.); Ace double, #M-123, 1965; 45¢.
5. *The Fireclown*, Michael Moorcock; Compact #F281 (London), 1965; 189 pp.; 3/6 (60¢).
6. *Rork!*, Avram Davidson, Berkley #F1146, 1965; 144 pp.; 50¢.
7. *A Plague of Pythons*, Frederik Pohl; Ballantine #U2174, 1965; 158 pp.; 50¢.
8. *Dune*, Frank Herbert; Chilton, 1965; 395 pp. plus map, glossary, appendices; $5.95.
9. *The Ragged Edge*, John Christopher; Simon & Schuster, 1966; $4.50.
10. *All Flesh Is Grass*, Clifford D. Simak; Doubleday, 1965; 260 pp.; $3.95.

[…]

Books (April 1966)

Under two hats—or would bi-focals be the better image?—I have, I suspect, the dubious distinction of being *the* Compleat S-F Reader. And every now and then I get fed up: I mean, to *here.*

If this tends to happen fairly regularly in November (see last month's angry column, written Thanksgiving week), it may have something to do with the surfeit of reading connected with the preparation of each annual volume of The Year's Best SF.... And now, with the profusion of fall book publishing....

Well, this year, as has happened before, I was just about set to take the pledge, convinced I would never do another anthology, already mentally writing letters of application for a decent, honest, job in say, advertising, or some intellectually stimulating spot in English teaching, when they pulled the switch on me. Just why it is that December and January magazines carry more good stories than other issues, I have never figured out; but I have now discovered that the winter books are better too.

(Of course I have *theories:* they have to be better, to get published at all in the "off-season"? Or the editors figure there's nothing to lose, and take a chance on the books that are just a bit *different*? Or they were supposed to be fall books, but the authors insisted on taking that extra bit of time for revisions?)

Possibly this annual renewal of faith has some connection with my tendency to read a lot more *outside* the field in December. (Partly reaction; partly anthology story-hunting through mainstream and afar fields; partly Christmas-coming, which brings on one of my semi-annual bouts of purely masochistic newspaper reading—studying splendrous ads for things I can't afford, and clipping reports on plays, concerts, and art shows I'll never get to.) One way and another, my horizons expand; and somehow or other, the hills of home look better.

[...]

There are two new Brunner novels, and the lesser of the two is up with the best of his earlier work. *The Day of the Star Cities*[3] is a carefully thought-out, colorfully written sci-fic puzzle story, dealing with the contrasting reactions of conformists and rebels to an alien invasion. But it is also more than that.

For one thing, the conflicting reactions occur within individuals as well as groups. Nor has the "conquest" of Earth occurred in any usual manner: the aliens came and established a few isolated and invulnerable Cities, completely disorganizing and disarming Earth's armies in the process—somewhat offhandedly turning back offensive weapons with no effort at retaliation. They have no interest in the exploitation—or welfare—of Earth outside their own cities. The responses of humanity, in humiliation rather than actual defeat, are varied and credible. Some scenes and incidents (the religious sects, the "weirdos," the mobster's castle) are especially well done.

More than anything else, it is the painstaking application of interior logic that makes this book *work*; and it is applied to the background situation, the interaction between characters, and the thematic material with equal rigor and comprehension. In *The Squares of the City*,[4] this same discipline is even more necessary, and more notable.

Star Cities deals with problems of multidimensional perception, and the capacity for adaptation to an alien environment. *Squares* turns (squarely) to what is essentially Brunner's major topic: government and politics. But more than anything else, it is a Games book—a novel about the many kinds of games that people play, and the many levels on which they play them, written by a shrewd gamesman and games analyst, for gameplayers and game-watchers both.

(Do not be misled: I am not talking about games/amusements; this is no trick-gimmick book. It is a serious novel which makes use of game analogies, games analyses, *and* game amusement to make its points.)

To begin with, the book is built on a chess game—a real game, which the reader is invited to follow as he reads, if he likes. (Being a dilettante at chess, I kept both eyes on the page, and took Brunner's—and Edward Lasker's—word for it that the Steinitz-Tchigorin game cited would play out if tried.)

Then, it is set in "an imaginary South American country somewhere around the place Venezuela holds on the map," where chess is *the* national pastime: as widely played and watched as baseball here, with its champions reaping the kind of homage only a heavyweight champ, or top pop singer, or Liz Taylor could get here.

One level deeper:—

The hero is a "traffic analyst whose work involves not just movements of hardware but of populations as well—specifically, a designer of the boards and fields on which the basic industrial and sociological games of society must be played. The villain is a former professor of theory of government who has found a live laboratory to work in, and boasts of having created "the most governed country in history." (Among other things, Brunner presents an exposition of the potential of currently known techniques of thought control that would make Orwell look positively cuddly to that man on the *Star.*) Most of the other major characters are prominently active in political, military, religious, or economic roles in the life-and-death game dynamics of modern society.

And then, between individuals, there is the constant interplay of the familiar personality games Berne discusses in his book.

All these relationships are further exposed and clarified by the fact that these characters also function (unknown to them) as living pieces in a monumental chess strategy being worked out between Vados, the dictator, and his chief domestic opponent.

The book is complex, but the complexities add richness rather than spread confusion. It is probably true, however, that the demands of the elaborate structure are responsible for one weakness of the novel: time and again, the author had to sacrifice opportunities for developing individual characters in full dimension, in favor of depicting interpersonal exchanges. If the book were half again as long as it is, there would have been room for more fleshing-out of the excellent skeletal structure; and if the individuals rang as true internally as they do in motion, what is now a first-rate science fiction novel and a good book by any standards, might have been a first-rate novel, with no qualifications. Perversely, of course, it was the very fact that it was science fiction that must have kept Brunner from attempting the bigger job: it is already half again as long as the average s-f novel, and Ballantine Books is entitled to one of the rare kind words permitted publishers in this column, for having sense enough not only to take the book, but to promote it rather more vigorously than most.

The Squares of the City is an impressive piece of work. Resting as it does on the previous achievements of *Star Cities* and *The Whole Man*, it leaves me very eager to see Brunner's next.[5]

I wish I could say the same about Mack Reynolds, whose history as a writer parallels Brunner's in several respects. Reynolds has demonstrated repeatedly that he is serious about what he has to say—when he bothers to say it. Far less frequently, but still memorably, he has demonstrated how well he can say it—when he takes the trouble.

Planetary Agent X[6] is Reynolds in top form thematically and middlin'-good stylistically, which makes for a science fiction novel both unexceptionable and unexceptional. Or novella, rather, for it is Part One of the book, the first 86 pages (originally "Ultima Thule" in *Analog*) which impressed me. (Part Two first appeared as "Pistolero," and rather reverses the qualities indicated above—except that the gain in treatment is not sufficient to make up for the loss in content. Both are unconnected episodes in the career of Bonny Bronston.)

The novella, then, deals with two vital strands of the politico-economic complex treated in Brunner's more ambitious effort. Reynolds offers the same kind of speculative integrity, informed logic, and inner consistency—with much more room for, but less work at, characterization and emotional development. The fact is, he handles political extrapolations so well that he hardly needs more than the right problem to turn out a readable yarn. This time, he examines the intricacies of the relationship between technology and political economy in social evolution, tossing in as he goes a simple effective home recipe for successful revolution and social upheaval, as learned by a rookie agent in the mysterious, improbable, but mostly entertaining "Section G" of the Interplanetary Bureau of Investigation.

If the characters are cardboard, the concepts are concrete—and there are some comic spots to keep the reading easy. (At the very least it should be required reading for the writers I was railing at last month, who think serfdom and surfeit will walk hand in hand at the writer's bidding.)

Raphael's *Code Three*[7] is susceptible to many of the same criticisms and praises as the Reynolds book—with the difference that this is a first novel, and as such, a most promising one. The subject here is the specific problem of large-scale continental traffic control in a near-future of vastly accelerated speeds and continually increasing mobility. Just as Reynolds has virtually trade-marked political science fiction, Raphael (in a handful of stories besides the two novelettes—"Code Three" and "Once a Cop," both from *Analog*—on which this book is based) seems to have taken over the Public Works Dept.—police and traffic and water control, mail, sanitation, and recreation services. I know of no other writer active in the field today (unless Arthur Clarke is to be considered active) who can work the means, methods, and materials available today into a day-after-tomorrow probability with so much clarity and conviction.

Once again, it is a matter of "homework:" the application of rigorous internal logic to the results of conscientious research—and once again, unhappily, conceptual kicks are about all you'll get here. An easy narrative style makes the lack of story—almost—unnoticeable; a good ear for dialogue—almost replaces any real characterization; light comedy—almost—covers for the absence of true emotional interchange between characters. And because the underlying structure is both solid and satisfying, the *almosts* are just enough to make the book not only readable, but well worth reading.

Besides which—one finds the scene here, the page there, which point to the possibility that Raphael can do more. Aside from one short story in 1959, he has been writing fiction for only four years now, and almost entirely for *Analog*, whose standards are evident in both the virtues and failings of this first novel—the virtues to a degree rarely reached in or out of that magazine. If Raphael goes on to achieve the emotional depths his work so far has only hinted at, there is a chance we may see a major talent emerge.

The last item on this month's quintet of homework-winners is a not-so-new book by Alan Nourse,[8] sent to me last August by the publishers with a letter which unfortunately identified it as a juvenile. I don't like juveniles, and there are always too many books on hand to review. It kept slipping to the bottom of the pile, partly because I *do* like Alan Nourse (and I *don't* like juveniles) and I wasn't even sure I didn't have a Policy against reviewing them.

It was too bad about that letter, because nothing else would have tipped me off. As it was, I finally reminded myself firmly that I had enjoyed everything of Nourse's I ever read, and opened it up, and I am here to report that I have still enjoyed everything of Nourse's I've read, and this one in some ways, more than most.

First of all, it is a remarkably *adult* book, in which the adult characters look, talk, and act like grownups, and the teenagers, realistically, do their best to *act* grown up. Second, it is a valuable juvenile, because it provides as good an indoctrination in the essentials of the scientific attitude and a modern philosophy of science as anything I've read short of such demanding works as Wiener's *The Human Use of Human Beings*.[9] Third, I learned something reading it. (Remember? Remember when you used to read science fiction and learn things about science?) This last item has been true of most of Nourse's work, but I always thought it was because he was a doctor who always wrote about doctors. This time the topic was the same one tentatively explored in Brunner's *Star Cities*—the extent of the human capacity to perceive, and to adapt to, truly alien environments. Both authors handled the concept thoughtfully and provocatively; but Nourse left me better informed.

I am not sure whether these comparatively objective values are more important or this subjective one: I believed these characters. The "Universe Between" and its inhabitants and psycho-physical properties were less convincing to me than the backgrounds of most of the other books—but that didn't matter; there was nothing in the invention that I had to *dis*believe while I was reading. And I was willing to work at not-disbelieving the background if necessary, because the people were not characters, but *people:* convincing representations not of the folks next-door, but of the highly intelligent research scientists they are supposed to be.

Juveniles, anyone? I have decided I do not have any Policy about them at all.

Notes

[…]

3. *The Day of the Star Cities*, John Brunner; Ace #F-361, 1965; 40¢; 158 pp.
4. *The Squares of the City*, John Brunner; Ballantine #U6035, 1965; 75¢; 319 pp. incl. author's notes and Introduction by Edward Lasker.
5. John Brunner has written to ask me to correct an error in my January column. His first sale he says, was "a [paperback] to a now defunct publisher" in 1951, and his first American sale, which preceded his publication in the Nova magazines, was "Thou Good and Faithful," published in *Astounding* in March 1953, under the pseudonym of John Loxmith.—J. M.
6. *Planetary Agent X*, Mack Reynolds; Ace double #M-131 (with *Behold the Stars*, Kenneth Bulmer); 45¢; 133 pp.
7. *Code Three*, Rick Raphael; Simon & Schuster, 1966; $3.95; (rev. from galleys).
8. *The Universe Between*, Alan E. Nourse; McKay, 1965; $3.95; 208 pp.
9. If you don't know it, or know it, but don't own one, the revised second edition of *The Human Use of Human Beings*, by Norbert Wiener, is in an Anchor edition (1954) at 95¢.

What Do You Mean? Science? Fiction?
Part I (May 1966)

I used to know what "science" meant: at least I understood the word well enough to believe that a statement like, "A revolution is occurring in science," made clear sense. At that time, the distinctions between "physical sciences" and "biological sciences," "theory" and "application," "research" and "engineering," "experimental" and "clinical" seemed perfectly obvious.

I also used to know what "fiction" meant. I knew the difference between a novel, a novella, a novelette, a short story, and a vignette: between "subjective" and "objective" narrative styles; between "psychological fiction" and the "adventure story"; between "realism" and "fantasy."

I never did know just what "science fiction" meant: in all the nights I stayed awake till dawn debating definitions, I do not recall one that stood up unflinchingly to the light of day. They all relied, in any case, on certain axiomatic assumptions about the meanings of "science" and "fiction."

Actually, when I first became involved in such debates—about twenty-five years ago—there was already a fair amount of honest confusion (among scientists) about the meaning of "science" in the 20th century. As dedicated—*addicted*—s-f readers, we had some awareness of the upheaval in process in scientific philosophy, following on the work of Heisenberg and Schroedinger, Bridgman and de Broglie: but as dedicated—*addicted*—s-f readers, we also made a complete, unconscious adjustment when we talked stories instead of concepts—"science" in "science fiction" meant (and for most readers—and writers—still does mean)—"technology."

What is viable in "science fiction" (whatever *that* may mean) today is coming from a comparatively small group of serious writers—in and out of the specialty field—who are applying the traditions of the genre and the techniques of contemporary literature to the concepts of 20th century science. The first results are already barely discernible. Science fiction is catching up with science. And the genre is returning from its forty years of self-imposed wandering away from the wellsprings of literature.

The two events could only be simultaneous. Art at any time can achieve validity only if it is rooted in the accumulated human experience of its day, and touches somewhere on the nerve center of the culture from which it springs. The literature of the mid-20th century can be meaningful only in so far as it perceives, and relates itself to, the central reality of our culture: the revolution in scientific thought which has replaced mechanics with dynamics, classification with integration, positivism with relativity, certainties with statistical probabilities, dualism with parity.

If it seems I am saying that there is no adequate literature in existence now—I am. If it further seems I am claiming a special literary validity for science fiction—I would be, except that as it achieves that validity, it ceases to be "science fiction" and becomes simply contemporary literature instead.

I must pause here to establish my lack of credentials. Although, as fellow science fiction readers, our knowledge of scientific history, and contemporary scientific concepts, is probably roughly equitable, and (for many of you at least) arrived at in rather the same manner (elementary courses at school, and wide and presumably intelligent reading since), our knowledge of literature is neither equal nor similar. I learned my definitions of "fiction" from pulp writers and editors initially: their rules were hard-and-fast, and the penalty for breaking them was hunger; or worse yet, working for a living instead of selling stories.

So when I say I knew what fiction was. I mean I really *knew.* Things like: a short story is limited to one main character, who must be involved in a conflict which is resolved before the end of the story: it can be told from only one viewpoint, which must not shift during the story. A novelette is still primarily about one character, though it is possible to develop one or even two subsidiary characters to some degree—the main distinction is that there can be more than one or two incidents involved in developing the conflict before the resolution: if you get good enough, you can occasionally shift viewpoints in a novelette without killing the sale. Things like that.

I found out by a combination of my own dissatisfaction with the rulebook, and by a very slow and extremely erratic catching-up process (still far from complete) in my reading that the rules I had learned were not only not universal but not particularly applicable to anything I wanted to do—except *sell.* I also found out that in the upper literary strata, it was possible to break them and sell; and in the way-out literary strata (where nobody gets paid for anything) it was almost required to break them.

I didn't find the rules in other areas any improvement; at least, I kept on enjoying *reading* s-f more than other contemporary work—until a few years ago. What happened, or started to happen, two years ago, I will come back to. Meantime, let me tell you about my great discoveries, and try to see them through the eyes of a genuine discoverer. Bear with me if I sometimes state the obvious; it was not so to me. And if some things I say are obviously not so—remember, I claim no authority: I am speaking only of my own experiences and discoveries.

It is not the Bomb or the pill (or miracle drugs or synthetic materials or space travel) that are forcing us to re-think the meaning of "science": these, after all, are comparatively mechanical, *technological*, applications of what I have been calling 20th century scientific concepts—although they of course began in the 19th. The reverberations of that conceptual revolution have by now shaken every branch of scientific investigation and human life. Indeed the failure of entrenched, established academic Humanism to comprehend the meaning of the rumblings from cross-campus (the "two-culture" phenomenon) was probably due in part to preoccupation with the local effects of the same conceptual explosion in the arts and social sciences.

It was not James Joyce or Henry Miller or Jack Kerouac or William Burroughs who made it necessary to re-examine the idea of "fiction." They were simply pioneers in the process of re-examination. The seeds of the upheaval, as in the case of the scientific revolution, appeared at the height of Victorian formalist-mechanist complacency—the beginning of modern social science (Darwin, Freud, Boas, Veblen…) with a focus on human motivations, rather than surface behavior.

What happened in the various sciences had its almost exact counterpart in literature, and most markedly so in "fiction," that curious prose form which, like physics and chemistry, anthropology and psychology (and their numerous and hybrid offspring) came into existence at a distinct area of human endeavor during the Great Crackup of the 17th century. I will not attempt here to argue the causes. I am inclined to the notion that the voyages of exploration and discovery of America, and the printing press, with its attendant revolution in communications, were major factors. Whatever the chain of causation, the result was as though a figurative planet composed of man's intellect, suddenly acquired so much additional mass, or velocity (or both?) that it flew out of orbit, breaking up and fragmenting under the strain. (Perhaps the settlement of America enlarged the "subjective mass" of the planet in men's minds? Or possibly just the first accumulation of the sheer bulk of paper under which we are nowadays, likely to be buried.…)

One might carry the metaphor further, and assume that the reduced planet, and its severed chunks, would have settled, eventually, into new orbits closer to the source of energy. Some bits would have been drawn into the sun and lost entirely: Divine Right went that way (and with it a substantial part of the certainty of divinity). Other pieces, the largest ones, would have been drawn back into the parent body very quickly, and become attached as discrete territories, no longer part of the amorphous whole: one might conceive of the establishment of national sovereignties this way, or of the broad demarcation of not-yet-"scientific" disciplines as they first appeared—naturalist, mathematician-astronomer, philosopher, and so forth. The intermediate chunks, settling into orbits somewhat closer to the sun at first absorbed more energy perhaps, and *grew*, moving back closer to the parent body with each increment of mass and velocity.

Take the fancy one bit farther, and picture the return of the pieces (rather as Planetarium lecturers are fond of presenting the image of an eventual falling-back of the Moon). At least one of the first returning bodies would have landed with tremendous impact—Newtonian physics, the laws of motion, gravitation, and the Calculus, containing within them (if anyone had thought to notice, or had energy to spare to think it through) a clear explanatory warning of descents yet to come.

The new literary form, fiction, may be considered to have made its (far less impactful) return as a clearly formed body somewhere about the middle of the 18th century. (Even fancifuller, one might postulate that the date went unnoticed, and is still argued, because it landed in the tropic sea of some enchanted voyage of exploration—quite possibly just out of sight of Alexander Selkirk's lonely island—and that it was in the nourishing warmth of these waters that the solid mass broke somewhat apart, and eventually attached itself to the land mass again as the full-blown novel and incipient short story.)

⚛

All metaphors aside, I believe it is significant that the fiction form took shape and name in the same intellectual-cultural upheaval from which the familiar "scientific discipline" emerged—that it achieved a discernible form and popularity just about half way between the beginnings of physics and anthropology, and that its later history shows so many parallels with those of nineteenth-century science.

We tend to think of the 19th century in terms of its own popular image of itself: a time of complacency and classification, of rationality, mechanistic philosophy, scientific certainties, technological, literary and artistic polish rather than innovation. Actually, there seem almost to have been two parallel 19th centuries: some things about the *other* one we are still finding out. But we do know that the groundwork for modern mathematics—the non-Euclidean geometries of Gauss, Lobachevsky, and Riemann, as well as Boolean algebra and the basis of symbolic logic, had already been worked out in 1850—when Kierkegaard was writing the first existential works, and Baudelaire was setting forth the principles of the Symbolist movement—all before either the publication of *The Descent of Man*, or the organization of the Periodic Table.

Fifty years later—just at the turn of the century, while Victoria still reigned, and Teddy Roosevelt brandished his Big Stick—Freud and Pavlov, Lorentz and Fitzgerald, Buber and Heidegger laid the foundations for thought control, space-time cosmology, and even the Ecumenical Council.

The first confused wave of reaction against these innovations came in the form of reinforced mechanism and increasingly "discrete" and complicated "classification": perhaps it was not so much *reaction* as an honest effort on the part of people trained in the formalisms of the nineteenth century to cope with the fascinating, staggering, new integrations while still using the familiar methods of separation and analysis.

Thus, the twentieth century opened to a compartmentation and fragmentation of knowledge unprecedented in scope, and probably in attitude. Within the physical sciences, separate but traditional disciplines were splitting and resplitting: chemists became organic or inorganic chemists—then bio-chemists or physical chemists, etc. They devoted themselves to theory or to application. In the "social sciences," the same phenomenon occurred. In both areas, the engineers took over—at least in popular esteem.

The reasons for this are both obvious and subtle, and it would require, I think, a complete separate essay to examine them satisfactorily. All that matters for purposes of this retrospection, is that two completely separate—and for a time increasingly separating—streams of intellectual endeavor proceeded, in dialectical fashion, from the origins of modern thought in the last half of the nineteenth century. The most obvious, and most comprehensible of these was for some time the essentially engineering-type application of bits and pieces of new conceptual discoveries by the best of the old-school mechanicians; the flood of electronic, aeronautic, and biochemical inventions; the sensational discoveries of the behaviorists and early cultural anthropologists; the economic determinists in politics and sociology; and the school of twentieth-century "realism" in fiction.

I cannot define science fiction, but I can locate it, philosophically and historically:

There is a body of writing of whose general outlines the readers of *Extrapolation* are, by common consent, already aware: that is to say, the "classical antecedents" from Lucian and Plato through, approximately, Kepler and de Bergerac: the "borderline" (both of acceptability and between periods) instances of *Don Quixote* and *Robinson Crusoe*, terminating probably (in general acceptability) with *Gulliver's Travels* and *Micromegas*; the "Gothic" vein which characterizes the first half, or two-thirds, of the nineteenth century, and continues as a major element well into the twentieth; the period generally considered as "modern," beginning with Verne, and achieving general popularity in the last two decades of the nineteenth century; and the specific area of American specialty science fiction starting in the pulp adventure magazines of the 1910s, and being consolidated by Hugo Gernsback as a discrete phenomenon in his specialty publications during the 1920s.

Assuming this to represent some general area of agreement on what we mean when we talk about "science fiction," I believe it is possible to distinguish within the broad area certain distinct and more reasonably definable forms:

1) "Teaching stories": the dramatized essay or disguised treatise, in which the fiction form is utilized to present a new scientific idea, sometimes (as with the *Somnium*, or the works of "John Taine" and other pseudonymous scientists) because of social, political, religious, or academic pressures operating against a direct presentation: sometimes (as with the typical Gernsbackian story, and a fair proportion of late nineteenth-century work) as a means of "popularizing" scientific information or theories, or (hopefully) sugarcoating an educational pill. (This is what used to be called by literary snobs, "pseudoscience," and should have been called "pseudofiction"—although in the hands of an expert it can become reasonably good fiction: Arthur C. Clarke manages it occasionally, although his best work—*Childhood's End*, for instance—is not of this type.)

2) "Preaching stories": primarily allegories and satires—morality pieces, prophecies, visions, and warnings, more concerned with the conduct of human society than with its techniques. These are true "pseudoscience" stories: they utilize science (or technology), or a plausible semblance of science (or technology) or at least the language and atmosphere, in just the same way that the scientific treatise in disguise utilizes fiction. And let me point out again (rather more enthusiastically than before) that some first-rate writing has emerged from this sort of forced marriage. (Perhaps the difference between the work of a marriage broker and a shotgun wedding?) Stapledon's *Star Maker* falls into this group, as well as Ray Bradbury's (specifically) sci-

ence fiction and a large proportion of both Utopian and anti-Utopian novels up through the turn of the century.

3) "Speculative fiction": stories whose objective is to explore, to discover, to *learn*, by means of projection, extrapolation, analogue, hypothesis-and-paper-experimentation, something about the nature of the universe, of man, of "reality." Obviously, all fiction worth considering is "speculative" in the sense that it endeavors to reach, or to expose, some aspect of Truth. But it is equally true—and irrelevant—to say that all fiction is imaginative or all fiction is fantasy. I use the term "speculative fiction" here specifically to describe the mode which makes use of the traditional "scientific method" (observation, hypothesis, experimentation) to examine some postulated approximation of reality, by introducing a given set of changes—imaginary or inventive—into the common background of "known facts," creating an environment in which the responses and perceptions of the characters will reveal something about the inventions, the characters, or both.

It is in this last area that the essence of science fiction resides: it covers a great deal of territory, shading at either end into the first two categories. Clearly, there is hybridization all through the groups—as for instance in satire (such as *The Child Buyer*, or *Player Piano* whose main devil actually is some specific aspect of science or technology.

For purposes of this discussion, I am not considering the space adventure story, the transplanted western or historical, as science fiction, at all.

In his introduction to *Future Perfect*, H. Bruce Franklin points out: "There was no major nineteenth-century American writer of fiction, and indeed few in the second rank, who did not write some science fiction or at least one Utopian romance."

I doubt that a statement quite so all-embracing could be made for all of Western literature, but if you take fiction, for the moment, to include *all* forms of story-telling (other than the documented reportorial), and allow science its broadest (and I think truest) meaning—the conscientious seeking after knowledge of the nature of the universe, the nature of man, and the nature of "reality"—then I believe Franklin's statement can be applied with few exceptions to the major story-tellers of Western civilization, at almost all times in almost all countries.

One of the exceptional times-and-countries was America of the first half of the 20th century. (There is, frankly, some question in my mind as to whether this period can claim any "major" writers. But within its own framework, it had accepted "greats"—and almost to a man, they shunned anything resembling either science fiction or fantasy—except such fantasy as clearly existed only in the mind of a character.)

My contention is that "realistic" fiction, rather than speculative or science fiction, was the transient oddity—as grotesque a product of nineteenth-century super-rationalism and mechanistic philosophy as Watson babies and the Stakhanovite movement. For nearly a half century, American writers were somehow impelled to choose, not only one *field* of writing (poetry, essays, journalism, drama, fiction, biography), but—within fiction at least—one *area*. "Serious" fiction writers wrote realistic fiction (with Cabell as the exception). "Slick writers" wrote "realistic" stereotypes for the glossy magazines, "pulp writers," for the pulps. (They at least had some variety of subject, if not style, open to them.) Offhand, I can think of four notable names other than Cabell who broke the rules: Philip Wylie, Conrad Aiken, William Saroyan, and Stephen Vincent Benét. (When Santayana published *The Last Puritan*, he added an epilogue explaining that it was really a work of philosophy more than a novel.) But the Name Novelists—with the single exception of Sinclair Lewis in *It Can't Happen Here*—stuck to realism exclusively; or if they didn't, their realistic work was all we saw. (I used a science-fiction satire of Farrell's in a recent anthology, and met astonishment everywhere; the truth is, Farrell wrote the story almost fifteen years ago, and *wasn't able to sell it*: it wasn't "Farrell!") Men of scientific or academic or professional standing who suffered from a compulsion to write fiction did so under pen names. Eventually, eventually the pulp adventure magazines broke up into "categories": detective, western, sea, sports, science fiction, fantasy.

This was the unique—indeed, baroque—situation, when the first magazines devoted exclusively to fantasy and science fiction were published here in the mid-twenties. It was a time for extremes and bizarre combinations. The richest country in the world was enjoying its richest years—in the cities—while mortgages foreclosed and the Big Depression gained its first beachhead on the farms. These were the years of prohibition and gangsterism, Bix Beiderbecke and Isadora Duncan; the Scopes Trial in Tennessee and psychoanalysis in New York; bottle babies and "back to normalcy." Heisenberg published his theories on quantum matrices the year after Coolidge's election, and announced his "uncertainty" principle the year before the Model A replaced the Model T. Alfred Korzybski's first book had been published here in 1921; Ruth Benedict and Margaret Mead were working with Franz Boas in the new field of cultural anthropology. Eugene O'Neill's *The Hairy Ape* and T. S. Eliot's *The Wasteland* had appeared in 1922, as had *Ulysses*, and the big American novel that year was *Babbitt.* In 1926, the "new criticism" was gaining adherents here, but Dali and Surrealism were still almost unknown on this side of the ocean; Goddard tested his first successful liquid fuel rocket; while Lindbergh prepared for his non-stop flight to Paris; Rudolph Valentino died, and the first sound film was made; Hemingway (in Paris) published *The Sun Also Rises*, and became an important writer overnight.

The War to End All War had ended a way of life in Europe: here, we were still clinging desperately to certainties where we could find them, flinging out wildly when we lost hold. If Darwin, Freud, and Einstein had made Our Trust in God less than certain, Edison, Ford, and Marconi had given us back something *solid.* We did our speculating on the stock market—not in our fiction.

"Scientification" in its beginnings was a pure extension of the most mechanistic realism: tomorrow's machines today. The early Gernsback magazines were confined almost entirely to the Teaching school of science fiction, and were further confined almost exclusively to technology in particular rather than science in general. (The exceptions tended to be pseudonymous works by scholars and scientists who had no other outlet, in the rigid framework of the academic Establishment, for speculation outside the sharply defined range of their own specialties.) John Taine (Eric Temple Bell) affords perhaps the best, though not only, example.

The others, such as *Amazing*, seem, in retrospect, to have contained endless expositions of technical, technological, technophiliac, and Technocratic ideas, set forth in ponderous prose, illustrated with cardboard figures spouting wooden dialogue—yet at the time, it was exciting stuff indeed. Perhaps it gave us only more hardware, and gave it dressed in olive drab—but it was *tomorrow's* hardware, and it was knowledgeably projected. There was vast scope of the reader's own imagination to operate in the cities and spaceships and satellites and time machines of the World of Science (Technology) and Progress to Come.

And of course, "scientification" was not the only game in town. For those who craved madder music and gaudier lights, there was always *Weird Tales* (established in 1923), where amid warlocks and werewolves one could still find a good supply of mad scientists, mutant plants, Unidentified Alien Objects, mysterious islands, hollow planets, hypnotized beauties, shambling neo-frankensteins, lost civilizations, and all the rest of the gorgeous panoply of Gothic romance—perhaps a bit worn from a century's heavy use by

Hawthorne, Poe, Mary Shelley, Wilkie Collins, Stevenson, Doyle, Haggard, Wells, *et al.* At times this Gothicism hardly showed the shabby spots at all in the bright purple and muted mauve lighting effects preferred by Lovecraft and Clark Ashton Smith—and was perhaps no less powerful in its symbolism than when it was first used.

Weird ran heavily to the Preaching school—allegory and fable, not satire—with the idea content almost exclusively limited to the battle between Good and Evil. Technological or scientific novelties introduced were usually fully exploited by the author; they left comparatively little to the reader's imagination. *But* the rare story (and they were probably no less rare in the fantasy magazines than in science fiction) that did contain some genuine speculative content was much more likely to be equipped with movable-joint characters and appropriate imagery in the background—plus a considerably more colorful and complex prose style. (When they were good they were really quite good, but when they were bad, they were Gothic *awful.*)

What I have described is of course an extreme differentiating characteristic, not so much of two specific magazines as of the prevailing atmospheres associated with "scientification" and "weird" as sub-categories of the magazine specialty field of science fiction: Gernsback and Lovecraft (who dominated *Weird Tales* though he did not edit it) as they look forty years after.

Actually, the near-total polarization imputed here was effective, if at all, only at the starting-point. Science fiction and fantasy of all sorts were still appearing regularly in a number of "all-story" pulp magazines in the twenties, particularly what one might call (absurdly) the "prestige pulps" (*Golden Book*, *Argosy*, *Blue Book*). And by 1930, there were two more specialty magazines: Street & Smith's *Astounding* and Gernsback's *Wonder* (first *Air Wonder* and *Scientific Wonder;* later combined in the single title: later yet *Thrilling Wonder*). In the decade following the first issue of *Amazing*, the admixture of story types, and overlap of author—and readers—was considerable. Although *Weird* retained its own distinctive flavor, several of its authors (Carl Jacobi, Clark Ashton Smith, C. L. Moore, for instance) adapting their styles somewhat, began to appear in the other magazines: other writers from the general pulp field, like Leinster and Williamson, made themselves at home, particularly in *Astounding* under Tremaine's editorship; and new writers, science fiction specialists from the beginning, established themselves (John W. Campbell. Jr., Harry Bates, and Clifford D. Simak and from England, John Beynon Harris—now John Wyndham—and Eric Frank Russell).

In the thirties, or more precisely in October 1929, it became abruptly apparent, even to the most dedicated believers in Progress as embodied in Free Enterprise and the Survival of the Fittest, that all was not necessarily for the best in this most solid of all possible worlds. Yet inside science fiction, there was no serious questioning of the virtue inherent in machines or of the inevitability of the accelerated growth of the super-technological civilization. (However blind the first viewpoint may have been, the second was absolutely clear-sighted.) The net effect was simply to soften the Technocratic tone, and make the evangelical aspect obvious. The problem-story took over from the treatise: how to *use* the machine, how to apply the techniques.

When John W. Campbell, Jr. took over the editorship of *Astounding* at the end of 1937, the field in general, and *Astounding* in particular, had acquired a solid nucleus of steady contributors of true speculative science fiction: and I do mean "nucleus." The number of thinkers capable of new ideas is never large; the number of those with even those rudimentary insights into human behavior and the story-telling knack that constitute the bare minimum capability of a writer of fiction is much smaller. There has never been any likelihood of much genuine speculative science fiction at any time: less so in a low-paid and low prestige isolated enclave of literature. The *astounding* thing is not that the quantity was small, but that there was any noticeable quantity at all. Much more astounding was the rapid growth of the nucleus during Campbell's first five years of editorship.

The list of new names in *Astounding* and *Unknown* in 1938 and 1939 alone contains more than half the important bylines of the first book publishing boom of the early 1950s: Asimov, de Camp, del Rey, Gold, Heinlein, Hubbard, Jameson, Kuttner, Leiber, Sturgeon, van Vogt. (Boucher, Fredric Brown, Hal Clement, George O. Smith, and James H. Schmitz came along in 1941-43.)

Thus the field gained strength: yet John Campbell has taken a good deal of criticism in these past years, from fans, writers, and critics inside the field; recently he has been subject to what might better be called abuse, mostly from people too new to the field, or too uninformed (i.e., Amis's churlish comments in *New Maps of Hell*), to comprehend Campbell's role as writer and editor in the decade 1935-1945—or how much of what has happened since derived from his impact at that time. If he has been a damaging influence on some writers in recent years, the evil he has done is still outweighed by the good—and one cannot but suspect—particularly considering Campbell's working habits—that those writers who have been trapped in the *Analog* Formula these last years (or intellectually raped by Campbell's enthusiasms) solicited the economic haven of the trap, and offered up their thematic honor more eagerly than otherwise. Since 1948, it has been easy for any writer who cared to, to resist Campbell's pressure; before that, *Astounding* dominated the market so completely that a case might be made against the man for literary despoilage at that time—if anyone cared to. Certainly it is true that Asimov, Sturgeon, Heinlein, Leiber, were revivified by the emergence of new and more literarily demanding markets in the fifties. But it is hardly reasonable to condemn Campbell for not improving things *enough*; the fact is, when he took over *Astounding*, the time was ripe for the qualitative, and quantitative, explosion that occurred. But it is equally true that Campbell was the right man for the right time—and perhaps also true that his peculiar limitations were as useful as his considerable abilities.

After the 1965 Science Fiction Convention in London, the *London Sunday Times Magazine* published a thoughtful profile of Campbell by Pat Williams, who suggested:

> ...Life to Campbell is a gigantic experiment in form, and earth the forcing-house—an impeccable vision, but one not warmed (in his theories, that is) by a feeling for the pain or personal potential of the individuals in the experiment. That kind of gentleness in expression seemed to disappear with Don A. Stuart.
>
> So that, ironically, as SF becomes increasingly respectable, John Campbell, its acknowledged father-figure, can't really claim his throne. He provides the continuity, he shaped much of the thought, he made many reputations. SF narrowed from the vastness of space to the greater complexity of "sociological" SF with him presiding.
>
> But now it is narrowing towards the highly-focused, upside-down detail of "inner space." The tone is personal and subjective, the quality of expression important.... None of this is Campbell's style.

I think Mrs. Williams was exceptionally perceptive in her interviewing, and intelligent in her assessment; if she missed a stage between Campbell and "inner space," it is understandable, because British science fiction has not gone through exactly the same development. It was never effectively cut off, as the specialty field was here, from the main streams of literature and scientific philosophy. In England, they had Priestly, Huxley, Collier, Stapledon, Lewis, Heard, Kersh, Russell, through the thirties and forties. Here, we had Campbell—and eventually, Anthony Boucher and H. L. Gold.

It may seem self-contradictory to say that Campbell is the "sociological science fiction" editor, and add that his great limitation is his essentially *engineering* frame of mind: but this is precisely the "useful" limitation I referred to earlier. In the deepest sense, Campbell was the linear and logical successor to Gernsback. He was as technology-minded and application-oriented as the rest of the field in the thirties, with this difference: that he had a broader concept of the scope of "science" (technology and *engineering*); he wanted to explore the effects of the new technological world on *people.* Cultural anthropology, social psychology, cybernetics, communications, sociology, education, psychometrics—all these, and a dozen intermediate points, were thrown open for examination.

There were two immediately noticeable effects: better stories and more and better speculative development. A third effect came inevitably on their heels: one I do not believe Campbell was looking for, and may not have noticed when it arrived—better writing.

The thinking improved not only because there were vast unworked areas to explore, but because these particular areas attracted writers of somewhat more flexible intellectual inclination—and most of all, because the editor *wanted* clear thinking; he was honestly (at the beginning) interested in learning about human behavior; he genuinely lacked (as yet) any preconceptions, or even strong opinions, about how the answers should look.

The stories improved because they were required to be about things that happened to people, rather than just to have people in them. (Nor could they be *inside* people—and as the "mainstream" has painfully learned, psychiatric introspections make little good fiction.)

The writing gradually improved because the essence of good writing is clear observation, and you cannot project human responses accurately without observing some humans closely first. It also improved, I think, through hybridization: "scientification" had been pro-machine; the Lovecraft school generally anti-machine. There had been some overlapping before, but now there was fluent admixture of those writers from both areas who were least satisfied with their own sub-genre patterns. Treatise Drab and Poe Purple studied each other with interest, and adapted toward a common center. The general result was not anything that could properly be called literary style; but it approximated a tolerable narrative prose—determinedly matter-of-fact, slangy, colloquial with a fair balance of color and economy.

There was even the beginning of characterization. In Asimov's robot stories an individual grew out of a prototype: Dr. Susan Calvin became more complex and believable in each story. And of course the robots were individuals: in fact, characterization for aliens, elves, androids, and others hit the field awhile before living breathing humans arrived. Some of Leiber's too-true witches may have marked the transition. Del Rey began to generate character in his protagonists. Simak was perhaps the first to do so with any consistency (in the *City* series). Sturgeon, at that stage, was creating memorable puppets: his characters were cut from no stock on which other authors drew, but the Sturgeon whole-cloth was no more genuine—just brighter colored and better designed.

In those first few years of Campbell's domination of the field, the basic pattern was set for the next twenty years: the application of technological development to human problems; the application of human development to technology.

And, my God, how the stories rolled out! *Beyond This Horizon*, *Gather, Darkness*, Asimov's robots, "Microcosmic God," "The Gnarly Man," "Elsewhen," "Helen O'Loy," "Mimsy Were the Borogroves," *Slan*, "Pride," "Smoke Ghost," the *City* stories, "First Contact," *Universe*, "Etaoin Shrdlu," "Nightfall," "Killdozer!," "Opposites—React!," "No Woman Born," "Nerves," "Adam and No Eve." One could go on and on, and the sad fact is that with all but a few, remembering them is better than rereading them.

It was in those bright days—in 1941, to be precise—that I discovered the science fiction magazines. Ten years later, I could still re-read every story I mentioned here, and a good many more, with almost undiminished renewal of experience: I know this, because I had cause to reread them, critically, when I began editing "theme anthologies" in 1952 (reading for reprint, you do not allow rosy memories to haze over the actual words). And by that time, there was some impressive new work to compare it with—some of it by the same authors, some by the next flood of new names of the early fifties—generally so much better *written* as to place great strain on the acceptability of the earlier work.

The stories I have mentioned did stand up to—*that*—re-examination. I tried some of them again recently, and will probably not do so again. They were every bit as good as I remembered—but it was not the prose (however good it looked by comparison at the time) or the characters; it was the ideas that were vivid and memorable—and they remain so; re-reading adds nothing. (There is not much of what we now consider good characterization in *Beowulf*, either. Idea-fiction, like pure myth, seems to work as well with solidly constructed prototypes—and there *is* a difference between a player's mask and a cardboard cutout, between Everyman and no-one-at-all. But when did you last re-read *Beowulf*?)

By comparison with the new work of the early fifties, the best of the 1940-period stories survived; they still do—on their own terms. But their terms have no more to do with today's science fiction than—let us say, *The Red Badge of Courage* has to do with *Gone with the Wind*.

I said earlier that Campbell's specific limitation was his "engineering mind," and that I thought this had been useful to him and to s-f. I think it was useful—indeed essential—for the role he played in his first years as editor; I think it was almost as useful—to the field as a whole, though not to his own position in the field—in its second phase.

A few months ago, I participated in a late night radio talk-program, on which John Campbell and two professors of physics from local schools were co-panelists. To everyone's surprise (particularly the MC's) we got into a hot-and-heavy discussion of objective-vs.-subjective reality. In the course of one exchange, I accused Campbell of confusing logic with hardware. He replied that there *is* no logic without hardware.

I do *not* believe Campbell would have said this twenty years ago. And I offer it here, not in definition of what I mean by "engineering mind," but of what happened to Campbell's attitude—and thus to American science fiction, which, in the late forties, he dominated almost entirely.

An engineer is a man who converts scientific reasoning into functioning technology. (If the word "technology" confuses anyone if applied to the social sciences, I offer my apologies—but I know no more appropriate term. I do *not* mean machines, and I do not mean "hardware"—artifacts. I mean useful constructs derived from scientific concepts, but not requiring scientific training or understanding to use. Geometry is part of our technology, and so is algebra—and so is symbolic logic, and so are the "tools" of psychometrics—and the generally less tangible tools of psychoanalysis. Learning theory is part of the body of scientific knowledge and inquiry: teachers' colleges offer education courses consisting of the *technology*, the techniques, and the catalog of material, which apply learning theory to the teaching process. It is irrelevant whether the theory is sound or the technology is well-designed; the definitions are the same.)

The way a good engineer works is first to absorb the theory applicable to his job; then to investigate the technology already available for the purpose; determine what is useful to him, and what he needs, to design specifically for the job: try out (as much as possible on paper or in his mind—perhaps in model form) as many ideas as possible *to find out what will work best to do the job*—what offers the best combination of economy, durability, adherence to specifications, ease of operation, etc.; and then construct a pilot model embodying the most of the best of what he has learned. His objective is not learning-for-learning's sake, but the accomplishment of a particular utilitarian goal.

There is today a field called "human engineering," and when the first School of Human Engineering is opened, John W. Campbell will be entitled to the deanship; I doubt that the full extent of his influence, once or twice removed (through his own writing and that of the authors he attracted to what amounted to a "movement" in those early years of *Astounding*-and-*Unknown*), will ever be fully tabulated. Campbell did not originate the ideas; he did not stimulate the emergence of the field; he was one of its earliest and most productive engineers.

And as it happens, the first phases of an engineering job are almost indistinguishable from scientific research; the only significant difference is that side-tracks are less likely to be followed for any length. There may be something interesting at the end of one or another of the by-lanes, but as soon as it becomes apparent that what lies that way does not concern this *particular* job, it is set aside, or referred to the man who is working on that aspect.

Because Campbell thought like an engineer, because there was a specific kind of information he was after, rather than knowledge-in-general, he was able to give shape and direction to the science fiction of the forties, and it was precisely the shape and direction it most needed. Because he was a *good* engineer, he kept his mind entirely open about the nature of the answers he would find, except that he wanted things that *would work in practice*.

Problem: Human nature is such that it has changed the natural environment of humans and is continuing to do so at an accelerating pace. How to adapt human nature to its new environment?

It was when Campbell began to think he had found the answer that the "Golden Age" of *Astounding* was over. (I think, in retrospect, that Dianetics was the line of demarcation. There have been several other Answers since then, but from [at least somewhere about] that time, he has been in the second phase of the engineering job.) He stopped asking questions and examining the available equipment, and started making designs and building models. *Astounding*, quite appropriately, eventually became *Analog*; but long before that, Campbell had lost his real impact on the field. He remains the honored Senior Editor; most of the "big name" s-f writers of today started by selling, or trying to sell, to Campbell. Most of the younger Writers, in America at least, grew up on *Astounding* and *Unknown*, and on the reject-overflow into other magazines. Mrs. Williams's characterization of John Campbell as "father-figure" is, I think, exact and precise.

But there is beginning to be—there already is in England—a body of writers at work who are conscious of no debt at all to Campbell—indeed, know him only as the didactic and "increasingly magisterial" (Mrs. Williams's phrase) figure of the past ten or fifteen years. It is these writers, on the whole, who are making the new science fiction of the sixties, and what they are doing will prove, I think, a more radical and more exciting—intellectually *and* artistically—departure than anything up till now.

What *they* grew up on was the specialty s-f of the fifties, and the increasing bulk of s-f writing from "outside" sources.

At the end of World War II, *Astounding* was the only monthly in the field; *Amazing*, *Fantastic*, *Weird*, and *Famous Fantastic Mysteries* were bi-monthlies; *Planet*, *Startling*, and *Thrilling Wonder Stories*, quarterlies—four magazines a month altogether.

Bit by bit, the paper—and author—shortage came to an end. By the summer of 1949, *Amazing* and *Fantastic* were monthly, *Startling* and *TWS* bi-monthly. There were three new titles: *Fantastic Novels* (bi-monthly), *Avon Fantasy Reader* (three issues a year), and Forrest J Ackerman's "semi-pro" *Fantasy Books* (once or twice a year)—seven magazines a month.

Then the Boom began. It seems appropriate to date it from the first issue of *Fantasy and Science Fiction* (Fall 1949); (as *The Magazine of Fantasy*—bi-monthly from January 1951; monthly in August 1952). *Galaxy* started one year later, a monthly from the beginning.

Other Worlds came November 1949; *Imagination*, October 1950. *If*, *Infinity*, and *Science Fiction Stories* followed shortly. Through the first half of the decade, new titles kept appearing, old-new ones dropping out. Publishing schedules fluctuated wildly on the second-string regulars; it worked out to between eight and ten magazines a month, on the average. (There were now four s-f magazines in England.)

But the American specialty magazines were no longer an index of the health or popularity of the field. Science fiction was appearing, infrequently, but regularly, in such places as *Collier's, The Saturday Evening Post, Esquire, Bluebook, Good Housekeeping, Ellery Queen*. Above all, there were books.

Before 1948, there were six anthologies of science fiction in print, all published during the forties: Phil Strong's *Other Worlds*, Wollheim's *Pocket Book of Science Fiction*, Julius Fast's paperback, *Out of This World*, the Healy-McComas *Adventures in Time and Space*, and Conklin's *The Best of Science Fiction*. In 1948-49, there were six more, including the first of the Bleiler-Dikty *Best Science Fiction Stories* annuals. There were at least another six in 1950. [Nineteen fifty-one] was when the Book Boom began. ([Twenty-two] anthologies alone, if memory serves.) The same thing was happening with novels and short story collections. By 1950 or 1951, Doubleday, Simon and Schuster, Pellegrini and Cudahy, as well as most of the paperback houses, were all firmly in the science fiction business, and there were half a dozen specialty houses.

Those were the surface manifestations of a transformation inside s-f which was, within a few years, to make the genre, in the special form in which it had existed for thirty years, moribund.

Books (May 1966)

"I know it's junk, but I like it."

Which [says Jules Feiffer][1] is *the whole point about junk. It is there to be nothing else but liked. Junk is a second-class citizen of the arts; a status of which we and it are constantly aware. There are certain inherent privileges in second-class citizenship, irresponsibility is one. Not being taken seriously is another.*

Feiffer's super-comic-book is a study in puzzles and paradoxes. Fifty-or-so (large) pages of honest Feiffer text surround 132 more of acknowledged absurd nostalgic junk. It is sadly that I must say that not only Batman and the Green Hornet and Mr. America (none of whom I much cared for even then), but even Superman and the Spirit (both of beloved memory) have not improved with age, any more than the comic-book colors are enhanced by good book paper.

Feiffer himself—whether as cartoonist or essayist—is anything but junk. Except to someone in my peculiar position, I am not sure his fifty pages of autobiography, social comment, and philosophy are worth $9.75 (allowing 20¢ for the value of a double-size comic book), and of course I didn't have to pay for it. But for me, his final chapter on the subject of junk was pure revelation.

"Junk is there to entertain on the basest, most compromised of levels," he says at one point. "*It finds the lowest fantasmal common denominator and proceeds from there. Its choice of tone is dependent on its choice of audience, so that women's magazines will make a pretense at veneer scorned by movie-fan magazines, but both are, unarguably, junk.*"

Or substitute for *veneer,* intellectual eminence; for *women's magazines,* the bulk of "category" science-fiction novels.

"The success of the best junk lies in its ability to come close, but not too close; to titillate without touching us. To arouse without giving satisfaction. Junk is a tease...."

Yes indeed. And I only wish I'd read it before I began belaboring the authors of good junk—*my* kind of junk, too—in an attempt to make them come through with the intellectual and literary satisfaction they keep waving just out of reach.

The final quote is as profound as it is paradoxical, concluding as it does a ten-dollar volume with a pop-art Superman cover, which carries twenty-five-year-old comics to the artbook shelf of (I am sure, many of) the same households where the originals were burned on sight.

"A junk that knew its place was underground where it had no power and thus only titillated, rather than above ground where it truly has power—and thus, only depresses."

With unwonted restraint, I shall ignore all the opportunities provided not only for comment on the comment and philosophizing on the philosophy, but for a marvelous multi-meaning word game of *junkie, junkie, who's got the junk*? (Is Feiffer peddling the junk here, or is the junk peddling him?) More significant is the restraint I intend to show in future.

Shortly after I inherited this space, we asked for readers' comments on the column and what they wanted in it. The results were gratifying, but omnivorous. They—you—wanted discursive essays on some books *and* complete coverage of all books of s-f-interest. It can't be done. There isn't time or space (Ed the Ed. having flatly refused to devote half the magazine to books). So—Feiffer to the rescue, with his twin concepts of *good junk* and *underground junk*. Policy statement follows:

> This column will no longer endeavor to provide complete coverage of s-f and associated books. Non-junk books, good or bad—those, that is, that seem to make an *effort to satisfy* the special tastes of the s-f reader—will be discussed at whatever length their merit, my interest, and the space, permit. In addition, the *good* junk (because, once more, entwined in rosy wreaths—it is *my* kind of junk, and I love it!) will be described or at least mentioned, and recommended, without such examination as might expose it in either sense destroy its junk-value by trying to impose responsibility on it, or give it depressant power by dragging it above ground.

Thank you, Jules Feiffer!

Last month, this column devoted much of its space to Games—the theory and application, especially in science-fiction, and most particularly in John Brunner's triple-ploy games-novel, *The Squares of the City*. Apparently Ballantine, who published that one, is making it an all-out games season, following up with two other volumes as different from each other as from the Brunner, but equally game-centered.

One of the most memorable Games stories in s-f is Robert Sheckley's "The Prize of Peril." His earlier story on the same theme, "The Seventh Victim," left a less lasting impression on me, but apparently had a more significant impact on Joseph E. Levine, of Embassy Pictures. The result is the movie, *The Tenth Victim* (Why be cheap?), and a "novelization"[2] of the movie, this time by the original author, under the same more generous title.

The idea, as you probably know by now, is a legalized murder-game, government-approved and TV-commercial-sponsored, designed to provide an outlet for individual aggressions, and thus eliminate the emotional pressure toward the greater destructiveness of organized international slaughter. Anyone who gets enough kick out of killing to be willing to risk getting killed registers for the Big Hunt, and the Victim-Hunter pursuits supply the viewing public with all the real gore and surrogate adventure it can use.

As social theorizing, one cannot take the hypothesis too seriously. Happily, neither author Sheckley nor director Petri requires it. The film publicity quotes Petri: "We are giving the lie to violence as glamour, as a heroic ideal by sheer exaggeration...." I have not seen the movie, but I gather its tone is much like that of the book, which is highly successful (and withal suspenseful) farce.

What fascinates me, and excites a new kind of admiration for Bob Sheckley, is that this rewrite, far from the usual padding-out and watering-down job, is not only very well done on its own, but applies a completely different technique to the original theme, perhaps *more* effectively.

The Game in James White's new novel, *The Watch Below*,[3] is also one of life-and-death, but in a very different way. This is a thoughtful and thought-provoking novel combining one of the great "classic" s-f ideas (the "Universe" ship) with two major themes of current interest: the problem of adaptation to an alien environment, and that of communication between alien cultures.

The actual space ship involved is—well, on the one hand it is a space fleet, of "Unthan" ships, filled with freeze-sleeping star-colonists and their supplies, seeds, livestock, etc.; manned (if one may use the word) by part-time skeleton crews. The *other* ship is not in space at all, but a giant empty tanker, half-sunk during World War II, with a handful of people aboard who manage to survive long enough in the vast empty holds to establish an ecology cycle for air and food from the supplies of beans on board.

From vastly divergent starting points—a fleet of high-technology water-dwellers embarked on a well-planned space voyage; and five desperate men and women seizing on every scrap of salvage to sustain themselves while waiting rescue from the half-wrecked, reef-grounded tanker—the two groups move into an intriguing parallelism. The theory that provided for only short duty tours for each Unthan, with long spells of freeze-sleep to endure the long trip, proves unworkable, and in the end two couples assume the responsibility of progenitors of the fifteen generations who will have to live out their lives on board the flagship to bring the rest of the fleet through. Meanwhile, back on the Atlantic, the *Gulf Trader* is wedged securely just enough below the surface to be passed over repeatedly with no effort at rescue or investigation.

On board the Unthan flagship, the two officers who sacrificed their own prospects of reaching journey's end, spend the rest of their lives setting down text and precept and ritual which they hope will enable the space-borne generations to survive the pressures of cultural devolution at least enough to be able to waken the main body of the crew when the time comes. And on the *Gulf Trader*, they start The Game.

The Game begins only as defense against boredom and panic. It begins as mutual exchange of life-histories, goes on to exercises in memory (as often fantasy as fact) of books, plays, music—all experiences and perceptions. The children born in the submerged ship-world have The Game and its retention-sharpening effects for schooling, entertainment, cultural matrix.

It would be unfair to the author's careful construction to tell more than this. I only wish White had managed to imbue this saga-scope story with more of the emotional conviction and quiet poetry of his best short work. There are flashes of it here, true: unfortunately just enough to bring to mind the warm immediacy of (for instance) his memorable "Christmas Treason." Perhaps if it could have been a longer book....

This month's non-junk award to James White—and a Gold Star to Ballantine Books for three-in-a-row with originality, content, and craftsmanship.

Starchild,[4] the Pohl-Williamson sequel to *Reefs of Space*, is a rather more routine far-space adventure, brightened by spots of colorful effective imagery in which some of the more vivid archetypes of traditional fantasy emerge in pseudo-science masquerade.

Even more routine, and with only its easy-reading slick writing to make it worth mention as a no-strain alternative to television, is van Vogt's *Rogue*

Ship[5]—another "Universe"-type voyage, with some extra effects provided by (what I found) some most confusing time-slippage metaphysics.

Shepherd Mead brings the aliens down to Earth in a tongue-in-cheek novel so slickly readable that its significance is almost lost between the pacing and the parody. Almost.

Between gentle pokes at saucer-watchers, beatnik artists, and homegrown engineers, and somewhat less gentle prods at Mad Ave, *The Carefully Considered Rape of the World*[6] tells a story of alien invaders using advertising-and-market-research control psychology techniques (plus odds and ends of alien super-technology) to take over for Man's Own Good. A household of improbable semi-beats proves just immune enough to the mass-media techniques to stir up some trouble for the genetic do-gooders—who have, however, some well-done genetics going for them. There is much freshness, and more surprise than you might think, in Mead's description of human reactions to the baboon-like "new-mods," the mutant improvement in the alien master-plan, and in the gradual exposure of the motives and methods of the invaders, even in the knowledgeable farce on Mad Ave mores and patois—and believe-it-or-not, in the way the whole thing ends.

Most surprising of all is the realization *after* the end that the freshness was not limited to the handling of (essentially familiar) components, but extended to the underlying thinking: that all the fun and froth rests on a reasonably respectable thematic base.

[…]

Notes

1. *The Great Comic Book Heroes*, Jules Feiffer; Dial, 1965; $9.95; 189 pp. (incl. 127 pp. of comics).
2. *The Tenth Victim*, Robert Sheckley; Ballantine U5050, 1965; 60¢; 158 pp.
3. *The Watch Below*, James White; Ballantine U2285, 1966; 50¢; 192 pp.
4. *Starchild*, Frederik Pohl and Jack Williamson; Ballantine U2176, 1965; 50¢.
5. *Rogue Ship*, A. E. van Vogt; Doubleday, 1965; $4.50; 213 pp.
6. *The Carefully Considered Rape of the World*, Shepherd Mead; Simon & Schuster, 1966; $4.95.

[…]

The Year's Best S-F, Eleventh Annual Edition (1966)

Introduction

I generally skip introductions myself—at least until after I read the book. But I hope you're reading this one, because you may be disappointed otherwise.

This is not a collection of science-fiction stories.

It does have some science fiction in it—I think. (It gets a little more difficult each year to decide which ones are *really* science fiction—and frankly I don't much try any more.)

There are two selections full of good honest hard-science stuff. The biochemical one is a sort of bible story, and the astrophysical one is about an astral 'pataphysician. And there are a couple of planet-type stories by Leiber and Clarke—two solid science-fiction names if ever there were one—about life (or death) on (or in or around) the moon.

I can also offer a galore of space ships, a gaggle of monstrous or otherwise odd alien creatures, and a fair-sized battalion of robots and other kinds of thinking machines, as well as some telepathists and general Wielders of Powers, some disembodied entities, and a mess of mythological and magical beings (one giant, one sorceress, a devil-sticks dancer, and assorted semi- and demigods).

But if you think that makes the book a collection of *fantasy* and science fiction, I'm afraid I still have to beg off—unless you choose to include under "fantasy" everything that is not rigidly "realistic"—assuming you know what *that* means. I don't.

What this book *is*, is a collection of imaginative speculative writing reflecting, I believe, clearly and sharply the problems and conflicts of civilized man today, and his hopes and apprehensions for the future.

The stories and poems and essays here have been selected from as wide a range as I could cover of books and periodicals published here and in England last year. About half the entries are from the genre magazines. The rest are from books and from such diverse sources as *Mademoiselle* and *Escapade*, *The Colorado Review* (and *Ambit* and *King* in England). The youngest author is an eighteen-year-old college freshman; the oldest a ninety-three-year-old (if still alive) Parisian legend.

You will, I think, find the attitudes, treatments, topics, as varied as the sources.

Some of it is even science fiction.

[...]

Summation

Burroughs would have been lost...Edgar Rice Burroughs, that is.

Since the days of his novel *The Warlord of Mars* things have changed in outer space. Yet William Burroughs, he of *Naked Lunch* and *Nova Express* fame, would have loved every minute of it.

At ten o'clock on Sunday morning, when the decent folk of London were still in their beds, delegates to the 23rd World Science Fiction Convention in London were discussing "The Robot in the Executive Suite," speculating on practical optimums for robot construction.

Only one lonely bug-eyed monster appeared at the convention—at the costume ball; and Penguin books had great difficulty in persuading a Dalek[1] to appear. Monsters and Martians get harder to find every day. Science fiction, since the good old days when Hugo Gernsback first named the genre "Scientifiction" and printed space operatics in pulp magazines, has come of a respectable age. Unlikely Martians are of less interest than what one British writer, J. G. Ballard, has called "inner space," a very real world. In the space age Jules Verne can't shine a candlepower before the reality of Gemini.

This was the opening of the *Spectator*'s report on the World Science Fiction Convention in London last August. The London *Sunday Times Magazine*, shortly afterword, came out with a special s-f section: an article on the Clarke-Kubrick movie [*2001: A Space Odyssey*], one on the BBC's (then) forthcoming s-f drama series, and a thoughtful profile of John W. Campbell, editor of *Analog*, which summed up:

> ...Life to Campbell is a gigantic experiment in form, and earth the forcing-house—an impeccable vision, but one not warmed (in his theories, that is) by a feeling for the pain or personal potential of the individuals in the experiment. That kind of gentleness in expression seemed to disappear with Don A. Stuart.

So that, ironically, as s-f becomes increasingly respectable, John Campbell, its acknowledged father-figure, can't really claim his throne. He provides the continuity, he shaped much of the thought, he made many reputations. S-f narrowed from the vastness of space to the greater complexity of "sociological" s-f with him presiding.

But now it is narrowing towards the highly focused, upside-down detail of "innerspace." The tone is personal and subjective, the quality of expression important.... There is even a literary magazine: *SF Horizons*. None of this is Campbell's style.

You may disagree with the views of either or both reporters (Bill Butler in the *Spectator*, Pat Williams in the *Times Magazine*). What is significant is that they had views, and expressed them intelligently; that neither one approached the job in the role of literary slummer, or even intrepid anthropologist among the fantasists, but simply and seriously as observers reporting on a field they knew and understood, and believed to be of interest to other readers.

I was about to say, it couldn't happen here—but I suspect the difference in attitude is not so much spatial as temporal. What has already happened there is just beginning to happen here.

Which is to say: the big news in s-f this year is mostly not in s-f—not on this side of the ocean. (Exceptions: the establishment of the SFWA, and Doubleday's expanded publishing schedule, under the supervision of Lawrence P. Ashmead, who looks to be the best thing that has happened to s-f book publishing here in a long time.)

In a sense, the biggest news this year is that it is harder than ever to locate on the literary map any reliable boundary line between s-f and anything else. The other side of the coin, whose tail is the lack of focus and *esprit* in the specialty field here, is, I suppose the diminishment of spirited opposition or snobbism directed at the field. To some extent, this is a self-reproducing cycle, to a greater degree, the changing faces on both sides are being shaped by pressures initiating entirely outside the local literary scene, particularly such adjacent areas as education, advertising, psychology, and the Think Factory phenomenon. The s-f label becomes ludicrous, not to say invisible, when advertisements like the star-sprinkled page with the cute little capsule through whose wide-vision window a cheery astronaut and his mouth organ illustrate the pitch: "Three billion people will look up to you...on Dec. 16, 1965, the Hohner Harmonica became the first musical instrument to be played in outer space" appear in the same sort of magazines which now publish such stories as "Game," "Somewhere Not far from Here," "The Girl Who Drew the Gods," "The Drowned Giant" (and Stanley Elkin's "Perlmutter at the East Pole" in the *Post*), with neither apologies, explanations, nor exclamation points.

I mention these titles in particular because they are neither whimsical fantasies, space-cowboy adventures, sex-and-spy spoofs, nor sprightly satires, but serious speculative fiction of a kind that actually had no market here a few years ago (bar the infrequent *F&SF* acceptance).

It is part of the same happy blurring of edges that Daniel Keyes's *Flowers for Algernon* was issued recently by Harcourt with neither labels nor disclaimers on the jacket—*and* that Gold Medal's Beaumont selection, *The Magic Man*, did specify "science fantasy" out front, when the earlier collections from which it was culled had avoided the tag like the plague-carrier it was known to be for a serious and talented young writer.

It almost seems that the trend is to using the label when it seems helpful, and omitting it when it does not. One hesitates to make any assumptions of such widespread sanity, but the magazine situation almost requires it. Some readers, and most writers, will already have noticed that this *Annual* contains no Honorable Mentions listing. For the last two or three years, the attempt to compile such a list has been increasingly frustrating. The diffusion is too great: Even if it were within my powers to be certain I have *seen* everything entitled to consideration in a given year, I no longer know where to draw the line.

I use poetry, and sometimes cartoons, and frequently newspaper pieces among the selections: Ought they to be covered in the Mentions too? What about British publications, and English-language books published in other countries? How about things like the *Christian Science Monitor*'s "Martian Papers," describing the amusement along the Canal at UFO-nuts who claim to have seen six-foot-tall metallic-clothed extraterrestrials? Or the deadpan stuff the *Realist* has begun to use (since they broke the s-f ice with Harvey Bilker's "Genetic Faux Pas")? How in the world do you decide on a listing for (almost anything from) Roger Price's inflammatory *Grump*? What about Fernando Krahn's cartoons in the *Reporter*? How about poetry? Or critical writing?

The answer, of course, was to mention all these other things in the Summation, which began to make the addition of the HM list not only burdensome to me and unfair to authors whose work I would not discover till two months, or two years, later, but foolish as well, since much of the highest-quality work was mentioned only off-list. The new answer is to omit any pretense at publication of a comprehensive listing. [...]

One way and another, I keep coming back to it. The important things happening in American s-f are not happening *in* it at all. We have writers comparable to Ballard in stature, for instance—but not in current achievement, and certainly not in influence within the field. Cordwainer Smith and Theodore Sturgeon have each published two new stories in the last eighteen months or so—and none of them close to the author's best work. Leiber has been productive: a *Tarzan* novelization, and thousands of words of magazine stories, some of them very good reading, all rather closer in period to *Tarzan* than to Leiber's own work of a few years back ("Mariana," "A Deskful of Girls," "The Secret Songs," "The Silver Eggheads," *The Wanderer*). Nothing at all from Alfred Bester for three years now, nor from Walter Miller for much, much longer. Kurt Vonnegut continues to do a novel every year or two that almost makes up for the rest of what's missing—but he is not in the same sense a part of the field here at all; his impact on other American writers is almost more from "outside" than Ballard's.

The novel generally acclaimed as the best American product last year was Frank Herbert's *Dune*—a long, and in part excellent, but completely conventional future-historical, admirable essentially for its complexity rather than for any original or speculative contribution. Certainly there is nothing in it to stimulate or influence the work of others.

As it happens, the stimulus is being provided from outside—and not just from England. It is coming from exciting new work in psychology and the allied sciences; from the *avant-gardistes* and poets who have begun using the images and contexts of s-f with or without concern for the sources; and from the impact of the belated translation and publication of people like Borges and Jarry.

It is interesting to speculate on what the difference in our thinking and writing might have been, if we had had Jarry as part of the s-f tradition, along with Verne and Wells. Jarry himself was reading these men as they wrote, Verne in his childhood, Wells in his prime. He responded to Wells (See "How to Construct a Time Machine" in the *Selected Works.*) but also *with* Wells, to the scientific discoveries of the turn of the century. In a sense, he is Jules Verne's left hand, as Wells might be the right.

But if we *had* had Jarry, would we have read him? From today's vantage point, a hectic half century of scientific revolutions and upheavals later, Jarry's responses are rather more in keeping with the direction of physics itself than were Wells's marvelously sane and rational civilized adductions.

But how long have we been prepared to see this? Did we not have to work our way (with pleasure) through Gernsback and "scientifiction" to Campbell's then-revolutionary 1938-1942 magazines, and then from E. E. Smith to Heinlein, Leiber, and Asimov—and again, to Boucher's revolutionary notion that a science-fantasy magazine could be *well-written*—to Bester, Miller, Budrys, Cordwainer Smith—before we were ready for either *Cat's Cradle* or "Terminal Beach?"

Or if Borges had been translated as he wrote, if the eight stories in *Ficciones* (Fictions) had been available in 1941, instead of 1962....

I remember vividly the excitement of discovering *The Star Maker* and *Odd John* in the early '40s Stapledon opened tantalizing and terrifying vistas of probability for me. For others, it may have been C. S. Lewis, M. P. Shiel, or E. R. Eddison: but there is no question that the impact of these powerful imaginative thinkers on a whole generation of writers was one of the major forces that moved s-f out of the technocratic-primitivism of "scientifiction" to the sociological-sci-fi of the "great days" of *Astounding* and *Unknown*, and further, to the psychological/semantic/psychiatric science-fantasy of the early years of *Galaxy* and [*F&SF*].

But that was as far as the impetus of that group of brilliant apologists of dualism could take us. The next step we had to reach—are only now reaching—essentially by bootstrap-climbing. So it seems cruelly ironic now to discover that our newest concepts, painfully evolved over a quarter century of speculative interchange from the combined traditions of magic and mathematics, physics and poetry, were already set down—in essays, stories, poems, allegories, sometimes unabashed plot outlines—before we were fairly started on the process, by one man drawing on the whole range of aesthetic/intellectual traditions that have since filtered through to us, from a dozen different sources.

Would we have arrived any sooner, or any saner, at the crossroads of communication where we now stand—where poet and pragmatist, scientist and surrealist, are equally frequently disconcerted to see themselves mirrored in each other's eyes—would we have come to this gathering place, the converging of the many roads toward "reality" traveled by twentieth-century thought, any more readily for the guidance of one brilliant mind far ahead?

Or did we have to get this far ourselves before we could make out the meaning of the light? Did Borges's work, and Jarry's, simply have to wait for the rest of us to catch up? Perhaps we had to go the Zen route before we could contemplate the statement "'Pataphysics is *the* science..." with equanimity (let alone delight), and wait for our learned Academies to convene

Conferences on the nature of time before Borges's "Tlön, Uqbar, Tertius Orbis" became comprehensible?

Perhaps we did. Perhaps each cultural island—whether a nation, genre, discipline, or single man—must grow its own way through the stages of naïve rationalism and hardware sophistication, before it can approach the recognition of the inalienable association between the concurrent-and-diverse "realities" of physics and metaphysics, mathematics and mysticism, psyche and soma, science and art.

Note

1. Unautomated man-sized UK version of Robbie the Robot—controls, mike, etc., are inside, as is operator.

Books (June 1966)

[...]

I am not going to tell you much about *Genocides.*[1] I'll save the analytical discussion for the almost inevitable hard cover edition some hard-headed publisher will eventually put out. Right now, I'd rather leave you to enjoy the story the way I did, without knowing too much in advance. Suffice it then—

This is a *different* book about alien "invaders" of Earth. The reactions of the survivors of the first "attacks" are presented with a compassion exceeded only by the clarity of the author's perceptions. This applies not only to the behavior of the survivors, but to the selection of them: survival in crisis is not (as so many s-f authors seem to think) a random factor. The circumstances of life after the "conquest," and the adjustments of various individuals to those circumstances, are handled with both insight and inner consistency. Disch is not writing about how it *ought* to be; he is stating, clearly and convincingly, how, in a given situation, it would be.

This alone would make the book, in the current dearth of thinking-man's novels, worth reading. But there is more.

Without twisting the behavior of his characters to conform to his own preconceptions of right-and-wrong, the author does manage to say a great deal about his concepts of morality, especially as applied to the nature of survival and the struggle for existence. But, as with most good fiction, it is not until the second time through that you stop to reflect on the philosophy; the first time you are too absorbed by the narrative and the personalities.

Personalities, I said, not "characters." There are people in this book I will not forget for a long time.

Finally, the book is *written.*

There is an occasional small clumsiness or unnecessary cuteness or cleverness in the prose—but for an author whose first work was published less than four years ago, those spots are very occasional indeed, and against them are to be weighed such passages as these:

> *There was in these forests a strange, unwholesome solitude, a solitude more profound than adolescence, more unremitting than prison. It*

> *seemed, in a way, despite its green, flourishing growth, dead. Perhaps it was because there was no sound. The great leaves overhead were too heavy and too rigid in structure to be stirred by anything but gale winds. Most of the birds had died....*

(Anderson, leader of the settlement, and his son, Buddy, are tracking through this forest on the trail of the community's vital herd of cows, stampeded by their only bull, and with Anderson's youngest son in futile attendance.)

> *The smell had become very strong; then at a turn in the path, they found the twelve carcasses. They had been incinerated to ash, but the outlines were clear enough to indicate which had been Studs. There was also a smaller patch of ash near them on the path.*
>
> *"How—" Buddy began. But he really meant what, or even who, something that his father was quicker to understand.*
>
> *"Jimmie!" the old man screamed, enraged, and he buried his hands in the smaller pile of still-smoking ashes. Buddy turned his eyes away, for too great sorrow is like drunkenness: it was not fitting that he should see his father then.*
>
> *There's not even any meat left,* he thought, looking at the other carcasses. *Nothing but ashes.*

Or the two very different characters, city-folk, swapping hysterically clever repartee as they watch their city burn. They keep their cool until the First American Bank begins to go:—

> *They had lived these last years in the safe deposit vault in the basement.... Their precious stores of scavenged cans and jars were still locked in the safe deposit boxes, and the canary was probably in his cage in the corner....*
>
> *Jackie was crying real tears.*
>
> *"Sad?" he asked.*
>
> *"Oh, not sad. Just a little déracinée. And annoyed with myself because I don't understand it." She snuffled loudly, and the tears were all gone. "It's so horribly like what they used to call an Act of God. As though God were the source of everything unreasonable. I like to know the reason for things." Then, after a pause: "Perhaps it was the termites?"*

"The termites!" He looked at her unbelievingly, and her cheek began to show its telltale dimple...

(The city begins to burn out.)

Here and there, scuttling about the rubble, the incendiary mechanisms could be glimpsed attending their business. At this remove they seemed really quite innocuous. They reminded Jackie of nothing so much as of Volkswagens of the early Fifties, when all Volkswagens seemed to be grey....

"Well, goodbye, Western Civilization," Jackie said, waving at the bright inferno, unafraid. For how can one be afraid of Volkswagens?

It is always a mistake to offer samplings like these; one sample leads to another, and to do the variety of the book justice, one has to include yet another. There is no space here for that. Just go buy the book—if you can find it. Certainly it is the best reading bargain you're likely to get for some time: a literate, perceptive novel, none of which you have read before in short story form or botched serial or "one shot" version in the magazine (and honest science fiction besides).

And it may be something of an investment, too, if (like many s-f readers) you have a bit of collector's blood: the first edition of the first novel of a young writer whose name will probably be better known outside s-f in a few years than it is inside the field now—assuming he finds a way to get his books not just published but read.

Just now, he is without doubt one of the two really bright new lights on the American s-f scene. (I have in mind Roger Zelazny, whose first novel is about due, I understand, from Ace; both writers began publishing in Cele Lalli's *Fantastic* within a few months of each other in 1962.)

Meantime, I have on hand another first novel, equally exciting in a very different way. Actually it is difficult to think of *Flowers for Algernon*[2] as a "first novel," nor is it so in any but the technical sense. That is, it is only half-new, and one has small reason by now to expect it to be followed by more. The book is an isolated event, rather than an early milestone on the path of a writer but a singular and significant event on several counts. In ascending order of importance:

Here is the proof that a first-rate novelette *can* be turned into an equally good novel; all it requires, I suspect, is that the author has something more to say on the subject, and has retained his full interest in saying it. Perhaps the very fact (or what I believe to be fact) that Danny Keyes, for all his literary skill, is not essentially "a writer," but a teacher (scholar? philosopher? preacher?) who happens to be exceptionally gifted in communication is precisely what made this possible. Keyes published four or five stories in the late fifties; all were well executed and thought provoking; "Algernon" alone (*F&SF*, April 1959) contained that special quality what does one call it? How do *you* think of it? *Excellence? Excitement? Creativity? Art?* Perhaps just: "Algernon" alone was a *memorable* story. He may yet do more fiction; but to date it would seem that this was the story he had to tell. The first time around, he wrote the essential parts; now here it is complete.

Next, on the matter of its publication: here is a first book by writer unknown, for all practical purposes, outside s-f. There is hardly a reader inside the field who is not familiar with either the author's name or the story title by now (*F&SF*'s *Best*, Ninth Series, 1959; my own *SF*, Fifth Annual, 1960; Asimov's *Hugo Winners*, 1962; all three in paperback more recently). Harcourt Brace & World—perhaps because they do not have "a science fiction line" and have not acquired some of the publishing preconceptions—are to be loudly applauded for having done the obvious and logical thing: they have wrapped the book in a quiet, tasteful, and appropriate jacket and described the story on the flap with neither apology for, nor repudiation of, "science fiction"; there is no need for label to tell s-f readers what this book is, and there is no label or other indication of second-class publishing citizenship to frighten off the non-habituated. (But they *did* get prompt advance copies out to specialty review sources; and I must apologize here, as I approach my final point, for not having reviewed this a month earlier.)

The fact is, when I got the book, I didn't want to read it. I remembered the story too well, and I did not want to read a padded out, watered down version. Unfortunately, the opening page supported this sad expectation; and now that I have read it all—without putting it down, once I got started—I think the only real criticism I would make concerns some of the changes on the opening and cloying pages.

The impact of the original story rested primarily in the author's extraordinary—perhaps unique—success in conveying an identifiable-and-identifiable-*with* subjective portrait of a subnormal intelligence. Charlie Gordon was a moron, and he was also a man; the reader could accept him as a fellow-human, share his fears and hopes and desperate needs. (Sturgeon has occasionally come close to accomplishing the same thing for me, but never so completely; offhand, I cannot think of another writer who has even come near it.) And as a fellow writer, I remember admiring the author's restraint in the later part of the story almost as much as his earlier achievement: he had sense enough *not* to try to do the same thing for Charlie's "superman" phase, I thought.

Well, now he has done just that; he has taken Charlie through intellectual, emotional, social, and sexual discoveries, and done it successfully. The technique is still one of restraint, and it is perhaps the only available technique for conveying an insight into the potentialities of a higher order of intelligence than that of either author or reader. (Sturgeon, again—in "Maturity," specifically—came close to accomplishing this; in the hundreds of intellectual-superman stories I have read, very few others have come anywhere near the mark: some parts of Shiras's *In Hiding* perhaps; an occasional spot in Clifton's short stories; the muted ending of *Odd John*....) Here, I think it is less the technique (the first person "Progress Report" method of the original story, assisted by occasional reminders, like: "Strauss again brought up my need to speak and write simply and directly so that people will understand me. He reminds me that language is sometimes a barrier instead of a pathway. Ironic to find myself on the other side of the intellectual fence."), than the feeling that the projected shadow of a giant in the "simply" written diary is *real:* that somehow the author has managed to discern the actual shape of—if not the giant himself, then—the shadow, at least.

The novel is fully as remarkable an accomplishment as was the original story. I am sorry to have to include even my one small quibble—that some of the revisions in the very first and very last *progris riports* seemed to me to detract from, rather than add to, the original image of Charlie. Perhaps it is only that the paragraphs are longer; there is a bit more continuity of thought; Charlie seems to observe or understand more of *other* people's reactions. Or, perhaps, it is just that I do not want anything to change in my own almost personal vivid recollection of Charlie Gordon....

Notes

1. *The Genocides*, Thomas M. Disch; Berkley, F1170, 1965; 143 pp.; 50¢.
2. *Flowers for Algernon,* Daniel Keyes; Harcourt Brace & World, 1966; 274 pp.; $4.95.

Books (July 1966)

This seems to be international Brotherhood Month in s-f. In my stack are two editions, one each British and American (slightly different), by Brian Aldiss; the first American edition of a well-established British novelist, John Lymington; a British edition of a previously unpublished novel by American author Charles Harness; and an American edition of a work by an American author, Joseph L. Green—based on a series of novelettes written for the British magazine, *New Worlds.*

The big good news is Harness's *The Rose.*[1] Some of you will already know that Charles Harness, after too long a silence, has started writing again; two short stories have already been published this year. Some will remember—in particular—"The New Reality" (*Thrilling Wonder Stories*, 1950, and *Best Science Fiction Stories*, 1951). Beginning at the end, let me inform you, as neither the cover nor title-page of the book will do, that "The New Reality" and a shorter story, "The Chess players" are included in the Compact volume.

"Chess players" is a good, funny story; anyplace except sandwiched between "The Rose" and "New Reality," it might seem better than that. As it is—the latter, you may recall, is the story of Professor Luce, the ontologist, who evades determined government control in his effort to prove it possible to change "reality." The novelette reads like too much of the high-idea-content work of science-fiction; the characters are there to argue out the theories; the action is faintly reminiscent of the photography of early silent movies; the dialogue might seem at home in magazine melodrama of the 1890s. I say all this, and add: even today, sixteen years after its pulp publication, "The New Reality" is a compelling piece of work. I couldn't put it down. (I read it, as it happens, for the first time in this volume, so there is no question of nostalgic attachment.)

"Rose" comes out of the same powerful philosophic context as "Reality," and though the prose style, as I look back at it, is only one degree farther removed from *Air Wonder* than in the shorter work, this time the concepts are integrated with a vivid story, and the characters are as convincing as they are bizarre.

The rose is a triple symbol, with significance to three people: for Martha Jacques, top-level scientist, it is the graphic pattern of the equation she is pursuing that will contain ultimate knowledge; for her artist-writer husband, Guy, as for Anna van Tuyl, psychiatrist and dancer, its meaning is more obscure through most of the book—but compulsively strong: a question to be answered, rather than an answer to be found.

It is understandable that this book found no market here when it was written almost fifteen years ago; no one was buying a mixed bag of surrealism and science at the time. What is surprising is that it found magazine publication at all; it appeared in the short-lived British s-f magazine, *Authentic*, in 1953. Rather more surprising is the failure of American publishers, who have scoured the bottoms of some much mustier barrels lately for book material, to uncover it.

I am certain there will be an American edition sooner or later. But my advice is, get the Compact book now—not just because it's now, or just for the two bonus stories, or for Michael Moorcock's knowledgeable introduction—but because Roberts and Vinter, who publish both Compact books and Moorcock's *New Worlds*, deserve a vote of appreciation for rescuing "Rose" from its dustheap—and quite probably for being instrumental, through the magazine's interest in his work, in getting Harness back to some new writing.

When I came back from England last fall, I had a copy of the Faber edition of *Earthworks*[2] with me, and I waited this long to review it because I understood Doubleday was publishing a slightly different version.

The differences are very slight indeed, more in format than anything else. Not, in any case, enough to do what I had hoped: connect the last half with the first.

It is hard to believe that the same man wrote both parts—or that he had the same story in mind when he did. I know it must be so, because the *good* part is what reads like Aldiss—and the characters and places have the same names.

Granted, it is difficult to live up to an opening like this:

> "The dead man drifted along in the breeze. He walked, upright on his hind legs like a performing nanny goat, as he had in life, nothing improper, farther beyond the reach of ideology, nationality, hardship, inspiration, than he had ever been in life. A few flies of ripe dimension stayed with him, although he was far from land, travelling light above the surface of the complacent South Atlantic. The tasselled fringe of his white sylk trousers—he had been a rich man, while riches counted—occasionally catching a spray from the waves.

"He was coming out from Africa, moving steadily for me."

Nor do I mean to say the opening paragraph is all there is. The whole first half of the book, as Knowle Noland exposes himself, his past, his fears, his stubborn lingering unattached hope, to the reader's rapt gaze, is Aldiss at his best: brilliantly written in part, excellently most of the rest; rich with evocative imagery; utterly convincing in characterization and action. But even in this part, some small flaws show in the social structure Aldiss builds bit by bit, in flashbacks, to account for the four-man crew of the endlessly sailing automatic freighter, the *Trieste Star*, of which Noland is Captain—and for the dead man transported from the coast of Africa to the ship.

In mid-book, the *Trieste Star* runs aground, the spellbound isolated situation is at an end—and the whole thing turns into a completely routine artificially contrived adventure-chase, which ends with an effort to make an effective scene out of Noland's conversion to the belief that assassination is an effective modern political weapon.

I'll tell you how good the beginning is: it's worth getting the book for the first half. (Chapter Six is a good place to quit.) Well, it's worth it in the book-club, or paperback; it seems to me for $3.50, you ought to get a full 154 pages worth.

FROOMB![3] is a strangely old fashioned-feeling book, full of exciting new ideas. It is stiffly, almost clumsily written; yet the characters (one feels, almost by separate effort of their own) emerge with startling credibility on the page. The plot continually jumps from one improbability to another and less acceptable one; yet you keep turning pages, some how, not just willingly but eagerly. I would understand it better if this were a first novel, by an unpracticed but vital young author. Lymington, however, is well-established in England, with five or six (I think) previous novels to his credit.

FROOMB is a catchword, a slogan, an explanation, the motto of the slightly future age in which the book is set; it stands for Fluid Running Out Of My Brakes. (One says, "Froomb!" in annoyance or despair. Or, critically, "He's gone Froomb!" Or, hiply, approvingly, "Froomb.") I won't tell you anything about the plot; it's too silly. But the ideas in back of it are *not*.

I hope Doubleday plans to do more of Lymington's work. I want to find out if they're all like this....

I'm afraid *The Loafers of Refuge*[4] was something of a disappointment too—and I hate to say it, because for some years I have been turning eagerly to Joseph Green's stories in *New Worlds*—including, or rather, especially, the "Refuge" novelettes and novellas—and enjoying them thoroughly.

The stories concern the gradual approach to cooperation and mutual understanding between the technology-oriented human colonists on Refuge and the native "Loafers," whose culture is built on the development of an empathic, quasi-telepathic relationship with the flora and fauna of the planet. (There are some lovely scenes, with Loafer controllers guiding the monstrous *grogroc* beast through the process of eating-out the insides of a *waquil* fruit, to make a new home for someone—or persuading the *whampus* to come to the surface of the water and be milked.) The handling of intercultural and interpersonal conflicts and approaches is carefully and effectively done. So is the structuring of the individual stories. The only trouble is—

The usual one. They called it a novel, but nobody bothered to turn it into one. Without the magazines to refer to, I cannot be certain, but it does not seem to me as though any revision was done at all: enough stories were selected to make a book-size thing, and they were lumped together and called a novel. (If there was any revision, it was in detail, not structure.)

On the other hand, now that you're warned, and since you probably have *not* read them before—just start with the understanding that every time you find that a new chapter involves a jump in time or continuity, you are beginning a new story. That way, it should work fine.

Notes

1. *The Rose*, Charles L. Harness; Compact Books, F295 (London), 1966; 189 pp.; 3/6 (60¢, including surface postage).
2. *Earthworks*, Brian W. Aldiss; Doubleday (New York), 1966; 154 pp.; $3.50. Faber and Faber (London), 1965; 155 pp.
3. *FROOMB!*, John Lymington; Doubleday, 1966; 187 pp.; $3.95.
4. *The Loafers of Refuge*, Joseph L. Green; Ballantine U2233, 1965; 160 pp.; 50¢.

What Do You Mean? Science? Fiction? Part II (August 1966)

I started reading science fiction in the early Campbell years, but my first science fiction story was published in June, 1948. I was living in New York then, working at Bantam Books; my first anthology (*Shot in the Dark*, because that's the way Bantam felt about it) came out in 1950; and I was active in the semi-official s-f professional group, The Hydra Club, all through its first hectic years from 1948 until 1952. Which is to say, I came into the center of professional activity just as the Big Boom was building up.

The qualitative changes in science fiction at that time may have been evident to people outside the still-small, but growing, fringe audience—but those of us working in the field were dazzled at first by the sudden proliferation of markets. When we began to notice the literary improvement, we tended to attribute it to the Boom: more markets with more money, demanding better work, more room for a range of editorial taste and personality. And all this, of course, was true—once it got started. As to what started it....

The Bomb did not produce the Boom. If anything, the anti-egghead reaction damaged the field—although there was a powerful indirect stimulus in the flood of "Preaching story," atom-doom writing, during the militant days of the atomic scientists' *Bulletin*, the United World Federalists and Garry Davis's World Citizen movement. Everyone got into that act—Philip Wylie, Leo Szilard, Pat Frank, an unknown writer named Judith Merril; but most of it was not labeled "science fiction" and did little to interest new readers in other kinds of s-f. What it did do was bring new writers into the field and break the ice with some book publishers and a few editors of national magazines.

The most important secondary effect of the Bomb was not felt until the height of the McCarthy era, when science fiction became, for a time, virtually the only vehicle of political dissent; but that was later, when the Boom was well under way.

More significant in 1947-1948 was the beginning of serious, official interest in space flight and satellites. We were trained sign-readers, remember; we knew the government was getting interested when (1) the Hayden Planetarium started its space symposium series, (2) *Collier's* worked the material into a glossy spread filling half the magazine, (3) *Destination Moon* was produced as a major film, (4) Viking brought out the first beautiful Bonestell-Ley volume, *The Conquest of Space*, and Wernher von Braun's name kept popping up in the papers. (That was 1948; I think the IGY [International Geophysical Year] satellite projects were actually announced in 1950 or 1951.)

A prophet can be honored in his own land; it all depends on the kind of news he brings. As prophet-in-chief of the Atom Age, John Campbell got nothing but trouble; whatever good the Bomb did for s-f occurred in books and national magazines. As prophet-in-chief of the Space Age, Campbell came into his own in the outside world. *Astounding* prospered, Campbell's own work went into books, and instead of (or in addition to) stealing his best authors, the big magazines interviewed and consulted him. (All this may have had something to do with his phase-change, too; it is difficult to be an open-minded expert.)

What part of *Astounding*, and later *Analog*, was not devoted to the successive Campbell Enthusiasms (Dianetics, Psionics, et al.), or the exposition of his hypotheses on education, religion, social organization, etc., remained (and remains) open to one highly developed type of speculative story, the so-called "new map" extrapolation, primarily as it relates to space flight and the technology associated with it.

"New map" stories are those that offer a detailed, sometimes highly technical, often very knowledgeable, explication of some as-yet unfilled-in area in a territory recently explored by the "concept" and "research" people, but open now to settlement and building-up by the "engineering" and "applications" men. It was to this kind of science fiction more than any other that the new readers of the Boom turned. Space was the trigger that turned them, but a thousand other frontiers of the Post War world held them.

All these factors, at least, and probably others I have overlooked, acted both on each other and on the reading public to produce the Boom phenomenon, and to improve the quality of the stories as the market spread. But the qualitative transformation had actually started before the Boom and had its roots essentially in the same ground that produced the infant space industry.

One of the more intriguing and less resolvable philosophic puzzles concerns the role a prophecy may play in its own fulfillment. There is no doubt that the prophets of modern science fiction acted directly on the chain of events simply by voicing their predictions. They were a significant conditioning factor on the acceptance threshold of society in general and of the scientific/technical segment in particular. How much of the work in the engineering phases of space flight and atomics, for instance, has developed along the lines of prevailing s-f views because that work is a logical development? How much because the work is being done by engineers and technicians who devoured *Astounding* and *Amazing* with their breakfast Wheaties, twenty, thirty, forty years ago, and knew roughly how it would all work before they got their first slide rules? Or how many of them started reading science fiction because of a previous technical orientation—and how many were oriented toward science-and-engineering by science fiction? One can only speculate.

Viewed historically, I believe that American science fiction functioned between the mid-twenties and 1950 as an *Encyclopédie* of the Space Age. The early "scientifictionists" were markedly evangelical; in 1925 they already knew that space flight, atomic power, servo-mechanisms, efficient world-wide video-audio communication, hydroponic farming, and chemical synthesis of needed materials *could* and *would* be achieved. The basic theories already existed; the engineering potential was already available. Only two things were lacking: financial incentive and public acceptance. By the time the (not precisely financial) incentive for crash programs on rocketry and atomics materialized during World War II, science fiction had already made the *idea* of such possibilities public property; and a thousand-and-one specific ideas for development had been tried out on paper and in fan-talk bull sessions.

At the end of World War II, there were few people outside the ranks of science fiction fans and rocket experts who "believed in" space flight—or so they said. Yet, there had already been enough belief in 1938 to panic the State of New Jersey when Orson Welles did his famous *War of the Worlds* broadcast. (Nobody "believed" *Buck Rogers* or *Flash Gordon* or *Superman* either; but everybody *read* them.) In 1950, a small percentage of *Collier's* readers had joined the ranks of Believers; the overwhelming majority still regarded the whole business, overtly, as anything from "crazy comic strip stuff" to "neurotic escapism" and "phallic symbolism." But the soil had been spaded, and the seeds *were* already swollen; it took less than two years of an official information campaign to convince the world that *Sputnik* was neither a hoax nor an obvious impossibility.

There is a rich field for future literary-sociological scholars in the chicken-egg argument implicit here, but it is certain that the publicity given to atomic power, space flight, and servo-mechanisms by science fiction, before the fact, was fully reciprocated by the publicity the developing facts gave science fiction in the late forties and fifties. (Often enough, the same people were involved as working scientists, popular science writers, and/or science fictionists: Willy Ley, Arthur Clarke, Isaac Asimov, John Pierce, Norbert Wiener, Harry Stine....) Or, egg-chicken-wise, the boost these developments gave to the Boom of the fifties was a feedback from the preceding twenty years of "scientifiction" and its successors.

That much we understood, at least vaguely, even at the time. The other feedback circuits operating inside publishing were less obvious.

First of all, those five great years of *Astounding* (and *Unknown*) had attracted not only new writers, but new readers—and continued to attract them, even after Campbell's own focus had shifted. Those were the same stories, that (*before* the Boom) filled the first two big anthologies, *Adventures in Time and Space* and *The Best of Science Fiction*, and made a whole new audience of book-buyers aware of s-f as something other than a successor to Tom Swift and Edgar Rice Burroughs.

When Campbell's personal interest and editorial influence moved from the exploratory to the analog-building phase, the magazine did not suffer. (By that time there were a lot more technicians than there had been ten years earlier; Oak Ridge was one of *Astounding*'s hottest sales areas.) But the "fringe" readers did suffer. Campbell had, in effect, created an audience for new speculative idea fiction, which his own magazine was no longer supplying. The Healy-McComas and Conklin anthologies renewed those readers' interest, while swelling their ranks.

At this point, the Campbell feedback circuit joined another one, in book publishing. Science fiction book publishing in the US all but disappeared in the thirties. We had *It Can't Happen Here* and Stephen Vincent Benét, plus some superlative peripheral work—William Sloane's memorable speculative-fantasy novels; Thorne Smith; some of Don Marquis; Philip Wylie's bits-and-pieces scattered through other books; Stewart's *Fire* and *Storm*. In the early forties there was Fearing's *Clark Gifford's Body*, and McHugh's *I Am Thinking of My Darling*.

In England, however, it was different. *Brave New World*, *The Shape of Things to Come*, John Collier's *Green Thoughts*, Olaf Stapledon's *Last and First Men* and *Last Men in London* had all appeared between 1931-1934: the next year, there were *Odd John* and *Star Maker*, Susan Ertz's *Woman Alive*, and E. C. Large's *Sugar in the Air*. In the forties (with Huxley, Collier, and Stapledon still going strong) came J. B. Priestly, C. S. Lewis, and Gerald Kersch, as well as the books edging curiously in-and-out of the boundaries of science fiction by such writers as Nevil Shute, H. F. Heard, Nigel Balchin, Dennis Wheatley, David Garnett, Alfred Nouyes, R. C. Sherriff, Rex Warner, Graham Greene, and a whole crew usually associated with the detective story—Agatha Christie, Dorothy Sayers, John Dickson Carr, Philip MacDonald, Marjorie Allingham, Leslie Charteris, Eric Linklater, etc. Then came Orwell.

Of course we had had some of the British stuff here all along—Huxley, Priestly, later Collier. (British books, then as now, were available here if you knew what to look for; I am talking about what was actually *written* and/or *published* here.) Between these and the comics and radio and the specialty field, science fiction was a recognized and accepted part of American culture in the mid-forties: it just wasn't a respectable part—not something a serious American writer would do, whether it was art or money he was serious about.

With the end of the war, and the run of atom-doom stories from Big-Name mainstream writers and scientists, the strands began to combine and the (not-yet-quite-Boom) book breakthrough began here: the two big anthologies, *Mr. Adam*, *The Big Eye*, *The Big Ball of Wax* and Ward Moore's exciting *Greener Than You Think*. America discovered Kafka and Graham Greene, *Charm* and *Mademoiselle* discovered Kuttner and Bradbury. *Collier's* published Wylie's "Blunder" in 1946, and Will Jenkins's "Symbiosis" in 1947—the same year the *Post* adopted Heinlein, and introduced Gerald Kersh to American readers.

And then came Orwell.

1984 was ponderous. It was obvious. It was somewhat less than original. But it had some good catchy phrases, and it was eminently respectable, both literarily and politically. (Even Joe McCarthy had to approve—a wonderful joke with no one to laugh at it, because American readers were no more aware than Big Joe himself that the author of this great anti-Communist document was himself a leading British Socialist.) Above all, it was a bestseller.

When the *New Yorker* published a Roald Dahl science fiction story in 1949, and E. B. White himself wrote one the next year (while Paul Gallico tried his hand at it in the *Post*), the breakthrough was complete.

The new crop of American science fiction writers—the people who began in *Astounding* between 1946-48, and the new names everywhere in 1949-50—no longer had to think of themselves as literary Untouchables—or even resign themselves to a choice of poverty or part-time, insofar as s-f was concerned. Nobody except perhaps Orwell, Huxley, and Wylie—was making money on the stuff yet; but it was already possible to write with one eye on the slicks and the other on book publication, knowing the specialty magazines were there to catch everything that missed.

Once again, the right man came along at the right time. Until Boucher and McComas started *Fantasy and Science Fiction*, in 1949, the Campbell-dominated specialty field had no place in it for the kind of stories Beaumont, Budrys, Clingerman, Cogswell, Dick, Henderson, Matheson, Miller, MacDonald, Moore, Nourse, Pangborn, Tenn, Vance, Vonnegut, and a score of others began to produce—as did Asimov, Bester, Leiber, Wyndham, and others, many of whom had virtually stopped writing until the necessary new magazine came along.

Anthony Boucher's role in the emergence of American science fiction from its self-made ghetto has never, I think, been fully appreciated—except among the authors writing for him at the time.

Boucher was neither scientist, worldsaver, nor prophet. He was a man of enormous erudition, catholic interests, discriminating tastes, overweening curiosity, and rich humor—a humanist in the best and widest sense, one of the most civilized human beings it has ever been my pleasure to know. He brought literary standards and literary status, both, into the specialty field. Already well established as author and critic in the then far more respectable neighboring field of mystery and detection, he was able to attract a large segment of new readers, including a fair sprinkling of intrigued writers, publishers, influential critics, and educators. He approached his editorship with a revolutionary concept: the idea that science-fantasy (as he preferred to call the whole field of rational-imaginative-speculative fiction) *could be well written.*

Boucher carried this to an unheard-of extreme. He would not buy a story just for the idea; he had to like the writing. And unlike most earlier editors, he was not style-deaf.

Neither was Horace Gold, the first editor of *Galaxy*, which began publication the following year (1950), but he was more deeply rooted in the traditions of the field. (Both men, by the way, first entered the field through Campbell's *Unknown.* And here is another curious bypath for those scholars-to-come: the re-mergence of the author-editor in s-f, at a time when the phenomenon had virtually disappeared from publishing.) Gold would not buy for idea *alone*, but he would settle for just-competent writing when the idea appealed enough (or do some heavy rewriting himself—one of the factors that eventually lost a number of *Galaxy* names to *F&SF*). What appealed to Gold was important, because it provided a counterweight to Campbell's restrictions.

Galaxy wanted psychiatric stories and social satires: no one could have written "Baby Is Three" (the core of *More Than Human*), for instance, or *The Demolished Man* or *The Space Merchants* for *Astounding*.

Galaxy was an immediate favorite among science fiction fans. It had Sturgeon, Heinlein, Leiber, and Bester almost exclusively for several years, and among the newer writers, Tenn, Pangborn, Kornbluth and Pohl. But what at first seemed marvelous freedom turned out to be as limiting (from the opposite end) as writing for Campbell. More and more, writers with fresh ideas and serious intentions turned to *F&SF*: there was one unbelievable period when Boucher, paying exactly half the word-rate of either of the other Big Three, was getting first submissions from a sizeable majority of the top names in the field.

Possibly the most significant thing about Boucher (equivalent to the importance of the word "engineer" applied to Campbell) was his respect for the manifold meanings of "literature": the history and traditions, the exercise of the craft, the working body of authors. His literary requirements were as powerful an attraction to writers as his sensitive critiques. (It was a not-quite-joke among writers that Boucher's letters of rejection could be more encouraging than another editor's checks.) And the writers, new and old, s-f specialists and names from all over, responded. (Most startling were people like Mack Reynolds, Philip José Farmer, Chad Oliver, Mark Clifton—idea-men, "Teacher-story" writers, who could not be bothered, elsewhere, with more than putting their thoughts down in competent language; when they published in *F&SF* it turned out they could *write*, too.)

Boucher's function as book reviewer was no less important than as editor. He had, at least part of the time, brilliant competition. For many fans, Damon Knight was the preferred critic; for others, William Atheling. But for the writers, it was Boucher's accolade that counted, and for thousands of new readers of s-f books, it was Boucher's guidance they trusted.

I said earlier that science fiction today is catching up with science: Anthony Boucher was the dominant force in the fifties when science fiction began to catch up with fiction.

Then, as had been true with Campbell, Boucher's special qualification became his limiting factor. He was the first editor in the field—perhaps the only one in this country who understood the specialty field as a phenomenon in the history of literature. Even in the first few years of *F&SF*, at the height of the magazine boom (there were more than thirty magazine titles in 1952) with his own publication the acknowledged prestige leader. Boucher had few illusions about the viability of the specialty field, or of the magazines in particular. His views on "The Publishing of Science Fiction" are on record, along with those of John W. Campbell and several other distinguished persons, in a symposium, *Modern Science Fiction*, edited by Reginald Bretnor (Coward-McCann, 1953).

Boucher anticipated a dropping-off of magazine popularity in favor of books, and a gradual re-union of the side-stream with the mainstream of literature. He saw the relationship of the category to the large body of fiction as an almost exact parallel with another category, detective fiction, whose development and specialized audience were in many ways similar. His blind spot was in his failure to recognize the essential element of opposition in the two fields.

As humanist and true aficionado of literature, Boucher was also something of a classicist: the forms and styles of fiction delighted him for their own sake. His emphasis was as much on science-*fiction*, as Campbell's was on *science*-(technology)-fiction. (By my way of thinking, Boucher had more comprehension of science, in the modern sense, than Campbell did—but it was less important to him. On the form/content seesaw, he counter-balanced Gold: Boucher would always settle for just-adequate thinking if the writing was good enough.) From the beginning *F&SF* suffered somewhat from a tendency to select for the elegant and stylistic (and occasionally precious) rather than the vigorous.

This emphasis was desperately needed in 1950. It was what made Boucher the right man at the right time. And it is what makes his influence, fifteen years later, almost as restrictive in its way as Campbell's. Boucher, or Boucher-as-was, is probably still the dominating influence on the specialty field here. What might have happened had he stayed with the magazine is hard to tell: I rather doubt that Boucher (1966) would be exerting the same subtly retarding force that the still-honored image of Boucher (1956) does today. But—with all due respect to some excellent editors since then (notably Robert P. Mills, Cele Goldsmith Lalli, Fred Pohl, and increasingly now, Ed Ferman)—there has been no sustained influence of equal intensity in this country since Anthony Boucher retired, and his editorial ghost is by now not an unrestricted asset.

The Boom, as such, broke in 1955. Book titles dropped off, but not all the way, and not for long. The marginal magazines folded, one after another—and stayed folded. Yet the list of stories appearing in general periodicals grew steadily year by year.

Today American science fiction supports only seven titles, two of which are reprint magazines and two bi-monthlies—thus, only four new-material magazines a month. But there is hardly a publication in which fiction appears at any time in any form—newspapers, trade journals, house organs, men's magazines, women's magazines, literary reviews, *every*thing—in which s-f does not sometimes appear. And the big market is still in books. The specialty magazines no longer dominate, or even represent, the genre.

All of this is much as Boucher, and Bretnor, foresaw it fifteen years ago. What they did not foresee was the back-water swirl of conservatism that would engulf the field in America in the first years of respectability, burying most of what was original or truly speculative in a flood of polished mediocrity and formularized paperback pap. They saw the specialty field remaining as a nucleus, and a breeding-ground for new writers (which it is), but not as the sad manifestation of a mystique-turned-cult; symptomatic are the interminable "series" stories, featuring the patterned exploits of a Beloved Character, and the long articles treating minor, and already unreadable, authors of twenty or thirty years ago as "master" writers of "classic" stories.

Nor could anyone have anticipated, fifteen years ago, the emergence of a British specialty field as a major force, not only in s-f but increasingly in contemporary British writing and publishing. (The tiny market in the UK supports two magazines a month, plus a modest distribution of the American magazines, and a paperback market as flourishing as our own.)

Reginald Bretnor came closer than anyone else. His own essay in *Modern Science Fiction*, "The Future of Science Fiction," still ranks as the outstanding critical insight into the nature and direction of the genre. It falls short, even today, only in its failure to specify the influence of certain forces outside the field. Bretnor saw, and described, the *shape* of the influences: he simply failed to identify the names and faces.

⚛

As it happens, Bretnor and Boucher are fairly-near neighbors in Berkeley, California; professionally and personally, they are congenial, with much in common in tastes and attitudes. Their expressed views in 1952 varied little in surface applicability, but radically in underlying philosophy.

Boucher was discussing the place in literature of an area of fiction whose special province is science; Bretnor was thinking about a fiction form emerging from the interaction between science and literature, and possibly embodying some synthesis of the two. "The emergence of science fiction as a genre," he stated as his first premise, "is rooted in our failure to understand the scientific method and to define it adequately for the average individual and the average scientist." And, second, "Science fiction is not a genre. Its scope is universal. It holds the promise of an entire new literature."

Some of his predictions:

(1) To say that science fiction holds within itself the seed of an entire new literature does not mean that science fiction as we know it, *is* that literature. Nor does it mean that we can now foretell the exact forms that literature will take when it evolves from science fiction *and* non-science fiction....

(2) ...The impossibility of stretching the "old maps" to fit the new terrain, or of preserving them by trying to exclude it, will become constantly more obvious. The unperceptive reader will react to this as he is reacting now, but even more intensely; he will demand and get, on levels appropriate to his own complexity, stronger and stronger "emotional shock" values in his non-science fiction....

(3) All fiction derives from the experience of reality. All fiction creates imaginary times, imaginary worlds, to be experienced only through acts of "the imagination." And the subjective reality of fiction depends, not on the spacio-temporal coordinates assigned to it, but on the author's direct or indirect experience of reality, on his frames of reference for the interpretation of reality, on his ability to abstract and synthesize fictional experiences, and on his selection of symbolic media capable of evoking these experiences completely for his readers.

(4) Therefore, the "serious" writer of non-science fiction...will find that the expansion of his frames of reference will neither force him to write about the future nor forbid him to write about "the present" and the past. If he determines to write science fiction as we know it now, he will learn that a hypothetical future is merely an interesting and plausible device particularly well suited to the presentation of those human problems and experiences promised by the nature of the scientific method and *by* its continued exercise. He will see that it is possible to write science fiction set in "the present" or the past—possible, and sometimes necessary, and usually just a bit more difficult.

(5) Eventually, we will again have an integrated literature. It will owe much, artistically, to non-science fiction. But its dominant attitudes and purposes...will have evolved from those of modern science fiction....

It is the evolution of that literature that I am discussing here. It has not yet achieved a distinctive form. It is, possibly, just now experiencing the inception of its first "Movement"—but up till now it has had not even that much cohesiveness. Yet, I presume to believe that I can see its directions, and recognize some of its early practitioners, and identify some of its immediate antecedents.

Only to the extent that I am able to do so does this essay become more than an annotation of Bretnor's earlier one. His thinking influenced me so strongly that I frankly did not realize, until I went back to the book for the references here, how closely I had paralleled his structure and reasoning, considering the state of science and the state of fiction as prerequisites to an appraisal of the state of science fiction. Our conclusions are very much the same; the difference up to this point has been only in the perspective of fifteen years, which has allowed me to fill in detail, and verify predictions.

In what follows, I am dealing with events-in-process, events moreover in which I myself am involved. I have not attempted to analyze the literature of the Boucher period as I did that of the preceding decade; I do not have sufficient perspective as yet to do anything but describe the overall mood and direction—or alternatively, itemize memorable individual stories, of which there were a great many during the fifties. In approaching the events of the sixties, I cannot begin to be comprehensive, and shall not attempt it.

Since Walter Miller redefined the term in 1959 with *A Canticle for Leibowitz* (which may be thought of as the climax of the "Boucher Period"), the number and diversity of *good s-f novels* is such as to require a complete essay in itself. There is no brief characterizing discussion possible of a collection of books which includes, for example, *The Child Buyer*, *Nova Express*, *Stranger in a Strange Land*, *Flowers for Algernon*, *The Crystal World*, *A Clockwork Orange*, *Dorsai!*, *Journey beyond Tomorrow*, *Cat's Cradle*, *The Wanderer*, *The Genocides*, etc.

One becomes involved not only in questions of style, approach, and treatment, but subject matter. The line of definition between "science" and "non-science" is difficult to find when stories and newspapers both are full of talk of the chemical treatment of emotional disorders, and psychiatric cures for somatic malfunctions; "subjective time"; "computer art" (and music and poetry); the Theory of Games (with its statistical predictions of human behavior); "brainwashing" (a precise technological/psychiatric operation, involving chemical, electronic, semantic, and physiological components); or even the existence of the "Think Tanks" as a growing facet of industry and government. ("R&D man" rolls off the tongue disturbingly like "R&A Director" or "R&B band.")

But in all this I believe I can see a direction—not of "science fiction," but of the "new literature" emergent from it. And again, because it is new, and still formative, it would take as much space to discuss, in any useful manner, the still very small body of work involved as to cover all the rest of the field since 1960. I am not going to attempt to define, explain, explicate, or justify any of the work I mention in this section. As with my first listing of the antecedents of "science fiction," I am only pointing to a location. In the first case, it was an area determined by much past discussion and definition-seeking. Here it is an area existing more in my own intuition, perhaps, than anywhere else.

Bretnor specified three "attitudes" of science fiction as significant in the role he predicted for it: "(1) it is not self-restrictive; nor is it restrictive of its readers; (2) it is not a literature of false dichotomies, conventionalized; (3) it is integrative." (The meaning of these attitudes is implicit in the following paragraphs.)

> In writing, as in the other arts, there have been a number of responses to the problem posed by the new complexity of knowledge and the breakdown of the older synthesis. Characteristic of almost all of these, especially in this century, is a peculiar process which can quite accurately be called the intellectual renunciation of "the intellect." Actually, this rebellion against "reason" is a revolt against the scientific method, reason's cold instrument in the old scheme of things. It is a revolt prompted by the failure to understand, and by a fear of the un-understandable. It has varied in degree; it has been more or less conscious, more or less deliberate. It has included such seemingly diverse phenomena as the complete Dadaist denial, the Existentialist dramatization of fashionable despair, and a highly verbalized insistence on restrictive neo-Aristotelian frames of literary reference which themselves are a retreat from the Aristotelian balance of the Renaissance. The trend, in our most "serious" fiction, has been increasingly toward a focus of all emphasis on "the emotions," on "feeling" rather than on "thought"—as though the two were mutually antagonistic and mutually exclusive.

And later:

> To science fiction, man is the proper study of the writer—man, and everything man does and thinks and dreams, and everything man builds, and everything of which he may become aware—his theories and his things, his quest into the universe, his search into himself, his music and his mathematics and his machines. All these have human value and validity, for they are of man.

Let me rephrase the opening of that last paragraph slightly: "Man is the *proper* study of any artist—man and" ...etc. Call it the Bretnor-Merril Uncertainty Principle; you cannot define or describe a man except in terms of the universe of which he is aware; you cannot define or describe the universe except in terms of man's orientation within it.

This is what I meant when I said at the beginning, "Art at any time can achieve validity only if it is rooted in the accumulated human experience of its day, and touches somewhere on the nerve center of the culture from which it springs." It is still possible today to read Greek drama and Elizabethan poetry with delight; it is *not* possible for a modern writer to create Greek drama or Elizabethan poetry—only to imitate them. I refer not only to the mutability of language and form, but to a complete cultural complex. In our culture, within the last quarter century, purely technological accomplishments have radically altered (though not *quite* erased) the meaning of a phrase like "American literature." The young American writer today is likely to owe as much to Kafka or Kierkegaard as to Whitman and Emerson. In the same way, our culture today—not "American" or "Indonesian" or "Eskimo," but our increasingly global culture—is inescapably involved with the implications of modern scientific thought; if not with its philosophy, then at the very least, with its artifacts and their influence on human existence. In the arts, as in the sciences, the conflict between the response to the new challenges, and the reaction against them, is still raging; and within the growing ranks of those who have begun to accept the new concepts there is further inevitable experimental dissension.

An explosive experimental dissidence was in progress when Boucher and Bretnor were writing their respective essays in 1952. Between Berkeley and North Beach, the distance is short and the traffic is heavy; but between pre-*Sputnik* science fiction and the pre-Burroughs Beats, there were no bridges of any sort to span a distance no one on either side thought worth measuring.

I claim no prescience here; I didn't take the San Francisco scene seriously enough to do more than glance at a few pages. But I must add I had done little more with the big guns of the twentieth century literary revolution. The fact is, I did not know that Jack Kerouac or Henry Miller, *or* James Joyce represented anything more revolutionary than the Great Obscenity Rebellion—on which ground I distantly approved of them. (Remember, I was the Noble Savage at large in the world of Literature—nor am I sure how much I have changed since.) The only real difference I saw between (what I have since learned to call) the *avant garde* and the Establishment was what appeared to be a greater facility with language and more attention to form in the latter group; but my indifference to Faulkner and Eliot was almost as massive. I simply was not *disenchanted.* Dis-involvement, "alienation," the "search for identity"—the whole "cool" scene—were, and are, so foreign to my outlook (and my concern with writing, in particular) that I rejected all of it, even in its most elegant forms.

I do not mean to present my own benighted state as representative of science fiction. Bretnor, Boucher, Knight, Blish, and a good many other critical observers were able to make educated distinctions between the varieties of literary experimentalists (they certainly did not, like me, confuse the *New Yorker* with *New Directions*). Obviously, Bretnor neither ignored what was happening across the Bay, nor dismissed it as cursorily as I.

But dismiss it he did—we did—validly, I think, insofar as it related to "science fiction." Or any fiction.

The one thing I did know by then was fiction. I had been reading it for twenty-five years, and writing it for seven, and by that time I knew what made it work, and what worked *in* it—and even a little about writing (as distinct from selling) it. I think I speak for an overwhelming majority of the other writers I knew when I add that fiction was the only prose form that mattered; you might do other things for the exercise, or for the money. You might write an exquisite prose style, or create unforgettable characters, but if you couldn't tell a story, you were simply out of it.

And the stuff they were doing on the bongo beaches—or on the Left Bank—just wasn't in it for fiction—wasn't and *isn't.* No matter whose rules you're playing, projection, not involution, is what stories are made of. Fiction is not poetry slowed down; it is drama spread out. Some narrative poems are also fiction, and some great fiction is also, in large part, poetry. In the hands of a good writer, a drama too subtle or complex to make a good stage-play may be a great story humor particularly (aside from slapstick) lends itself more readily to the flat-page technique than to the stage, where there is no technique equivalent to prose narrative for distortion of perspective. But stage or page, comic strip or Greek chorus, the only thing you cannot dispense with in story telling is externalized dramatic action. It can be realistic, symbolized, dreamlike, anticipatory, remembered; it may be witnessed, experienced, heard-of, imagined. It may illustrate any theme, convey any mood, dramatize any insight, act out any idea. It may have two characters or three or four or, rarely, more. (Almost always, when you get past three, they fall into alignments and groups, becoming for purposes of the *story*, two or three composite figures. But it cannot have *one*.

There are stories with only one person on stage, and a few with only one person evident: but when that happens, some part of the environment acquires an animistic character. (Back in the wings a Manichean devil chuckles wickedly at the protagonist's efforts to overcome malicious—or malignantly indifferent—nature.)

There is no protagonist without an antagonist; in a story the confrontation between the two is acted out. Given these two basics, you may be as subtle or interior or stalemating as you please; you may not have a *popular* story, but you will still have a story. With less than those two essentials, it may be poetry, it may be essay, it may be monologue; it is not drama, and not fiction.

Psychiatric introspection makes fiction only when it involves remembered drama, symbolized drama, or delusional drama; a recital of symptoms, like a travelogue, may be frightening, fascinating, even beautiful, but it is not a *story*. Equally, the Battle between Good and Evil—or Life and Death—or Man and Woman—becomes drama instead of treatise only when the principles become principals, capable of *acting out* the conflict.

Obsessive introspection and agonizing reappraisals of morality seemed to be the whole range of subject matter for the serious science-fiction writers, and they did not seem to know how to turn this stuff into *story*.

The Beats of course were not trying to write fiction. I don't believe it ever occurred to me, in 1952, that they might be trying *not* to write fiction. (If the idea crossed my mind, it would have been as an example of absurd perversity.)

As for the "literary" types, the Quarterly and Review writers, the backbone of *Atlantic* and *Harper's* and *New Yorker*, they were trying all right, and mostly doing a poor job of it. Their diction was graceful and their insights often profound, but they (literally) did not seem to know which way was up—by which I mean, they wrote in limbo, not on Earth, nor elsewhere in any real or sharply imagined universe. In this, it seemed to me, they could claim no distinction from the slick women's magazine writers or comic strip continuity writers.

The Beats seemed to me a crude, sometimes grotesque, malformed variety of the Establishment Litterateurs. I have no doubt at all that that is exactly how science fiction looked when viewed from North Beach. Oppositely oriented, there was not sufficient interest in either rebel camp to discover how similar our views of the middle really were. To the literary-artistic *avant garde*, science fiction's struggle for literary respectability, for acceptance by the very Establishment they had contemptuously abandoned, gave us a clownish aspect; their attempt at total rejection of modern technological society made our determined involvement with its dynamics look like a crude, sometimes grotesque, malformed variety of 19th century "materialism." They were too involved with the dynamics of meaning and expression, and the search for new modes of language and literature appropriate to the ambivalences and relativistic realities of modern life, to concern themselves with unorthodox experiments in interpretation of these realities, or with any philosophy more complex than existentialism. Our rockets and planets and alien creatures, unconnected with their immediate realities, appeared as absurd caricature-symbols of (not just "neurotic" but) childish "escapism." To us, their howls and bongo rhythms and cut-up-fold-ins were, just as obviously, the rococo entertainments of sterile decadence. We were much too intent on communicating our intellectual insights to have time or patience for experiments in unorthodox form.

Bretnor's view of "science" and "non-science" fiction suffered from the same limitation afflicting most "mainstream" critiques of s-f; it contrasted the *best* science fiction with the *bulk* of the rest. When he attacked the "anti-intellectualism" of "non-science" fiction, he was penetrating and accurate; but when he claimed an "integrative, non-restrictive" nature for s-f, he was talking about what he knew it could and should be—not what, for the most part, it was, or is.

There were people, in 1952, who understood emotionally/intellectually that both intellectual/emotional components of man were indivisibly meaningful: that new ideas required new forms, that new modes of experience demanded new techniques of expression: but most of them were mathematicians, cyberneticists, and air- or space-craft designers. A very few (like Bretnor) had begun to comprehend that the same principle applied to literature, and fewer yet (I know of three) had attempted the application.

Although I did not think of it that way at the time, retrospectively, I believe I would identify Cordwainer Smith's first science fiction story, "Scanners Live in Vain" (*Fantasy Book*, 1950), as the first effective—and possibly deliberate "integrative" effort I read. The impact of the story was tremendous, and baffling. Both Fred Pohl and I recommended it promptly to Robert Heinlein for the anthology (*Tomorrow, the Stars*) he was then preparing for Doubleday. But I could not understand my own response. The piece was so "clumsily" written; the prose, the structure, the characterization—everything was subtly *wrong*. In the arguments that followed its publication, I was one of those who contended (wrongly) that "Cordwainer Smith" was not a pen-name, because the story was so "amateurish."

"Scanners" was neither the first such effort, nor the best early one: just the first *I* saw. It is a reasonable inference, since "Smith" is an accomplished linguist, and—according to his "momentary prologue" in *Space Lords* (Pyramid, 1965)—particularly fond of the French Symbolists, that when he turned to science fiction writing he was already familiar with the work of Alfred Jarry; it is almost as probable that he also knew some of Jorge Luis Borges's work.

(Boucher knew of Borges; he did the first English translation of Borges's fiction for *Ellery Queen's Mystery Magazine* in 1948: "The Circular Ruins" appeared in *New Directions*, and there were at least three others in the next five years. But Boucher used none of them, and—incredibly—overlooked, or decided against, translating "Tlön, Uqbar, Orbis Tertius" for *F&SF*.)

For most of us, however, Borges and Jarry might as well never have existed until after 1962, when Grove issued *Ficciones*, New Directions published *Labyrinths*, and *Evergreen Review* had its all-Jarry "'Pataphysics" issue; at that, it took two or three years for word-of-mouth for more than the handful of two-camp people who then existed to become aware of what had been written in Paris in 1900 and in Argentina in 1940.

To all intents and purposes, it was 1962 before American readers heard of Anthony Burgess, either—or of J. G. Ballard. Only one Ballard story appeared here before then, and I am happy to say it was his first published story, "Prima Belladonna" (from the British magazine, *Science Fantasy*), reprinted in my *Second Annual SF* in 1957.

[Nineteen fifty-seven] was also the year that David R. Bunch's strange grim short stories began to appear; he was the first writer, as far I know, to grow up with a foot in both camps. From the beginning he was published simultaneously in the "little magazines" and in *Amazing* and *Fantastic*. Post-Beat rather than Symbolist, Bunch had none of the bright-fairy-tale appeal of "Smith" (who had done nothing after "Scanners" till 1955, when "The Game of Rat and Dragon" appeared in *Galaxy*; he got into full swing only in 1958-59). Bunch is still a highly controversial figure in American s-f—and I think almost unknown in England.

R. M. McKenna's "Casey Agonistes" came out in 1958. Again, the impact was explosive; but this time we were a little more ready, a little more knowledgeable—and McKenna was available for comment. He knew exactly what he was doing, and was able to convey a great deal of it to other writers.

A diffused cumulative influence began to be visible in 1958-59 with tentative approaches to the new direction like Carol Emshwiller's "Pelt," Knight's "The Handler," Leiber's "Mariana," Sturgeon's "The Man Who Lost the Sea." The next year, Vance Aandahl emerged suddenly from nowhere (and apparently returned there, after three years of ill-received exciting new work). That same year Brian Aldiss's "Shards" and "Old Hundredth" appeared here. In 1961, it was R. A. Lafferty, with a bright humorous streak that made his approach more acceptable to the magazine audience.

And we are back at 1962, when Thomas Disch and Roger Zelazny began publishing strange provocative stories in *Amazing* and *Fantastic.*

There have been others since—Norman Kagan and Sonya Dorman, most recently—but most of what has happened has not been in the American science fiction magazines, at all.

I do not know exactly when William Burroughs's influence began to make itself felt among the Post-Beat writers here—or whether there were other influences inside the group preceding him. But by 1962, the San Francisco little magazines were experimenting—wildly, sometimes satirically, not often successfully—with their own "integrations," a good deal more consciously and enthusiastically than "science fiction" as a whole. Out of that group and/or affected by its widespread influence, began to come a steady trickle of stories, appearing most frequently in the better men's magazines (*Cavalier*, *Escapade*, sometimes *Playboy*, the late lamented *Nugget*), and in *Mademoiselle*, and *The New Yorker*.

And, of course, there have been others: a scattered handful of stories approaching the same area from the Establishment end, or simply developing independently in the obviously appropriate direction for our times: George P. Elliott, John Anthony West, Donald Barthelme, John Updike, and most notably Kurt Vonnegut. But the main stream of the new integration has not been in this country, at all.

⚛

The shortest route across the Golden Gate turned out to be by way of England. That it should have developed mainly in E. J. Carnell's magazines is appropriately absurd for modern writing. That I should have been a box-seat observer was pure happenstance.

At least six different s-f magazines were started in England and Scotland between 1949 and 1955: the two that survived were *New Worlds* and *Science Fantasy* (now *Impulse*), both founded and edited (until 1964) by Carnell.

Carnell was a latter-day Gernsback—but it was not only another time, but another country—and besides, Technocracy was dead. Carnell had the same energetic optimism about science fiction, the same persistent evangelical streak, something of the same sort of curiously innocent capacity for astonishment by the world's wonders as Gernsback did—and the same head for business, as well as a remarkably similar indifference to, or unawareness of, literary technique.

Also he had a vanishingly small budget, and one of the things he did about it was to turn agent on the side. From the time he heard about my Annuals, Carnell was sending me stories—anything he thought I might *possibly* like; shortly afterwards, he began sending me the magazines regularly.

Once again, I must avoid attempting an inadequate history or appraisal of the development of what is now a conscious, if somewhat elliptical infant "movement," centered around *New Worlds*, under the editorship of Michael Moorcock, *and* around a point in space in British poetry determined by the relative positions of Peter Redgrove, George MacBeth, D. M. Thomas, Bill Butler, *Ambit* magazine, a bookshop called Better Books, and I don't-know-how-many other factors. (I hope to accomplish a more knowledgeable survey when I complete an anthology of the British "new wave" now in preparation for Doubleday." [*England Swings SF*, 1968]) But there is no doubt that the outstanding figure in this movement is J. G. Ballard, both in terms of his own work, and of the influence he wields.

I have discussed Ballard's work at considerable length in a review of his two most recent books (*The Crystal World*, 1966; *The Impossible Man and Other Stories*, 1966) in the August 1966, issue of *Fantasy and Science Fiction*. Some of what I had to say there, while primarily applicable to Ballard, could be generalized to serve as a description of the nature of the "new literature" I see emerging:

> Because he has borrowed so much from the surrealists, and works for direct conveyance of concepts (however abstruse) through imagery, sensory clues, symbology, and associative language and structure, rather than overtly verbalized intellectualizations, it is easy to think of Ballad as the unconscious purveyor of potent magic-in-fantasy. To some small extent, this is probably true.... But for the most part, he is an intensely conscious and purposeful speculative writer, and the modes he elects to use are those best suited to his vital interest in the philosophic basis of the contemporary revolutions in both scientific thinking and artistic expression. He is concerned with relationships rather than isolated definitions; with the synthesis of varieties of acquired knowledge, rather than the further dissection or analysis of the parts; with the opposites to be found in apparent equalities, and the identities to be derived from contrasts. The most recent stories are reaching toward a slightly different area of exploration and experimentation, but the main focus of the first ten-year phase was on Time—most specifically, man's orientation in Time, in the universal flow of event, the place of the hour, or flower, or single human consciousness, in the birth-to-death movement of cosmos, planet, species, culture....
>
> Ballard climaxes his first decade as a writer—and in another sense, the first phase of his career—as a point where the criteria of genre criticism are totally inadequate to judge his work: and while most of what he has done in the last two years comes off satisfactorily (and occasionally brilliantly) under examination by the established rules of "serious" literary criticism, those rules are themselves far short of satisfactory for examination of most of his work. In the phase he now seems to be entering (to which "Terminal Beach" was a preliminary—as, five years earlier, was the far less complete "Voices of Time"), either set of standards will be about as useful as one axis on a sheet of linear graph paper for charting the course of a rocket: by using *both* axes, we can determine two dimensions of the trajectory; without some fairly sophisticated mathematics (the as-yet unformulated critical vocabulary) we have no way of indicating the third dimension.

And here, clearly, I must stop. I can deliver no comprehensive summation or resounding conclusion, because there is no adequate critical vocabulary, as yet with which to make wise statements about a literature so new-born that we hardly know how to distinguish hunger from temper from lung-exercise in its cries. Fifteen years from now, someone else will have to point out the errors and omissions.

Books (August 1966)

Almost fifteen years ago, in a critical essay on science fiction as yet unsurpassed for acute analysis or predictive accuracy, Reginald Bretnor[1] amused some readers, antagonized others, and drew vigorous agreement from a few, when he said of s-f:

It is not a genre. Its scope is universal. It holds the promise of an entire new literature.

He based his statement on a careful survey of contemporary writing and thinking, in and out of the science fiction field. I cannot take the space here to review Bretnor's article in full; I commend it heartily to anyone who can find a copy. But I want to quote two passages here in preface to a discussion of two new books which stand, I believe, at the opening gate to that "new literature":

In writing, as in the other arts, there have been a number of responses to the problem posed by the new complexity of knowledge and the breakdown of the older synthesis. Characteristic of almost all of these, especially in this century, is a peculiar process which can quite accurately be called the intellectual renunciation of "the intellect." *Actually, this rebellion against "reason" is a revolt against the scientific method, reason's cold instrument in the old scheme of things. It is a revolt prompted by the failure to understand, and by a fear of the un-understandable. It has varied in degree; it has been more or less conscious, more or less deliberate. It has included such seemingly diverse phenomena as the complete Dadaist denial, the Existentialist dramatization of fashionable despair, and a highly verbalized insistence on restrictive neo-Aristotelian frames of literary reference which themselves are a retreat from the Aristotelian balance of the Renaissance. The trend, in our most "serious" fiction, has been increasingly toward a focus of all emphasis on "the emotions," on "feeling" rather than on "thought"—as though the two were mutually antagonistic and mutually exclusive.*

And later:

To science fiction, man is the proper study of the writer—man, and *everything man does and thinks and dreams, and everything man builds, and everything of which he may become aware—his theories and his things, his quest into the universe, his search into himself, his music and his mathematics and his machine. All these have human value and validity, for they are* of *man.*

Bretnor spoke of science fiction as "integrative…not self restrictive…not a literature of false dichotomies, conventionalized…." In this, as in much of what he had to say about the specialty field *per se*, he was writing more of what science fiction should and could be than what it ordinarily is. As it turned out, his predictions concerning the move towards s-f by "mainstream" writers and publishers, and by the reading public in general, were startlingly accurate, and much more so, it has seemed, than his expectations for what would happen in the field itself. But the premises underlying his argument were more significant than any of his conclusions, and they concerned the moving spirit of our age, from which all expression in art and literature must eventually flow: the revolution in scientific thought which has replaced mechanics with dynamics, classification with integration, certainly with relativity, dualism with monism, facts with probabilities. In the arts, as in the sciences, and in our whole culture, the conflict between response to the new challenge and reaction away from it, is still raging, and within the growing ranks of those who have begun to accept the new concepts there is further inevitable experimental dissension.

But, dimly, not yet the actual shapes, but the foreshadows of emergent forms are beginning to make themselves felt. In literature, at least English language literature, the reactive forces have been vigorous and effective, but in the last decade or two, even the literary Establishment has loosened its grim clutch on dying "realism" while within the enclave of American science fiction, where the first efforts had been made, a backwater reactive swirl seemed for a while to be burying all that was original or truly speculative in a flood of polished mediocrity and formularized paperback pap.

This is still largely the case; most of even the best writers in the field do no more in the way of idea originating than filling in intricate detail on their "new maps." The literary explorers here are mostly "fringe people": writers who neither identify themselves with s-f, nor align themselves against it, but make use of its unique properties when and as needed. For various reasons, the situation in England is different: the "realism" reaction was never as strong; major writers and thinkers there began making use of s-f techniques in the thirties, instead of the fifties; the specialty field grew up in the shadow, if not the smile, of literary respectability.

Whether such background distinctions provided a more favorable atmosphere for the development of a writer like J. G. Ballard, or whether Ballard himself was a prime factor in keeping the British field from following the lead (or tail) of the regressive movement in the previously dominant American magazines, is not even a matter of importance. What does matter is that at least one fully qualified writer has now developed to occupy the position for whose description we have as yet no adequate critical language—a literary outpost rather closer to the lonely prominences of the Argentinian, Borges, the Parisian, Jarry, the Swede, Martinson, than to his closest English language neighbors (Kurt Vonnegut, William Burroughs, Cordwainer Smith, Joseph Heller, David Bunch, Anthony Burgess, are among them); somewhere in the direction that Kuttner and Moore were perhaps the first to point to from inside science fiction; the ground Sturgeon and Miller approached and abandoned; from which Aldiss and, more often, Leiber, have brought back magical reports; where McKenna had only begun exploring when he died; where, perhaps, Zelazny, Disch, Lafferty, and a growing school of young British writers (with perhaps Langdon Jones and George Collyn at the fore), may find their way.

(My apologies for any notable omissions; I did not set out to compose an honor roll, but to describe a rough circle.)

A year ago in this space, reviewing *The Drowned World* (July 1965) I said I thought Ballard "well on his way toward becoming the first truly conscious and controlled literary artist s-f has produced." It is time now to dispense with cautious qualifiers. With the publication of *The Crystal World*[2] and *The Impossible Man*[3] (his fourth novel and seventh short story collection—five in this country), Ballard climaxes his first decade as a writer—and, in another sense, the first phase of his career—at a point where the criteria of genre criticism are totally inadequate to judge his work, and while most of what he has done in the last two years comes off satisfactorily (and occasionally brilliantly) under examination by the established rules of "serious" literary criticism, those rules are themselves far short of satisfactory for examination of most of his work. In the phase he now seems to be entering (to which "Terminal Beach" was a preliminary—as, five years earlier, was the far less complete "Voices of Time"), either set of standards will be about as useful as one axis on a sheet of linear graph paper for charting the course of a rocket: by using *both* axes, we can determine two dimensions of the trajectory; without some fairly sophisticated mathematics (the as-yet unformulated critical vocabulary) we have no way of indicating the third dimension.

In a brief discussion of *The Drought* here (Jan. 1966), I said it was "a more easily readable book than *The Drowned World*, and almost certainly a better *novel*. Whether it is a better book—because Ballard does not really write novels anyhow—will take time to determine; the significance seems to keep seeping up to the surface of the mind for a long time after the book is closed." I started to write the same opening comments, almost word for word, in regard to *The Crystal World*, until memory nagged, and I checked the earlier review. The only differences would have been in the omission of the parenthetical phrase, disqualified by the publication of *CW*, which is indeed—among other things—a novel, and a good one; and in the closing thought, which would have related more to another comment in the same review: "it is becoming almost impossible to review a new book of Ballard's all by itself. The author is building from book to book, and from story to story, in such a way that although each unit is meaningful on its own terms, it assumes full dimensions only in the context of the whole body of work." This is true to varying degrees for all but a double handful of the short stories—and a first novel (*The Wind from Nowhere*, *F&SF* "Books," July 1965) which one assumes to have been Ballard's only major experiment with "writing for the market." In general, it is the richest and most rewarding stories that gain most from associative reading—and this applies above all to the curious thematic-trilogy of (for want of a better word) novels, in which *The Crystal World* serves as bridge and climax to *The Drowned World* and *The Drought*. (And by the way, for what it's worth, my feeling six months later—with only minor seepage still going on—is that *Drought* was indeed the "better book.")

CW is emphatically the best novel of the three, not only because of an observable increment in both craftsmanship and maturity, but because of its particular function in the trio. Where *Drowned World* examined time-past in terms of psychophysical and geophysical evolution—a return to the womb-of-the-world—and *Drought* explored the drying-up of life in time future from the platform of the culture complex of man's accomplishments till now, *CW* presents us with a (literally, physically) crystallized pattern of time-now—the frozen present, infinite moment, immortality in the instant of I *am*. In the first book, archetypal figures were moved by powerful blind biopsychic forces to fulfill—or reenact—their mythic roles; in the second, elaborately evolved and multi-faceted allegorical personae picked their way through an elegant/decadent choreography of desuetude and devolution on a dying earth; the third book is actively inhabited by individuals entirely alive and aware in the only moment of reality we know at all—the eternally passing present we call *now*, where the focus in space expands as time narrows down, and action shots of life in process are not only possible, but inevitable.

The twentieth-century novel is primarily concerned with the interplay of immediacies and intimacies in interpersonal relationships; in these terms, *CW* is a brilliant success compared to its companion pieces—and a respectable accomplishment relative to the general body of contemporary literature. As a speculative work—and it *is* that—only the most superficial part of its content is self-contained; the larger, and deeper, statements are to be found only in the dynamics of its relationships with the other two books and to lesser degrees, with some of the short stories.

The closely timed publication of *The Impossible Man*, containing as it does a near-complete sampling of the spectrum of Ballard's work of the last four or five years, serves as a tidy complement to the new novel. It seems unlikely that this was purposeful on the part of the publishers, since the book is obviously a cleaning up collection (leaving only two of the first-decade stories not yet in book form: "The Singing Statues," which will be in a forthcoming Doubleday collection, and a fragment, really, called "Prisoner of the Coral Deep"), but it was most fortuitously done for my purposes here, and I recommend reading them together—if of course you know where to *find* Berkley books. (In view of some of my recent remarks about Berkley, I should mention here that I *did* receive a review copy in advance of publication—and then of course I waited to discuss it in connection with the novel....)

The collection includes nine stories, three of them new, and only three previously published in this country. Between them, they cover almost all of Ballard's stylistic range, from the literary conventional "Drowned Giant" up to, but not including, the earlier examples ("Terminal Beach," "Voices of Time," etc.) of the experimental forms of his newest work; and provide a remarkably inclusive set of views of the vivid/haunting, grotesque/stark, fearsome/beautiful prospects and images of Ballard's unique and persuasive inner landscape. Here are the sand beach and desert, the waiting ocean, patient river basin, echoing wind-carved rock galleries, dark grottoes and sunlit gardens; the crumbling mansions and abandoned hotels, streaming high-speed highways and jostling crowd bodies; the stalled ship-turned-dwelling, the sand drifted ruins. Of the most familiar sights, only the biological laboratory, and the billboards and white masonry block buildings are missing, but there is a hospital, and giant canvas screens stand in for the geometries of blocks and boards. Here too are the hypnotic, brilliant insects, soundless snakes, and frightening birds; the prismatic brights and darks, the inversions of light and time and mortality. Every major theme of that first decade is somewhere here, emerging as topic in one story, deep underlay in another; almost all of them interwoven with symbols, ideas, images relating to the three novels.

It is no happenstance that the least "related" story is not only the best piece of proper fiction in the book, but probably (technical and artistically) Ballard's best short story to date. "The Drowned Giant" is almost a model of the contemporary conventional concept of short fiction. Indeed, there is a quaint academic-literary rhythm to the prose, and a formality in the narration (neither one, oddly enough, unusual for Ballard) quite sufficient to eliminate that "contemporary," if it were not for the effective use of superimposed mythical and naturalistic symbology ("Modern" since Kafka and the Melville renascence) and, more importantly, the altogether mid-century cultural mold of the community in which the drowned giant is cast up.

The story has already been selected for two major anthologies. I expect it will make itself at home in a good many more, not limited to s-f. In fact, I confess myself bewildered at its selection by the members of the SFWA for the first Nebula Awards collection, supposedly limited to "science fiction." It is a remarkably good story: superior symbolic—but not speculative—fiction, and neither by the literary snob's nor the sci-fi fan's definition, conceivably "science fiction."

"Giant" is significant *within* the context of Ballard's work primarily as an index of his literary development. Almost as though he were testing himself from time to time, a small but consistent part of Ballard's output has fallen into a special group of what can only be regarded as exercises in formal fiction. Usually on traditional "gothic science fiction" themes (appropriately updated in rationale, costume, fittings, setting, and dialogue), most of them contain rather more scientific/technological furniture than "Giant"; some of them completely satisfy the specific demands of "solid science fiction"; but where the speculative element remains, it is carefully limited: the themes are either small chunks broken off the main body, or—as with "Giant"—completely separate one-time ideas.

There have been perhaps ten such stories in the ten years (and that first, learning, novel). The other one in the current collection is "Rites of Passage," and a comparison of the two gives a clear picture of the gain in craftsmanship and control during the four-or-five year interval between them. In the meatier stories, where other kinds of impact are involved, this kind of progress is far less consistent.

It is quite reasonable to assume that the surface of the prose was best tended in these more formal stories simply because they *are* closer to the surface—intellectualizations of concepts, rather than dimensional images, the almost single-handed work of the Professional who is one of the essential personalities of the complete writer. It is the Prophet whose vision informs the work, the Poet who conveys the vision; the Professional (if he is strong enough) maintains a balance between them, and (if he is even stronger) learns enough from both of them so that he is increasingly able, on occasion, to function without their active participation. (When he starts feeling too strong, he sometimes decides to do without the others altogether—but *that* lecture is for other authors, not Ballard.)

"Passage" and "Giant" are the only stories in the book that are less than uniquely and specifically (the composite) Ballard. On the opposite end of the spectrum are "The Gioconda of the Twilight Noon" (1964) and "The Impossible Man" (new in this book), both containing some of the most powerful symbolic punches Ballard ever pulled: or perhaps "pulled" is the wrong word. The title story is sharply thought-provoking, and "Gioconda"—almost a straight interior fantasy "psychological story"—is powerful, ugly, fragmentary, and unforgettable. But both are extreme instances of the "incomplete" story—perhaps "unbalanced" is most accurate, in terms of my Poet and Prophet analogy arid in both cases, I believe, for the same reason: these stories belong thematically to the "second phase," which Ballard is only now beginning to be able to cast into appropriate forms. (There is a string of these irritating, fascinating, *almost* and *a-bit-too-much* stories, going back at least six years to "Manhole 69" and "The Waiting Grounds." These, more than any others, enrich each other, and gain both abstract meaning and human impact from relation to each other, and to the main body of work.)

Because he has borrowed so much from the surrealists, and works for direct conveyance of concepts (however abstruse) through imagery, sensory clues, symbology, and associative language and structure, rather than overtly verbalized intellectualizations, it is easy to think of Ballard as the unconscious purveyor of potent magic-in-fantasy. To some small extent, this is probably true, in the side-stream of "pre-writings" represented most powerfully here by "Gioconda." But for the most part, he is an intensely conscious and purposeful speculative writer, and the modes he elects to use are those best suited to his vital interest in the philosophic basis of the contemporary revolutions in both scientific thinking and artistic expression. He is concerned with relationships, rather than isolated definitions; with the synthesis of varieties of acquired knowledge, rather than the further dissection or analysis of the parts; with the opposites to be found in apparent equalities, and the identities to be derived from contrasts. The most recent stories are reaching toward a slightly different area of exploration and experimentation, but the main focus of the first ten-year phase was on Time—most specifically, man's orientation in the universal flow of event, the place of the hour, or flower, or single human consciousness, in the birth-to-death movement of cosmos, planet, species, culture.

"The Reptile Enclosure" (1963), "The Delta at Sunset" (1964), and "Storm-Bird, Storm-dreamer" and "The Day of Forever" (both new here) are all directly in this central flow, each closely related in theme, structure, imagery or style to one or more of the three novels. "Storm-bird" actually takes some of the same characters and one setting from *The Drought*, engaging them in an entirely different symbolic expression of the same compression of future time:

> *At dawn the bodies of the great birds shone in the damp light of the marsh, their grey plumage hanging in the still water like fallen clouds. Each morning when Crispin went out onto the deck of the picket ship he would see the birds lying in the creeks and waterways where they had died two months earlier, their wounds cleansed now by the slow current, and he would watch the white-haired woman who lived in the empty house below the cliff walking by the river. Along the narrow beach the huge birds, larger than condors, lay at her feet. As Crispin gazed at her from the bridge of the picket ship she moved among them, now and then stooping to pluck a feather from the outstretched wings. At the end of her walk, when she returned across the damp meadow to the empty house, her arms would be loaded with immense white plumes.*

The same boat, the same river, the same woman with even the same name, Catherine York—though Quilter of the book becomes Quimby here, and Crispin is not at all Dr. Ransom. Feathers for sand drifts, and a chain reaction of hormone-forced crops and giant birds instead of a molecular chain sealing off the seas—how many ways to tell evolutionary time? But it is a different world, and suddenly, it is *not* after all the same woman who bears the same name and appearance.

If you have not read *The Drought*, I imagine you will find "Storm-Bird" exotic, exciting, provocative, chilling, and memorable. If you have read *The Drought*, you may well feel as I did, naggingly irritated at first, partly with what seems sheer author's laziness, partly at the off-center, out-of-focus feeling each time something different turns out the same, or something clearly the same proves different after all; but sometime before you have finished, the new and old have vibrated into place together, leaving a slight double-vision blur whose net effect is somehow to intensify credibility far beyond the limits of sharp clarity of visualization; and you will approach the final impossible confrontation with almost unbearable awareness of the loving urgency of loneliness in guilt on one side, and the unmoving ineradicable hope of the hopelessly victimized, across the river. The effect is purely explosive.

"Enclosure" and "Delta" are less closely aligned to any one of the novels, though both are closer to the regressive *Drowned World* than the *Drought* end-game. I would venture a guess that "Enclosure" was written a good bit earlier than its 1963 publication (as "The Sherrington Theory") in *Amazing*: the idea so dominates the treatment that it seems much more like one of the "unbalanced" first approaches than something written *after* the return to the sea of *Drowned World*. As for "Delta"—I have read this story at least half a dozen times since I first saw it in the British *Terminal Beach* collection last fall, and I still do not know what it is, in a story that seems unextraordinary *between* readings, that moves me as strongly each time.

"Day of Forever" appears to be a variant handling of the basic concepts of *Crystal World*, somewhat after the manner of "Storm-Bird" and *Drought*, but except for some vivid scene setting and evocative premise-stating (*At Columbine Sept Heures it was always dusk...the time whose hands were almost frozen on the dozen clocks. The dead clocks that stared down from the municipal towers and deserted towns were the unique flora of the desert, the unused keys that would turn the way into his dreams...*) it seemed to me that all the author had to say had already been stated more strongly, and more subtly, in the novel, or for that matter in the earlier novelette, "The Illuminated Man" (*F&SF*, Jan. 1964) that was actually the first version of *CW*.

In many ways, the story that has most to offer toward all enhancement of the values of the novel is the much earlier "Screen Game"; but it would not matter which novel I was talking about, because this is a Vermilion Sands story.

Nothing I have said about the development of Ballard's work applies here. It is not uncommon for a young writer, in his first or near-first work, to produce one piece far beyond his actual capacity, not to be equaled or surpassed until years and volumes have gone by. And if he has the patience and persistence to work back to a conscious, controlled, possession of that initial power, it often turns out on later analysis that the early reputation maker had somewhere in it the seeds of every mode, thought, construct, in the author's later work. The phenomenon is, for some reason, unusually apparent, in science fiction.

Ballard has come a long way in ten years. He has already regained and passed by his first burst of power. His very latest stories even show indications of style, and perhaps content as well, that were not germinating ten years ago. But in all the work of that first ten years, I do not think one can find anything that did not first see the light of print in *Vermilion Sands*.

It was inevitable, I suppose, that if other authors write one such story, Ballard would write five, but he was traditional enough at least so that his first published story was one of the five: "Prima Belladonna" (which I am happy to say introduced Ballard to American readers, in my *Second Annual SF*) began:

> *I first met Jane Ciracylides during the Recess, that world slump of boredom, lethargy and high summer which carried us all so blissfully through ten unforgettable years....*

In the first page, the Vermilion Sands atmosphere is indelibly established. The narrator owns a "music shop" just off Beach Drive. He is sitting on the balcony of his apartment, upstairs from the shop, with two friends, an architect and a ceramicist,...*yarning and playing i-Go, a sort of decelerated chess which was popular then....*

> *I usually put a couple of hours in at the shop each morning, getting off the orders and turning the beer.*
>
> *One particularly hot lazy day I'd just finished wrapping up a delicate soprano mimosa wanted by the Hamburg Oratorio Society when Harry phoned down from balcony.*
>
> *"Parker's Chloro-Flora?"*

As for Jane: *The gossips at Vermilion Sands soon decided there a good deal of mutant in her, because she had a rich patina-golden skin and what looked like insects for eyes.*

If you do not already know the story, it is in Berkley's 1962 collection, *Billenium*, and will be reprinted next year in Doubleday's *Vermilion Sands* collection. Meantime, we have "Screen Game," and Emerelda, whose insects were real, and jewelled, at Lagoon West, *where the highway forks to Red Beach and Vermilion Sands.... Only a year earlier this had been a well-kept private road, but the ornamental gateway lay collapsed to one side, and the guardhouse was a nesting place for scorpions and sand rays.*

> *...we followed the road as it wound like a petrified snake above the reefs.... A few abstract sculptures stood by the roadside. Once these were sonic, responding to the slipstream of a passing car with a series of warning vibrators, but now the Lincoln passed them unrecognized.*
>
> *...the tires cut softly through the cerise sand, and soon we were overrunning what appeared to be the edge of an immense chess hoard of black and white marble squares...the huge wreck of Lagoon West passed us slowly on our left. Its terraces and balconies were deserted, and the once marble-white surface was streaked and lifeless. Staircases ended abruptly in midflight, and the floors hung like sagging marquees....*

Ballard once described Vermilion Sands as an "exotic suburb" of his mind; if so, he is an exotic suburbanite (which is not far from the truth either), because here above all is where we find the merging-place of all the extremes and opposites in the sand sea, light dark, freezing burning alternatives of Ballard's "inner landscape." In Vermilion Sands, the weather is always brilliant or storm-wracked, or both at once, but never mild, and all vistas are surrealist compositions. In "Screen Game" in particular—besides Emerelda, the woman-on-the-balcony, the sensual-untouchable, ice-sheathed sex symbol of *Drowned World*—the shifting screens and painted flats deceive the eye (and "I") in preparation for the flat-walled bunker-maze in "Terminal Beach"; the double-level allegorical-character construction of *The Drought* starts here with Charles Van Stratten's reasons for financing the *avant garde* film, *Aphrodite '70;* and insects head-set with rubies and emeralds presage the trees and birds and fabulous crocodiles of *The Crystal World.*

It would seem time, and past time, to say something about *CW* itself. I have done nothing else, really. Its significance as a speculative work—or as science fiction, if you prefer, because both in the basic Bretnorian sense, and in the casual meaning of the term, it is that—is to be found essentially in its position in relation to the other work I have discussed. Its peculiar enchantment can no more survive discussion and dissection than can any magic. I have marked endless passages in the book for quoting—but it seemed more important to use the space in other ways. Many of you will already have read "The Illuminated Man," in which the novel itself was almost entirely undeveloped, but the images, the settings and symbols, the taste and texture were already close to complete. Two brief bits, then—the one the author himself chose to preface the book with, and one on that crazy crocodile:

> *By day fantastic birds flew through the petrified forest, and jeweled crocodiles glittered like heraldic salamanders on the banks of the crystalline river. By night the illuminated man raced among the trees, his arms like golden cartwheels, his head like a spectral crown....*

> *...As he paused by the boat feeling the crystals along its sides, a huge four-legged creature half-embedded in the surface lurched forwards through the crust.... Its jaws mouthed the air silently as it struggled on its hooked legs, unable to clamber more than a few inches from the hollow trough in its own outline now filling with a thin trickle of water. Invested by the glittering light that poured from its body, the crocodile resembled a fabulous armorial beast. Its blind eyes had been transformed into immense crystalline rubies. It lunged toward him again, and Dr. Sanders kicked its snout, scattering the wet jewels that choked its mouth....*

As for the usual reviewers' things to say, I could tell you that this is a book about the transformation of time and light into matter, or about the psychophysiological implications of leprosy (Dr. Sanders, the protagonist, is a doctor attached to a leprosarium) or discuss the sharp divisions into black-and-white, dark-and-bright, that run through the book. I could tell you about Dr. Sanders's relations with the two women (dark and bright), or talk about the conflict between the desire for immortality and the drive to self-immolation. But to expand on these is not only unnecessary, it is destructive. Ballard's particular artistry is his ability to present composites, to work with harmonics. Rephrasing his statements, recasting his images, isolating individual notes, can do nothing but reduce their effectiveness.

I could make critical noises, admiring his phrase, "the dark side of the sun," deploring his reliance on certain descriptives (most notably, "like a Fabergé gem"), or discuss his relationship to Hawthorne, for instance, or his debt to the Surrealists. But these are trivia—the sort of thing scholars may find it worth saying in twenty years, if Ballard goes ahead as he now seems to be going. I have already said everything important except this:

If you don't want to bother reading any of the rest, read *The Crystal World* anyhow. If you have liked Ballard before, this will delight you; if you have not, it will probably surprise you.

Notes

1. "The Future of Science Fiction," by Reginald Bretnor, in *Modern Science Fiction*, ed. Bretnor, Coward McCann, 1953.
2. *The Crystal World*, J. G. Ballard; Farrar, Straus & Giroux, 1966; 210 pp.; $4.50.
3. *The Impossible Man*, J. G. Ballard; Berkley #F1204, 1966; nine stories, 160 pp.; 50¢.

Books (September 1966)

[...]

The Ninth Galaxy Reader[1] is—like *Galaxy*—a very mixed bag, everything from excellent to inane. Outstanding are Richard Wilson's "The Watchers in the Glade" and L. A. Lafferty's "Slow Tuesday Night;" Wilson is moody and dramatic, Lafferty outrageous and hilarious, but both are solidly spectacular stuff in the symbolic vein, first-rate examples of the new kind of s-f. Harry Harrison's "How the Old World Died," Fred Pohl's "The Children of Night," and Larry Niven's "Wrong-Way Street" are all superior science fiction of the sort that typified the best in *Galaxy* in the fifties. Roger Zelazny's "The Monster and the Maiden" and Damon Knight's "An Ancient Madness" are highly mannered fairy tales: the Zelazny, short and sharp, was the more effective for me—but I am not much of a fairy-tale buff. In addition, there are three standards by Brian Aldiss, John Brunner, and Lester del Rey; a blunted savagery by Philip José Farmer; and a dull joke by C. C. MacApp. Overall, the book leaves a curiously bad taste; its one cohesive element is a sort of Black Humored dim view of humanity, not so strong in most of the individual stories as to be actively unpleasant, but mounting in cumulative effect.

The new *If Reader*[2] is less representative of the magazine. *If* has been following a consistent policy of introducing at least one new writer per issue, and this would have been a considerably more interesting collection (and quite possibly a better-quality one) if Pohl had resisted the understandable temptation to throw in the best "names" available—unfortunately seldom represented in *If* with their best work. (This last applies to Keith Laumer, one of the early *If* discoveries, but now a budding "name" himself, represented in the magazine almost exclusively by the endless *Retief* stories; the sample included here is very standard stock.) Best-of-book are Fred Saberhagen's "The Life Hater" and Jonathan Brand's "Long Day in Court" (both authors originally introduced in *If*), and John Brunner's "A Better Mousetrap." Leiber's "The 64-Square Madhouse" is great fun for chess buffs, but otherwise far from his best. Robert F. Young, Jerome Bixby, A. E. van Vogt, and Pohl himself contribute tiredly professional retellings of old ideas.

Also on hand is the reprint edition of *The Best from F&SF*, Eleventh Series[3]; this is the one with Cordwainer Smith's "Alpha Ralpha Boulevard,"

Vonnegut's "Harrison Bergeron," John Anthony West's "George," Davidson's "The Sources of the Nile."

The newest thing in series anthologies of course is Damon Knight's *Orbit 1*,[4] the first volume of a book-periodical of original s-f. It emerges as a most uneven volume leaning more to polish than profundity, rather stronger on technique than concept. It is an excellently readable collection, but—

Of the nine stories, there are no more than four I am likely to read a second time, and of those four, only two "needed" a book like this to achieve publication. The outstanding inclusion here is Richard McKenna's posthumous "The Secret Place," long overdue for publication, and by itself, I suppose, justifying the existence of the book. Almost the same thing might be said of James Blish's "How Beautiful with Banners," if he had finished the story he began. Rich, meaty, absorbing in its opening pages, it seems to run out of content half way through: a woman more complex and believable than any character of Blish's I have ever read turns into a scientifictional spinster stereotype; a compelling emotional experience seems to degenerate into a pale dirty joke. Yet the first part is so extraordinary that I know I will return to it, ignoring the dropoff afterwards. I do not understand why the McKenna has not seen print before now; I can see why a book of this sort would be necessary for the publication of the Blish. The same applies to Sonya Dorman's "Splice of Life," for somewhat different reasons: it, too, is flawed, for me at least, by what seems like a last-minute insertion of a science-fictional rationale in what is otherwise a strong, satisfying, and completely unclassifiable story—this last characteristic making it an unlikely sale for any magazine I can think of. Virginia Kidd's "Kangaroo Court" is the fourth valuable find here—less potent than the McKenna in its symbolic content, but a solid piece of science fiction wrapped up in some elegant prose. There are, also, a somewhat overwritten good idea by Kate Wilhelm, a beautifully smooth mood piece with not much idea at all by Poul Anderson, a shrill giggle by Allison Rice, a gorgeously colored bottle of bird-woman relish by Tom Disch, and an unoriginal but strongly written underwater story by Keith Roberts. Of them all, only the Kidd and McKenna seem to me to fit Knight's stated aims: "...to put together a collection of unpublished stories good enough to stand beside an anthology of classic science fiction."

Another Knight offering accomplishes this aim, except for the "unpublished" specification: *Cities of Wonder*[5] is probably both the best collection and the most-published one of the present group, containing as it does, Forster's "The Machine Stops," Blish's "Okie," Benét's "By the Waters of Babylon," and Heinlein's "'It's Great to Be Back!'" as well as Don A. Stuart's "Forgetfulness," Miller's "Dumb Waiter," and Kornbluth's "The Luckiest Man in Denv." Slightly less familiar ("unreprinted" previously—which is to say, previously reprinted only in "collections," not anthologies) are Ballard's "Billenium," Kuttner's "Jesting Pilot," and Aldiss's "The Underprivileged." Robert Abernathy's "Single Combat" is, I believe, reprinted here (in any use of the word) for the first time—and *high* time. Not a bad or even half-bad story in the lot, and more than half are very good ones. If there are more than two or three you haven't read, it's worth buying; for that matter, it's worth buying anyhow, to give to someone new to s-f.

Next on the list are three period-piece collections, two of which present themselves as comprehensive showcases of "modern" science fiction, although the definition varies considerably. Sam Moskowitz's *Modern Masterpieces*[6] starts with E. E. Smith and goes through Philip José Farmer, containing only three stories (out of 21) first published in the past fifteen years; and only one from a source outside the American science fiction specialty magazines—Ray Bradbury's "Wake for the Living," from a 1947 issue of *Dime Mystery.* Christopher Cerf's *Vintage Anthology*[7] has only three (out of 20) stories published *more* than fifteen years ago: the earliest is Martin Gardner's 1946 "No-Sided Professor," from *Esquire*, the most recent new story by William Styron, published for the first time in the anthology; only nine selections are from the American specialty publications, with other sources including *The Saturday Evening Post* and *The Harvard Lampoon*, the British science fiction magazines, translations from the Polish and Spanish, etc.

The difference in the two books is clearly stated by the editors. Where Moskowitz deplores the fact that (after Farmer introduced Sex to science fiction) "...it was the *completeness of* the usurpation of the strongholds of scientific wonder, action, and romance by stories of a philosophical, psychiatric, or sexual bent that posed a danger," Cerf proclaims that "space-age fiction," dating from the end of World War II, "has helped to turn science-fiction writers away from technology as an end in itself, and, consequently, has led them to subordinate their scientific imagination to an increased concern with human attitudes and emotions, on the one hand, and with the field of sociology on the other. This new trend," he adds, "has succeeded in raising noticeably the literary standards of the science fiction story."

Only five authors appear in both anthologies: Sturgeon, Wyndham, Simak, Bradbury, and Clarke. (Typically, Moskowitz represents Sturgeon with the 1941 "Microcosmic God," and Cerf with the 1956 "And Now the News.") *Masterpieces* adds to those already mentioned some well-tested, tried-and-true selections by Leinster, Williamson, del Rey, Heinlein, van Vogt, Asimov, and Leiber, and a shocking total of ten stories for which I have not found any previous book publication (although I believe two or three *have* appeared in collections not on my shelves), by Smith, Campbell, Wyndham, de Camp, Bloch, Bradbury, Henry Kuttner, C. L. Moore, Edmond Hamilton, and Eric Frank Russell. Unfortunately, my remarks earlier about avoiding untested selections were not entirely sardonic; there *are* some re-readable stories in the s-f magazines more than two or three years old that have not yet been reprinted anywhere—but most of them are either precocious examples of (what I call) *modern* science fiction, just coming into its own (and apparently unrecognized as yet by either Moskowitz or Cerf), or they are for one reason or another unavailable. Moskowitz's desire to make use of his vast knowledge of the field to add some freshness to his book is understandable—but on the whole, unfortunate. The Campbell and de Camp (both of which I suspect *have* been in collections), are the only entries in that last group that add anything much to the book.

Cerf has been much more discreet. He includes only four items previously unreprinted in any form: the Styron original, the *Lampoon* item (a short-short by John C. Brust), and selections from José María Gironella's fascinating *Phantoms and Fugitives* and from *The Modern Polish Mind* ("I Kill Myself" by Julian Kawalec). In addition to these and the five overlap authors, he includes Roald Dahl, Idris Seabright, Martin Gardner, C. M. Kornbluth, Robert Sheckley, Damon Knight, Fredric Brown, J. G. Ballard, Avram Davidson, Alfred Bester, and Walter M. Miller, Jr.

[...]

Notes

1. *The Ninth Galaxy Reader*, ed. Frederik Pohl; Doubleday, 1966; 203 pp., 12 stories; $3.95.
2. *The If Reader of Science Fiction*, ed. Frederik Pohl; Doubleday, 1966; 252 pp., 9 stories; $4.50.
3. *The Best from Fantasy and Science Fiction; Eleventh Series*, ed. Robert P. Mills; Act M-137, 1966 (reprint); 254 pp., 16 stories; 45¢.
4. *Orbit 1*, ed. Damon Knight; Putnam, 1966, 192 pp., 9 stories; $3.50.

5. *Cities of Wonder*, ed. Damon Knight; Doubleday, 1966; 252 pp., 11 stories; $4.50.
6. *Modern Masterpieces of Science Fiction*, ed. Sam Moskowitz; World, 1966; 518 pp., 21 stories; $6.00.
7. *The Vintage Anthology of Science Fiction*, ed. Christopher Cerf; Vintage Books, 1966; 307 pp., 20 stories, plus biographical notes; paper, $1.65.

[…]

Books (November 1966)

I wish I had seen the movies.

I keep promising myself I will not review "novelizations" without finding out first what the author was working from.

It is time, of course, that a book, any book, must properly be judged on its own: when the feely-smellies, or dream-helmets, or whatever, have relegated the quaint "talkie" to their dusty cans forever, the books will remain, at least in scholarly libraries, as part of the author's record of accomplishment.

Still, it would be nice to know how much of the James Bond element in the two recent offerings by major names in s-f derived from the films, and what part of the scientific and philosophic content is the nominal author's work, but I have had these two books for two months now, and have *not* got around to seeing the movies, so—

If you are one of the many readers who abandoned *Fantastic Voyage*[1] after the first installment in the *Saturday Evening Post*, you may have made a mistake. (As it happens, I have not seen the *Post's* version either—but I have heard the reactions of those who started it, and I have seen other *Post*-cut serials, most notably the hash-up of Richard McKenna's *The Sand Pebble*. I may be throwing old stones unfairly here; perhaps the magazine version of *Voyage* is identical with the book, but—) As it happens, *Voyage* is at its weakest in the opening chapters; even if it appeared exactly as in the book, the first installment might well have been the last for Asimov fans, when there was no chance to riffle through the rest and see what was to come.

Because I am an Asimov fan, I prefer to make the assumption that the amusingly banal characters and the straight Gernsbackian plot were part of the situation-as-given. I further assume that, aside from the amount of money that must have been involved, Asimov's reason for doing the book was the opportunity afforded him by the basic plot element (as old as the field, and still fascinating) of a journey—literally with (laser) gun and, if not camera, at least radio and periscope—through the vascular canals. Oddly enough, Asimov the Biochemist has hardly ever combined with Asimov the S-F Writer in the past: almost all his work, and certainly the best of it, has been on psychological and sociological themes. This time, the Good Doctor takes us on a not-so-fantastic-after-all tour of his own domain, and the result is fascinating.

My suggestion is to start with Chapter Four. The exciting part, the voyage itself, begins in Chapter Five, and I would say to start there, except for some "Briefing" (the chapter title) in Four. If you find yourself at all confused about the characters, you can go back and skim through Three—but with a little patience, you can save that effort: you've seen them all in a hundred movies already, and you'll identify them.

For that matter, if you've been around more than fifteen years or so, you've read them before; they are the stock complement of the Good Old Days of Scientifiction—all of them but the hero, who as a matter of fact, starts out as "Granite" Grant and winds up as "Good Old Charlie" Grant. It is this sea(blood?)-change that makes me wish I'd seen the film: I suspect Ike may have added something to the original script.

The other "novelization" is Fritz Leiber's fat-and-fanciful new Tarzan book,[2] where, again, I confess I had to force myself through the beginning; again, was glad I did so; again, for self-evident and rather more valid reasons, found myself confronting many old familiar characters (but a few new ones too); and, again, find myself wondering how much of the (gradually-developed) Secret-Agent-for-World-Peace characterization of Tarzan is Leiber's.

Perhaps this difficulty with openings is a natural hazard of "novelizing," where the author starts out with a predetermined background, plot, and set of characters, and must work his way gradually (and I suppose as unnoticeably as possible) inside them before they begin to acquire conviction. At any rate, in both books the break occurs when the introduction is over and the action begins: in this case, it is only when Tarzan is out of the airplane and tweeds, and back in the jungle, that Leiber's Tarzan evoked for me the same awed breathlessness that Burroughs's original awakened thirty or more years ago.

[...]

I don't know whether it is James Bond again, or Viet Nam, or the '30s replacing the '20s as the current pop fad, but spy-intrigue, political conspiracy, economic manipulation, and the strategy and tactics of revolution appear to be the key themes in a whole new batch of novels, with heroes and villains ranging from official Secret Agents and the world power combines to guerrilla leaders, underground cell members, and spying double agents.

Of course, Poul Anderson, Keith Laumer, Mack Reynolds, John Brunner, and others have been doing this sort of thing for some time. But—except for some of Reynolds and Brunner—the emphasis has usually been either on swashbuckle or satire. There is some of both in the current crop, but also an underlying vein of genuine speculative interest in the causes and effects of political intrigue, and its mechanisms, which is more than welcome in a field rather badly overplowed.

Perhaps the '30s fad *is* the major influence, because there is also a noticeable return, in many of the books, to the inclusion of some element of scientific speculation, or at least information, in science fiction. Frank Herbert, for instance, has buried some brilliant ecological extrapolation in *The Green Brain*.[3] (The Secret Agent this time is a beautiful lady scientist Mata Hari.) Like *Dune* (*F&SF* "Books" March 1965), the novel is over-contrived; unlike *Dune* (where the ecology of the desert-civilization was presented as a novel-within-the-monumentally-long-novel) the basic concepts here run straight through the book, and while sometimes submerged by the complexities of the plot, they are essentially related to it. Also, the considerably shorter length makes the action-adventure move faster, and the idea development stand out more.

As an addition to the memorable line of Mutated Insect stories, the book falls short because of *plot* incredibilities and stock characters. But there is some exciting and convincing jungle-adventure action, and the first absolutely valid and intriguing Giant Insecti that I can recall.

As an attack on short-range know-it-all thinking involved in "pest" extermination campaigns, and our present attempts to supplant the natural biota with a premature planned-ecology based on the infant science of biochemistry, the book is both exciting and important. (But I wish the author had not succumbed to the same anthropomorphic-teleological thinking he attacks: his Giant Insects are directed by a Giant Brain which, of course, is, or was, human.)

The giant quasi-insects in Keith Roberts's *The Furies*[4] are a different breed altogether. Roberts is an extraordinarily prolific and talented young British writer, and I think it is unfortunate that he is being introduced in this country with his highly derivative science fiction rather than some of the charmingly original fantasy that has appeared in the British magazines. (Equally unfortunately, I think, he has elected to publish his sensitively-characterized sci-psychological stories, in both countries, under a completely independent pen-name.) The astonishing thing about *Furies* is that it contrives to be so readable while saying nothing at all (informationally, thematically, any other way) that has not been said, and well said, over and over before. As with his story in *Orbit 1* (reviewed here in September) *Furies* is a compound of other people's ideas handled just-that-little-bit-better. This time it's guerrilla warfare against invading e-t's—but don't confuse it with Eric Frank Russell on that account; Roberts writes about real people, and sometimes frighteningly real-seeming invaders.

Two other new novels are rather more serious in their consideration of the nature and strategies of revolution—although on the surface Allen Kim Lang's *Wild and Outside*[5] is anything but serious. This is a funny, charming, plotful story about the damnedest secret agent ever: Eddie Keenan of Earth and the Mets, star shortstop and draftee, out to civilize the planet Melon with a quarterstaff and a baseball bat. And underneath it all, there is some of the most consistent, coherent, sociological thinking s-f has ever seen. Laugh along with Lang; then settle back and think it over.

Heinlein's *The Moon Is a Harsh Mistress*,[6] on the other hand, is very sober indeed about its lessons in political economy and military and revolutionary principles; if you happen to be of the Heinlein-Anderson (or Nietzsche-MacArthur-Goldwater) school of thought in these matters, you can take his premises seriously. Otherwise, my advice is to suspend your disbelief as willingly as, for instance, you probably will do in order to accept the computer-with-personality who (which?) is one of the alternate protagonists of the story. Given the two premises (that a computer can develop an ego; and that the determining factors in political-economic conflict are weaponry and military tactics) the book is a fascinatingly detailed narrative of colonial rebellion, soundly structured and excitingly told.

The fact is that revolution makes good story. Lang succeeds by basing his book on the solidest of conceptual bedrock, developing a strategy that cannot help but succeed, and then tossing in, as tactics, every bit of slapstick and/or colorful romance that comes to hand. Heinlein's strategy is at the least highly improbable; but he bulwarks it with magnificently realistic tactical detail—and he has another advantage. Whatever else he is doing, whether his mood is investigative, whimsical, or preachy, Heinlein never forgets that the business he went into was story-telling and he manages to tell a story, and tell it very well, on the way.

One *possible* minor exception to this dictum is the new story, "Free Men," in Ace's *The Worlds of Robert A. Heinlein.*[7] But I prefer to believe that the lack of resolution here is the fault of a writer grown accustomed to much longer lengths, rather than a failure in Heinlein's native narrative sense. The other stories, familiar as they are, bear re-reading well enough to support my basic contention ("Blowups Happen," "Searchlight," "Life-Line," "Solution Unsatisfactory").

The contrast between the Lang and Heinlein novels recurs in a comparison between Heinlein's short story collection and Leiber's *The Night of the Wolf*.[8] I must disqualify myself from any evaluation of the merits of the Leiber collection—but I can say that the two volumes taken together provide an entertainingly instructive illustration of two basic modes of science fiction. Leiber's logic is in his underlying situation and character development; Heinlein's is in the impeccable organization of plot and puzzle components. Heinlein may commence with the most wildly improbable hypothesis; Leiber may elaborate with the most bizarre details; both manage to sustain a conviction of plausibility for the duration of the story, and to leave something of color as well as thought behind.

[...]

Notes

1. *Fantastic Voyage*, Isaac Asimov; Houghton Mifflin, 1966; 239 pp.; $3.95. (Novelization from the screenplay by Harry Kleiner, based on an original story by Otto Klement and Jay Lewis Bixby.)
2. *Tarzan and the Valley of Gold*, Fritz Leiber; Ballantine, 1966; 317 pp.; 75¢.
3. *The Green Brain*, Frank Herbert; Ace F379, 1966; 160 pp.; 40¢.
4. *The Furies*, Keith Roberts; Berkley F1177, 1966; 192 pp.; 50¢.
5. *Wild and Outside*, Allen Kim Lang; Chilton, 1966; 139 pp.; $3.95.
6. *The Moon Is a Harsh Mistress*, Robert A. Heinlein; Putnam, 1966; 383 pp.; $5.95.
7. *The Worlds of Robert A. Heinlein*, Robert A. Heinlein; Ace F375, 1966; 189 pp. (author's intro and five short stories); 40¢.
8. *The Night of the Wolf*, Fritz Leiber; Ballantine U2254; 221 pp. (four novelettes); 50¢.

[...]

Books (December 1966)

Our ancestors were afraid of magic; we are afraid of the word. Except for children, anthropologists, and s-f writers, no one uses the word in its proper meaning—which is, simply, that class of phenomenon and experience which we can neither explain nor explain away. In a culture whose firmest faith is the concept of linear cause-and-effect, the popular inclination is to deny the "reality" of any incomprehensibles which cannot be classified as "miracles of modern science." What is left over is manifestly either error of observation, outright trickery, or gullible "superstition."

Our ancestors were comforted and sustained by their myths; we admit to none. Except for children, psychologists, and s-f writers, no one accepts contemporary mythology in its true sense—which is, of course, the symbolic projection (personification, objectivization) of unconscious knowledge. In a culture so antagonistic to the concept of magic as to exclude it even from religion (rejecting all revelation for rationale; favoring the manifestation over the inspiration), the popular inclination is to deny the "reality" of any awareness whose source is unnamable. Persistent symbolic figures originating outside the bestiaries of scientific classification (Dinosaur, Germ, Neanderthal Man, Astro/ Cosmo/naut, Miracle Drug, Hell-Bomb, and of course Scientist, both Noble and Mad) are, manifestly, distortions of observation ("folklore" and—usually—"flying saucer"), deliberately perpetuated illusions ("false religions," "red propaganda"); or simply "imagination" (good as in "creative," bad as in "neurotic").

But we continue to create and cherish our mythic symbols. (Add, for instance: Auschwitz Ovens, Coca-Cola Bottle, Jack-and-Jackie, Thinking Machine, Pinup Girl/Marilyn Monroe, etc.) What we lack is the codification of the myths themselves. "Myth" is in a sense the mathematics of unconscious symbolism, the means by which we organize and recognize the raw symbols which are our only means of communication with our own nonconscious selves. The mnemonic device of the myth maintains the symbolic language in available, accessible form.

The as-yet unformulated contemporary mythology is the map modern man must use in the search for his soul. And how desperate that search is becoming is evident not only in our private and personal disorientations (sexual "abnormality," suicide, drug addiction, etc., as well as the official statistics on "mental illness"), but in our public, institutional confusions as well (cold wars, dirty little wars, price wars, gang wars, race wars, space race, etc.).

An increasingly large part of serious speculative fiction, in and out of "science fiction," now concerns itself with the examination and analysis of mythology, and a significant, if smaller, segment with the creative search for viable modern myths. Most of these latter attempts, inevitably, emerge as imitations, rationalizations, or cosmetic-modernizations of the no longer vital mythotypes of the agrarian and nomadic cultures of the past. But here and there, one feels the authentic thrill, if only for a chapter, a scene, or a page, as bits of the new Passion are articulated.

Eight recent s-f novels fall within this mythotropic movement, combining to produce in interchange something a bit more than the sum of their statements.

Edgar Pangborn's *The Judgment of Eve*[1] is set in the dawn of a new culture, following on the devastation of the "One Day War" and the plagues and mutations that followed it. The story is told by a scholar of some centuries later, endeavoring to piece out the substance of one of the basic myths of his own time. In the retelling of one of the most enduring of folk tales (the three princes seeking their fortunes in competition for the hand of the beautiful princess), Pangborn is attempting neither to rationalize the legend nor to justify it in terms of the present or possible future. He makes no effort at the sort of realism which is the usual measure of the atom-doom story—indeed—deliberately bypasses the period of degradation and dissolution.

Eve is the story of a beginning—not individualized but abstracted. A culture has grown from this conception to a point where it can now inquire into its own origins; but the mythic significance of Eve herself and the man who wins her—mythic mother and father of the new world—is of less importance than the role of the myth itself in nurturing the new culture.

The whole thing is a job that could not have been done by any writer less skilled, less tender, or more sentimental than Pangborn, who has managed to demonstrate the life-giving function of myth in—if not an actual myth—a most effective fairy-tale.

In Avram Davidson's *The Kar-Chee Reign*[2] the setting is again a devastated civilization—this time as the result of the invasion of Earth by the Kar-Chee, whose super science planetary mining operation has tumbled whole empires into the sea, altered the faces of the continents, and left only small enclaves of humanity clinging, in various degrees of primitivism and reconstruction, to isolated pockets of still fertile land.

When the story opens, there is already an established mythology, in the process of rigidifying into ritual, based on the invaders and their powers. More accurately, there are a number of such incipient cults, and it is the confrontation of two of them which opens the way for an effort at resistance. In the course of the rebellion itself, a new mythology is created.

Davidson's treatment falls a good bit short of the poetic strength of Pangborn's. The book lacks the simplicity and classic proportions of *Eve*. But it offers some meaty material for consideration of the complex functions served by mythology.

The vital role of the viable myth in the formation of a culture is directly opposed by the restrictive nature of moribund ritualized myth, and most "conventional" science fiction has (in keeping with the general cultural posture) concerned itself with the myth-breaking, rather than myth-making necessities. Jack Vance's *The Blue World*[3] is a colorful and absorbing instance of development along these more traditional lines.

On a predominantly marine world, the descendants of a space voyage known as "The Escape" maintain a precarious foothold on tiny island settlements. The several castes into which these People of the Floats are born all trace their origins to the colonizing crew! For each caste—Hoodwink, Smuggler, Bezzler, Malpractor, etc.—there is a traditional job, and ritual training:—

> "When the Ship of Space discharged the Firsts upon these blessed floats, there were four Hoodwinks among the Two Hundred. Later, when the towers were built and the lamps established, there were hoods to wink, and it seemed only appropriate that the Hoodwinks should occupy themselves at the trade...."

The mythology that has grown up on the complex base of the writings and artifacts of the crew members, and the terrifying powers of the Kragen, the giant native sea-dwellers, has hardened into a ritualistic strait-jacket, suppressing all exploration and development. Vance, at his inventive and dramatic best, develops this through a beautifully paced adventure story (including much carefully-thought-out utilization of the marine ecology) to a traditionally satisfying collapse of the barriers of ritual ignorance under the assault of pragmatic experimentation.

Ursula Le Guin's first novel, *Rocannon's World*[4] is in a similar sense a successful version of a (different) standard science-fantasy approach—removed from plain-fantasy sword-and-sorcery not only by its displacement to a remote planet, where elves and gnomes and winged steeds blend into the landscape without offense to the reader's sensibilities or credibilities—and where the anthropologist-hero from a galactic civilization is sustained as a reasonable element in the story, by cutting him off from his base world and its scientific resources—but even more, as a result of the charm and delicacy of the writing. Nothing here to keep you up thinking all night, but a pleasant few hours of reading.

Claude Nunes's (also first) novel, *Inherit the Earth*,[5] fails to achieve either the poetic, speculative, or dramatic satisfactions of any of the books already discussed, but it does pose a problem intrinsically fascinating, and for the first half of the book, at least, sustains a high level of both narrative and speculative interest. In a sense, its failure after that is a more vital contribution to the happenstance-symposium exchange effected by this whole group of books than either Vance's attack on myth-as-superstition, or Le Guin's nostalgic reshaping of yesterday's myth figures. The protagonists here are artificially developed doll-size humanoids, whose origins and initial situation are such as to remove both fear of death and pressure of hunger from their biopsychic composition: presumably the culture they create as they take over the abandoned radioactive earth will be either without myths, or so different in its basic symbols as to *appear* mythless. But Nunes chickens out: by the end of the book, the creatures have begun to die and hunger, and the statement-by-default appears to be simply that there is no drama to be found in the absence of the essential human myths.

As it happens, three of the books in this group are first novels, all of them, by further coincidence, the work of writers who were first published during 1962. Of the three, Roger Zelazny is the only one whose reputation is already solidly established by his magazine work: *This Immortal*,[6] in fact, appeared originally in a shorter version in this magazine ("...And Call Me Conrad," *F&SF* Oct. & Nov. 1965).

It is unfair, I suppose, to judge a book by one's expectations—but it is also inevitable: a Grade B novel by a Grade C (or unknown) writer will always look better than the same Grade B from a Grade A man. With this in mind, I regret to say that I found *Immortal* an impressive disappointment: impressive for its poetry, its technical skill, its occasional philosophic insights and character asides; disappointing as a novel, both in conception and structure.

Superficially, the book might be classified as "conservative" s-f, in the same sense as the Vance and Le Guin. Actually, it is better described as reactionary. Zelazny's response to the common feeling of myth-loss is an attempt to refurbish the old forms of positing a devolutionary process (radiation-induced) in which the figures of ancient Greek mythology reappear "naturally": not so much the new-wine-in-old-bottles of the usual old-myth-justification or sword-and-sorcery as an attempt to decant the old stuff into new ones. Let it be said for the author's technical skill that he carried out the exercise expertly within the framework of the book; but though he never spilled a drop, last night's champagne in today's plastic flask is still warm and flat—and likely to be confusing, as well.

The old myths have not lost their power to enchant; they have simply lost the power of myth, because their images are no longer those in which we clothe our archetypes. The sabertooth has succeeded Cerberus as a symbolic figure; the browsing brontosaur evokes more responsive overtones (or inner-tones?) than Cyclops brooding in his cave; the eternal exile comes to mind more readily in blank-faced body-bristling space armor than in the Greek or Roman draperies of either Odysseus or the Wandering Jew. There is no way to turn this psychic clock back, however much we might prefer the (now) mellower symbols of a less complicated world.

I cannot leave this discussion, however, without adding that, though the plot and story elements are conventional (for s-f), and the thematic content confusingly inverted, the style and treatment are (for s-f) almost revolutionary: alternately intensely-intimately-tender and tough-hard-boiled in mood, essentially introspective in tone, much more preoccupied with personal moralities and ethics than group mores or behavior, the treatment is very close to the Hammett-Chandler school—something rarely attempted and much less often realized, in any variety of s-f. And as was sometimes true of Hammett, and almost always of Chandler, the writing itself covers all varieties of excellence, from glib to superb.

Samuel Delany, as it happens, also began publishing in 1962. To the best of my knowledge, nothing of his has ever appeared in a magazine, and *Empire Star*[7] and *Babel-17*[8] are his sixth and seventh novels, all published by

Ace. I think it would be fair to say that, with Zelazny and Thomas Disch, he represents the most promising of the new American s-f writers so far.

But Delany offers no such firm grips for dissection and discussion as Zelazny does. Before reading these two new books, I had seen only one other (*The Ballad of Beta 2, F&SF* "Books," Nov. 1965). Since then I have gone racing through the other four, and in the storm of impressions left behind, I can say only this much—

There is, in Delany's work, a mythic-poetic power comparable in its intensity and creative effects only to the work of such names as Sturgeon, Ballard, Vonnegut, Cordwainer Smith. His style is undeveloped—indeed, still highly derivative of both Sturgeon and Smith. He mixes the most melodramatic absurd cosmic *shticks* with shockingly powerful images and insights. (E. E. Smith and van Vogt aren't even *in* it with extra-super-galactic Delany space opera.)

He tosses basic concepts of time and space and mathematics (but valid ones; not pseudo-surface jargon) around as dizzyingly as he juggles dazzling psychological insights and aesthetic theorizings. He likes the word "multiplex," and it suits him.

The total effect of his books is the exact opposite of Zelazny's novel: the surface is confusing; the essence is marvelously clear. If I go back and read through the novels again, perhaps by the time the next one comes along, I will be able to articulate the components of my excitement. Meantime—I don't know where he came from, where he's going, or quite clearly what he's doing now—but this is one of the people who has begun to carve the new myth out of the void. I hope he can keep it up. I want to read more.

Notes

1. *The Judgment of Eve*, Edgar Pangborn; Simon & Schuster, 1966; 224 pp.; $3.95.
2. *The Kar-Chee Reign*, Avram Davidson, and *Rocannon's World*, Ursula K. Le Guin; Ace double G-574; 138 pp., 117 pp.; resp.; 50¢.
3. *The Blue World*, Jack Vance; Ballantine U2169, 1966; 190 pp.; 50¢.
4. *Rocannon's World*—see note for *The Kar-Chee Reign*.
5. *Inherit the Earth*, Claude Nunes, and *Dawnman Planet*, Mack Reynolds; Ace double G-580, 1966; 127 pp., 117 pp. resp.; 50¢.
6. *This Immortal*, Roger Zelazny; Ace F-393, 1966; 174 pp., 40¢.
7. *Empire Star*, Samuel R. Delany, and *The Tree Lord of Imeten*, Tom Purdom; Ace double M-139, 1966; 102 pp., 152 pp. resp.; 45¢.
8. *Babel-17*, Samuel R. Delany; Ace F-388, 1966; 173 pp., 40¢.

Books (January 1967)

Two pieces of information came my way this past month—neither one entirely surprising, both a bit shocking in their effect on me. The first, and sadder, item, I will leave for last; the second was more of a reminder than a discovery—the celebration of the one hundredth anniversary of the birth of Herbert George Wells.

That is to say, it is more than seventy years now since the publication of *The Time Machine*, and almost thirty-five since the production of *The Shape of Things to Come*, the two works which effectively span Wells's career as a writer of "scientific romances."

I knew this before. But the fact is, I have been in the habit of regarding Wells simply as one of the rather-better contemporary writers. I don't think I have ever re-read anything of his—and it is perhaps the lack of any impulse to do so that accounts for the "rather." I have simply read his stories (some of them quite recently), not with that faint almost-inevitable adjustment I make for even the best of the turn-of-the-century writers, nor with the slightly exaggerated attentiveness one may bring to that which classifies, by age and virtue, as "classic," but with the spontaneous interest and pleasure that, for me, derives specifically (and all too seldom recently) from good science fiction.

It was somewhat startling, then, to be forcibly reminded that *The Island of Dr. Moreau*, for instance, was already fifty years old when I read it. I had even then read any number of later, and duller, variations on the theme; I have read many more since, and none of them stay as fresh and exciting in my mind.

I have *not* re-read Wells, and I should have to do so to be sure of this, but I incline to think still that he was not, in the usual sense, a "great writer"—at least not of fiction—but rather a genuinely original thinker. The "mainstream" novels, after all, have not lasted as well as the science fiction, and of the s-f, the most vivid, memorable titles are not primarily those that dealt with specific technological and biological extrapolations, on the precise predictive scale now considered "solid science fiction."

The Time Machine, *Things to Come*, *Dr. Moreau*, "The Invisible Man," *The Food of the Gods*, "The Country of the Blind," *The War of the Worlds*, "The Man Who Could Work Miracles"—these all contain the essence of Wells. His utopian dreams are dated; but his visions—both glorious and terrifying—of the age of scientific man are as contemporary and meaningful today as they were in 1900, because they were about ideas, not gadgets. They deal not just with isolated instances, but with the nature of the interaction between man and his own inventions, between the natural and technological worlds, between conditioning and reasoned thought.

The War of the Worlds caused even more of a sensation when Orson Welles broadcast it in 1938, than when it was first published forty years earlier—not just because of the effectiveness of the broadcast, but because its underlying statement, only vaguely visible in 1898, was terrifyingly clear in the tension of the thirties. It was not (just) a story about Martians or their machines of war, but a powerful prophetic statement of the implications of truly scientific global war. *The Shape of Things to Come* was more direct statement on the same theme, but it remained, for more than thirty years, the most memorable film of its kind,[1] not because of "special effects" or monsters or metal marvels, but because it grew out of the same deep-rooted comprehension of the realities of modern war for real people. Even the seemingly light fantasies are, again and always, essentially concerned with the still-desperate conflicts and ambivalences of modern man, in search of the new kind of soul he needs to abide in the world of his own making.

It is obvious to me that I have under-rated Wells, till now, in at least one respect, and I suspect I have done him too little honor in another way, as well. The popular habit of regarding fiction values the prime component of "greatness" in contemporary prose Writers is insidious, and clearly inadequate.

The general function of fiction is to provide surrogate experience, sensations, insights, activities, emotions. Its principal residue (beyond the remembered pleasure which is the legacy of any art) is in the personality rather than the intellect of the reader: an increment in perception, a growth of empathy, and emotional potential. This function is served as well, though differently, by drama, bardic poetry, and some forms of graphic art.

The little literary province currently known as science fiction is essentially a medium for readers, not viewers; a stimulant for the mind rather than a tranquillizer for the soul. Whether it acts as science lesson or social criticism, gadget-extrapolator or philosophic depth-probe—whether its objectives are an infusion of information or an interpretation of ready-known facts—its determining characteristic is that it must leave the reader in a state of heightened mental activity.

Ideally, when good science fiction is also good fiction, it accomplishes both purposes. In practice, the combined accomplishment is almost vanishingly rare, on any really significant level. But there are other kinds of good or even great writing; Wells perhaps utilized the fiction form, not so much for its unique values as simply to make use of its current popularity as entertainment to gain a broader audience for philosophic writing.

The use of science fiction as a popular medium for philosophy is familiar; fantasy fiction as a vehicle for symbols and images of the less conscious level otherwise largely confined to poetry, is equally traditional. The current emergence of what appears to be a combination of these modes—the use of science fantasy as rationalized image, to make a multi-leveled statement of intellectual and symbolic content—is too new a process to be "assessed" in any realistic manner. But the significance of the trend is already established beyond question. It is not confined to writers inside the narrow enclave of category science fiction, but its most direct line of development has occurred there, and its practice at the moment seems most successful in the hands of writers whose major background is in s-f.

The trend is typified in England by J. G. Ballard. Until a short time ago, its outstanding American practitioner was the man known as "Cordwainer Smith," the late Professor Paul A. Linebarger of Johns Hopkins University.

This is, of course, my other piece of news, and I take what small satisfaction is available in paying his true identity the respect we have been obliged to give to the Smith façade until now.

I did not hear of his death until a month after it happened. The news was not surprising; he had been ill for some time. I knew him, not closely, but gratefully, and could not seize the opportunity for closer acquaintance provided by the coincidence of our residences in Washington last winter, because the strain imposed on him by visitors was obvious. I find it difficult now to separate the sense of loss of a remarkable human being from the feeling of deprivation as a reader. Both because his loss is too recent, and his work remains too new, I shall not be so presumptuous as to attempt any general discussion of his accomplishments in this article. When the inevitable re-publications and comprehensive editions of his work appear, I will undoubtedly have much more to say.

For now, those who valued his work as I did will want to know that at least one book is currently on the stands—a grouping as demi-novel of the four Casher O'Neill stories, under the title *Quest of the Three Worlds*.[2]

Examining the new books against the renewed background of Wells, and from the advanced position reached by "Smith," the most noteworthy is probably Fred Hoyle's *October the First Is Too Late*[3]—certainly his most exciting piece of fiction, conceptually, since *The Black Cloud.* Although it lacks some of the plot-and-structure qualities of the last two *Andromeda* novels (for which one assumes the collaborator, John Eliot, must have been primarily responsible), this book for the first time seems to me to be written at a level commensurate with Hoyle's best non-fiction work. The theory of time around which the book is built is both fascinating and abstruse, and Hoyle makes full use, this time of his unique capacity to distil complex abstractions into simple, lucid, and very readable prose.

I shall not attempt to emulate his success, but limit myself to recommending the book to anyone interested in the current investigations of time. In addition to the basic exposition, the situation Hoyle derives from his time theory is as bizarre, intriguing, and imaginatively provocative as anything in recent fiction. Time has cracked, as it were: the entire globe is broken into a crazy-quilt of time zones. Between Honolulu where the narrator is situated, and England, the gap is only two weeks; but France is almost half a century behind them both—still fighting World War I; Greece in the Periclean Age; the USSR in a vast and featureless Ozymandian future. North America appears to be in the 18th Century.

The possibilities implicit in the situation are immediately apparent, and Hoyle starts out to develop them with originality and thoughtfulness—not just the customary scientific and philosophic explorations of past and future civilizations, but—for instance—the conflict of historical and commercial-tourist interests in classical Greece, and the marvelously complicated economic and political shifts and stresses in Europe, as England explodes into the world of 1918 with the technology and post-empire pacifism of the sixties.

Unfortunately, Hoyle develops these possibilities just enough to fascinate—and tantalize—and then falls back into not one, but both of the conventional time-travel-story routines: the extrapolation of an early period of history, as viewed through the time traveller's eye; and the vision of tomorrows maybe-Utopia. As tends to happen with Utopias, things get rather dull and disappointing.

But at least he was willing to try. If the plot falters before the ideas, nevertheless there is a steady stream of speculation. This is first-rate science-fiction; and while it is not "literature" in the sense in which we usually measure the artistic merits of fiction, it ranks very high (or some sections of it do) in that province of literature known as "belles lettres," in which the speculative essay is a special and important art.

Rosel George Brown's long-overdue first novel, *Sybil Sue Blue*[4] is something, believe me, *else*. You have never read a science fiction novel anything like this before, and if you have read any other kind of novel very much like it, I'd appreciate being informed. Sybil Sue is the swingingest mama since—well, *since*. She is a policewoman, forty or close to it, passionately devoted (in no definite order of precedence) to her job, her beautiful sixteen-year-old daughter, her (probably) dead space-exploring husband, Gin-and-'gin, and good cigars. Her skill with a rabbit punch or wielding her stiletto heel is fabulous. In the right light she can pass as her daughter's classmate, but her sex habits are definitely not teen-age. She is very fond of men, and they of her.

This (first only, one hopes) Sybil Sue book recounts her adventures rounding up the benzale pushers from Radix.

And the damnedest part of it is that under all the froth and fun and furious action, there is more acute comment on contemporary society than you are likely to find in any half dozen deadly serious social novels.

In what I believe to be another first novel[5] Gertrude Friedberg (whose "Short and Happy Death of George Frumkin" in this magazine three years ago will be remembered by others beside myself) proposes an idea I have actually not read before. It is not a large dramatic theme, but it is original, and even more astonishing, combines some sound speculation with good writing and effective story-telling. It would be damaging, I think, to the first part of the book to discuss the essential idea here, but I will drop a possibly misleading clue: I think she has been reading Hoyle.

[...]

Notes

1. It is too soon to say, I suppose, but the chances are that *Dr. Strangelove* will endure, as well.
2. *Quest of the Three Worlds*, Cordwainer Smith; Ace F-402, 1966; 174 pp.; 40¢.
3. *October the First Is Too Late*, Fred Hoyle; Harper & Row, 1966; 200 pp.; $3.95.
4. *Sybil Sue Blue*, Rosel George Brown; Doubleday, 1966; 183 pp.; $3.95.
5. *The Revolving Boy*, Gertrude Friedberg; Doubleday, 1966; 191 pp.; $3.95.

[...]

Books (February 1967)

> "About once every hundred years some wiseacre gets up and tries to banish the fairy tale. Perhaps I had better say a few words in its defense....
>
> "It is accused of giving children a false impression of the world they live in.... I think what profess to be realistic stories for children are far more likely to deceive them. I never expected the real world to be like the fairy tales. I think that I did expect school to be like the school stories....
>
> "...the two longings are very different...a child does not long for fairy land as a boy longs to be the hero of the first eleven. Does anyone suppose that he really and prosaically longs for all the dangers and discomforts of a fairy tale?—really wants dragons in contemporary England? It is not so. It would be much fairer to say that fairy land arouses a longing for he knows not what, it stirs and troubles him (to his life-long enrichment) with the dim sense of something beyond his reach and, far from dulling or emptying the actual world, gives it a new dimension of depth. He does not despise real woods because he has read of enchanted woods; the reading makes all the woods a little enchanted...."

C. S. Lewis speaking, in a paper prepared for the British Library Association in 1952, "On Three Ways of Writing for Children," one of thirteen assorted, selections—essays, lectures, an interview, an introduction, polemic, three short stories, or chapters of an unfinished novel related only by (the masterful prose and) a common thread of interest expressed in the title: *Of Other Worlds.*[1]

Two of the short stories were originally published in *Fantasy and Science Fiction* ("The Shoddy Lands" and "Ministering Angels"). A third, "Forms of Things Unknown," appears for the first time in this collection. I will not discuss them here, beyond advising readers who have somehow never read any of Lewis's fiction, to do so. I am in fact constrained from discussion by Lewis's own urgent argument in the lecture, "On Science Fiction," also published for the first time in this volume. He assails the contemptuous criticism of s-f by people who neither know it nor enjoy it: "Who wants to hear a particular claret abused by a fanatical teetotaler, or a particular woman by a confirmed misogynist?" My own attitude is nowhere so extreme, but I confess I rarely find Lewis's fiction as effective as his writing *about* fiction (or almost anything else). I am, however, in a minority, and the chances are you will enjoy the stories more than I do. As for the rest–

In addition to the paper on science fiction and three pieces dealing with children's books and/or fairy tales, there is a charming one-page introduction to one of his own children's books (*The Lion, the Witch, and the Wardrobe*, in the Narnia series), called "It All Began with a Picture..." and an angry "Reply to Professor Haldane" (also previously unpublished), defending the trilogy, *Out of the Silent Planet*, *Perelandra*, and *That Hideous Strength*, against Haldane's criticisms–and in the process providing a fascinating insight into the author's mind. "On Criticism" is another lecture appearing here in print for the first time. Although it addresses itself specifically to the author/critic, on how to "improve himself as a critic by reading the criticisms of his own work," it is as cogent a commentary on the purpose and function of literary criticism as I can recall, and should be required reading for authors *and* critics both. "Unreal Estates" is the taped discussion between Lewis, Brian Aldiss, and Kingsley Amis, recorded for publication in *S. F. Horizons 2*, shortly before Lewis's death, a piece probably familiar by now to many *F&SF* readers.

My own favorite of them all is the opening selection, "On Stories," originally published as a contribution to the 1947 volume, *Essays Presented to Charles Williams* (Oxford University Press), in which Lewis expresses with unique clarity and comprehension, the essential *virtu* of all the many kinds of story that make up "s-f."

[...]

Re-readability is, of course, the test for anything, but under certain circumstances it becomes too severe a test. Since the time, a year ago, when I filled this column with my own personal Discovery of England, I have been trying keep up with s-f publishing in both countries, and have been developing an acute case of double-image vision in the process. I write, at the moment, from London, where some of the more interesting new books this season include William Tenn's *Time in Advance*, Frederik Pohl's *Alternating Currents*, Kate Wilhelm's *Andover and the Android*, and Donald Barthelme's *Come Back, Dr. Caligari*. (Last winter saw the first London publication of a critical volume not to be confused with the C. S. Lewis book, Lloyd Arthur Eshbach's 20-year-old *Of Worlds Beyond*.)

The time gap tends to be narrower crossing the ocean westward. Most British books appear in the US within six months or a year, if they appear at all; but, for instance, there is the E. J. Carnell series of anthologies of origin stories, *New Writings in S. F.*[2] The ninth volume has just appeared here, and the second is either just out, or just about to be, in New York. (As it has worked out, I have read the first two of these, and the seventh and ninth: Number Seven is outstanding, with two good-average entries by James White and R. W. Mackelworth, three superior jobs by William F. Temple, John Rankine, and Robert Presslie, and two genuinely memorable stories, Keith Roberts's "Manscarer" and "The Man Who Missed the Ferry" by Douglas R. Mason….)

[…]

Which brings me back around to the matter of re-readability. Although the Aldiss volume is a selection rather than collection, covering his first eleven years of short story publishing (1954-1965), four, at least, of the fourteen stories have never been published in the US, and two of these, as well as two others, were new to me. Of the ten I had previously read, I was impressed to find myself rereading almost all with fresh interest—and at the same time disturbed to realize that with the exceptions of "Psyclops" and "Old Hundredth," everything I first read more than two or three years ago *was* fresh: I did not so much remember the stories, as remember having read them.

This is not true for all of Aldiss's works; there is a rich assortment of titles I still recall in wide-vision, full-color mentascope, even without the aid of a refresher collection. There is another author with whom I have experienced this sort of thing, and there are probably a good many parallels to be drawn between Aldiss and Theodore Sturgeon. Certainly Aldiss is one of the very few others who can tell an essentially unimportant story so well that I enjoy it just as much after I've forgotten it. Nor is this simple "story-telling" facility: it is (in both authors) a brightness of imagery, a warmth of empathy, a *caring* about even the most insignificant character, that communicates itself to the reader intact (…the sort of man who *can* find it in his own back garden…).

And of course—again for both authors—when they get hold of something solid in a story, it is *entirely* memorable. Thus, from this volume, I think I will recall "Not for an Age," "Dumb Show," and "Man on Bridge" (…) as vividly ten years from now as I still do the two titles mentioned above. A high percentage, after all, particularly from a collection selected by the author himself.

[…]

William F. Temple's *Shoot at the Moon*[4] is a good solid mainline astronaut adventure, with an intriguing grouping of not quite credible but entertaining characters, a few scenes on the Moon that gave me genuine chills, and a fast enough, smooth enough pace so I read straight through.

John Brunner's *The Long Result*[5] is a bit disappointing after *The Whole Man* and *The Squares of the City*: a touch of preachiness, perhaps, which may be responsible too for the feeling that the tempo is a bit *off*. But the basic idea, as usual, is solidly thought through, and interestingly developed. A thriller of sorts, I suppose, with a hero employed by Earth's (interstellar) Bureau of Cultural Relations exposing the vicious "The Stars Are for Man" League.

Harry Harrison's *Make Room! Make Room!*,[6] is included in this listing because (like his last two novels) it was first published in England, is a good fast-paced colorful book, offering a somewhat fresh approach to the over-population theme. I found Harrison's premises rather shaky, but the reasoning and plotting built on them very solid; the end did not quite sustain my interest, but the central part of the book was strong enough to make me entirely forget my quibbles with the underlying hypothesis. The writing and characterization are back to Harrison's usual standard (back from last year's disastrous *Plague from Space*). Good reading.

L. P. Davies's *The Paper Dolls*[7] is published as a mystery, and I suppose it is one—but more in the mood of Margery Allingham than any of the sixties-thrillers: some very convincing English countryside, and a modernized-Gothic plot with mutant telepaths, superstitious farmers, remote-control murders, and some first-rate story-telling that carries you through the improbabilities.

Inner Circle,[8] by Jerzy Peterkiewicz [aka Pietrkiewicz], is difficult to describe briefly. Three narratives are interwoven: *Surface* is a future world, featureless except for the Hygiene Boxes, squashingly populated, in which the "inner circle" consists of the narrator, his two wives and two adopted brothers, linked in a whirling circle to maintain a spot of empty space to call their own under the pressure of seething thousands all around them; *Underground* is a present-time story of social and emotional dislocation—the "inner circle" is the Circle Line of the London Underground; *Sky* is the story of Eve's last years, after Eden, and the "inner circle" is part of the magic sign distinguishing humanity from the beasts. The three narratives interrelate only—only?—on a symbolic level. The book is lavishly and wittily illustrated by F. N. Souza, and I am not quite certain whether it was the text or the drawings that affected me most. I am not even certain it is a good book: only that it fascinated me, and continues to echo in my mind. Not for the prudish.

Notes

1. *Of Other Worlds*, C. S. Lewis; Harcourt Brace & World, 1967; Bles, London, 16s.
2. *New Writings in SF 1*, E. J. Carnell, ed.; Bantam F3425, 1966; 147 pp., five stories; 50¢.

[...]

4. *Shoot at the Moon*, William F. Temple; Simon & Schuster, 1966; 249 pp.; $4.50.
5. *The Long Result*, John Brunner; Ballantine U2329, 1966; 190 pp.; 50¢.
6. *Make Room! Make Room!*, Harry Harrison; Doubleday, 1966; 213 pp.; $3.95.
7. *The Paper Dolls*, L. P. Davies; Doubleday Crime Club, 1966; 216 pp.; $3.95.
8. *Inner Circle*, Jerzy Peterkiewicz; Macmillan of London, 1966; 185 pp.; 36s.

Books (March 1967)

The topic for today's sermon is Sex.

(And the next line, of course, is supposed to be "…and now that I have your attention…." Actually, I'll be getting back to sex. Meantime—)

Two of the most-discussed and best-selling books of the fall publishing season provide, in their contrasts as well as their common points, some basis at last for understanding what the "science fiction" category label, as currently used in book publishing, actually signifies. Although neither volume uses the label anywhere on its jacket, each of them is an excellent example of a familiar type of s-f: two very different varieties, lying at opposite ends of (but clearly within) the traditional spectrum of "science fiction."

The fact that one of these is a comic-strip book and the other a 700-page novel of extraordinary literacy does not in either case detract from the solid s-f virtues of either one. Nor should the habitual reader of the genre be put off by the pretentious *apologias* enclosing both books (in the jacket-flap copy of one, and in the introductions and postscripts to the other). Oddly enough, though quite in keeping with the inversion layers of the publishing climate these days, the comic book comes from Grove Press, and the serious (and possibly important, as well as "Important") novel from Doubleday.

Barbarella is essentially space opera of the good-old *Planet* or *Startling* variety, comparable in plotting, pace, color, and (most of its) content, to the happiest memories of Ed Hamilton and Leigh Brackett, the early Ray Bradbury, and the emergent Jack Vance.

Giles Goat-Boy is a philosophic-picaresque novel of the general type of Pangborn's *Davy* or Sheckley's *Journey Beyond Tomorrow* (in *F&SF* as *The Journey of Joenes*) the education-and-adventures of a uniquely innocent and potent young hero, through whose eyes and actions, in an analogous other-universe, our own society is explored.

Virtually the only points the two books have in common are precisely those factors which set them apart from category s-f publishing, and three out of four of these factors are size: They are both big books, one in length, the other in format.

[…]

They are both big sellers: *Giles* is doing so well that Doubleday is reissuing a revised hardcover edition of Barth's last novel, *The Sotweed Factor*. *Barbarella*, according to the jacket, sold 20,000 copies of its original French edition at art-book prices—and this does not include, presumably, the figures for its underground sales since being reportedly banned in Paris

They are both Big critically—I mean, *in*. John Barth, of course, has been a favorite of the Literary Establishment for some time, and now bids fair to inherit the #1 spot on the college campuses from Tolkien. As for *Barbarella*, I quote from the jacket copy, which quotes from the French literary weekly, *Arts* (a serious and respected journal, *honestly*): "*Barbarella* recaptures the spirit of the American comic strips of the early days when even the impossible was possible. It has the same audacity and originality, the same mixture of fantasy and humor, beauty and horror, cruelty and eroticism. In its physical appearance, and inspiration, in its heroine and its themes, *Barbarella* reflects not only filmic and literary techniques, but also certain conflicting ideals of our times.

"*Barbarella*...is the archetype of the modern female. She is the modern vamp, the woman who offers herself from billboards, ads, and movies...the liberated woman, who constantly controls her own destiny rather than submitting to the dictates of men...a creature of the future who, confronted with the monsters and robots of an unknown planet, is put to the test like a medieval knight or the heroes of old.... Barbarella is not only desirable, capricious, and fascinating; she is also in quest of the absolute."

Other quotes include: "the first comic strip for grown-ups," "a truly mythic character," "a modern epic," and "the incarnation of the eroticism of today."

With which we come to the fourth, and most significant, factor separating both the pleasant absurdity of the one book and the possible sublimity of the other from what is published and sold as "science fiction": I *said* I'd get back to Sex.

And indeed I will—after a brief pause for novel identification. That is, although *Giles Goat-Boy* is much concerned with sex, sexuality, and sexual behavior, and although these elements are responsible for much of what is good in the book, it is by no means a "sex novel," nor even a novel primarily about Sex. So before I get into my Sex Sermon, it seems best to pause and fill in something of the context and character of this wonderfully complex and even more wonderfully enjoyable novel.

My first, and probably only adverse, comment is a recommendation to skip the introductory matter, where the author, in various personae, explains why a book of this sort is really Okay, if not indeed Great—and incidentally, why he doesn't give a damn whether you like it or not (which I very much doubt is correct—and I for one am weary of the reverse-sell). Beyond these thirty-odd roman-numeraled pages is a second title page, which reads:

R.N.S.

The
Revised New Syllabus
of
George Giles
Our Grand Tutor

Being the Autobiographical and
Hortatory Tapes Read Out at
New Tammany College to His Son
Giles (,) Stoker

By the West Campus Automatic
Computer
And by Him Prepared for
the Furtherment of
the Gilesian Curriculum

The excerpts above are from the first chapter; after which, George meets a wonderful human called Lady Creamhair, who arouses him, with peanut butter and fairy tales, to a recognition of his own membership in the race. George is then prepared by Max for his eventual entrance into New Tammany College. His education during this period convinces him that he has a very special destiny: that indeed he is the predicted new Grand Tutor, who will have the power to enter the Belly of WESCAC, the giant computer, and change its AIM, so as to end forever the terrible threat of a totally annihilative Campus Riot III with either Nikolay or T'ang College, or both of them.

Armed with his goatherding stick, protected by an amulet made of the testicles of Freddie, the greatest buck of the herd, and accompanied by Max and by G. Herrold (a lowly library assistant who lost most of his mind under WESCAC's deadly EAT rays while rescuing the infant-George from the

Belly), the Hero-to-be sets out for West Campus. On the way, he encounters the beautiful Anastasia (who, quite by accident, lures G. Herrold to his death); Croaker, the half-savage giant from one of the newly emergent Frumentian colleges; Maurice Stoker and his blackleather-motorcycle retinue of Powerhouse guards; and Peter Greene, the paper and plastics tycoon responsible for the roadside signs, *Keep Our Forests Greene.*

George soon learns that others besides Max are cynical about the realities of the Finals, Graduation, and Commencement Gate, but perseveres in his own faith and gains acceptance as a Special Student by forcing an entrance to the registration area (the first in all studentdom to do so since mythic times) through the fabled Scrapegoat Grate (overcoming the ritual opposition of Stoker in the traditional role of Dean O'Flunks). George then wins an Assignment from WESCAC, completion of which will qualify him for his Finals and, presumably, enable him to oust the false Grand Tutor, Harold Bray.

The Assignment is a list of seven tasks "to be done at once in no time": George must *Fix the Clock*, *End the Boundary Dispute*, *See through My Ladyship*, and perform other largely ambiguous labors, which bring him into close association with Dr. Eblis Eierkopf, of the lenses, mirrors, and measurements, and Classmate X of the Student-Unionist Nikolya College, and....

And so it goes. Education, theology (the Enos Enochites, the Moishians, etc.), science, politics (the Quiet Riot and Creeping Student-Unionism), psychiatry, social protest and social conformity (the *Beists* and the Midpercentile class), all come in for a share of the action. Barth does not have much to say that is new or startling on these topics, but he says so much *to the point* about so many things, and does it with stunning style and uproarious comedy. Whatever else may be happening, whenever anything is happening (aside from purely philosophic discussion), Sex also rears its variously lovely, ugly, wistful, joyous, painful, funny head.

Giles might have been a good book without the sex (I say doubtfully, because I can't imagine it that way), but it would not have been the *very* good book it is—and certainly not the first-rate science fiction it also is: because with all of Barth's acute observation and piercing comment on other aspects of human behavior, the only really speculative, experimental thinking in the book concerns the varieties of sexual and quasi-sexual relationships and activities worked out between the characters.

Barbarella, for that matter, would be a rather routine planet-story strip—a slightly fresher, more plausibly motivated, less careful though more colorful *Flash Gordon*—if it did not, as advertised, "incarnate the eroticism of today." To the extent that this description is accurate, the strip gains credibility: the girl-on-her-own either seeking sexual companionship or simply using sex as a ticket (or a bit of both) is a valid modern phenomenon, rather more believable as the central figure of an adventure series than the under-sexed high-minded Boy Scout of the space patrol, or Tom Swift of the trading ship or intergalactic governmental service. But "eroticism of today," while partially accurate, is quite inadequate as a description of Barbarella's adventures, which include a variety of experiences not yet available for testing in the flesh, and it is these incidents that supply the only real novelty of the strip.

Now as it happens, I like Sex as a topic, and I am heartily in favor of more and gustier public discussion. I enjoy reading and writing about it, and I like good pornography at least as much as any other good fiction. Those who feel otherwise will not care for *Barbarella*, and I suppose there are still some among us for whom *Giles* will be spoiled by its sexual content. But whatever the individual reader's preferences in subject matter, or prejudices in morality, I think there will be few who do not recognize—whether with delight, indifference, or horror—that however things *should* be, our society actually is in the midst of a tremendous upheaval in interpersonal behavior in general, and sexual mores in particular. The surface manifestations we are witnessing right now are only the first disturbances of a major groundswell. The combined, and in some ways conflicting tensions produced by nuclear anxiety, the population explosion, and the leisure byproduct of automation, along with the proliferation of psychochemical drugs of all sorts and the new technology of contraception, all coming hard on the heels of what a short time ago we still thought of as the Freudian "revolution"—all these, inevitably, are going to result in radical (and I mean "from the roots") changes in sexual attitudes and activities everywhere. (Changes which will be accelerated, I should expect, by the intercultural exchanges that have already begun, and will increase with the imminence of global television: if the Eskimos or the Samoans do it…?).

No doubt there will be back-swings as drastic as the experimental movements. We can anticipate, over the next generation or two, virtually every range of puritanism and licentiousness, of individualism and togetherness, of homo- and hetero- and auto- and ??-sexuality, in fits and fads and wild pendulum swings. We can—and some of us no doubt will—simply refuse to think about it. There are still some people who prefer not to think about the reality of chemical warfare, or of space travel, or DNA, or thought control, or antibiotics. But for better or worse, these things are now part of our conscious knowledge, and thus increasingly affect our personal lives. The same is true, without question, of the Pill and the Loop and time "psychic energizers" and tranquillizers and pep pills with which, more and more, we pre-determine our emotional states.

It is time, and long past time, for some of the same kind of hard-headed speculative thinking that science fiction contributed to space flight and atomics to be done in interpersonal psychology and sexology. The startling thing is not that it should appear now in a book like *Giles*, but that there has been so little of it *inside* science-fiction up till now.

Of course, a few things have been done. But by and large, what sex there has been in s-f has been conventional and "decorative" rather than speculative or exploratory. Except for some cautious handling of miscegenation themes, multiple marriage, and homosexuality (all greeted as radical and exciting within the field), almost all discussion has been impersonal or lavishly symbolic.

There are reasons, of course, and not all of them have been publishers' timidities, but few of them are applicable now. In particular, the new willingness of book publishers to handle longer novels in category publishing should make it more possible for s-f authors to deal adequately with intense personal topics. *Barbarella* is a good direction sign, and *Giles Goat-Boy* a fair start. But based on past performances under conditions of extreme limitation, I cannot help wondering what—for instance—Sturgeon, Aldiss, Heinlein, Leiber, Farmer, Zelazny, Ballard, Disch, Moorcock, Delany might do, if any of them really *tried?*

Books (May 1967)

Once upon a mundane time, before the first satellites went up to weave their orbital spells around the Earth—in the remote and disenchanted days when "pseudoscience" was the librarians reference term for space fiction—in that vanished past of a decade or more go, it was fashionable among learned critics to speak (often at length, always with condescension, sometimes with fury) of the phallic symbolism of the rocket as the underlying appeal of the "escapist fantasies" of science fiction.

I rather miss those angry old men now. It would be comforting, with space de-pseudoed, to hear the eminent distinctive voices still crying out against the (ab)use of non-fantasy rockets as virility symbols in the battle for potency between two great world powers. But it is no longer *in* for intellectuals to patronize man's yearning for the stars or his phallic fascinations. S-f and the Literary Underground made the highbrow-pop hit parade together, roughly coincidental with the Beatles, Op Art, and the God-is-Dead movement. The heavens are under attack in more ways than one. I am waiting now for the late-comer critic who will emerge with a mouthful of insight about the New Symbolism of Space and its Significance in Modern Man's search for New Gods to replace the One whose recent death has been so widely publicized by other learned doctors (with special claims to intimacy with the deceased).

On second thought: why wait? Listen, out there—

Space fiction is two kinds of things today: adventure stories and symbolic speculation. The adventure stories are *about* space flight; they are no longer what we real-true-*inside* readers of the stuff call science fiction. But, after a comparatively planet-bound period these last few years, the rockets have come back to science fiction in a new way. The flight into space is a symbol of the "expanding consciousness"; it is a symbol of growth; and it is, just now, very much a symbol of the search, not for god alone (although that exploration too is going on), but the meaning of god, and of man's search for god.

I do not mean to suggest that the treatment of religion in s-f is new: far from it; only that it has acquired a new importance, a new incisiveness, and perhaps most of all, a new element of compassion, or depth—a recognition of the subjective "reality" of religious experience to the individual human being. Although it was not the first of its kind, Walter M. Miller, Jr.'s *A Canticle for Leibowitz* is probably the landmark-work setting off the new kind of religion story from the (generally more "sociologically oriented") earlier sort.

(It is an intriguing coincidence, by the way, that the final section of that novel, "The Last Canticle," was published in this magazine during the same International Geophysical Year, 1957, in which the first satellites went up.)

In any case, a very large proportion of the more seriously speculative work now being produced is closely concerned with one or more aspects of what might be called the religious functions of man. And there seems to be an intensification and concentration of interest beginning to take place.

Four new novels in any case, have succeeded in exciting me as I read in a way that very little has done recently.

Frank Herbert's *Destination: Void* (Berkley, 50¢) is a meaty examination of the nature of "consciousness," of the "ego," and of "life," by a small group of highly trained people whose personal survival depends on learning enough to build these attributes into an electronic computer. In *Night of Light* (Berkley, 50¢), Philip José Farmer is concerned with the nature and significance of "miracles" and "divine manifestations," and the ethical and theological conflicts posed by diverse manifestations in a universe no longer conceived of as uniform in its "realities." Clifford D. Simak explores differing concepts of "Immortality" and the relationship between belief-in-survival (whether in the flesh or spirit) and social mores, in *Why Call Them Back from Heaven?* (Doubleday, $3.95). The fourth book, not published as science fiction, is described in the jacket flap as "the most brutal fairy tale since Anderson and Grimm yielded the form to Tolkien, C. S. Lewis and Golding." *The Scorpions*, by Robert Kelly (Doubleday, $3.95), centers on the question of the efficacy of the several most customary modes of defense (ritual, fetish, insight, faith, reason, violence, to name a few) attempted by terrified mortals in the face of the expanding unknown of the "known" universe.

In one sense each of these books, individually, is unsatisfying; considered as conventional novels, they offer a particularly well-rounded variety of failings. Farmer has tacked together two widely separated episodes in the career of John Carmody, the criminal-turned-priest with whom many *F&SF* readers are familiar; the book suffers not only from the characteristic stiff joints of such novelettes-become-novel, but also from the unhappy improbable-quasi-caricature feeling so many "series character" stories seem to acquire in the introductory scene-setting sections—and of course, there are two such bits to get through in this one. But the last halves of both sections are internally related and powerfully modeled, in full depth and dimension.

Simak seems to have compressed most of his thematic content into a tiny portion at the end of the book, in order to make space, within a standard-length category book, for a disappointing action-adventure midsection. But the beautifully balanced opening, in which character, plot, and context form an inner-motivated unity, provides basis enough to take the reader through the comparatively empty middle, to the extremely provocative, though sketchy, conclusion.

Herbert's book has the vices of its virtues. It is a "puzzle story" of the memorable (but largely unreadable) type characteristic of the best idea-stories of the early Campbell *Astounding.* That is, the characters and setting seem to be devised essentially as components of the puzzle and tools for its solution. After the manner of such stories, the book consists almost entirely of dia- and monologues, both interpersonal and interior, which set forth the progress of the argument, and of engineering sessions at the electronics bench, in which the pretty girl hands parts and pieces to the inspired engineer—with a bit of hot math thrown in for emotional kick. Yet these primitivisms are easy to ignore (are perhaps proper because they *can* be ignored?), in favor of concentration on the genuinely, and consistently, exciting pursuit of ideas which constitutes the true action of the book.

Kelly comes from a different tradition entirely. His prose (or, as often, prose-poetry) is a consistent delight, and he can impart an illusion of reality to the most trivial, clichéd, and inane characters. He works in the true tradition of the symbolists, and does it knowingly, charmingly, and effectively. But so many of his concepts and characters *are* trivial-to-inane, and if not exactly clichéd (because contemporary), distressingly derivative. His protagonist seems to be compounded of equal parts of Nero Wolfe, 007, the Dharma Bums, and Alistair Crowley; his imaginative scope suggests a landscape of Henri Michaux's projected in cinemascope on the sides of the Batmobile. It is only a mastery of narrative and description (perhaps equal to Michaux's) that carries one on to the (deliberate) irresolution of the non-ending.

Four frustrating books—yet in Kelly's campy, careful nihilism, as in Herbert's scientistic positivism (*Destination: Void*, despite its title, is the only book of the four that presumes anything like an answer to the questions posed), and in the more moderate approaches of the other two, I did find that special kind of excitement that has become all too rare in the new novels—the particular kind of thrill that creates the "science fiction addict" and can only originate in the author's own excitement in exploring unmapped territories of the mind.

Simak, for instance, deals with the effect on society of the kind of deep-freeze potential immortality we have heard so much about recently. He describes a rigid neo-puritan culture, a world of penny-pinching, body-saving, emotional isolationists, living as unremittingly for the Next Life as every fundamentalist Christian did, because any man or woman who fails to provide an adequate investment sum to grow for him while he is frozen, will be unable to compete in the reawakened society. A truism, actually: the same phenomenon that pressures the high school student to work for nothing but grades, in order to be admitted to college, or the university undergraduate to work for nothing but grades in order to be admitted to graduate school, the graduate fellow to, etc., in order to gain a research fellowship. (There it changes; the research fellow works for publication, not grades, to get a professorial appointment.) It is belief in the future that makes us capable of sacrifice; absolute belief in literal immortality, of whatever sort, makes us virtually incapable of non-sacrifice.

The only free men in such a society are the outcasts. In the world of Forever Center, this means the rare criminals who have had a "death sentence" and walk as living ghosts through the rest of their natural lives, aware that when they die, it will be for the last time, and forever; or those less finally cut off, who retain their right to a new life, but wear the brand of ostracism, so that they are unable to work in any way to prepare for the next world.

From this base, Simak poses problems relevant to all concepts of immortality and the basic premises of most Western concepts of God.

Farmer tackles a different aspect of religious belief. By presupposing a planet on which verifiable miracles actually occur, and where, through a form of mass telekinesis, the entire population can and does at intervals literally *create* a flesh-and-blood god, he poses two vital questions:

> 1) If it is true that Man created God in his own image, rather than God giving life to Man, does that diminish the "reality" of the created Being? Is God less "real" for being the created rather than creator?
>
> 2) If Man does create God, and the image in which the creation is patterned varies with every culture and time and place, is one God

> more "true" than another? Does the God of the wisest and most virtuous people outrank the manifestation of a thieving nomad tribe, for instance? Is a Galactic God more powerful, or more valid, than a local planetary one?

Kelly and Herbert are both less Christian and more catholic in the questions they raise; neither one presupposes the importance of any literal manifestation of deity; they are more concerned with the way in which man can relate to his own concept of godhead to the advantage of his inner satisfaction and outward efficacy. In many ways, these two books are opposite numbers, examining from very different platforms much the same problems of consciousness, ego, and the meaning of life.

Kelly starts with a hero convinced he has attained a fair degree of wisdom on these matters, living a carefully ritualized and insulated existence, in which he is almost totally isolated from communion with other people: as psychiatrist, he is mirror or camera to his patients; as a private man, he surrounds himself only with people who will function as mirrors or servants. He is then taken out of his temple/office/home, and must test the validity of his wisdom in direct contact with life.

Herbert proposes a dynamic concept instead: "…consciousness is a field phenomenon.… It's not introspection, not sensing, feeling, or thinking.… It's not synonymous with awareness. It's neither subjective nor objective. It's a relationship…" and later, "*Emotion…the characteristic that gives us our sense of person, the thing that summates personal judgments. A process in capsule form that can occur out of sequence.* Here was a break with all machine concepts of time—emotion as process, an audacious way of looking at time." […]

It is not possible to point out all the ways in which these four apparently unrelated approaches intersect with each other to achieve a geometric progression of ideation. I do want to take a bit of space, however, to return to the business of symbols.

Part of the reason for the success of each of these books, even in limited terms, is the accuracy (or intuition) with which the backgrounds, the imaginative elements of the environments, were selected in each case. *Only* an alien planet could supply the appropriate symbolic level for Farmer's concepts. Herbert's novel would have been a dull, not-much-dramatized essay if the same project were being researched in a ground laboratory; but in an exploratory space ship, with all the knowledge of the universe as the potential reward, imminent death the penalty for failure, and no help at all available from parent Earth (beyond the training and equipment already provided before the departure), the search for "self" *and* "god" acquires emotional importance even in the absence of either plot-action or credible characters.

In some ways, the *absence* of the spaceships, or near-absence actually, in the other two book provides a clearer indication of the significance of their use as symbols. In Simak's novel, space has ceased to represent a frontier; it is real estate, being processed by Forever Center for the eventual reawakening of millions of bodies. All frontiers, physical and spiritual, are barred to this life, postponed to the next. But most impressive of all is Kelly's grounded pseudo-spaceship: an impregnable Rolls Royce, equipped with what amounts to an astronaut's life-system, for all practical earthbound purposes—carrying its own food and drink and toilet facilities, equipped with defensive and offensive armament, and totally opaque for womb-like privacy.

I think this is only the beginning. I am waiting impatiently to see what will come next: not just the other books undoubtedly on their way already, but the ones we'll see *next* year, building on what has been published so far.

Books (June 1967)†

In this month's "Books" column, Merril reviews two nonfiction books, The Supernatural by Douglas Hill and Pat Williams and Intelligent Life in the Universe by I. S. Shklovskii and Carl Sagan. The two books "span the full topical spectrum of science fantasy: the extra-galactic to the extra-sensory, dybbuks to Dyson spheres, laserphones to lycanthropy."

The first volume on the supernatural covers topics such as magic and witchcraft, spiritualism and psychic investigators. While Merril finds interest in the supernatural, she reject both the "supersceptic" and the evangelist. This volume, however, find an intelligent middle ground.

The second volume was written by two astronomers, one from the US and one from the Soviet Union. Although the two could never met in person, and despite some ideological differences of opinion, Shklovskii and Sagan offer an engaging report from the vanguard of astrophysics. Both texts are simplistic enough for the average reader and, yet, contains the essentials.

† Full text in the E-book version.

Quotes from original "Books" column.

Books (August 1967)†

In this short "Books" column, Merril notes the rapid pace at which SF titles are being published, though "a shocking proportion of them are not worth mentioning." Among the dross, however, she finds eight novels to comment upon, if ever-so briefly. She notes that part of the problem with novels and novel writing is economics. The novelist commits a great deal of time in writing a novel, and therefore, the author has a tendency to write something familiar, something tried and true. For story writers, however, they have a short-term investment in the product. In addition, they have more—and more varied—markets to which they can pitch their story. They can afford to take greater risks. Consequently, she finds many of the story collections are better than the novels. She offers ever-so-brief comments on eight collections.

† Full text in the E-book version.

Quotes from original "Books" column.

Books (September 1967)

> *The purpose of this volume has been to display both by word and example what the editor means when he uses the term "sense of wonder" in relationship to science fiction. In the process, three truly marvelous short novels have been rescued from pulp oblivion.*
>
> *Beyond the considerable entertainment quotient of these stories, it is hoped that their examples may make a significant enough impression so as to bring about not a substitution of this type of story for what is being written today, but an incorporation of the elements they contain into the mainstream body of modern science fiction.*

The volume in question is *Three Stories* (by Leinster, Williamson, and Wyndham in his John Beynon Harris incarnation, Doubleday, $3.95). The editor, and author of the didactic seventeen-page introduction, is of course Sam Moskowitz (known through science fiction fandom as just SaM).

I have read SaM's commentary, though I confess to skipping his synopses of *Gulliver*, *The Odyssey*, and *The Time Machine*, and just skimming some pages of history of "The Golden Age of the Scientific Romance" (as represented primarily in *Argosy* and *All-Story Weekly*, 1906-1919), and I am not much clearer about what he means when he says Sense of Wonder, but I have pretty well decided that my own problem is not so much atrophied SoW as undeveloped SoN.

N is for Nostalgia, and on this SaM is an expert, even by the standards of Pop Culture. I don't know if it came out of a surfeit of newness and change, or perversely, just that nothing *really new* has happened lately. (I mean, it's *ten years* now since the last Real Breakthru—and no men on the moon yet, no cancer cure, no global war, time travel, anti-gravity, immortality pill.) Whatever the reason, the big N is *in*, and anything from Aubrey Beardsley through left-wing Americana of the thirties will put you with it.

And of course, science fiction is ahead of the field; the program *Inside S-f* has been underway for years. We have ERB cults and Conan clubs and EE-Smith concordances, but most of all, we have SaM. From the horse's mouth:

> *We see on every side nostalgia becoming the secret ingredient that today moves the more mature adults to experience again some of the exhilaration associated with their youth. [Using dime-novel collectors*

as an example, SaM explains that rereading an old book] became a trigger for nostalgic remembrance, in detail, of the innocence and bittersweet of their youth. It was a literary windshield wiper which cleared the mist from memory, enabling the mature mind to view with understanding the wonder of a youthful day forever past....

The child or teenager who originally read the dime-novel truly had that sense of wonder within himself. The child grown old re-stored the memory of those past....

It is legitimate to ask, can the author induce a sense of wonder in the reader without the existence of a special mental receptivity and appropriate subjective conditions of age and timing?

Before I give you his answer, I must pause to assure anyone unfamiliar with SaM's work that he is in deadly earnest: SaM is perhaps the only American writing critical copy today who has less understanding of camp than Susan Sontag. And he makes that clear:

The sad part about the revival of "comic" hero characters is that they are making their way with the adults as satirization *of themselves.*

Two Broadway musicals supplied SaM with the answer to his troubling question: *Superman* and *The Private Life of Sherlock Holmes.* He says:

It never was the intent of the creators of Superman to convince anyone above the age of twelve of the reality of their character. No adult could hope to retain an interest in so far-fetched a character except *as a satire.* [But] *a Sherlock Holmes story, read for the first time, holds the same sway over the imagination of an adult as it does for a child.*

And so:

The answer is in the positive if he [the author] combines sincerity with his relation and creates a mood that will engage the emotion as well as the intellect of his reader.

How does all this apply to science fiction? It seems there was a survey in the *Science Fiction Yearbook* for 1957 which showed that only 12½% of the readers of s-f were over 40. Allowing for the probability that what this actually means is that 12½% of science fiction fan club and convention members ten years ago were over 40, it is as recent as most census figures, and as representative as most polls: at least 1% and possibly 2% of the total readership. In any case, SaM wants to know why more of his (and my) generation are not interested in his (and my) favorite reading matter. Is science fiction "less necessary" as one grows older?

> *...Has a man or woman after forty either relaxed in the attainment of an acceptable degree of creature comforts and economic security, or resigned him or herself to distinct limitations and, in either case, found that science fiction is no longer a bright roadmap of the future and that it offers no escape from the reality of their situations?*
>
> *This should be true only if the sense of wonder is generated only in the individual with the content of science fiction merely a source of ignition. However, if a sense of wonder can be made an ingredient of the story...it should be possible to revive the feeling, no matter what the age of the individual.*

I have quoted all this because, after reading it myself, I am not honestly sure whether I am arguing with SaM or agreeing with him, when I say: although I will be 45 on my next birthday, and that birthday is not very far away, I guess I am one of the *less* mature adults, because I haven't yet started getting my biggest charges out of *remembering* my biggest charges. Nostalgia, for me, is a sleepy sort of thing—maybe maudlin at a beery 3 a.m.—perhaps more sentimental in a lingering summer twilight—but either way associated with a low pulse-rate. It certainly is not what makes me read science fiction.

It all makes me wonder if maybe my SoW hasn't been operating all this time after all? I've been sitting around with the rest of the gang all these years while SaM gave us hell for losing our SoWs, and I kept thinking I had no business arguing back, because I have the sort of guilty thing, see? about being the only one in my age bracket (apparently) who didn't start reading the stuff when *Air Wonder* began. (I mean, I was three in 1926, and perfectly able, to read—well, all right, not *perfectly*—and I sat around spelling out Kipling and Carroll and Milne when everyone else was already digging those truly marvelous stories. I could plead financial incapacity; I didn't have my own allowance yet. But when I did get it, I blew it on stuff like Keats and Housman and Whitman. Anyhow—) I didn't actually come to s-f till the ripe age of 18: the 1938-42 magazines. (Ragged starting dates due to financial problems again—no more allowance; I started in the 2nd hand magazine stores.)

I have gone back since then, and read some earlier work. And at least one thing SaM said, I know I do agree with—his comment on Sherlock Homes. Believe it or not, I never read a Holmes story until 1949, and then read every one I could get my hands on. The same thing was true for some science fiction

(I'll get down to some specifics later): but one thing I know I don't agree with SaM about is his choice of examples to demonstrate *whatever* he was saying.

I gave all three of these "truly wonderful" stories an honest try, and I even got all the way through one of them.

Leinster's (1934) "Mole Pirates" I *almost* managed to finish. After the first third, I skimmed my way through to the end, because—no matter how absurd his story, Leinster has the basic storytelling-gift. I had to know how it came out—but I didn't really care *why*, and it was too tedious following the twists and turns on the way. The story is about this Desperate Scientist Criminal who steals Jack Armstrong's—I'm sorry, Jack Hill's—Wonderful Invention, a machine that can travel through solid matter, and uses it to satisfy his psychotic need to Rob, Rape, Loot, Steal, Despoil, and Slaughter. It is full of stuff like this:

> *He flung a switch and vacuum tubes glowed. A curious, ghostly light appeared above the white-painted sheet of metal on the table.... "I am going to coordinate all the atom poles in this piece of brass," he observed. "Around the shop, here, the men say that a thing treated in this way is dematerialized. Watch!" [The block is exposed to "the field," and—] Instead of a solid cube of polished brass, there was the tenuous, misty outline of a cube.... He swept his hand through the misty block.... A skeptical silence hung among the reporters.*
>
> *"If that brass was still there, an' it would pass through anything else, it'd slide right through the sheet metal an' drop through the floor!"*
>
> *"Radio-activity," said Jack. "The only exception. When coordinated matter is bombarded by radio-active particles, some of the atoms are knocked halfway back to normal. This paint has thorium oxide in it...."*

This must have been exciting speculation in 1934. For that matter, the basic idea remains speculatively interesting: people are still writing science fiction about aligning atoms to make matter inter-penetrative. But the newer stories are easier to read (even when they are no better or more enduring than this one) just because they are in the idiom and use the storytelling conventions of the sixties. (Leinster's story starts out vaguely *wrong* for today's reader, because an invention of this sort is being developed privately and displayed to the press with no security protection. Perhaps the editors were wise to maintain the period-piece effect by keeping the original spellings of words like coordinate and radio-active. It helps hype up the necessary SoN.)

As for the Williamson, I cannot tell you of my own knowledge what it is about, except that an anti-gravity machine turns out to be a time machine instead, and (according to SaM's careful introductory description) the plot derives from S. Fowler Wright's *The World Below*, in which a man *disembarking from his time machine saves a female-like creature from death.... At times when his energies are depleted, she is able to impart to him, with a touch, some of her own, to enable him to carry forth an urgent venture. Though there can never be anything physical between them, a strong emotional tie does develop.*

This identical situation is taken by Williamson and in "The Moon Era" developed into a relationship between alien and human in mutual peril of such delicacy and feeling that the story becomes a complete success in the tradition of A. Merritt, conveying the elements of constantly new wonder and mystery....

Here is how it is conveyed by Williamson:

He rose, agilely enough for one of his seventy years, and led the way from the long room. Through several magnificent rooms of the big house. Out into the wide, landscaped grounds, beautiful and still in the moonlight.

I followed silently. My brain was confusion. A whirl of mad thought. All this wealth whose evidence surrounded me might be my own! I cared nothing for luxury, for money itself. But the fortune would mean freedom from the thankless toil of pedagogy. Books. Travel. Why I could see with my own eyes the scenes of history's dramatic moments!...

I have enjoyed Jack Williamson's later work too much, and I have too much respect for the ability he has since developed, to be willing to go on reading that—particularly after learning from SaM that the story itself is directly derivative from Merritt and Wright, two writers I did *not* find still-viable when I went back to try them out.

The one I did get all the way through was the Harris/Wyndham: it is even possible that I might have read this story on my own if I'd come across it on the sort of idle day I used to have when there was nothing I *had* to read. It is written in English, with no offensive stylistic mannerisms; it has a solid hook at the beginning: the viewpoint character is tolerably convincing (and must have been overwhelmingly so in 1933). Even the bat-like aliens living in caves on an asteroid, enslaving captive humans, provide a couple of scenes the first time they appeared that will stick with me. I can see why this one would have stuck in SaM's memory; on two counts at least (besides the literary quality) it would have been an extraordinary story in the thirties. The aliens are neither gods nor devils, but simply castaways, surviving the only way they can. (They even let the surplus, non-useful human leave peaceably.) But what must have provided the greatest impact—in 1933—was the use of the dramatic new brainwashing discoveries of the Behaviorists. The aliens use infant conditioning techniques to accomplish the enslavement of their victims to the total satisfaction of the slaves themselves.

Which brings us to the core of the matter. Harris (Wyndham) wrote his story at just about the same time that another British writer, Aldous Huxley, wrote a book with the same gimmick—probably inspired by the same recent work in psychology—but where "Exiles of Asperus" can still claim to be readable, *Brave New World* is a major contemporary novel, as vital today as when it was published.

It is too easy to say: Huxley was a better writer. I am not at all sure he was that much better, or that (beyond a certain level which Wyndham automatically attains) prose and rhetoric are that important in the durability of a novel. The essential difference, I believe, is that "Exiles" is, like the other two stories in the Moskowitz collection, nothing more than a plot wrapped around a gimmick; *Brave New World* used the gimmick to construct a statement of significance about the world we live in.

I have never heard a word from SaM about the Sense of Wonder in *Brave New World.* Perhaps if I ever do find out what he does mean when he says it, I'll decide that—by his standards—I have gone and lost mine after all?

[...]

Books (November 1967)

They call it The New Thing.

The people who call it that mostly don't like it, and the only general agreements they seem to have are that Ballard is its Demon and I am its prophetess—and that it is what is wrong with Tom Disch, and with British s-f in general.

There is a certain uneasiness in finding oneself the publicly appointed Defender of an undefined Faith. But the more I read of (what must be by simple subtraction) The Old Thing, the more inclined I am to take on the championship of TNT—especially as the very lack of definition provided by the innovators of the term leaves me in the happy position of being able to describe my own parameters. What sort of game is it that fits so agreeable a name?

I assume it is my enthusiasm for Ballard's work, and for much of what is being done by the group of new "*New Worlds* writers" in England (commonly, and erroneously, thought of as Ballard disciples by OT supporters here), that has identified me with TNT. I am now, as it happens, preparing an anthology of British s-f for Doubleday, which should make much clearer by example than I can possibly do by precept, some of the specifically British directions of TNT [*England Swings SF*, 1968]. But any sub-classification of new s-f writing which begins by including such basically dissimilar—and versatile—writers as Ballard and Disch can hardly be limited to the area cultivated by *New Worlds* and the late lamented *Impulse*. The American counterpart is less cohesive as a "school" or "movement": it has had no single publication in which to concentrate its development, and was in fact, till recently, all but excluded from the regular s-f magazines. But, for the same reasons, is more diffuse and perhaps more widespread. Without reference to such names as Barth and Barthelme, whose s-f qualifications would, I am sure, be hotly debated by TOT supporters, there is a clear vein of native NT running at least from Philip Dick to the American aspect of the split-Disch, and including among its more notable practitioners Kurt Vonnegut, David Bunch, Kit Reed, and above all, the late Cordwainer Smith. Add the less well-known (inside s-f) work of Carol Emshwiller, Vance Aandahl, Harvey Jacobs, and a score of others barely known in the s-f magazines. Remember that the antecedents of TNT begin (at least) with Kuttner, show up prominently in the best work of Sturgeon and Leiber, some of Kornbluth, most of McKenna, and good part of Budrys—not to mention memorable excursions into the area by Knight, Bush, Laumer, and Asimov, for instance. Finally, consider the nature of most of the recent work of such current OT favorites as Roger Zelazny, R. A. Lafferty, Samuel Delany, and Harlan Ellison.

The Thing isn't so New: it is nothing more than the application of contemporary and sometimes though mostly not very experimental literary techniques to the mind of contemporary/experimental speculation which is the essence of science fiction.

I have in front of me samples of the most recent work of at least half of the best currently active writers (British and American) of American science fiction: novels by Dick, Disch, and Delany, and two anthologies, one of which calls itself *World's Best Science Fiction 1967*,[1] while the other—*Orbit 2*[2]—spreads a big black catchline over its title, proclaiming, "The Best *All New* Science Fiction Stories of the Year."

The first of these collections is edited by Donald A. Wollheim and Terry Carr. Carr generally expresses a more open attitude toward TNT than most American editors; Wollheim is probably as solid an OT man as you'll find in the business. Quite possibly it is just this combination of editorial attitudes which has maintained the generally high level of this series—and predictably, the stories in this year's grouping tend to level out to a fairly even balance between old- and new-style selections. Predictability by name or source falls down almost entirely otherwise. Although there are four selections (out of the book's total of twelve) from *New Worlds*, and three selections which might fairly (though by no means emphatically) be described as examples of TNT, there is only one of those three which originally appeared in *NW*: Brian Aldiss's excellent "Amen and Out," a funny and tender (among other things) treatment of religion, robotics, and immortality (among other things). On the other hand, "Behold the Man"—also about religion, also from *NW*, and written by the editor of that magazine and chief spokesman for TNT, British style, Michael Moorcock—is a highly effective, completely conventional (in s-f) treatment of a Freudian-conventional view of the hero of that other NT, Jesus Christ.

Just to even things out, the farthest-out story in the book, and the only one to which the NT label can be unequivocally attached, was written by one of the most emphatic and influential opponents of (British, at least) TNT: Fred Pohl, editor of *Galaxy*. And the third NT item, R. A. Lafferty's "Nine Hundred Grandmothers," was published in *Galaxy*. (At the risk of further confusing the issues, I must add that I found both of these below-par both for the collection as a whole, and for their respective authors.)

The two Zelazny inclusions, again, criss-cross my line of definition: "For a Breath I Tarry" is written in a breathless quasi-poetic style usually associated with TNT, but there is not a breath of fresh idea in its crossbreeding of two of the hoariest plots in s-f; "The Keys to December" is exciting, complex, absolutely TNT speculation on education and religion (among other things) structured and styled in such a way as not to seem out of place in a collection of, say, the best from *Analog*. (Both stories appeared in *New Worlds*.)

Best-of-the-book, I'd say, are the Aldiss and Moorcock and Bob Shaw's (conventional, even sentimental, but vividly evocative and inventively consistent) "Light of Other Days," from *Analog*. The rest of the line-up consists of three good-ish stories by Philip K. Dick, Avram Davidson, and Paul Ash and two undistinguished entries by new authors, A. A. Walde and Dannie Plachta.

It is worth mentioning that in their brief preface the editors speak of the "relative scarcity of genuinely new ideas" in science fiction today. I think they are right—for traditional (which is to say, OT) science fiction: the new ideas today cannot be adequately written in the style of the gadget-and-gimmick ideas of the golden age of the American science fiction magazines. Just how true this is is made unhappily clear, I think in Damon Knight's *Orbit 2*.

This is the second of the Putnam-Berkley series of anthologies of original s-f. The jacket and flap-copy specify "science fiction," but I note that Knight has omitted a generalizing preface this time, and I expect he was motivated at least in part by the impossibility of reconciling the contents with his own frequently-stated concept of science fiction. Of the ten selections here, only Kate Wilhelm's "Baby, You Were Great" and (just barely) Aldiss's "Full Sun" would satisfy any reasonable traditional definition of science-fiction-proper.

Once again, there are three stories that might be described as TNT, but only one that is unarguably so—and this time I am pleased to say I also found it distinctively the best piece in the book: Kit Reed's story of adolescence, pop music, alienation, and dieting (among other things), "The Food Farm." McKenna's "Fiddler's Green" was probably unpublished previously precisely because of the way it straddles traditional fantasy and TNT: trimmed of its overlong simplistic-fantasy introduction, this might have been an exceptionally powerful symbolic exploration. Lafferty's "The Hole on the Corner" also seems to me a bit less economical in the writing than his best work, and somewhat looser-woven conceptually, as well.

In addition the book contains a straight mainstream story of no great merit by Philip Latham, a transplanted mainstream (medical missionary) story by Ted Thomas, an anti-heroic-fantasy by Gene Wolfe, and two delightfully literate but otherwise routine sword-and-sorcery stories by Joanna Russ.

The outstanding quality of the collection, in fact, is its literary merit. The book is eminently readable—but when you have finished, the sad note struck in the Wollheim-Carr introduction is even more strongly in evidence. Only in the Wilhelm, McKenna, and Reed selections is there any content worth chewing on; for the rest, ingenuity replaces idea, and technical excellence conceals conceptual emptiness.

And there's the crux of it: the people who find TNT uncomfortable now are the same readers and writers who turned away from The Old Thing of mainstream fiction twenty, thirty, or forty years ago for the explosive exploratory delights of The New Things science fiction was then offering—and who seem not to have noticed that speculation about space travel and the Marvelous Machine has become as routinely OT today as summer movie reruns on TV. There is a highly selective sort of blindness that afflicts the members of Establishments (call it the *Let 'em Eat Cake*! syndrome), and it does not discriminate between powerful governments, entrenched academicians, and loyal science-fictionists. It is what makes some people see all bearded men as Beatniks (or, thirty years ago, as Russians), and what made space science fiction look like romantic/escapist junk to parents, educators, and librarians right up till 1957. Presumably it is the same myopia that made the phrase "Black Power" seem no more than a political slogan to Congress—and allows the solid Science Fictioneers and one-time Futurians to look, for instance, on the Mothers of Invention (or the Fugs, or even Beatles) as well as pop art, student protest, the new sexual revolution, psychedelics, and a multiplex of other manifestations of the silly-sounding phrase, Flower Power, as collegiate antics comparable to goldfish-swallowing and phone-booth-cramming.

The Brave New World of the Flower People is not always comprehensible to me—but neither was nuclear physics when Heinlein and del Rey and [Cleve] Cartmill turned me on to atom power a quarter century ago. TNT is what Campbell gave us then, what Gold and Boucher gave us a dozen years later, and what looks as weird to some of our Establishments today as *Weird* looked to the readers of *Ballyhoo*.

But don't get me wrong: *Ballyhoo* had its good points, and so does some of the OT. (I mean, I even dig Jane Austen.) And *Weird* was pretty bad most of the time; so is a lot of The New Thing. But when it is bad, it is usually because the author's technique was not adequate to handle his concepts—rather than because his basic ideas were too old, too stale, or too flat to matter.

Philip K. Dick is admired, if anything, even more by Old Thing adherents than by TNT people. Yet, he is virtually the only established American s-f writer who demonstrates a consistent awareness of the facts of life in this country today.

Perhaps because his work is so colorful—and sometimes so garbled—Dick does not seem to be as highly regarded for the acumen of his political/sociological observations and projections as he deserves: this in spite of the fact that *The Man in the High Castle* is generally considered (on both sides of the Thing fence) to be his best book, and it is certainly the one with the least pyrotechnics and the most fully-developed socio-economic extrapolation. Since then, his work has been, in general, more flamboyant but more complex in concepts; and ambitious in scope, but seldom as fully realized.

The three recent novels under discussion here—*The Crack in Space*,[3] *The Zap Gun*,[4] *Counter-Clock World*[5]—are all somewhat more restrained: less infuriatingly *disconnected*, than most of the interim work (notably last year's *Now Wait for Next Year*—and the elusive quality of something-extra, a note quite graspable *plus*, which pervaded *Next Year* and *Palmer Eldritch*, is (if also somewhat modified) beginning to be more comprehensible.

That is to say, I think I have at last discovered what it is that at once delights and annoys me in the particular kind of *brightness* characteristic of Dick's work of the last five years or so—and it has to do with his appropriation of a very specialized and very contemporary aspect of pop art: an approach probably excellently well suited to his content—and incidentally, but relevantly, extremely irritating to me.

Pause for story identification: *Zap Gun* is the Romeo-and-Juliet story of Lars Powderdry, weapons fashion designer for Wesbloc, and Lilo Topchev, his opposite number in Peep East, set against a fascinatingly postulated near-future of intensely controlled economy, in which the two great powers maintain stability by the conduct of a false war, fought in mock-up on tabletops, while the "concomodies" on the UN-W Natsec Board think up ways to adapt the weapon designs to practical civilian use. *Counter-Clock World* contains one of the very few future-projections of the present Black Power movement in which there is any genuine comprehension of the issues, motivations, and directions of today's "insurrection," along with further comments on our anticulture, and some cogent asides on the character of contemporary matrimony—all thrown into a really unbelievably banal plot set in an amusing, sometimes-satiric, lightly-scatological reverse-time fantasy, whose burlesque-and-bathos effects almost neutralize the political concepts completely. *Crack in Space* uses abortions and human deep-freezing, a pleasure-satellite run by a two-headed mutant, and lots of fast action to veil a meaty account of economic and race issues in an election campaign.

In all three books, Dick makes use of every available color-and-motion effect—as well as his innate magnificent sense of timing—to create a spell-binding effect which carries the reader easily through the countless *non sequiturs* and logic-gaps of his plots. In every case, it takes aliens or supermen to get things resolved. The characters, going through a series of disconnected but (each time) briefly, convincing motions and emotions, seem to be painted entirely in primary colors—

And it was with that thought that the flash of insight came to me. Phil Dick is not writing novels, but comic-strip continuity—and when you chew on that thought a bit (even if, like me, you have trouble swallowing it) you may recognize that it is *not* a Bad Thing, after all. Dick is writing what the British critics like to call a "novel of ideas" rather than a "novel of manners." It doesn't matter what sort of nonsense he makes use of, to carry his concepts—as long as he can hold the reader, and as long as the idea-cargo itself comes through intact. He may offend my sense of fitness—but I learned to read out of Victorian novels. My children learned mostly out of comic books, and the public school adaptation of comics known to the Ed Biz as Visual Aids.

It may be pushing things a bit, but this view of Dick made me take a new look at Disch, who is represented here by two of his less New-Thing-y efforts: *Echo Round His Bones*,[6] and *Mankind under the Leash*[7] (an expansion of the magazine story, "White Fang Goes Dingo").

It is time, I think, for me to make an admission: when I wrote my wildly enthusiastic review of Disch's first novel, *The Genocides*, I had just finished reading the book. I still stand by what I said—but had I waited a week to set it down on paper, I should have said it much more mildly. Disch has a spell-binding trick of his own, and it resembles Dick's only in being intensely visual. The difference is, on one level, the reverse of the point about novels of manners and of ideas: Disch is concerned primarily with character interactions, and he uses his idea content, ordinarily, to construct a showcase for the behavior of his characters. But he focuses on only two or three individuals—and "focus" is the key word here. These are not comic-strip types, but movie characters: the caricature element is gone, and in its place is the illusion of depth which the motion picture added to the still photograph. The foreground figures are in full focus, and for the most part fully realized; the others at any point are "extras" whose illusion of reality need not be sustained an instant longer than it takes them to cross the screen (unlike the comic book, where the reader can always turn back).

Once again, what sounds like an indictment is meant as an observation of interest. In spite of what I think—or rather, how I *react*—I not only do not *think* there is anything wrong in this technique, but suspect that they are excellently well adapted to the authors' purposes as well as the readers' tastes.

[...]

Samuel Delany's new novel, *The Einstein Intersection*,[8] left me as divided in response after first reading as the Disch and Dick novels—but for very different reasons. I read the book at a gulp, delighted page by page, and disappointed at the end, without quite knowing why. When I went back to skim through and refresh myself before writing about it, I found myself re-reading instead: and found out it was the gulping that gave me that faint indigestion the first time.

Do not let the easy story surface and lyrical language mislead you: this is a dense mixture, heavily concentrated, double-distilled. If you cannot read slowly, with care—attention to each (believe me!) carefully-wrought sentence—if the pace carries you along too swiftly—then go with it, but go back afterwards, and discover what you missed (or some of it; I suspect I will find more next time, and perhaps more again after that). The epigraphs and excerpts [from] the author's travel diary that precede each chapter are not there for any of the usual reasons (decoration, counterpoint, vanity)—or least not for those reasons alone; they are integral to the tight-woven complexity of Delany's multi-level fabric of statement.

If the book has a serious flaw, it is in the over-tight weaving, the too-careful pruning and packing of meaning into deceptively simple and rhythmic language: that is, that it is in large part closer to poetry than prose, without any of the typographical, linguistic, or structural formalities which usually serve as clues to the reader to proceed more attentively than he expects to do with an adventure novel (let alone an adventure novel in cheap paperback format with a lurid red demon-thing on the cover).

Then again, I expect I'd have had that uneasiness at the end even if I had paid proper attention all the way through the first time. I had the same kind of thing when I finished Richard McKenna's *Sand Pebbles.* ("Endings to be useful must be inconclusive," says one of the quotes from Delany's journal.)

That is to say: this is a charming book, a gay book, a story of true love and roving adventure, full of strange music, a song of changelings and dragons and a Dove and a devil; where Orpheus battles Billy the Kid, and is saved from the Minotaur by a compassionate computer; but it is also and absolutely a story about where-it's-at, right here, right now.

I cannot imagine a book about the world I live in that could leave me feeling satisfied at the end: which is one of the more important basics of The New Thing.

[...]

Notes

1. *World's Best Science Fiction 1967*, Donald A. Wollheim and Terry Carr; Ace, 75¢.
2. *Orbit 2*, Damon Knight, ed.; Putnam's, $4.95.
3. *The Crack in Space*, Philip K. Dick; Ace, 40¢.
4. *The Zap Gun*, Philip K. Dick; Pyramid, 50¢.
5. *Counter-Clock World*, Philip K. Dick; Berkley, 60¢.
6. *Echo Round His Bones*, Thomas M. Disch; Berkley, 60¢.
7. *Mankind under the Leash*, Thomas M. Disch; Ace double, 50¢.
8. *The Einstein Intersection*, Samuel R. Delany; Ace, 40¢.

Books (December 1967)

In an introduction to his big new (wide-screen-spectacular) anthology, *Dangerous Visions*,[1] Harlan Ellison takes pains to point out that *his* New Thing is not the same as Michael Moorcock's (editor of the British *New Worlds*), or my own. He is absolutely right. I hereby relinquish, cheerfully, all claim to the dubious title: I have enough trouble with the old confusions about "science fiction" without acquiring a new label, already splintered.

I am a trifle more reluctant to hand over my own abbreviative tag of last month's column, but in all fairness, I concede that the associative connotations of TNT are far more suitable to Ellison's taste *and* image than to mine: surely he is s-f's most explosive popcorn package and snap crackling firebrand; and from the evidence of this book, *his* New Thing is characterized specifically by pyrotechnic style and shock content.

Dangerous Visions was originally advertised to the authors invited to contribute as a collection of "unpublishable" stories—that is, stories either unsold or unwritten specifically because of "taboo" themes or unconventional treatments that made them unpalatable to the existing markets.

The idea for such a volume has been in Ellison's mind for some time; I was myself involved, several years ago, in a painfully abortive effort to do a similar collection. (I was to be the anthologist; Ellison was editor at a publishing house far better forgotten.) The useful outcome of that venture, I felt, was my discovery that there is no such thing as a (good) unpublishable story today. There are non-commercial stories which will go only to low-paid or unpaid markets, and there are highly specialized themes which will be bought only by appropriately specialized publications; but the only (good) story that approaches unpublishability is the oddity whose treatment is at variance with its themes, and even these *eventually* find homes. (Virtually every story on the list for that earlier volume has now, been published: for instance, Sturgeon's "Noon Gun," a glowingly mantic narrative of a young man's love—not lust, went finally to *Playboy*; and Leiber's "Snow White," a sympathetic-viewpoint story about a necrophiliac, appeared recently in a publication called *Taboo*.) Presumably, Ellison made the same discovery I did, because the emphasis in his introduction to the completed anthology is much more on his concept of The New Thing than on the Dangerous Visions idea. And certainly the large majority of the inclusions would seem quite in place, for instance, in the pages of this magazine. (I would estimate that there are less than half a half-dozen, out of thirty-three, which *might* have had to go outside the range of American s-f magazines for publication: probably the Emshwiller, Bunch, and Sladek stories; possibly Delany's, Ballard's, and Spinrad's. But every one of these would have found a home either in the literary reviews or in England—and half of the rest could have gone to popular general fiction magazines as well.) It is not that the book is lacking in literally Dangerous Visions, but that (with one exception—well, perhaps two—) they are dangerously familiar, as well: incest, atom doom, the death of God; brainwashing and personality absorption, the mechanization and/or institutionalization of humanity, overpopulation, automotive suicide, and some varieties of cannibalism considered as popular sports: they are all quite horribly familiar themes in or out of s-f or your daily newspaper.

(But your paper has not yet reported on the theme set forth in Samuel Delany's "Aye, and Gomorrah...," and I am sure it has done little more than hint at the eventuality discussed in Philip Dick's "The Faith of Our Fathers." Neither have your regular science fiction magazines. For which reasons, I shall certainly reveal neither one here.)

The Dangerous Vision has become a commonplace of our society; the forecasting of such visions is one of the chief roles science fiction has played in the past twenty or thirty years. Yet this book, which began as a direct request to presumably stifled authors to voice their most terrifying, shocking, or extreme viewpoints, is (with two—well, perhaps three—exceptions) most effective in those stories which concentrate on literary values and technical excellence, rather than idea content.

(Carol Emshwiller's female-viewpoint examination of the ambiguities of "Sex and/or Mr. Morrison" may disturb some readers—but where are the extrapolations and projections of legalized homosexuality and abortion? female sexuality in the era of the Pill and antibiotics? rioting and assassination as political-action patterns in the US? the cumulative effects of widespread use of various drugs? the possible worlds of Black Power and/or Flower Power? The Rand Corporation, and your daily newspaper, both make predictions freely....)

What it all goes to prove, presumably, is that the established s-f writer can write much better than he usually does, and will—given a half-reasonable rate of pay, and (apparently) unlimited stylistic freedom: also that very few are inclined toward innovative or experimental techniques, since all but a handful (whose presence establishes the parenthetical *apparently* above) elected to put their best literary feet forward in a decidedly conventional style. What it proves about the writers' thematic interests is less certain when one considers the nature of some of the work published elsewhere by authors whose contributions here are notably non-violent intellectually (Aldiss, Ballard, Brunner, Bunch…)—or the names missing from Ellison's list of authors invited-but-not-included (not mentioned and not present: Vonnegut, Disch, Dahl, Gary, Borges, Jacobs, Heinlein, Burroughs, and add your own—one way or another—controversial names). The thematic content of the final selections bears a fair resemblance to the themes most clearly recurrent in Ellison's own work.

The whole book, in further fact, is rather more like an Ellison collection, in which other authors are quoted at length, than like an anthology in the usual sense. (There is some justification for this, inasmuch as the editor is in small part the publisher: that is as he explains in one of his introductions—Ellison not only took no editorial share of the publisher's advance for this book, but added considerably to the funds provided in order to produce a book of this size with better-than-average payment for the authors included.) Even more than editorial selections, the extensive and often painfully personal detailed introductions confirm the evidence of Ellison's earlier collections of his own work: as writer and editor, he is a man of vision, boldness, determination, generous loyalty, intense sensitivity, strong beliefs, unbelievable egocentricity, and very nearly complete lack of taste.

With any reasonable care and editorial judgment, one standard-length anthology could have been selected from this giant, to match and perhaps surpass any previous collections of imaginative fiction. As it stands, the total wordage breaks down into four roughly equivalent portions: one quarter is composed of twelve titles ranging from good to superb; one quarter consists of four stories of remarkable, but flawed, quality—each or any of which should have been susceptible to marked improvement with discerning criticism; one quarter are fair-to-good stories, which would neither grace nor quite disgrace an average-good issue of *F&SF*; and one quarter (almost exactly by length) is composed of commentary by Ellison or about him (including Asimov's forewords and the personal material on Ellison contained in some author comments)—comprising one of the least pleasant autobiographies I have ever been unable to stop reading.

I am not going to comment further on the introductions, except to say that when I found myself so disaffected that I began distrusting my own judgment if Ellison seemed to agree with it, I solved the problem of not being able to ignore the notes by reading them straight through first, and (after a suitable interval) going back to the stories without prejudice. As a further happy accident, the reading copy I had was an advance set of galleys provided by Doubleday and auctioned off at the NYCon a few [weeks] ago—so that I am quite unable as I write to give in to the temptation to quote from the introductions, or refer to them specifically. I have notes only on the stories I considered most worth discussing.

I am, therefore, able to state with full enthusiasm and no sour overtones, out of memories still vivid in my mind, that those top twelve stories alone are worth the price of the book (high as it is, and even adding in the possible cost of getting trapped into reading the introductions). If $6.95 is too much for you, let me urge you at the very least (while waiting for the paperback) to find a friend or library or friendly bookdealer, and open immediately to the end of the book: Delany's "Aye, and Gomorrah…," without doubt *the* outstanding selection in the book.

The rest of the best list includes: Dick's "The Faith of Our Fathers," (among other things, the first worthwhile piece of science fiction I have seen on psychedelics—among, as I said, *other* things); Emshwiller's "Sex and/or Mr. Morrison"; Joe Hensley's sensitive "Lord Randy, My Son"; Sonya Dorman's gutsy (very) "Go, Go, Go, Said the Bird"; Fritz Leiber's haunting and evocative "Gonna Roll the Bones"; John Sladek's bitter "The Happy Breed"; Kris Neville's sardonic "From the Government Printing Office"; R. A. Lafferty's oddly romantic "Land of the Great Horses"; J. G. Ballard's quiet/classical "The Recognition"; Norman Spinrad's malignant "Carcinoma Angels"; and Keith Laumer's thoughtful "Test to Destruction."

None of these are stories to hear about, but to read. The four that make up the second quarter of my grouping above, however, need some discussion.

Philip José Farmer's "Riders of the Purple Wage" is perhaps the one story in the book that would not have been published anywhere else—in its present form. It is certainly one of the most entertaining—and least "dangerous" selections, and it suffers only from the fact that it is not quite good *enough* to sustain its highly specialized humor for more than 30,000 words. It is a cheerful, careening combination of neo-Joycean word-gaming and science-fiction imagery, homespun philosophy, homeloomed psychiatry, and witty comment on the contemporary scene—particularly in the arts and academia. But so much of the humor is (Joycean or s-f) in-group, that I suspect there is a relatively small audience eager for such a large dose. I myself laughed delightedly for 10,000 words, grew quieter for another ten, and then put it down to finish—as a duty—later on. (Turned out the only plot point was a lovely pun on *Finnegans Wake*.)

Some incisive editing might have done a great deal, also, for the stories by Robert Silverberg and Frederik Pohl: both of these seemed to me to be written with an emotional involvement, and on a level of prose, right at the (rarely-touched) top of both writers' considerable powers—and both concluded with endings that seemed so feeble by comparison as to be virtually unrelated to the body of the story.

Finally, and sadly, I must add that one other story besides Farmer's would have to be judged homeless without this book—except that Sturgeon wrote it, and there are enough others like myself who are so hungry for new Sturgeon that someone would surely would have published it anyhow. I must add, first, that I know the story would not have been written at all except for the existence of this book—and, second, that I took such delight in the sheer texture of the Sturgeon prose, and the glimmering in-out-sights of the Sturgeon images, that I was halfway through (it is a *long* novelette) before I let myself realize that I already knew what the big shock ending was going to be—and that I was neither shocked nor enlightened.

I cannot amplify this charge, of course, without further nullifying the already weak surprise-ending structure; I can only wish someone had made him go back to work on it. Read it, of course; you'll love it—just don't look for satisfaction at the end.

Besides, with a title like this you hardly need a story: "If All Men Were Brothers, Would You Let One Marry Your Sister?"

Summing up, then—

I am afraid Ellison's New Thing resembles to a great degree the same New Thing Anthony Boucher and J. F. McComas brought into s-f in 1949: the not-so-radical-really notion that literary standards could and should be applied to science fiction. A *good* thing, but—

But, among other things, it needs an outstanding editor to use that principle as the main line of guidance—an editor with taste.

In last month's column, I discussed Samuel Delany's novel, *The Einstein Intersection*, which describes the adventures of Lo Lobey. When Lobey approached the big city for the first time, he saw billboards, with a beautiful woman pictured on them. The first one said:

"The Dove says: 'One is *nice*? Nine or ten are so much *nicer*!'"

The next one said: "The Dove says: 'Though ten are nice, 99 or 100 are *so* much nicer.'"

The same philosophy that substitutes shock for insight, and spectacle for imagery, really *believes* ten is nicer than one, and 100 nicer than ten. As for me, I am happy indeed to see ten good stories instead of just one—but sorry to feel that many readers will inevitably miss the good ones because of the dross they are bedded in.

I do not believe that showmanship equates with artistry; there is no job like a snow job to turn me *off*. Ellison Disneyland is undoubtedly in tune with the Grate Society—but that's not what I read science fiction for. I wish this book had had an editor for the editor. But—

It was Ellison who had the idea, and who carried it through, and made it work. It has some *very* good stories in it.

[...]

Note

1. *Dangerous Visions*, edited by Harlan Ellison; Doubleday 1967; 552 pp.; $6.95.

Books (February 1968)

You probably can't buy a copy. I found it in a stack of remainders at one of the Marboro Bookstores in New York, and maybe they still have some. Your public library ought to have it.

It was published in 1965, and I remember thinking, when I read the lukewarm reviews, that it was a book I ought to have a look at. But no one else I've shown it to seems even to have seen any reviews, so I suspect the ones I saw were in England.

All of which is sad indeed, because Hortense Calisher's *Journal from Ellipsia* (Little, Brown) was undoubtedly the best science fiction novel of 1965, and a strong contender for that matter against some of the first-rate books that have appeared since (*Flowers for Algernon*, *The Crystal World*, *Giles Goat-Boy*, *The Einstein Intersection*, for instance), whether you judge by literary virtue or solid science fiction content.

This is the story of a visitor to Earth from Ellipsia (where ellipsoid creatures inhabit an ellipsoid planet in perfect equilibrium and timeless stability—where there are no pronouns but We and Ours—where One and One always make One). Eli—the name the One adopts on Earth—has come to Earth as part of an intergalactic conspiracy of exchange-visits, and the story is primarily concerned with (his?) education by and of an Earthwoman preparing to go to Ellipsia. (He?), like a few other misfits from elliptical society, is endlessly fascinated by the variety, variability, mutability, of earth's biology and culture, and by the phenomenon of sequential time: just as Janice, (his?) opposite number, is lured by Oneness and simultaneity, serenity, smoothness.

The story is told in alternate, sections from the viewpoint of Janice's former lover, Jack Linhouse, a British-American academic, and as the direct narrative of Eli, delivered at Janice's "memorial" service.

It is funny, serious, suspenseful, poignant, philosophical, and lots more: it even builds to a climax, and then sustains it. (I mean, something *happens* at the end.)

Ask your library. Or maybe some bright paperback publisher will do something about it.

Meantime, *Inside S-f*, the Big Waking-up Day seems to be arriving: that is, the science-fiction infield has begun to discover that something stranger than rockets is going on—that there's a revolution going on Out There.

Of course, as soon as I say that, I have to rush to modify it in two different ways. Phil Dick has known about it all along; so have Phil Farmer, Fritz Leiber, Ted Sturgeon, and a few others. But with the exception of such peripheral writers as Kit Reed, Carol Emshwiller, David Bunch, etc.—who have worked the vein mostly in short stories—American genre writers have kept whatever thoughts they were having on the Revolutions (Youth, Sexual, Black, Psychedelic, et al.) pretty much to themselves—even to the extent of being noisily impressed by the "inventiveness" of Phil Dick's novels.

The second modification suggests some possible reasons for the first, and perhaps accounts for the scant use such otherwise with-it young writers as Disch, Zelazny, and Delany have made of The Scene: the publishers have clearly been convinced that Hip is Hip and Stef is Stef, and never the twain. But the category gap is closing: one of the four crossover novels on hand today was published by Pyramid as part of their regular s-f line. Berkley has made at least a half-way move with an (hot, boy! translated from the *French*) item called *Sexualis '95*, about "a world totally engaged in the pleasures of eroticism"; and even *Dangerous Visions*, which I reviewed here before seeing a copy of the finished book, has come out with a near-illegible "psychedelic" lettered jacket. And there are rumors all around of more to come. Meanwhile—

The main features for today represent a complete range from commercial category s-f, to a privately published mimeographed novel out of San Francisco.

In the middle are Grove's latest William Burroughs book, *The Soft Machine* ($5.00), and Dial's *Logan's Run* ($3.50), by William F. Nolan and George Clayton Johnson. *Logan's Run* is going to surprise a lot of people: although it carries no special label to that effect, the whole book (size, jacket-art, paper, type-face) has the somehow-look of that special sub-sub-category, the Teenage Science Fiction Novel. And, indeed, it is just that, in all respects but one: it is set in the not-too-far-future, with a cast entirely composed of teenagers, a Secret Agent hero, lots of fast action/adventure/chase stuff, and some solid gobs of what seems to be reliable science talk. The difference is just that in this one (from the flap copy), "Multi-level chronic and glass cities provide their residents with neighborhood LSD parlors. Sex is unlimited and marriage is nonexistent.... No one is allowed to live past the age of 21."

Interestingly enough, *Logan's Run* and *The Soft Machine* make use of almost identical elements—gimmicks, images, thematic content—to achieve radically different effects. In both books, you will find every variety of colorful-familiar s-f menace being manipulated in complex spy-intrigue conspiracy situations; both are concerned with an essentially *irresponsible*, machine-governed society; sex, drugs, death, violence are the main preoccupations of the characters in both books, and the central character of both is in flight from the law most of the time, covering incredible areas of space in, effectively, non-time.

Yet where *Logan* contrives to present all this hash seriously, and even compellingly (for the duration of the reading), piling the incredible on the grotesque so swiftly and smoothly that the ugliness goes almost unnoticed, and only the immediate danger facing the hero is significant on any page—it is a totally forgettable book the next morning. Burroughs on the other hand disports his BEMs and metal monsters with a sort of terrible gayety, clearly conscious of their character as clichés, and handling them lightly to achieve maximum impact from their familiarity; indeed, he turns his own most original and terrifying images into clichés-of-a-sort in the course of the book, by repeating scenes and fragments of scenes, sentences and fragments of sentences, in changing juxtapositions, continually. It is not a single-sitting book; I tended to read only short pieces at any one time, and even then, to jump around in the book. But behind the perfervid activity there is meaning, and the images do not fade easily.

Chester Anderson's *The Butterfly Kid* (Pyramid, 60¢) and Willard Bain's *Informed Sources (Day East Received)*, again, have a number of vital elements in common, but the contrast between the two books is even sharper. Both deal with a takeover-plot using psychedelic drugs; both make extensive use of the author's own familiarity with "underground" and Hippy circles. But—

Butterfly is clever, glib, sometimes funny. A pop Group foils the Invading Blue Lobsters, and prevents them from loading New York's water supply with the dread Reality Pills (producers of "public hallucinations"—whatever your subconscious wants it will objectify, whether it's butterflies, a halo, an orchestra, or a personal bodyguard of gods and goddesses). The setting is Greenwich Village, twenty years from now—and mostly the West Village at that, which every reader of the *New York Times Magazine* knows by now is strictly tourist country, Teenybopper Land; and the book reads like a tourist job, a fast and facile ten-day-wonder, ground out fast when the author realized that if The Scene was acceptable to *Times* readers, it might be all right for science fiction too.

This impression is confirmed, by the way, by the photograph and bio lines on the back cover, which show a vastly bearded and mirror shaded young man, stove pipes (à la pad) in the background, (pot?) pipe in hand, with the information that he "writes for most Underground newspapers, has made an Underground film, runs a singing group, and commutes between the Haight-Ashbury section of San Francisco and Middle Earth."

Like, *too* much!

The physical appearance, make-up, construction, and structure, of *Informed Sources (Day East Received)* put me off just as much as the back cover of *Butterfly*: it is as self-consciously non-commercial-underground as the other book is over-commercial-hip.

IS is gimmicky, written in newswire cablese, with what few explanations and explications are offered filtered into the text so slowly that most of the opening is sheer bewilderment. It is published under the coy colophon of "The Communication Company"—if indeed "published" is an appropriate word to describe a mimeo job presumably done on a basement machine under dim light; sloppiness of reproduction is altogether Unforgiveable in a book which relies on typographical effects and makes use of unfamiliar language and abbreviations to the extent this one does.

And besides, it is angry-autobiographical, and at this point I think the News Biz is probably as over-exposed as Mad Ave. All in all, I approached it with considerable resistance, and did not really expect to get through the first 30 pages. Certainly I did not expect to stay up reading till 2 a.m., once I got through that first 30.

What it's got going for it, I think, is that the self-conscious Hashbury air is in this case absolutely genuine—and the author is a well-informed source, not only about wire services (he worked for three years in the San Francisco AP office), but also about the P(eripheral) U(nderground) M(ovement) which provides the background for the Great Green Dreams Conspiracy.

"Day East Received" (I found out somewhere inside the book) is the label under which the San Francisco office of the AP files each 24 hours of teletype messages from the East Coast. This book gives 24 hours worth of wire messages on the (presumptive) death of a legendary character named Robin the Cock. Conflicting "eye witness" stories, elaborations, interpretations, opinion roundup interviews, and you-name-it flood the wires between New

York, San Francisco, Dayton, Portland, Honolulu, Dubuque, Milwaukee, Miami, Boston, Baltimore, and points elsewhere. Between Flashes and Bulletins, the IS (Inform Sources) attempts to conduct routine business of its distinctive service: including the over-tricky bit of reviews of the novel itself and some hilarious send-ups on standard news services (the weather report, the Top Tunes listing, etc.). Through all this, a conspiracy is being conducted, almost-but-not-quite off-wire by members of the P.U.M., and—

And that's enough. I won't give it *all* away.

[...]

Books (March 1968)†

In this month's column, Merril discusses a number of nonfiction books about science and space exploration. She argues that, in the early days of science fiction fandom, a love for science fiction and a love for space flight were synonymous. Early fans were proponents of space flight, and much early science fiction was propaganda for space flight. On the other hand, actual rocket scientists tended not to align themselves with science fiction and fans—except for Willy Ley. Further, she notes that Isaac Asimov and Arthur C. Clarke were scientists with the "courage of their convictions," who outwardly aligned themselves with SF. She then turns to Clarke's "literary exhibit of the actual birth of the space age." She suggests that Clarke has the ideal experience and perspective for the book: as an insider and outsider in the development of space flight, and as a true citizen of the globe. Next, she covers Asimov's nonfiction book on life in the universe, which she finds to be one of Asimov's best books, in its prose, its style, and its "sheer humanity." The third book she addresses is the joint venture by US astronomer Carl Sagan and the Soviet astronomer I. S. Shklovskii, which also examines the question of "intelligent life in the universe,"

Merril then turns from the respectable and mainstream field of space travel to the "bizarre," from a book that collects essays on various bizarre topics, to Vincent Gaddis's collection on UFOs, poltergeists, and other "oddities," to Cohn Clair's collection of "classical and medieval writings" on Unnatural History, to Otto Binder's collection on flying saucers, and, finally, Ivan Sanderson's work on an "assortment of marvels."

† Full text in the E-book version.

Quotes from original "Books" column.

Books (May 1968)

The author's name is Miguel Angel Asturias.[1] The book costs $7.95, and it has just won a Nobel Prize for Literature, which would be irrelevant except it probably means it will take a bit longer to come out in paperback, but also means that if your local library doesn't already have it, they can be persuaded to buy. Presumably a variety of book clubs are also rushing it onto their lists. But if you have no other way to read it, sacrifice a bottle of scotch or a first-run movie date or a bag of grass or whatever your thing is, and buy the Delacorte edition of *Mulata.*

This is the book about Celestino Yumi, also known as Hayumihaha, and later as the dwarf/wizard Chiltic, and his wife Caterina or Catalina or Zabala, who is also the witch Giroma, and about the corn-demon Tazol and the terrible seductress without a name, the Mulata. Or these at least are the central characters in a fabulous adventure which mingles science and sorcery and sociology, magic, myth, and materialism, allegory and earthiness, sex, religion, politics, priests, peasants, bears, boars, porcupines, devils and demons and democrats, and *lots* more. Think of H. Rider Haggard at his peak, then add Leiber's dark eroticism, Sturgeon's tenderness, Farmer's earthiness, Ballard's vivid juxtapositions, Dick's surrealist timesense, Cordwainer Smith's sophisticated symbolism, Walter Miller's bitter insight, Zelazny's myth-analysis, Delany's mythopoetry, Aldiss's great laughter, Disch's erudite despair, Simak's dignity-in-simplicity—what more can I say? This is the kind of book that might have happened here if *Unknown* had had a chance to grow up. It is fun; it is frightening; it is fascinating. Read it.

I was less impressed by another "outside" book, the much-publicized *The Master and Margarita* by Mikhail Bulgakov, which I read in the shorter Grove Press version, translated by Mirra Ginsburg (available in paperback for 95¢). A recent serious intellectual review began by acknowledging the book as "a masterpiece" and concluded by calling it an "incomplete work of art." Incomplete it is; a masterpiece, hardly; a work of art, doubtfully. Three separate strains run through the book, never successfully integrated: a rather sentimental reconstruction of the Passion with Pilate as the civilized, sensitive, ambivalent protagonist; a slapstick-buffoonery satire of the Soviet literary/intellectual Establishment; and a fine evocative fantasy of witchcraft and demonism built around a particularly intriguing characterization of the Devil manifested in modern Moscow.

Well worth reading, if you dismiss the notion of a suppressed masterpiece before you start—but even then a good deal less rewarding than R. A. Lafferty's treatment of some similar themes in *The Past Master*. This is Lafferty's first novel, the first original published in the new Ace Specials line, and probably the first "category" science fiction book in the decade since *A Canticle for Leibowitz*, to be considered as a valid successor to Miller's classic novel. It is going to be a hard act for Ace to follow.

You could describe it as a novel about Thomas More in Utopia, but that would be a laughably simplistic description of a complex, subtle, colorful, and highly sophisticated book, which manages, at half the length, to touch on almost as wide a range of marvelous, mystical, and maniacal phenomena as the Asturias novel. Page for page, in fact, I suspect it jams in as much incident and imagery, as well; and if I must add that it does not quite achieve the same depth or impact each time, this is less a criticism than an accolade, in that it is possible to compare the two books, at all.

To some extent, any discussion will sound like a comparison, because the topics here, besides Utopia, are Hell and the nature of devils and of The Devil; politics, affluence and poverty; psyche and psychology; magic, theology, technology, cosmology, and the human condition. The setting is, mostly, a planet called Astrobe in the fairly far future, and the characters (in addition to More, transported from old Chelsea) include the child-witch Evita who is 200 years old; Rimrock, the "ansel," a telepathic mutant sea-creature; Paul, the outlaw astronaut; Father Oddopter of the green-robes, a monk whose duty it is to kill the devil every day; King Charles the 612 of the Feral Lands; some Programmed People of Astrobe; the lungers of Cathead; some killer machines; Walter Copperhead, the necromancer; and the rulers of Astrobe, headed by a triumvirate described in the opening paragraphs:

> *The three big men were met together in a private building of one of them. There was a clattering thunder in the street outside, but the sun was shining. It was the clashing thunder of the mechanical killers, ravening and raging. They shook the building and were on the verge of pulling it down. They required the life and the blood of one of the three men and they required it immediately, now, within the hour, within the minute.*

The three men gathered in the building were large physically, they were important and powerful, they were intelligent and interesting. There was a peculiar linkage between them: each believed that he controlled the other two, that he was the puppeteer and they were the puppets. And each was partly right in this belief. It made them an interlocking nexus, taut and resilient, the most intricate on Astrobe.

Cosmos Kingmaker, who was too rich. The Heraldic Lion.

Peter Proctor, who was too lucky. The Sleek Fox.

Fabian Foreman, who was too smart. The Worried Hawk.

"This is Mankind's third chance," said Kingmaker. "Ah, they're breaking the doors down again, how can we talk with it all going on?"

He took the speaking tube. "Colonel," he called out. "You have sufficient human guards. It is imperative that you disperse the riot. [It] is absolutely forbidden that they murder this man at this time and place."

"Foreman," said Peter Proctor softly within the room. "Whatever you are thinking this day, do not think it so strongly. I've never seen the things so avid for your life."

I restrain the impulse to quote more at length. Lafferty magics me with humor, anger, and love, and with unpredictable corner-of-the-eye perspectives and perceptions, but above all, I suspect, with his word-music. And yet—

—yet there is something missing here, something a little bit less than complete. I do not think it is simply a lack of my own kind of logic: I do not have to *agree* with Lafferty's manner of reasoning to be both enchanted and—can I say?—*ideated* by it. Perhaps it is actually as much lesser instance of the same lack I feel much more forcibly in two other recent novels by two of my favorite authors, Clifford Simak and A. J. Budrys.

I must hasten to add, after that introduction, that I *liked* both these books; I enjoyed reading them; they are both well-written, satisfying as stories, and thought-provoking. Most of the science-fiction-labeled novels I see are either unreadable or totally forgettable, and even the small balance remaining—the books I feel are worth at least mentioning here—can claim nothing more than competence in execution combined with a clever concept somewhere or a colorful image somewhere else, or maybe even both together. I can understand why people want to read them, but not at all why anyone wants to write them. (I think it is shortsighted practicality for a clever and competent man to write a novel just because a publisher is willing to sign a contract with him; if there is nothing in particular he wants to write *about*, he can make a good deal more money in a variety of other ways.)

But those are *other* books. None of this applies to either Simak's *The Werewolf Principle* (Putnam, $3.95) or Budrys's *The Amsirs and the Iron Thorn* (Fawcett, 50¢). Both Simak and Budrys had something to say, and I think it may have been something worth hearing: at least the hints they gave me left me feeling as though I had missed something *important*. What baffles me with these two books is: Why would two men of far more than routine ability, with sufficient prestige *and* publishing connections not to have to worry unduly about conforming to standard editorial restrictions on length, format, or style, have selected the magazine-style category-science-fiction novel as a vehicle for concepts completely outside the form?

By "outside the form" I mean, in Budrys's case, that all his most telling points could have been made more effectively in a present-day novel, which did not weaken the pictures he drew by making them appear to be exaggerated. He was not writing about where we are going, or what might be, but about where we *are at*! (Okay, Ajay: I am with you in everything you say about canned kicks, empty erudition, pseudo-sophistication, super-security, and valueless victories; and I don't even demand that you come up with a solution—I cannot believe you meant to imply that ignorant barbarism is any more blissful than ignorant civilization? But the portrait of decay would be sharper and stronger if the faces of the characters were not lost in an unlikely future.)

The damnedest thing is, Budrys manages to make the whole improbable and inappropriately conceived thing first-rate reading—while you're reading. Imagine what a talent like this could do with all the stops pulled out?

The Werewolf Principle is "outside the form" in a different sense. Simak's symbolic structure is well-selected and carefully modeled. His choice of a near-future world is absolutely right, because he is talking specifically about choices that lie only a short time ahead of us, and developmental paths we have already—largely unconsciously—embarked upon. Both the special nature of the protagonist, Andrew Blake, and the triple personality with which he is endowed are integral to the theme—as is Blake's preoccupation with identifying and comprehending these aspects of himself throughout the first half of the book. Then, when the introduction is completed, and the stage cleared for the beginning of the action—we are abruptly initiating the final sequence, tying up plot-ends, and rushing into the final clinch.

There was much more to be said; it was an ambitious concept, obviously thought through seriously and with care; it deserved something more than to turn into a (very) well told routine novel.

[...]

Note

1. Translated by Gregory Rabassa.

Books (June 1968)

Election year, USA.

The world holds its breath: lives, livelihoods, the welfare and integrity of people and peoples all over the globe hang in the balance with every shift of power in the US or USSR. The world watches, waits, listens. We talk.

Speeches, debates, discussions, panels, symposia, lectures, letters-to-the-editor, political advertisements, pamphlets, articles, poems, songs, records, cartoons, books.

And more books. Not just the predictable biographical, autobiographical, analytical, eulogistic, polemical, and predictive volumes by and about the candidates and would-be candidates, but a veritable river, spate, flood of argument, narrative, pejorative, paean, satire, sloganeering, data-processing, policy-interpreting, philosophical, scientistic, spiritual, idealistic, pragmatic, prejudiced, protesting, and patriotic literature in every possible guise and disguise.

Not just another Presidential election, but a time of grave decision on issues we will probably never have a chance to reconsider: a time of crises as immediate and important for this country as those of the 1860s, as vital to the rest of the planet as those of the 1930s. A time of national dissatisfaction without historical precedent: I doubt that anyone from the President down is satisfied or optimistic; never has US prestige been so low with its own citizens—never before has the phrase "my country, right or wrong," been so charged with ambivalence.

Twenty years ago, when the seeds of the monstrous issues of today were sprouting in the ideological fallout of atomic victory, science fiction proved to be by far the most effective medium for prophets and propagandists. Nuclear and biological warfare, the population explosion, automation, possible planetary pollution, technological proliferation, were all topics indigenous to the genre, and (then) so little understood by most of the reading public that they could neither be treated as given in "realistic" novels, nor taken straight in non-fiction (on any level below the rarefied, militant one of the *Bulletin of Atomic Scientists*).

Then, in the fifties—Eisenhower, and Sen. *Joseph* McCarthy—the science fiction magazines were, for a while, the only pop arena in America for the dissemination and examination of nonconformist and dissident ("subversive") ideas. The use of the genre for this purpose became so familiar to a growing body of "mainstream" writers, that at least one new-won enthusiast swung considerable critical weight behind his conviction that political and social criticism was the *only* valid use of science fiction.

S-f writers generally refused to be limited to this aspect of the field; but the science fiction idiom was adopted by other mainstream writers, and even more by journalists (columnists like Buchwald and Baker, *Mad*-type satirists, documentarians like Hersey) as a standard vehicle for political comment.

Today, the science fiction infield is actually far behind the "underground" and even much of the mainstream, in the extent and intensity of its criticism of the status quo. Nor is the medium intrinsically particularly well suited to the examination of intergroup confrontations and institutional moralities. Nevertheless, it seems that every philosopher, politician, moralist, or people-watcher currently without platform has, this year, bethought himself of Swift, Wells, Bellamy, Huxley, and Orwell, and sat himself down to construct a novel around his own analysis of the ills of society or his individual recipe for salvation.

Since many regular writers of s-f can also be described as unemployed philosophers, a number of "message" novels and a general trend toward political themes are evident on the regular lists of publishers specializing in the genre. Others—depending on the author's reputation and political position—come from mainstream publishers, and some are even privately printed.

As most readers of this magazine already know, I too have certain strong political biases. I also like to believe that I am capable of recognizing literary merit even in a book entirely opposed to my own way of thinking. But art and propaganda are poor bedfellows at best, and even in the books closest to my own convictions, I have found none so far that merit high praise for their purely literary virtues: the best one can say of some is that they contrive to be entertaining while instructive, and of others that they are provocative enough in content to compensate for novelistic ineptitude. In any case, I make no claim, in this period of political passions, to a detachment amounting to perversity, which would permit me to admire the logic of a book whose premises I consider seriously in error—or recommend for pre-election reading a convincing argument for the Bad Guys.

What I can do, in an (only slightly reluctant) effort to be "fair," is open this column to opposing views; I, therefore, invite anyone who feels that books representing his views are being slighted or ignored here, to submit reviews to this space.[1]

The Report from Iron Mountain on the Possibility and Desirability of Peace first appeared in shorter form in *Esquire*, and was then published by Dial at $5.00; both versions were introduced by one Leonard C. Lewin, presumably an editor at Dial, who presents the document as the final report of a "Special Study Group" convened (by "unnamed government administrators of high rank") in utmost secrecy in the summer of 1963, and as quietly disbanded in the fall of 1966, after its own decision to suppress its findings. The publication of the Report is purportedly due to determined opposition to the idea of suppression by one member ("John Doe") of the 15-man commission.

"...the unwillingness of Doe's associates to publicize their findings," says Lewin, is "readily understandable," since their recommendations were based on the conclusion that "lasting peace, while not theoretically impossible, is probably unattainable; even if it could be achieved, it would almost certainly not be in the best interests of a stable society to achieve it."

The deadpan approach slips only occasionally, and then only by the tiniest margin, into obvious farce—and I kept trying to explain away these small clear signs of send-up, *wanting* the "Study Group" to be real, wishing I could believe that there were high government officials prepared to sponsor, read, and act on a report so cynically realistic:

> "We find that at the heart of every peace study we have examined... lies one common fundamental misconception...the incorrect assumption that war, as an institution, is subordinate to the social system it is believed to serve.
>
> "...Although war is 'used' as an instrument of national and social policy, the fact that a society is organized for any degree of readiness for war supersedes its political and economic structure. War itself is the basic social system...which has governed most human societies of record....
>
> "Wars are not 'caused' by international conflicts of interest. Proper logical sequence would make it more often accurate to say that war-making societies require—and thus bring about—such conflicts.

> "...'war' is virtually synonymous with nationhood. The elimination of war implies the inevitable elimination of national sovereignty and the traditional nation-state.
>
> "The war system not only has been essential to the existence of nations as independent political entities, but has been equally indispensable to their stable internal political structure. Without it, no government has ever been able to obtain acquiescence in its 'legitimacy,' or right to rule its society. The possibility of war provides the sense of external necessity without which no government can long remain in power ...."

In this vein, the book describes the functions of war from economic, political, sociological, ecological, cultural, and scientific viewpoints; then considers possible substitutions for the various functions, and concludes that none of the "war surrogates" considered are sufficiently "technically feasible, politically acceptable, and potentially credible to the members of the societies that adopt them," although the closest single substitute— "development of an acceptable threat from 'outer space,' presumably in conjunction with a space-research surrogate for economic control"—is considered "unpromising" only in terms of credibility. ("New, less regressive, approaches to the creation of fictitious global 'enemies' invite further investigation.")

I have traced here, very sketchily, the line of reasoning presented under the subhead, "Political" in the successive sections of the book, not because it is either the most incisive or the most likely to shock, but because it provided the final evidence of the fictional character of the book. Quite clearly, no administration capable of recognizing the callous truisms expressed here could possibly mismanage the conquest of Vietnam as badly as it is now being done; nor could a government of—after all—decent, civilized, twentieth-century Americans conceivably participate in the inhumanity of the present conduct of the war unless it had first come to believe its own mythology about the nature and purposes of the conflict.

Iron Mountain is neither fiction nor science, let alone science fiction—but it is the essence of politico-socio-economic science-fiction compacted into the fictionally scientific "Report" form, which has provided one of the great vehicles for contemporary s-f. The lack of plot is insignificant; the book is guaranteed to stir your adrenalin, no matter what your views: there is something in it to infuriate *every*one.

There is more science and better fiction in *The Cassiopeia Affair* (Doubleday, $4.95), a novel by Chloe Lerwick and Harrison Brown (one of the early post-WW II, anti-Bomb, atomic scientists), which takes as its theme the impact of the discovery of an intelligent extraterrestrial planet on terrestrial international affairs—and more specifically, on the political and personal conflicts of two distinguished American scientists, one Einstein/Oppenheimer figure, the other a Teller-type. Although the personal dramas are sometimes compelling, and the narrative is well paced and well told, the book lacks either the extrapolative logic or the excitement of *Iron Mountain*.

Hayden Howard's *The Eskimo Invasion* (Ballantine, 75¢), on the other hand, is one of the worst-constructed novels I have ever read—and one of the most brilliantly radical examinations of the philosophic and spiritual/moral premises on which, essentially, *all* aspects (however opposed) of contemporary American thinking are based. The book was first published as an extended series of short stories in *Galaxy*—of which the first was excellent, and the others increasingly tedious. It is a method occasionally utilized successfully by an accomplished and experienced novelist. This is Howard's first novel, and the stories, strung together, are almost as dreary as they were separately—until the explosive final sequence fits them together. The warm, affective opening should carry you a good way into the body of the book, and you can then look forward to four or five more exceptionally moving and convincing scenes *en route*. But even if it goes very slowly much of the way, it is a book to be read, and not skimmed too much.

[...]

In much time same category is *Let Us Reason Together*, "A Novel of Election Year, 1968," written and published (paperbound, varityped-offset) by Thomas Morrill (Dupont Press, 1403 Stone Road, Tallahassee, Florida 32303, $2), whose name will be familiar to readers of that unique journal, *The Worm Runners' Digest*, as the author of the memorable "Alice's Adventures in Evolutionland."

I wish I could say that Morrill has the same flair for Swiftian savagery that he had for Carollian pastiche. This is a heavy-handed leaden-footed novel about President Lyman P. Jimson (and his wife, Bug), his boyhood companions, Joseph (now General) Arim and Junior Sexton, now known as Ex. Other characters include Marylin and Robby Colleny, Nick Dixon, and a cross-section of dissenters and conspirators in "The Underground." *MacBird* did it better—or anyhow funnier—except for one thing: this book has something *more* to say, and the reader with the capacity for endless conversations, expositions, and set-scenes characteristic of Moskowitzian ("classic" 1930s) science fiction will find it worth the effort before he is done. I say this in full expectation, and with the warning, that not one in a thousand readers is likely to find himself in full, or large, agreement with Morrill's thesis, which builds from the premise that American entry into World War II was the initial error from which the Vietnamese involvement grew, and from which a true Police State is in process of growing. But you may be surprised—and upset—at the way the lesser premises cling together, given this foundation.

Also, I *think*, privately printed (Arcturus Pub., 1044 Lake St., Oak Park, Ill.) is Lowell B. Mason's *The Bull on the Bench*, the life story of justice Thomas Bullock of the Supreme Court of Moovalia—the sovereignty which replaced the United States of America after an atomic Doomsday effected some swift gene-switching in humans and cattle both:

"With humanity spiritually impotent, and cattle freed of their muteness, the latter forged ahead…adopted the Constitution…drew up a Five Year Plan…issued Position Papers, Proclamations, Directives, and Orders in Council. With that splendid generosity common to all who find it easy to take other people's property, cattle proceeded to care for their ill-fed, ill-clothed, and ill-housed relations still wandering about in open pastures."

The author was a "Federal Trade" Commissioner under President Truman, to whom the book is dedicated, with a nostalgic reference to the Truman Credo, "If You can't stand the heat, get out of the kitchen!" Those whose political memories, like mine, go back to pre- (Joseph) McCarthy times, will understand me when I say this is a truly Trumanesque book: knowledgeable rather than intellectual, more humorous than witty, not dirty but earthy, riddled with inconsistencies yet punctuated with sudden satisfying insights of a sort that seem to have vanished entirely from my world. This is a morality-tale of the nobility of the Individual in the sinful morass of Welfarism. It would be nice to believe; it was refreshing to read; it is sad to have to remember, at the end, that the last claim of technologized man to that kind of simplistic Honor went up in mushrooming smoke over Hiroshima, on Mr. Truman's orders.

Patterned like *The Bull*, Olaf Johannesson's *The Tale of the Big Computer* (Coward-McCann, $4.00), translated by Naomi Walford from a Swedish novel by the pseudonymous scientist/author, is a "future history" of the evolution of life on earth through the age of humans and the "Symbiotic Age" to the beginning of the true Computer Age. It may be full of telling points; I wouldn't know: it was too dull to read.

Note

1. The most interesting reviews will be used in the letters column which began in the May issue. Please limit comments to 250 words.—Ed.

SF 12 (1968 hb, 1969 pb)

Introduction: Fish out of Water, Man beside Himself

> We do not know who discovered water—[a small folder. Picture: orange fish against streaks of green and blue.]—but it was almost certainly not a fish. [And inside:] Anybody's total surround, or environment, creates a condition of nonperception.

It might have been intended as the essential statement on the motives, mode, and *modus operandi* of science fiction. Actually, it was an advertisement for a firm of industrial consultants, quoting Marshall McLuhan.

> ...sudden relevance to contemporary thinking. He orbits in the same system as R. D. Laing and McLuhan....

That one was from a "mainstream" London review of *The Disaster Area*, a collection of stories originally published in the s-f magazines of the fifties and early sixties.

Well, one has one's little snobberies: best-seller philosophy, pop technology, two-culture professors—obviously, McLuhan. But I had just discovered Laing. And Edward Hall, Eduardo Paolozzi, Sagan and Shklovskii, John Barth. And suddenly, *Sgt. Pepper*!

Take *Sputnik I*—October 1957—as a not-so-arbitrary dividing line. Until then, the only body of literature seriously attempting to discuss contemporary man (meaning, man in a self-made synthetic environment) was science fiction.

But...the times they are a changin'...Dylan and Heller, for a start. Eisley, Koestler, Fuller, Hoyle. And now: Ornette Coleman, Claes Oldenberg, Ed Emshwiller; Jarry and Borges, Burroughs and Michaux, Vonnegut and (sudden relevance!) Ballard—all popping up big, "in," no longer enclave heroes but cultural phenomena...getting better all the time.... Okay, so I read McLuhan.

In 1952, Reginald Bretnor wrote a brilliant predictive essay for his critical anthology *Modern Science Fiction*:

> In science fiction, man is the proper study of the writer—man, and everything man does and thinks and dreams and everything

> man builds, and everything of which he may become aware—his theories and his things, his quest into the universe, his search into himself, his music and his mathematics and his machines....
>
> Science fiction's emergence as a genre is rooted in our failure to understand the scientific method and to define it adequately.... This new awareness...is growing, despite educational conventions which inhibit it, despite a literary convention which almost universally excludes it....
>
> Eventually, we will again have an integrated literature. It will owe much, artistically, to non-science fiction. But its dominant attitudes and purposes...will have evolved from those of modern science fiction.

Asturias, Bulgakov, Singer, Nabokov, Martinson, Grass, Cortázar. *Transatlantic Review*, *International Times*, *Cavalier*, *Ambit*, *The Realist*, *Esquire*. Kubrick, Fellini, Lester, Godard, Ralph Nader, Mark Lane, Dr. Spock, Malcolm X, The Diggers, Bertrand Russell's War Trials, *Ramparts*, *Report from the Iron Mountain*, Burgess, Elkin, Updike, Hawkes, Friedmam, Calisher, Southern, Landolfi, Martin, Barthelme. What do *you* read? or read about? The Delphi prediction; RNA memory transfer; moon landings; artificial hearts; multimedia, light shows, psychedelic art; "God is dead," buttons and badges, "Reality is a Crutch." (Some of it is new; some is just starting to *happen*. Trotsky called it the Theory of Combined and Unequal Development.)

I read McLuhan. In 1951, in *The Mechanical Bride*, he said:

> No longer is it possible for modern man, individually or collectively, to live in any exclusive segment of human experience or achieved social pattern. The modern mind, whether in its subconscious collective dream or in its intellectual citadel of vivid awareness, is a stage on which is contained and reenacted the entire experience of the human race. There are no more remote and easy perspectives, either artistic or national....
>
> The magic that changes moods is not in any mechanism. It is critical vision alone which can mitigate the unimpeded operation of the automatic.

When that was written, "mainstream" fiction was still straitjacketed in a "realism" left over from the certainties of nineteenth-century mechanics and pure reason, and the science fictionists were almost alone in their efforts to seek new, remote, enlightening, if difficult, perspectives. Last year another Lit Prof, Robert Scholes, published a book called *The Fabulators* (Oxford):

> The writer who is willing to accept the word as his medium…must move away from the pseudo objectivity of realism toward a romance or an irony which will exploit language's distinctly human perspective on life. In competition with the cold and lidless eye of the cinema the sightless book must turn to the dark world of the imagination, illuminating it by the uniquely human vision to be found in words.…
>
> Fabulation, then, means a return to a…less realistic and more artistic kind of narrative: more shapely; more evocative; more concerned with ideas and ideals, less concerned with things. I am not proposing here an airy program for the future. I am talking about what is going on all around us.

SF: Speculative Fabulation. A satisfactory solution at last for my abbreviation-in-search-of-an-extension?

"Science fiction" now means many different things to many people; but what it meant that was, for a short time, important, is no longer so. Bretnor was right, and the time is now: his "integrated literature" is "going on all around us."

My favorite button-badge says *Reality Is a Crutch.* You will find much "nonrealism" about "reality" in this book, and a good bit of "realism" about "nonreality"; also much more about men, media, and the "McLuhan Age," among other things.

What they have in common could be called *outerness.* Maybe what s-f really stands for is Space Fish?

[…]

Books (August 1968)

May Day, 1968: Yesterday, I was rushing to finish a column, already overdue, when I was interrupted by the telephone. I heard the news, no more credible for being not entirely unexpected than was the assassination of Martin Luther King a few weeks earlier. On that earlier occasion, there was the radio to listen to through the night, and by morning I had heard the words often enough to understand that the inevitable had occurred: that a man of larger-than-life love, anger, faith, and endurance had ceased to endure: that his plans and passions were now and evermore *stopped*, with only framed and dated stop-action records of the past to guide the hundreds of thousands hoping to follow him out of the wilderness of now, into a future whose promise no longer shines so bright.

Yesterday, in my less public incredulity, there was only the telephone to force belief, but after one has said often enough to the shared friends and fellow-losers, *He is dead!* the statement, willy-nilly, gains some meaning—and deadline be damned.

Today, almost convinced, I approach (what I still tend to think of as) "Tony's column" almost—understanding—and later than ever. ("We never seem to communicate except by Special Delivery," he wrote one time, late to answer a query I had been late to send.) But of course there will be no fast-finish now. In a way, I have to learn how to write all over again.

For almost twenty years, every word I have written for publication has been addressed in part at least to Anthony Boucher. These columns, above all, have been done with an awareness of audience so acute he might have been looking over my shoulder as I wrote. (We never did find time to write those letters we both kept promising each other: these last few years—he was not well, and I was travelling—we had almost no correspondence. But there was at least this quasi-monthly "letter home," to try to show that I was working, learning, that I *cared.*)

I think most writers have some such single-person audience, one ideally-understanding-and-ultimately-critical reader—a teacher, fellow writer, editor, friend, to whom specifically they address themselves. Now (as soon as complete conviction comes—right now I still feel Tony up behind my shoulder—probably snickering softly at my refusal to look around and notice him and stop this morbid mawkishness) I suppose I shall have to learn to write broadcast.

Well, for this time at least it will be more like a collaboration. It is an appropriate one for the purpose: the column I was working on yesterday borrowed its theme from an extraordinary book, *Dynamics of Change* (of which more below); perhaps the dynamic will be seen more clearly by going a bit farther back to look at it.

For some time after his retirement from *F&SF*, Tony continued to do an occasional s-f review column for the *Times Book Review*, and an annual review of publications for my *Year's Best SF* anthologies. His review of 1962, in the *Seventh Annual*—about the time his column stopped appearing in the *Times*—began:

> "I have been trying for some time to discover why I, as a reviewer, am so much more resentful of uninspired routine books in science fiction than I am of similar publications in the mystery-suspense field....
>
> "I see now that it is because s-f is a form which, more than almost any other, by its very nature demands creative originality. The detective story and even the more modern psychological crime novel are—like the western, the love story, the historical romance—fixed forms, in which the creative challenge lies largely in seeing what the author can do within established boundaries. S-f is—or perhaps better, should and must be—a literature of stimulus and fresh horizons.
>
> "Put it this way: You are not going to complain if a large number of sonnets sound, superficially, a good deal alike; you are fascinated by what each poet manages to do within the sonnet. But if all the free verse you read, from countless diverse hands, sounds pretty much the same, you are justified in thinking that poetry is in a hell of a state.
>
> "A conventional, competent, uninspired murder novel or western is a perfectly reasonable commercial commodity. Conventional, competent, uninspired s-f has no reason for existing."

There *was* no reason—or at least very little. But nowadays—

Making money may not be a good reason for writing conventional, competent, uninspired s-f, but it is a very potent one. Science fiction is "in": or

I should say, "science fiction," because it is the label and not the substance that sells. There is an enormous, and growing, audience of both readers and viewers who will buy anything with the label provided it *is* conventional, competent, and uninspired: provided, that is, that it does not dangerously overstimulate virgin mentalities. Publishers and producers have discovered that they can sell, and sell well, anything with a spacecraft, giant computer, mysterious alien, strange, large, monster, or anything else *sufficiently incredible and incomprehensible* to these spinster imaginations. And the producers and publishers are now prepared to pay, and pay well, those authors who can wrap up sci-fi idioms and images in glossy packages guaranteed to blow no minds.

In 1952, Boucher (who was first president of the Mystery Writers of America, and an ardent supporter of the early abortive efforts to establish the SFWA) said in his article in Bretnor's *Modern Science Fiction*, "I know a man who has been turning out a steady 30,000 words a month and selling all of it—the equivalent of five or six book-length novels a year. His annual income from writing has been $3600. There must be some way of being just as poor with less effort." Things were not very much better when he wrote his tirade in the *Seventh Annual*—so it is hardly surprising to find so many of the suddenly big Names of s-f willing to swap their second-class literary and financial citizenship for wall-to-wall installations of Formula Imagination. The surprise, if anything, is that a handful of the established people *still* saw no good reason to stop thinking with their mouths open—and that some of the others (perhaps having caught up on their bills and maybe having had a short holiday) are now backsliding again into intellectual doorbusting, riskily speculative literary ventures, and general imaginative excess.

Whatever the reasons, the Dynamics of Change are clearly in operation, and writers who have been purring along smoothly on their Own Thing tracks, lavishing spit-and-polish on the brasswork of some favorite Fantasticke Engine (or else streaking by so fast in a cloud of technosociogobbldelogical steam that no one could notice there was no engine at all) are suddenly turning up grappling with new raw clumsy genuine home-made *concepts*. Some of them are too big to handle easily, or too bulky to handle convincingly, and some of the handlers are a bit out of practice. But it doesn't really matter if they're wrong or right: they're right where they belong, I mean—

Science fiction is not *science*: its job is not getting the answers, but asking the questions. It doesn't have to turn out to be "right"—just turn up what's "wrong"; and, maybe most of all, question the meaning of both words. ("…if it has a more serious function, it is less that of pin-pointed prophecy than that of creating in its readers a climate of acceptance of new wonders and a willingness to think at least one step ahead…." From "Science Fiction Still Leads Science Fiction Fact," *N.Y. Times Magazine*, 1957.)

So it's getting better (she said sourly), getting really better all the time.

The way you can tell is the way it's getting worse: I mean the *way* its getting worse. The Dynamics of Change are more dialectical than Euclidean, and when you get the swing of it, you can almost compute the progress vector by the force of the accompanying reaction blast. Remember—the pubescent child is pimply, clumsy, and gawky, an obvious loser in the Natural Selection; the fiercest riots are not in Alabama or Mississippi, but in Newark and Detroit; just before the divorce is when the sweet-talk is stickiest; pollen makes flowers and hay-fever both. *And* if some of the more thoughtful new books are lumpier in texture, uglier in flavor, gloomier in color, or cruder in shape—well, there's lots of the familiar predigested stuff around, if you prefer it.

"You will be required to do wrong no matter where you go. It is the basic condition of life, to be required to violate your own identity."

"We're all someone's tool. That's what society means."

The first quote is from Philip K. Dick's *Do Androids Dream of Electric Sheep?* (Doubleday, $3.95). The second is from Brian W. Aldiss's *Cryptozoic* (Doubleday, $4.50). Both lines are delivered by sages; both times the protagonist accepts the dictum with a sense of enlightenment and release. Although their speculative contents and story structures are very different, both books seem to me to be concerned fundamentally with the interface between institution and intuition, and any discussion of this duality today is in some respect an investigation into definitions of morality and of sanity. John Brunner's *Quicksand* (Doubleday, $4.50) and Alan F. Nourse's *The Mercy Men* (McKay, $3.95) are less complex books, in which the same duality, essentially, is exposed in—again—two radically different narratives of overt individual madness.

Brunner and Aldiss both conclude with split-level endings: In *Quicksand*, the choice is between "realistic" and "science-fictional" explanations of the ultimate tragedy; in *Cryptozoic*, the alternatives are simple personal tragedy, or an individual transcendence which will serve in time to mitigate the collective doom of which it is a part. *Androids*, like *Mercy Men*, has a "happy" ending—for the protagonist, if not the reader. Although Brunner's is the only story set in present time, all four books deal in some depth with overlapping aspects of the psychotogenic factors most apparent in contemporary western civilization, particularly as they affect the capacity, and the need, for human communication.

Quicksand gives us a psychiatrist working in a mental hospital, maintaining a precarious personality balance in the face of corrosive authoritarian pressures, status-structure stresses, professional and social hypocrisies, and domestic hostility and deceit. When the encapsulated idealism-fantasies which have provided his only internal support are attacked and exposed by a seductively defenseless patient (alien or alienated—the reader is left to take his choice), the disintegration of the doctor's personality is complete.

In an insidiously quiet, indeed quite/rather British/polite manner (very different from Brunner's usual tone), the book poses one vital question after another: Who are the really insane? Who are the controllers, and who the controlled? What do you mean, "freedom"? That sort of thing. But it only poses, never probes—out of politeness, one almost feels, or would, if one had never read Brunner before. The hero, or antihero, is a Mitty without the courage of his own daydreams, a man whose very fantasies are grey-on-grey, and whose fears are a virtual catalogue of neurotica (his mother, society, his boss, an unknown God, his body, and of course his own emotions). A man, in short, grimly over-representative of our culture and, more prototypically than ironically, a psychiatrist: the purblind leading the purblind.

Even this might have made for a fable of power, if the environment from which the little man flees were equally apropos. But I had a bit of the feeling I get when *Playboy* lectures on the New Morality or Betty Friedan on the Feminine Mystique—a sort of displacement-in-time which might be as gently nostalgic as a Jack Finney story if it were less earnest. Women's rights were fought and won many years ago; I know there are millions of women living underprivileged existences today and projecting their frustrations on a delusion of A Man's World—but the battle they have to fight is with their own infant conditioning, not with their husbands. I know there are millions of American boys who persist (in the face of high school pregnancy statistics) in believing that The American Girl must be tricked, lured, or bribed into bed, but the "sexual revolution" of the sixties (as distinct from the twenties) starts with full knowledge that sex is popular with women too, and concerns itself more with the varieties of sexual experience than with its outworn proprieties. Brunner's Paul Fidler, similarly, seems to drive himself to his destruction in a Model-A, the victim of an early-Freudian culture of the sort in which—I know—millions of people still live, but which, as setting for a contemporary novel, provides little opportunity to do more than peer through keyholes at the most central problems.

Nevertheless, this is one of Brunner's best books to date: solidly constructed, strongly composed, and vividly successful in the effectiveness of those keyhole-glimpses.

Nourse's *Mercy Men* is a deceptively simple, action-packed story which approaches many of the same problems from just about every possible opposite direction. The view is from the future, and an ugly one it is, nothing relieved by its moments of utter plausibility. Here, a volunteer subject in a giant research foundation is "cured" (of the trauma earlier induced in him by the same medical-elite powers) by a sort of homeopathic application of carefully controlled dosages of physical and emotional violence, structured falsehood, and personality invasion; the result seems to make him as acceptable to his nightmarishly deranged world as it has become to him. I should like to think that the author's intent was ironic but his approval or disapproval of the world he has shown is irrelevant beside the fact that so much of *what* he shows has a brutally authentic and convincing ring. In fact, the book is in many ways an illustration of my earlier comments on concepts and crudities: only superficially "conventional," it is certainly *not* "uninspired," and it departs from Nourse's usual pleasant competence in two directions at once: the writing is rougher and the thinking is tougher.

Aldiss's *Cryptozoic* also concerns itself with power structures on several levels, including the psychiatric and political; but its main speculative preoccupation is with man's orientation in time. The concept presented here is one I do not believe has been treated before in fiction except in miniature, in carefully localized short-term situations in short-length stories. I am not going to try to describe it. Aldiss needs the whole book to depict it; I think I should need one at least twice as long. And any attempt to describe rather than to depict would be doomed: on the rational level, the concept is clear enough—but quite irrational. The book is full of petty inconsistencies and internal contradictions. And yet—

There were moments, over and over, when (in "bellyfeel," not words) I *knew* what he meant. What he has hold of, I think, is a poetic concept so *right* intuitionally that the very attempt at analysis on the surface level of verbal consciousness shatters it unrecognizably. And considering the flaws in the rationale the author provides, it does not much matter whether that "rightness" is purely symbolic or prophetically "scientific." What does matter is the excitement, long gone from most of the genre, of snatching at, and sometimes seizing on, a strange, alluring, and frightening avatar of Truth, most maddeningly out of reach in a nonetheless rock-sure surreality. (Quick note—no, *no!* I do not mean it is a "surrealist novel"!) Read it.

Do Androids Dream of Electric Sheep? does not suffer from any of the assortment of novelistic shortcomings which qualify my admiration for the other three books: Dick has apparently worked his way through to a methodology that gives him much more control, and makes his ideas much more accessible to the reader. In a review of his work some months ago, I compared his techniques to those of the comic strip, and I understand there were readers who took this as denigration. If it seemed so, it was probably because the comic strip itself is simply not a congenial form to me: I don't like the flat bright colors, and stylized images. But I recognize that in this particularity I am stranded almost alone on the far side of a generation gap (with people twice my age, since it is my own generation that first took the comic book to heart)—and it has never stopped me from *reading* (well, some) comics, or from recognizing the value of the form as a message-medium.

In any case, I have read, I think, every one of Dick's books from cover to cover, even when he infuriated, frustrated, or baffled me (as for a while he was doing regularly): at the least there was always the same sort of thing I found in the Aldiss novel—flashes of awareness of a concept entirely outside my own bag, and not successfully communicated, to me, by the author—but clearly worth reaching for, and coming back to.

Whether I have acquired skill at reading Dick, or he has, as it seems to me, begun to organize his material more successfully, this time I experienced none of the jump, frame confusion I have suffered from in the past. This is a rich book, which deals with aspects of the whole range of conflicts, dualities, dichotomies, and interchanges approached in all three of the others described here—and is nothing like any of them. Some of the elements will be familiar to regular readers of Dick's; others are new. This is a world of falling population and sublethal fallout dust, of Wilbur Mercer and the black empathy box, of religious devotion to living animals and merciless extermination of androids, of "specials" and bounty hunters, mood consoles and the inescapable Buster Friendly. Every one of these things is meaningful in context, and the context is constructed to contain all the meanings and multiply them.

Perhaps the best thing I can say is that there were still some ideas I'm not sure I know whether I liked, or agreed with, or fully understood but I assume I will see them from some other angle the next time around.

And I can say with some certainty that the Happy Ending is *supposed* to make you weep.

[...]

Tony never said *Goodbye;* he always said *God bless.* When he said it, I always thought it quite possible that God really would.

Goodbye, Tony, God bless.

Notes

1. *The Dynamics of Change*, edited by Don Fabun; Prentice Hall for the Kaiser Aluminum Corporation, 1967, $6.95.

[...]

Books (September 1968)

In the heart of Pennsylvania, at a famous university, there is a man who teaches a (full credit) course called *Prophecy and Prediction.* This is even more extraordinary than it sounds, because—in direct violation of all established institutional practice—Professor Philip Klass is not only peculiarly well-equipped to teach such a subject, but it was precisely because of his demonstrated ability to practice prophecy commercially that his lack of some of the more ordinary academic qualifications was considered immaterial when he was invited to join the faculty of the English Department at Penn State.

That is to say, he happens to be an outstandingly good science fiction writer—and please note I said *prophet,* not prophesier. He is not an Elder Statesman of Space, one of those proto-engineers who, in a sense, *invented* space travel and atomic power (and television, and a number of other pleasant and unpleasant facts of modern life) in the early "scientifiction" magazines. When his first story was published, in 1946, most of these items were already on—or on their way to—the drawing boards of the "real" engineers (who—like Klass—had received much of their education and inspiration from those pre-designers of the thirties and early forties). But while the Young Engineers were applying themselves to the task of turning other men's *predictions* into everyman's artifacts, the Young Writer calling himself "William Tenn" set himself a course of apprenticeship in the rather more outré business of *prophecy.*

Professor Klass today makes a sharp distinction between the two words, and I am not at all certain that my definitions match his. I am only sure—after reading (the new and re-reading the old in) the six volumes just released by Ballantine in "celebration of William Tenn"—that by *my* definition he learned his trade brilliantly. I find myself as much impressed today by the accumulated work as I was twenty years ago by the marvelously inventive and richly comic young writer (who was two-light-years and nine published stories ahead of me at the time). But I am impressed now by different stories (few of them written then), and for different reasons.

The specialty s-f field—like most ingrown enclaves, I suppose—has had an unhappy history of glorifying its best writers to destruction. In 1948,

William Tenn had already established himself not only as a lightning innovator and bang-up storyteller, but as "One of the rarest birds on the science fiction horizon, a true humorist." (In 1949, "Venus and the Seven Sexes" set him beyond doubt in a Klass of his own.) Retrospectively, I suspect that this early image as First Funnyman of Fantasy did his later reputation—and quite possibly his writing as well—incomparable damage. Certainly it seems probable that some of his long silences in recent years have resulted at least in part from an editorial and critical reluctance to relinquish an image long since grown constrictingly smaller-than-life. I hope, now that he seems to be producing again, that the large-but-misbegotten effort Ballantine is making to contain the old image in a—wildly, absurdly—inappropriate new one (Rediscovered Primitive) does not result in similar damage.

The six books just issued consist of Tenn's only novel, *Of Men and Monsters*, published in full for the first time, and five short story collections. *Of All Possible Worlds* (hereafter mostly, *APW*) and *The Human Angle* (*THA*) are reissues of collections first published in 1955 and 1956; *The Wooden Star* (*TWS*), *The Seven Sexes* (*TSS*), and *The Square Root of Man* (*SRM*) are new selections of pieces originally published between 1946 and 1967. At a total price of $4.50 for the six books—one novel, one novella, one critical essay, nine novelettes, and 34 short stories—there is a prodigious amount of good reading here. Unfortunately, there is also an unpardonable scattering of the author's commercial apprenticeship efforts spread through all five books—unpardonable, that is, when so many of his better stories were incomprehensibly omitted ("Firewater," for instance, or "Time Waits for Winthrop"). Also—

[...]

The fact is, Tenn's work, at its best (or even its high-grade median) resembles absolutely nothing written by anyone else. None of it is easy to describe, and the best is impossible. One can say a few things in general: that some of the concepts and moods are so immediately contemporary as to be frightening—considering that all but a handful of these stories were written more than thirteen years ago; that the satire at its most effective is an unforgettable, nearly unforgivable, fusion of savage and tenderness; that the pure strain of Tenn humor (as distinguished from satire, or gags) is as unique, individual, unpredictable, and irresistible as—well, there is only one modern standard for this kind of thing—*Catch-22*.

[...]

Of Men and Monsters is the full story of the young man known as Eric the Eye, whose initiation rites into the adult world of Mankind (consisting of 128 people) were described in the *Galaxy* novelette, "The Men in the Walls," in 1963. (The original story is now the first of three parts in the novel.) It is a rich mixture of anthropology, poetry, prophecy, and adventure—the story of the turning-point in the future of (what we now call) mankind, whose remnants, at the opening of the story, are scattered in degenerated tribal groupings, living a ratlike existence in the walls and floorings of the monstrous houses of alien invaders of Earth. Out of the conflicts of traditions and superstitions (Ancestor Science and Alien Science; the warriors and thieves of the Male Societies and food-processors and omen-tellers of the Female Societies; "Mankind" itself and the "Strangers": back-burrowers, outlaws, and the legendary Aaron People) in a time of desperation, a new human society is patched together, to mount a distinctively Tennian return invasion.

The book has everything one might expect—wealth of invention, perfection of pace, solidity of structure, consistency, craftsmanship, giggles, and *prophecy.* If it disappointed me somewhat, it may have been just the lack of freshness stemming from the long time between the writing of the beginning and its completion—or it may have been the equally long time between my reading of the beginning and of the rest (I am a bad serial-reader, and I ordinarily take pains to avoid reading in the magazines the earlier or partial versions of anything I think I may later be called upon to review in book form).

It is, in any case, the first novel we have had from a unique, an uniquely *readable*, writer: as stands, it is easily one of the best of 1968, and one hopes it is a promise of much more, soon. At the very least, the book manages to do what no more than a handful of writers—new or old—on the current scene can do: to combine narrative excitement with sophisticated, entirely contemporary, meaning.

Of that handful, one of the most distinguished, and certainly the most practiced, is Fritz Leiber, whose *Swords of Lankhmar* (Ace, 60¢) can no more be considered just as a "Sword and Sorcery" novel than *Of Men and Monsters* is simply a "catastrophe" story.

There are a number of curious parallels (and inversions) between the two books. For one thing, Leiber, too, has some men in the walls—but most of them are (any way you look at it) rats. Here, too, are small cooperating-while-competing tribal groups summing up in tiny numbers all of mankind: here too is an island universe in which parables enact themselves; here too is a constant contrast/comparison/questioning of the roles of science, magic, and tradition.

And, as it happens, here too the novel grew out of a comparatively remote magazine novelette—"Scylla's Daughters" in *Fantastic* in 1961. If it does not seem to suffer from that fact to the same extent as the Tenn book, it may be simply because Leiber has been writing about Fafhrd and Mouser so long that *they* have, in a sense, learned to grow along with him.

Or, it might be simply that the novel is not attempting to do anything as profound and complex as *Of Men and Monsters*. Which is not to say there is anything superficial about *Swords of Lankhmar*—except its surface.

There can be very few readers by now who are not familiar to some extent with Nehwon, the bubble-universe of Lankhmar, Quarmall, Ilthmar, the Sinking Land, the Salt Marsh, and the Frozen Sea, inhabited by Fafhrd, the giant red-beard barbarian-from-the-North, and the slim swift stealthy leather-clad dirksman, the Gray Mouser, as well as a variable population of Mingols, Ghouls, sorcerers, princes, sailors, warriors, dragons, rats, cats, and other miraculous creatures, not least of which is the endless supply of beautiful maidens either in, or distributing, distress.

Well, *this* time there is a marvelously seductive albino rat-girl and her evil merchant father, who are leading a revolution of the rats in Lankhmar Below, plotting to seize power from the decadent sadist-effeminate Glipkerio, Overlord of Lankhmar Above. For Leiber-lovers, it is enough to say that this book bears about the same relation to the early adventures of Fafhrd and Mouser as "The Night He Cried" did to Mickey Spillane—or perhaps more accurately, *The Wanderer* to a book by Louis Adamski. For anyone unfortunate enough not to know Leiber, or to those who (like myself) ordinarily avoid Swords-and-Sorcery by *anybody*, I can only say:

Try it. You may be surprised.

(And add, to those with weak stomachs: Forget it. You may be too surprised.)

Meantime, one can dream of the book that (after all) *might* come along (next year? the year after?) with Tenn's careful craftsmanship and literary balance, Leiber's vitality and lusty-gusto—*and* the narrative power and piercing intelligence of either one.

Or, on (what is it? fourth?) thought, there is a further factor, present in both these books, which is essential with all the rest: otherwise, Joanna

Russ's *Picnic on Paradise* (Ace, 60¢) might be just the brilliant combination described above. For lack of a dozen pages to discuss it, I will call it simply Prophetic Power: the binding energy that holds a novel of ideas together, provides the essential unity between theme, plot, and background, situates the most fantastic or unlikely characters and locales in a subjective matrix of "reality."

This is, of course, Miss Russ's first novel, and as such, it is quite startlingly superior: I cannot think when I last enjoyed so much reading anything so unconvincing.

I mean, I didn't believe any*thing*: not the character of the protagonist, nor (except in brief flashes) any other characters; not the situation in which they were placed, the world in which it occurred, or the final outcome. I did not, and do not, believe that a battle-scarred super-annuated (twenty-six, long past her prime for her time) adventuress from ancient Tyre is likely (let alone *necessarily*) the psychological, physical, and moral superior of people from a civilization four millennia later where "super-diets and hybridization from seventy colonized planets had turned all humanity...into Scandinavian giants"—and nothing in the improbable sequence of events described convinced me of it, even temporarily. (These include the use as an expendable Special Agent—untrained and unbriefed—of the only human being ever recovered from the past by an expensive and power-consuming time probe; a limited war being fought with elaborate ground rules for possession of a planet whose only value is as a resort area—where accredited tourist/neutrals cannot be lifted off-planet from a base manned by an interplanetary agent; complete vulnerability to the effects of drugs used as common-place refreshers and tranquillizer on the part of those most habituated to their use, while the only character totally unaccustomed to there can fight off their effects—and *lots* more.)

The overtones in all this are an oddly-assorted and overall-agreeable admixture of Leiber and Laumer (Mouser and Retief) which combine well with the pure Russ components, but nowhere add up to the "straight science fiction" the book purports to be. And I suppose it is, actually, only its false-science-fiction front I am complaining about, because actually, while I was reading, I didn't *care*.

Joanna Russ *writes* so well, it doesn't really matter if she makes sense. When it all got too much for me, I didn't stop: I just switched over to a (highly necessary) willful "suspension of disbelief," and went on reading into the small hours of the night, for the sheer pleasure of the prose, and delight in the imagery, color, and content of one vivid scene after another.

She could have made it easier for me if she had set the thing up as the fantasy it is. Or she could, with remarkably little change, have written it as a modern novel, and made me *believe*, easily, that a scrawny primitive battleax from, say, Peru or Viet Nam, was basically tougher and earthily smarter than a tourist new from New York. Maybe the next one—The fact is, *whatever* she does with the next one, I'll be there reading. The girl can *write*.

And who knows? Maybe she can learn the Prophet Business, too.

Books (November 1968)

[...]

Leave your preconceptions behind...when you open Samuel Delany's new *Nova* (Doubleday, $4.95). My own problem was the opposite of my friend's with *2001*: I came to this book with an anticipation keener than any I have brought to anything since—well, probably Vonnegut's *Rosewater*—looking for (at least an approach to) the Great Novel I (still) expect from the author of *Empire Star*, *Babel-17*, *The Einstein Intersection*, "The Star-Pit," "Aye and Gomorrah," and (now) *Nova*: and what I got instead was a first-rate jim-dandy solid provocative science-fiction novel.

It took me a while to realize I had no honest cause for complaint—a while longer to discover I damn well *did* have cause—longer yet to understand (first) why I was so irritated, and (eventually) the *real* reasons to be annoyed with the book.

Delany is in an almost unique position in s-f today: everybody loves him. The "solid core," the casual readers, the literary dippers-in, the "new thing" crowd—Delany is all things to all readers. It is an untenable position—unless, of course, he gets as good as I think he will eventually be. Swift, Melville, Carroll, Twain, Conrad are all read by children as well as litterateurs, their plots are reducible to comic book format, while their themes are subtle and complex enough to sustain reading after delighted analytical reading.

Well, Delany is not Swift or Conrad—yet; but his seven previous novels and scattered shorter works have already placed him out of the judging in the transient-writer class; and as the work of an apprentice-great, *Nova* must be regarded as more of a fascinating exercise than a satisfactory achievement. *But*—

What is wrong with the book is simply that the author tried to do—not *too much*, but *enough*: he tried to write a modern novel on all the levels required (by the same standards I am applying) of a contemporary work: if he did not *quite* succeed, it is well to remember that neither has anyone else—yet; and few other attempts have managed to stand up meanwhile as, at least, solid entertainment.

Here is what I wrote after my first reading of the book:

Nova is a deceptive book in several ways. Don't let the first page stop you; the book is *not*—except superficially—a *Planet Stories* superficiality. And don't rush in to identify with anyone too soon; it may take a while to decide whose viewpoint you are using.

The protagonist, the hero, and the viewpoint character are (in order of appearance, not necessarily identity) a 19-year-old gypsy-born spacehand-and-minstrel named the Mouse; a cosmically wealthy and powerful space captain named Lorq Von Ray; and a wandering scholar and spacehand called Katin.

The book is intriguingly, but unnecessarily, complex—mostly written underwater, as it were; that is, under the surface of a (too) familiar space adventure plot, aswarm and sparkling with the strange and rich biota of Delany's inner world.

There is, for instance, the Mouse's "sensory-syrynx," an instrument which can produce a complete multi-media show—visual, musical, and olfactory display; a recurrent theme involving Tarot lore; a carefully constructed cultural context in which the 20th century serves as the classical period of a culture 1000 years older, whose technological and philosophic beginnings are rooted in the transitions of today. There are the Illyrion furnaces which have made whole planets habitable and space traversable, great glowing pits called *Hell* here, and *Gold* there—and tiny battery power packs primed by micrograms of the same stuff, which run the wondrous syrynx and Katin's tiny recorder. There is a gorgeous physiological/astrophysical/political philosophic construct in parallels; and a sweep of action from Athens to the Pleiades, with fiery fights, drinking bouts, mosques and museums, diver-hunters and cyborg-spacemen—and with all this, the book is somehow lacking. I do not know what it lacks; perhaps if it had come after *Empire Star* and *Babel-17*, and before *The Einstein Intersection*, I should have found no lack, at all. But, just as I went on from the first banal page, simply because it was Delany, and I could be sure of finding the richness and excitement I did find, so I went on from history lesson to battle scene to gorgeous syrynx session to Tarot lore, hoping I could be equally sure of learning why they were all there together. I think an explanation was given to me in the last pages—and I do not think it satisfied me. But never mind: the fans will love it.

That was the first time around; I have now read the book—to be precise—two and a half times (the third time, only those passages marked the second time for re-examination), and when I started to retype that earlier comment, I thought the word *unnecessarily* must have been a typographical error. Alas, not so: the error was not mechanical, but (doubly) human—the reader's and writer's both.

There is nothing in this book that did not *have* to be there—from the blind drunk of the spacebars to the wicked gorgeous Princess, Ruby Red; from the syntax-inversion of the Pleiades speech-pattern to Katin's erudite lectures; from the cool halls of the Alkane Institute to the hole in the stellar doughnut. The problem is rather that some elements are so compressed as to be almost invisible, and I question whether any reader who lacks the responsibility of recording his opinion will work as hard as I did to find, and put together, all the pieces in a book so readily readable and pleasingly paced on the surface that there is no real cause to wonder how deep the channels underneath may flow—and small sign of their turbulence.

These are (at least some of) the ways you can read *Nova*: as a fast-action far-flung interstellar adventure; as archetypal mystical/mythical allegory (in which the Tarot and the Grail both figure prominently); as modern-myth told in the s-f idiom with powerful symbols built on solid science fiction clichés; as a futuristic vehicle for a philosophic complex of political/historical/economic/sociological ideas; as an experimental approach to literary criticism.

Among other things, the book examines: the nature and value of scholarship, mysticism, "progress," and the varieties of the creative experience; the significance of the "instinct for workmanship" (the quote is from Veblen, not Delany) and the alienation phenomena of the industrial and (current) electronic revolutions; the relationships between the psychophysiology of the individual and the ecology of the body politic. Each of the three central characters (or the three aspects of *the* character?) suffers a variant form of alienation, rooted in different combinations of social, economic, geophysical, cultural, intellectual, and physiological factors. Through one or another of these viewpoints, the reader observes, recollects, or participates in a range of personal human experience including violent pain and disfigurement, sensory deprivation and overload, man-machine communion, the drug experience, the creative experience—and interpersonal relationships which include incest and assassination, father-son, leader-follower, human-pet, and *lots* more.

The economy of Delany's writing is both maddening and delightful—and *almost* accomplishes what he seems to have been trying to do. (For instance, the culture-vista opened up when the Lunar scholar, Katin, says to the gypsy Mouse: "If somebody had told me I'd be working in the same crew, today in the 31st century, with somebody who could honestly be skeptical about the Tarot, I don't think I would have believed it. You're really from Earth?") But even 279 closely written, richly embroidered, tautly thought pages are not enough: it is too much of too many, and too little of each: and—add odd complaints—it is too easy to read, on the easiest level.

If you let yourself go, it will run away with you; since the author failed to set up stop signs, the reader must either make his own (put the book down and pace the room once between chapters?) or plan on a second, slower reading after the fun of the first. Or settle, of course, for a good read, and never mind mining out the gold.

For two writers so disparately individual in concept, mood, style, background, and viewpoint Delany and R. A. Lafferty have certain startling distinctions in common. There are other notable stylists and fine prose writers in s-f today; but—in very different modes—Lafferty and Delany are currently *the* two outstanding poetic writers (language both lyrical and precise; images exact and evocative). There are other evolving new concepts and working out appropriate new techniques for contemporary multiplexities; and there are many others writing action-adventure yarns in the s-f idiom; but I can think of no others who so frequently manage to combine these apparently contradictory efforts.

But their greatest similarity also contains their most symptomatic difference. Among the characters in both men's stories, a strange breed of children appear repeatedly: hardheaded/mystical creatures with electric personalities and powerful capacities. In Delany's stories they are most often young teenagers whose essentially heroic proportions and proclivities (like almost all Delany characters) are dramatically flawed, or defective, or incurably disadvantaged, in some one area. Lafferty's children are mostly prepubescent, and perfectly normal—except for a total lack of (parental or personal) inhibition; and a sort of amplification—of reality which permits them to act out archetypal childish fantasies on a grand-opera heroic scale.

Lafferty's first novel, *The Past Master*, was in another vein altogether. *The Reefs of Earth* (Berkley, 60¢) is an utterly charming book in which a group of clever, nasty, appealing children somehow won my complete sympathy, approval, and delight, while indulging in as crude, self-centered, and sadistic a series of Adventures as ever any noble, absurd, admired, epic (real or fictive) Hero.

Of course, the Dulanty kids, comparatively speaking, had cause. Even, to some extent, ethical justification.

First of all, they were not Earth people, but Pucas, and although all seven had been born on Earth, they were raised as Pucas, naturally, which meant their values and standards were basically different. When their parents began to disintegrate under the combined effects of Earth Allergy and Earth boredom, Elizabeth—the oldest—was nine; Helen and John, the two youngest were six. (I never did figure out how old Bad John was, but then he was usually invisible anyhow.) They were "faster and more intelligent than Earth children, and half of them—" (Elizabeth, Charles, and Helen) "—looked like angels or like handsome Earthlings. Their cousins, Peter and Dorothy and John and Bad John, looked like potato-faced goblins, like real Pucas."

The older Dulanty's had been sent to Earth as what you might call missionaries, in a Puca sort of way, or maybe traders, or spies. It didn't work out too well.

> "They had a hard time getting along with the people of Earth, and it wasn't entirely the fault of the Earth people. It was after coming to Earth that they sowed their seven children (Bad John is included in this count). The children were thus citizens of Earth if they wished to be. Moreover, it was believed that by their birth on Earth they would have immunity to Earth Allergy, that killing sickness.
>
> "'Earth is, after all, one of the four worlds,' the Puca instructors had instructed them, 'Earth people are, comical though it seems, our cousins in blood. So far, the blood between us has been bad blood....
>
> "Well, the Dulantys (and a few others) had been working at the problem for ten years and more. They had riot achieved accord.
>
> "Of the sisters, Veronica looked like an old potato, and Witchy was of an unearthly ('tis a Puca abhacht and not a pun) beauty. But who can say which was the more beautiful where they came from?

> "Henry Dulanty was tall and heavy. He looked like the ogre out of a fairy tale. He was. Earthers retain memories of earlier Pucas with such heads and hulks.

But the Earthers have lied about the ogre. He was the finest fellow you'd want to meet—in the daylight—not in the dark.

> "His brother Frank was tall and lean. All four of the parents had a striking goblinish strangeness in their appearance, though Witchy's was shimmered over with beauty.
>
> "There is no use kidding about it. The Puca themselves are not handsome. And the people of Earth (they deserve that, they have so little else going for them) are.... Mostly, the Puca, if they happen to be born of a pretty appearance and face, are able to maintain it while they are young. But with the coming of maturity, the shattering profundity of the developing Puca character will smash and bevanish that pretty mask and replace it with a deeper face, intricate and ugly and of a high humor...."

Most of the story concerns the adventures of the children after they arrive at the unhappy but logical conclusion that it has become necessary for them to kill everyone on Earth, except of course, themselves. They had to start with their parents because the Allergy had already disintegrated the adults' capacities and vitality beyond repair. They were too sentimental, really, to kill their parents, whom the loved, by hand, so they made a Bagarthach verse and sent it against them:

> *"We'll wither Witchy with a prank,*
> *And kindle them in flames like roses—*
> *Veronica and Hank and Frank—*
> *And give them all Apotheosis."*

They meant it to work by burning the house down that night, but they were not as experienced with Bagarthaches as they thought they were; it worked all right, but not quite the way they expected.

The next person on their list was wicked Coalfactor or Stutgard, and John was supposed to handle him with an ax that same night, while the house was burning. That didn't work either, because someone else got there first. But they were learning all the time, and once they managed to get hold of some transportation, and set off for the Green River on Fulbert Fronsac's fishing raft, the *Île de France*, they began to be able to do some fair amount of damage.

It is necessary to remember, of course, that in the world of the Dulantys, death is a very different condition from that visualized by Earthmen. (Even those of us who profess to a belief in an "afterlife" rarely attain the sort of awareness of pleasures and problems that is native and natural to the Puca mind.) This being true, murder is a considerably lesser crime, apparently, than unkindness. As for theft and deception, these are very relative acts for people who can change physical "realities" simply by imagining them different, and then making a Bagarthach verse to confirm the change.

I mean, this is an utterly horrifying, completely captivating, funny, tragic, pulse-quickening, music-making Novel of the Absurd. It may not stick with you like *Past Master*, but—well, I don't know, maybe it *will*.

What I'd *really* like, though, would be the book where the Dulanty kids square off against any half dozen assorted Delany kids. The Dulantys being younger, I think it would be fair to throw in their natural access to assistance by offstage Puca (dead or alive) adults. WOW!

[...]

Books (January 1969)

Chicago, 28 August, 1968:

Daley City, they're calling it, Fort Chicago, and now Prague West. Barbed wire and security checkpoints. Chemical Mace and police clubs; sequin-spangled Humphrey Girls—street-scene Yippies, sleepless, beaded, bandaged, bearded—V-signing clean-for-Geners, earnest smiles and angry eyes; incongruously babyblue bright helmets of Chicago's Finest, and the long slow convoys of army-drab Guards on Lake Shore Drive.

The kids I drove out here are a backroom squad, not-so-clean Geners, doing their thing here the way they were doing it in New York, with silk screens and paint stains, but working on cloth now, block-letter STOP THE WAR posters for delegates to smuggle, folded, into The Hall.

The buses and taxis are on strike. The kids tell me, wear your McCarthy button, and any McCarthy-stickered car will stop. What will they do when the miracle doesn't occur? If they get through the plank battle today, nominations will happen tonight, and the mood here is more and more mortuary—a growing feeling they may even Dump the Hump tonight and Draft Byrdman—if the Kennedy Heir Presumptive doesn't come forward: whoever it is, it won't be McCarthy.

If he agrees to a fourth party, they'll get some sleep and get back to work, I guess; and if he doesn't—

The SDS is waiting on the corners, and the police make the Yippies look better all the time. Black Chicago growls and glowers and grins in the ghettoes (except for the watchers patrolling the Loop: "Go home, sister—no black blood spilled here tonight."), but what happens if the next reporter the cops club down and Mace spray on the ground is black?

From here and now, the batch of books I brought out to review seem remote and pallid…

Milford, PA, September:

Too remote. The peace plank was defeated, the kids' cloth posters made some prime TV time, and all the savagery of the streets up to that point seemed nothing at all beside the film clips the networks (finally aroused) began showing alternately with the Amphitheatre Nominations coverage that Wednesday night. *The whole world is watching*, they chanted in the streets, while Delegates' Ladies aimed cocktail glasses from the windows of the Conrad Hilton at the cops below. Next morning, I phoned Ed Ferman in New York, warned him there'd be no column from me, packed up the typewriter and drove up to Lincoln Park. Later, I drove a Medic team between the hospital station at St. Chris's church on the near North Side, and Michigan Avenue. ("Don't mind her, she's a good kid," the med student said when the nurse student screamed at him: "She's just been gassed. It makes them irritable.") For two days afterwards, I interviewed medics and patients, first at the headquarters of the Medical Committee on Human Rights, then at the Free Theatre, took names and addresses of people there was no time to talk with on the spot. But no one who wasn't there wants to believe it the way it was: some of the publishers I approached made it clear they'd be glad to discuss a new science fiction anthology....)

And here I am, with the same stack of books, and some more. Some of them are pretty good reads, too. But almost all of them are—remote.

"Reality" is a crutch: a crutch we need, to cope with a universe whose multiplex phenomena are still beyond the scope of our small range of two-, three-, or (marginally, occasionally) four-dimensional perceptions. What first attracted me to the esoteric pulp-magazine cult of science fiction, almost thirty years ago, was its "realism"—as distinct from the pastoral, psychiatric, and/or patriotic fantasy-worlds of almost all popular and "mainstream" fiction of that time. The future histories and space-flung landscapes of Heinlein, Leiber, Simak, Sturgeon, de Camp, Boucher, Brown, del Rey, Cartmill, Jameson, *et al.*, actually bore a recognizable relation *to the world I was living in.* I found a complete literature aware of, and dealing in, the technological and sociopolitical facts of life as I knew it, in those pre-Pearl Harbor years of World War II.

It was a truly esoteric cult, in that its members shared wisdom hidden from the world outside: it was also a true "ghetto" in that a public ("outside") consensus of ignorance, not any lack of evangelism "inside," preserved the "secret" nature of the group. For fifteen years, through and around the forties, the science fiction magazines maintained an open, continuous, and almost exclusive forum for speculation, debate, and poetic vision stemming from such self-evident phenomena as: the dynamics of Big-Business-and-Bureaucracy (in trade unions, education and government, as well as business); the economic and anthropological implications of an accelerating technology on the verge of atomic power, robotics, space flight, and computerized high-speed decision making; the incipient conflict between nationalist, racist, cultural, and religious patriotisms and the ecumenical imperatives implicit in the developing technologies of communication, transportation, and warfare.

Through the forties, science fiction was ahead of the game: when the news of Hiroshima broke, s-f readers were dismayed at the manner of the coming of atomic power—not stunned by its existence. In some respects, we stayed ahead well into the fifties: when *Sputnik I* went up, we amused ourselves watching our neighbors, teachers, and literary critics shift from talk of escapist phallic symbolism to awed despair at the USSR's "incredible breakthrough."

But more and more through the fifties, through the dark age years of Joe McCarthy and the witchhunt, alike-with-Ike conformism, and crypto-*1984* anti-egghead sentiment, the best we could do was a holding battle against the smothering forces of (the manifold meanings of) "security." The first (brief, post-Hiroshima) s-f boom was over, and here and there security agencies got up dossiers on nearby science fictionists, but on the whole they wrote us off as nuts. Still, we were the only a-bit-subversive game in town, and we got to be an In Thing with the highbrow crowd. The dawn of what eye-rubbing editors at *Time* and *Newsweek* and the like called interchangeably, The Space Age and The Science Fiction Age caught us, so to speak, with pants up. Sudden public respect for science fiction's strange prophetic powers, and the bit of prose polish we had acquired rewriting old ideas when all the new information was classified (at least physics and chemistry and bacteriology—the old hunting grounds) started the field on its second boom, and we even sprouted an infant Establishment that grew into the mid-sixties with respectable new-found security of its own and a vested interest in continuing to purvey profitable what *The New Yorker* last year called "the futures of yesterday." (Overpopulation stories were going so well, for instance, the field as-a-whole managed to overlook the technological breakthroughs of the Pill and the Coil until they had become commonplace. I suspect s-f readers were just a bit *more* astonished than subscribers to the *Reader's Digest* when Roman Catholic priests and parishioners rebelled openly this fall against the Pope's ruling on the Pill!)

Today, approaching the seventies, the strange agglomeration now labeled "science fiction" seems at last actually to have become the Escapist Literature a bunkered public once hoped it was—and for which, I guess, unhappily unblindfolded they now embrace it.

This is not to say there are no writers in the field who are aware of, and working with, the revolutionary (technological, political, artistic, scientific, philosophic) concepts of 1968. (I mean, there are also a few breakaways from Johnson and Humphrey among the big labor leaders.) But—much as the fatcat former organizers, who got their own heads busted in sitdown strikes in the thirties, now uphold clubbings and gassings of hairy demonstrators in the name of Law and Order—the bulk of s-f seems determined to continue examining the same-new things it first discovered in 1938.

One thinks of perhaps ten or fifteen science fiction Names (Leiber and Simak, Dick, Herbert, and Farmer, Aldiss and Ballard, Delany, Disch, Zelazny, and Lafferty, perhaps Moorcock and Spinrad; add a scattering of newer or less "in group" names: Bunch, Jacobs, Reed, Emshwiller, Hayden Howard, Langdon Jones, Peter Tate, K. M. O'Donnell, come first to mind…) who seem fairly consistently to be cognizant of, and concerned with, at least some of the areas of exploratory excitement and explosive upheaval occurring in (for instance—and this list is even less inclusive than that of authors' names above) biophysical psychology, existential psychiatry, behavioral therapy, the technology of education, and the communicative arts.

Doubleday is the biggest publisher of hardcover science fiction in the US; there are six Doubleday books in my stack, four of them designated as science fiction. *Twilight Journey* ($4.50) is a British import in which L. P. Davies deftly hashes up a mixture of scraps from sleep-teaching, sensory deprivation and dream experiments, and *Nineteen Eighty-Four* leftovers, to concoct a fast-reading updated Svengali Special, topped off with a reassuring conclusion in which the Dedicated Scientist snatches humanity's prospects from the jaws of Malevolent Bureaucracy with an anti-tape tape. This one is so smoothly put together, you will find you have read it all before you really begin to be annoyed.

Theodore Tyler's *The Man Whose Name Wouldn't Fit* ($4.95) is almost an exact inversion: sophomore slapstick, freshman prose, and Hollywood-stock characterization here almost conceal a smartly conceived light farce constructed from relevant, quite contemporary, elements which produce a number of small but gratifyingly fresh turns of thought. Mr. Cartwright-Chickering is retired abruptly, three years beforetime, from a comfortable executive office, because the new computer payroll system cannot process names of more than twenty characters. Dr. Nathan Osgood is a brilliant (not black, but) brown-skinned physicist—for a rival computer firm—suffering from his daughter's taunts of Uncle Tomism. Together with Mr. C-C's ex-secretary and her formidable mother, they launch a neo-Luddite revolt armed with water pistols containing a plasticidal fungoid solution—sudden death to computer tapes! From there, I'm afraid, it gets into some very routine foreign-spies-and-presidential-chats stuff en route to the rosy ending. But it does sparkle a bit on the way, and in some of the flashes of communion between the two bewildered grandfathers, it does maybe *just* a bit more.

Not quite enough, though: for that real old-time s-f satisfaction, you have to do more than make pertinent comments of contemporary relevance. (*That's* what "mainstream" is supposed to do.) The third Doubleday novel, *not* published under the science fiction logo, is the only one of the three that really qualifies—barely. And frankly I hate to mention it at all, because *Kings of Infinite Space* ($4.95) falls far short of the book anyone who still treasures *The Small Back Room* and *Mine Own Executioner* as I do might have expected from Nigel Balchin when he turned his attention to NASA and the astronautical pageant. An intelligent speculative examination of the philosophic, scientific, and human values of the Space Race has long been overdue. This book *should* have been it. Balchin seems to be asking the right questions; I suspect the answers are so weak for the same reason that an (usually) unusually sure-footed suspense-and-story-pacer produced such a stumbling hesitant plot—made inadequate homework. The jacket says the author (a Londoner) spent four weeks at space centers in the US gathering material for the book. It wasn't long enough. (Query: *why* do American publishers insist on changing British spelling and distinctive usages, but refrain from blue-penciling the curious dialogue recorded by the peculiarly British ear for the unfamiliar American voice?)

Nevertheless, this is at least a thoughtful book by an observer with a well-trained questioning mind. For those who do not know Balchin's earlier work, its reward will considerably surpass its disappointments.

I cannot say as much for Keith Laumer's two-title short-shrift volume, consisting of one novella and one long novelette ($3.95). The first, and longer, piece, "The Day before Forever," is a mixture of cryogenics, neo-zombies, suspense, violence, secret passages, and slick psychiatry so confusing in retrospect that I cannot even say with any certainty that it had no idea-content. "Thunder-Head" is slower paced and genuinely moving enough in the beginning, with its lonely figure of a forgotten sentinel of Earth's far-flung space empire, so that its ultimate bathos is actively offensive:

"I'm sorry, Admiral," he said a moment later. "He's dead. Frozen. Both of them."

The admiral came up, knelt at Carnaby's side.

"I'm sorry, Jimmy," he said. "Sorry...."

"I don't understand," the general said. "He could have stayed up above, in the station. He'd have been all right there. What in the world was he doing down here?"

"What he always did," Admiral Carnaby said. "His duty."

Laumer, whose early work included such dark perceptive visions as "Cocoon" and "A Trip to the City," and whose long series of Retief stories began as sharp satires on conventional diplomacy and nationalist/racist idiocies, seems to have taken on himself of late the odd role of Defender of Dead Pasts.

(To double my digression for a moment: on that Wednesday night in Chicago last month, about ten o'clock, two authorized medics attached to the 15th floor first aid station in the Hilton, fully outfitted with white coats, red crosses, and the required room-key, were not permitted to enter the hotel with a—hairy, hippie-type—gas victim in serious condition. At the same time, same night, and same entrance, a neatly hair-trimmed young man in business suit and tie—who happened to be an official parade marshal for the Yippies—walked past the guards with neither key nor pass nor delegate's tag. The rule of thumb in Daleytown that week was: *If it has hair, hit it!*)

The title story in Laumer's other recent novelette collection, *Greylorn*, from Berkley, is a solidly constructed, well-told space adventure classic with equal parts of technology-puzzle and battle-suspense—Laumer at his yarn-spinning best for 50 pages. On the fifty-first, the last loose end is tied into place, when a reporter asks the hero how he knew that the cargo of naked bodies in the enemy ship were actually civilized beings, and not, as represented, "slaves, or rather domesticated animals."

"How could you be so sure, Admiral? They had no clothing, no identifying marks, nothing. Why didn't you believe they were cattle?"

"Because," said the Admiral, "all the men had nice neat haircuts."

(Did I mention that all this takes place in an interstellar civilization sometime around the 25th Century? Well, the military values are long-lived: loyalty, duty to the death, and haircuts.)

The other two Doubleday short story collections are something else again. Kate Wilhelm's *The Downstairs Room* ($4.95) is outstanding for its title story, and for at least five others: "Baby, You Were Great," "The Planners," "Windsong," "How Many Miles to Babylon?" and "The Feel of Desperation." These last two (and a few others in the collection) fall outside even my elastic usage of "s-f" as "speculative fiction"; but the extraordinary thing about the whole collection is that every one of the fourteen stories does satisfy at least my minimum requirements for *contemporary* fiction. That is, each and every one is about something, and the something is in each case a relevant, pertinent component of "Reality, c. 1968." In all but three—"Unbirthday Party," "The Plausible Improbable," and "Perchance to Dream"—I also found, if little in the way of original speculation or creative conceptualization, at least some valid new insight or unexpected perspective on problems and challenges that are clearly connected to my current reality-crutch. On top of all this, Kate Wilhelm is a born story-teller—and even more important for me she has a rare capacity for vivid image making. There are some scenes in the first group of titles mentioned that I doubt I will *ever* forget.

The other Doubleday collection, John Barth's *Lost in the Funhouse*, describes itself neither as science fiction nor short stories, but "Fiction for Print Tape, Live Voice," and everything in it (as well as a whole that is somewhat more than the sum of the parts) is, emphatically, speculative fiction of a vitally necessary sort, examining one of the most actively eruptive open-ended processes of this decade—namely, the (r?)evolution of fiction itself.

Aside from a small enclave of experimental writers (mostly more ghettoized than science fiction ever was), the prose forms have been the slowest of the communicative arts to respond to the insistent demands of new concepts and new complexities for new forms, new vocabularies, and new syntaxes: certainly, it is the medium most resistant to dramatic change (if only because it is such common property, unlike the specialist arts of poetry, music, painting, etc.).

The new Barth collection less a series of forthright experiments than an inter-related set of studies examining the difficulties and dissatisfactions of the serious modern writer, and pointing toward a few possible directions (mostly along the illuminated forking paths Borges alone has so far trod successfully). Unfortunately, this does not make for exciting reading: it is a truism, all too true, that the writer as character is the dullest of protagonists—except of course to other writers. Required reading, I'd say, for any practitioner of fiction today, and otherwise of dubious interest, except perhaps for "Night Sea Journey" and "Anonymaid"—and the opening selection, "Frame-Tale," which you can enjoy at a glance in your local bookstore.

Please understand, I am not making any special accusations against the Doubleday Science Fiction list: with the largest hardcover program, they publish both the best and worst, and much more (including the titles above) that is outstanding in neither way, but creditably representative of what writers are writing and readers are buying just now. ("Creditably" because their average is a good deal better than in the paperbacks or magazines.) The fact is, "Science Fiction" (the Established Category) has developed a peculiar imperviousness to the impact of the new ideas of the near-seventies: you are simply more likely to find the "breakthrough concepts" in *Esquire* than in *Analog* (or *Galaxy* or even *F&SF*) these days.

Whether this trend is to be laid primarily at the door of the readers, writers, or editors, and what the root causes of this categorical insensitivity may be, are questions I hope to pursue in future columns. (Readers are welcome to join in.) But I suspect the answer is partly in the nature of the new concepts, concerning as they do values and relationships more than measurements and tables of organization—call it "software"—and partly in the nature of the Creeping Establishment-ism that has accompanied s-f's current popularity.

I have not taken a recent title-count, but Ace is, if not the biggest, then one of the biggest paperback publishers of original s-f: the Ace Specials, in particular, provide some of the best (literary *and* conceptual) work in the paperback specialty field. In its first eight months, this line has published three first novels of superior merit: Lafferty's *Past Master*, Russ's *Picnic on Paradise* (both previously discussed here), and Alexei Panshin's *Rite of Passage*. Panshin's book was squeezed out of this column several months running, with the fortuitous result that it can now be considered with his second novel, *Star Well.*

Panshin, after the manner of this decade, begins his novelist's career with full accreditation: he has published a suitable number of increasingly good short stories, served his time with distinction in the fan press, attended the Milford Science Fiction Writers' Conference, worked as an editorial assistant, and published a scholarly-yet-readable volume of criticism (*Heinlein in Dimension*, Advent, recently reviewed here). If ever first-novelist might have been expected to display expertise, Panshin was it: surprisingly, he does.

Rite of Passage was published with cover blurbs from some impressive names: "…a fully realized, lived-in world.… A better first novel than most people's tenth…" Blish; "An impressive portrayal of the psychological and moral coming-of-age of a young girl whose upbringing and background are truly of the future…" Brunner; "…the power of a born storyteller…the start of what is sure to be a notable career…" Silverberg; "he has captured the feelings of a young girl, at the point in her life where all young girls are most beautiful and most pathetic…" Zelazny.

I am in full agreement with Blish and Silverberg. Some—male—readers may also agree with Brunner and Zelazny: for my part, I felt that the author's only real mistake was in his choice of viewpoint character; it is a rare talent—and seldom an inexperienced one—that can write successfully in the first person of the opposite sex, and this is the one area in which Panshin is clearly and unequivocally out-pointed by Heinlein.

For of course the most important single thing about this book is—for better *and* worse—its Heinleinesque character. (I cannot help wondering how much of the enthusiasm expressed on the jacket was at least subliminally evoked by this aspect of the novel? Or how many other writers in this field understand—as Panshin clearly does—the extent to which Robert A. Heinlein, as idea-originator, form-progenitor, and values-formulator, still stands as father-figure to everyone reared—as writer *or* reader—in the American s-f specialty field of the forties and fifties?) Panshin, in any case, emerges as the first clearly successful challenger of the master on his own grounds. That is, he demonstrates a narrative sense, structural soundness, and capacity for internal consistency that rank with the best in the field, and his argument with Heinlein's attitudes is solidly presented in a context embodying overtones (not imitations) of much of the best Heinlein from *Universe* to *Podkayne of Mars*. (I except, in passing, certain titles of which *Beyond This Horizon* and *Stranger in a Strange Land* are notable exemplars.)

The story, told in first-person by a teen-age girl, concerns the coming-of-age "Trial" (by planet-dropping among the "Mudeaters") of adolescent members of a nomadic starship society. It is in the on-planet scenes that I feel Panshin sometimes outdoes Heinlein: here and there I caught echoes of the excitement with which I first read Kipling's account of Kim's adventures on the Great Road. I also found Panshin's Elder Philosopher, Mr. Mbele, more agreeable than any Heinleinian counterpart since *Waldo*. Panshin loses a bit in his viewpoint character: Heinlein does understand the pubescent female better. All in all, it is high praise for Panshin to say that I think it depends on which man you agreed with to start with, whether Panshin or Heinlein comes out on top. My complaint, by the same token, is that a young man of Panshin's demonstrable talent, in 1968, should have elected to write his first novel not just in the (then revolutionary) structure and format initiated by Heinlein in 1938—but *on the same conceptual grounds.*

Still (I told myself) now he has performed his own *Rite of Passage*, conducted his ritual battle with the clan chief and proved his manhood. Perhaps the next novel will apply the same vitality, color, interior logic, and narrative power to Panshin's own ideas, in Panshin's own voice.

Almost it does. *Star Well* is the first of a projected series featuring a dashing dandy of the spaceways, Anthony Villers. An introduction by Samuel Delany describes it as "a gallery of gamblers, duels and double-crosses, a minuette of manners and manners mangled. . . ." It is all that, and it *does* have the vitality, color, interior logic, and narrative power aforementioned—plus, I think, Panshin's own voice. A good read: a fun book: it goes quickly enough to take to bed with you at night, and you can be sure it won't keep you awake *thinking.*

Well, that's science fiction, I guess: great escape literature.

Books (February 1969)

[…]

One hesitates to use the word *novel to* describe both John Brunner's quarter-million-word globo-vistar macroscopic, *Stand on Zanzibar* (507 large-size small-type pages from Doubleday at $6.95), and Bob Shaw's tidy little *The Two-Timers*, containing barely (if any) more than ten percent of the combined word-total of all four books (191 plenty-of-whitespace pages, an Ace Special, 60¢). Shaw confines himself modestly to five main characters and four main sets for a psychological thriller set a scant twenty years or so in a future with virtually no sociological changes and an apparently much reduced rate of technological innovation—aside from what might fairly be called mixed-media time travel. Brunner spreads literally dozens of detailed characters over as many meticulously constructed settings in his teeming and frenetic world of 2010—utilizing the basic techniques of Dos Passos's USA trilogy for sequential closeups and longshots on the mores, morals, and minutiae of politics, industry, education, entertainment, drug habits, dress fashions, computers, commercials, sex, slang, and all the et ceteras of Greater New York and Ellay in North America, The Republic of Beninia in Africa, the Guided Socialist Democracy of Yatakang in the Pacific, and all points between.

The other two novels are from Clifford Simak and Roger Zelazny. Zelazny's *Isle of the Dead* (another Ace Special, 60¢) is one shorter and maybe 5000 words longer than *The Two-Timers* with as many planets as Shaw had locales, and at *least* four times as many characters (of whom about one-fourth are less than ornately bizarre), in a 32nd Century adventure tale about a galactically wealthy, system-hopping hero—a worldscaping planetary architect-contractor and (also by profession) not-quite-immortal god. Both *Isle* and Simak's *The Goblin Reservation* (Doubleday, $4.95) belong to that special and, recently, all too rare sub-category first clearly delineated in *Unknown* (of blessed memory) which gave rise to the need for the term, science-fantasy: the genre of supernatural science, of the technology of magic, matter-of-fact fantasy, the territory just this side of weird-gothic-horror, fantastic whimsy, and sword-and-sorcery. But the two books, inevitably, are as far apart in style, theme, and concept as the genre permits.

Simak, predictably, stays with the traditional category-novel length: 55-60 thousand words (192 standard pages); he also maintains a median time-distance (26th century) and a familiar setting (the wooded countryside of the northmidwest): there ends the expected. The Goblin Reservation is a forest preserve for all varieties of Little People: trolls, fairies, leprechauns, et al., as well as goblins. It is administered by the College of Supernatural Phenomena, located next door to Time College (and its adjunctive Time Museum) on the Wisconsin Campus of Planetary University. The cast of characters includes, besides Little People, a ghost (named Ghost), a banshee, a biomech (Sylvester), Alley Oop (a Neanderthaler), one dragon, William Shakespeare, a generous handful of imaginatively (even for Simak) constructed extraterrestrials (only two types with more than walk-on parts), and roughly a dozen straight humans (assorted academics, one artist, one cop, one conman, one each professional waiter and hostess).

Do not be misled. *The Goblin Reservation* is neither Disneyland whimsy nor latter-day Robert Nathan—any more than the twisted dwarf, cruel lady, knife artist, and psychopathic killer of Zelazny's melodrama (not to mention Shimbo of Darktree Tower, Shrugger of Thunders—the deific alter ego of megamillionaire Francis Sandow—or the central image of Sandow's favorite creation, the gloom-shrouded Isle of the Dead itself) are really either Grand Guignol or H. P. Lovecraft. Beneath the (separate, indeed opposed, but equally) simplistic surface of each book (slaphappy stereotype symbols and sweetness-and-light in the Simak; a sort of Playboy-Philosophy sophomore sadism, cynicism, and calculated shallowness in the Zelazny), the comic-book images resonate at surprising depths. The greatest fault of both books, in fact, is (startlingly, for *both* authors) in the story-telling. But never mind—the images are bright, and they last well; the symbols ring true. One feels Zelazny has at last emerged from his long spell of preoccupation with veneers—that Simak is approaching a new level of meaning as significant as that he found with his first Webster Family stories. Both stylistically and story-wise, these two books are inferior to much of what each author has done before. The fact remains that I could not put either one down till it was done.

I cannot say the same for either Shaw or Brunner, although—again—for different reasons in each case.

The Two-Timers is a beautifully *fitted* piece of work: [...] and where Brunner's detailed visualizations rather outgrew his basic vision—Shaw's novella is paced and laid out (almost *staged*) precisely to fit its dimensions—which are small. Unlike last year's bombshell "Light of Other Days," the book offers nothing new in its time-travel theories or techniques, nor does it provide the sort of thrill of insight that lifted the prize-winning short story completely out of class of other clever *Analog* techno-gimmick stories.

Two-Timers is an admirably competent sci-fi thriller. *Stand on Zanzibar* is something, very, else.

In a sense, Brunner has written the first true science fiction novel. That is, he has taken a true novel plot, developed it in proper novelistic style, and at the same time extrapolated fully, in accordance with all the basic science fiction rules, a future environment whose initial assumptions provide not only the background for the story but an essential component of its central conflicts. The "classic" science fiction novels of the past have ordinarily achieved their fame by doing (either) one of these jobs *so* successfully that any simply passable performance of the other was acceptable.

I still remember the *world* of Heinlein's *Universe*, for instance, vividly; but the individuals in it—except for the physical attributes of the two-headed hero—are gone beyond recall. The members of the Gestalt group in Sturgeon's *More Than Human* are impressed in my memory as indelibly as children I have known and loved myself; so is the "personality" of the Gestalt itself; I cannot remember at all what rationale was provided for its existence.

A third type, of course, is represented by Miller's *A Canticle for Leibowitz*, which provided continuous "close-ups" in the form of a series of shorter stories containing the necessary balance of intellectual and emotional count, leaving the reader to fill in the parts between for himself. This approach has been, till now, the closest to the "true science fiction novel": or, on second thought, there was an earlier example—Frank Herbert's *Dune*, which I (alone, I believe) found flawed in logic and consistency, as well as pretentious and dull. It did, however, fulfill in theory, if not (for me) in effect, the job Brunner, has now, to my mind, done for the first time with minimal—but at *least* minimal—success.

It is a success which raises some questions about the worthiness of the endeavor, however. Within his established premises, Brunner conducts himself brilliantly: I do not complain this time of any internal inconsistencies; but the more detailed and believable his world of 2010 became, the less believable (while equally detailed) seemed the behavior of his characters. Question: is it *possible* for a writer in one culture fully and adequately to project the mores and emotional responses of realistic human beings in a (realistically) different environment?

Next question: is it possible to spread out this *much* detail about a world conceived in the author's mind (and—inevitably—dedicated to the proposition that his own logic is supreme) *without* getting to sound a bit pompous and pretentious?

I am not answering these questions, but asking them. I expect the answers will come from the other ambitious efforts that will assuredly follow now. It will be interesting, finding out.

Meantime, one can explore the book itself. I make no attempt to describe or summarize here, because any brief picture would be misleading. Read it straight through, or dip and skim: there's *something* for everyone, and an impressive amount overall. (The book is so full of a number of—fascinating—things that it doesn't really *matter* whether they add up to that increasingly ambiguous term, A Good Novel.)

Fritz Leiber (July 1969)

For thirty years, Fritz Leiber has been entertaining, inspiring, irritating, enlightening, and delighting a growing audience for fantasy and speculative fiction. He has received every honor and award the field has to offer, as well as some distinctive personal tokens of esteem, from a following which includes the entire spectrum of the curious multi-genre currently known as "science fiction": the weird-and-macabre, whimsical and "heroic" fantasy, hardware-sci-fi, sociological speculation and political satire, psychological symbolism and *avant garde* surrealism. He is as highly regarded by the New-rock Generation as by the Old Guard collectors of 1926 *Amazings*—and perhaps most of all by his colleagues inside the field ("a writer's writer"). Yet, his name is hardly known outside the genre.

This paradoxical state of affairs is in part due to his very range and variety. Leiber is equally the Romantic and the Realist: a Shakespearean, scholar, and surrealist; poet, prophet, pamphleteer, pacifist, and profligate; occasional painter, sculptor, collagist, and pianist; sometime fencer, serious chess-player, novice canyon-climber. He has been a (Phi Beta Kappa) philosophy student, stage and screen actor, preacher, college teacher, factory worker, editor; has written (aside from s-f) encyclopaedia articles, Lovecraftian horror, popular science, political tracts, comic-strip continuity, plays, poetry, and critical and scholarly works; he is a frequent contributor to fan magazines and amateur publications, an inveterate letter writer and omnivorous reader.

There are authors one admires, authors one agrees with, and authors one loves. The first two sorts are taught in schools, displayed on coffee tables and book shelves, discussed at cocktail parties, bought as gifts, and generously lent out. Leiber gets borrowed, tattered, and read.

Fritz is my good friend, and has been for nearly twenty years, but the fact is I fell in love with him half a decade before we met. This is not to say my passion is a purely literary one: simply that the man and his work are not separable.

Anyone in the author-meeting business (critic, editor, anthologist) quickly comes to know that the writer of the grisliest murders will turn out to be a tidy, milky little man; the author of a Noble Doctor story probably suffers from chronic acne complicated by gout; and the authoress of those innocent ladies' romances will undoubtedly be not just a tart, but a *tweedy* one. Not so Leiber. (Indeed if one were to invert his literary multiple-personality, he would be left with no character at all.) In appearance as well as manner, he could step into any one of dozens of characters he has written (and on one occasion at least did so with notable success): in fact the "noble barbarian" of the Fafhrd and Mouser stories is so nearly a self-caricature that he is known as "Faf" to his family. The rhythms of his prose are those of his speech; his letters and conversations seem to pick up where the last story stopped and run into the start of the next, if not in topic, then in theme and style. Writing about him, I find it difficult to remember whether this phrase or that image was from the public or private communications.

As critic and editor, I have had to learn to guard against underrating his work on just this account: the best of his stories are often the "transparent" ones that leave me feeling it was after all just a lovely letter from Fritz.

That this kind of *personal re*sponse—although less accountable and much less self-conscious—is shared by thousands of other readers has been made clear on several occasions. The November 1959 issue of *Fantastic*, for instance: Leiber had just come out of one of his recurrent dry spells, and editor Cele Lalli bought up all his new material until there was enough to fill an issue; the magazine came out with a big black headline across its cover—LEIBER IS BACK!

Or that "memorable occasion" mentioned above, when I saw—and heard—an ovation from hundreds of fans and fellow-writers when Leiber took an award at a convention hotel fancy-dress ball. The costume? A cardboard military collar slipped over turned-up jacket lapels, plus cardboard shoulder insignia, an armband, and a large spider black-penciled on his forehead, to turn him into an officer of the "Spiders" in the Change-war of *The Big Time* and "No Great Magic." The only other component was the Leiber instinct for theatre.

Leiber was born on the day before Christmas in Chicago in 1910, and plunged immediately into the study of Shakespeare: until he was six, he toured the country with the repertory company in which his parents were actors "...memories redolent of grease paint, spirit gum, curling colored gelatins of flood- and spot-lights.... I learned most of *Hamlet* at age 4 when my father was first learning it...") During his school years, he spent long winters in Chicago with two prim Germanic maiden aunts; summers, he was at home with his parents on the Jersey shore, learning more Shakespeare, stagecraft, and theatrical mores.

In 1932 he took a B.A. with honors in Philosophy from the University of Chicago, and went into the ministry: "Ran two Episcopalian 'missionary' churches in New Jersey as lay reader and minister while attending the General Theological Seminary in NY (here a missionary church means one without a resident priest).... I had to get christened and confirmed quick for this odd junket which I tackled most sincerely with the feeling, which 'Beezie' Mandeville [the Rev. Ernest W., of Middletown, NJ] approved, that I could view the job as one of rational social service rather than religious conviction and vocation. In about five months I found out this wasn't so and I worked out the 'season' and quit."

The next year he was back at Chicago doing graduate work in philosophy. Then a year touring with his father's Shakespearean company, and two years of (mostly male ingénue) bit parts in Hollywood, followed by a brief unsuccessful attempt at freelance writing—and back to Chicago again as a staff writer for the Standard American Encyclopedia (an extraordinary reference work, some of whose oddities are revealed in last year's *New Worlds* story, "The Square Root of Brain").

In the summer of 1937, the time of that first abortive try at "being a writer," two significant events occurred in the literary world: Howard Phillips Lovecraft died, and John W. Campbell, Jr., became editor of *Astounding*, and very shortly afterwards began gathering material for a new publication called *Unknown*, where Leiber's first story was published in 1939.

His interest in fiction had started at college, where most of the time left over from his education in Utopian Socialism, pacifism, fencing, and chess (the only subject in which he now has an official "expert" rating) was devoted to long literary correspondences. The most significant of these were with H. P. Lovecraft (and other members of the Lovecraft Circle) and with his friend Harry Fischer, of Louisville. It was in letters with Fischer that the characters and some of the background of Fafhrd and the Gray Mouser were first developed, and it was one of these that sold to *Unknown* and brought the author an immediate following among "heroic fantasy" fans. (Curiously, it was the second in the series, "Two Sought Adventure," that Campbell bought. The first, "Adept's Gambit," a far better story, did not see print until the publication of Leiber's first collection, *Night's Black Agents* by Arkham House in 1947.)

Between 1939-1943, there was a scattering of stories in *Unknown*, *Weird*, and *Future*. Meantime the Leibers (there was now a wife and infant son) left Chicago for Los Angeles again. A year teaching drama and speech at Occidental College was followed by another (very) brief try at free-lancing in 1942: just long enough to write the two novels that would place him firmly in the top rank of science-fantasy, and keep him there through his first long dry spell of five years.

Conjure Wife (later filmed as *Burn, Witch, Burn!*) combined traditional witchcraft and a realistic contemporary setting derived largely from the year at Occidental; *Gather, Darkness!* went further in two directions, at least, using the apparatus and literature of witchcraft in juxtaposition with technological extrapolation and political prophecy to create one of the first truly modern science fiction novels.

If he had written nothing more, Leiber would still be a leading genre author. I have reread both books in the past year, and I approached them nervously. Few quarter-century-old fond memories can stand intimate revisiting. These did. If I were coming across them for the first time today, I think I would respond with the same sense of discovery and astonishment I had in 1943.

The two novels were published almost simultaneously: *Conjure Wife*, complete, in the April *Unknown*; *Gather, Darkness!* as a serial starting in the May *Astounding*. By the time they appeared, however, Leiber had given up full-time writing again, and taken a war job as an inspector at Douglas Aircraft. (After a long strugglewith his pacifist beliefs: "I very slowly came around to the view that the anti-fascist forces had been justified and 'right' in WW II.") In 1945, he joined the editorial staff of *Science Digest*—back in Chicago—where he stayed for twelve years. His literary productivity throughout this period was uneven both in quantity and quality. Only in the past ten years has Leiber finally settled down to full-time writing; and only now is he really coming into his own.

There are good reasons why the sixties should be a time of recognition for him. In the television age, an audience of viewer-readers responds warmly to the specifically (and increasingly) theatric quality of his work: everything he writes has as much of the stage as the page in it. The best theatre, of course, is that in which the illusion is most complete, where the audience need not "suspend disbelief" but can just *believe*. Unfortunately for the actor (or playwright), however, the more convinced the audience, the less *impressed* it is likely to be. ("Everything was so natural.") And when the "play" itself is constantly in work, as it were, changing focus, subject, style (with every story), a naïve audience, particularly, will attend with delight, leave with bemusement, but fail completely to credit the skill behind the illusion.

The s-f audience of the sixties is vastly more sophisticated literarily, as well as scientifically, than that of the forties. And, of course, television has accustomed the reader/viewer to the idea of the familiarly convincing character and sustained theme displayed in a constantly changing, and frequently fantastic, series of situations.

And then, of course, science fiction and short stories are both "in": and Leiber's short fiction, more than that of any other writer, reflects the development of the several sub-species presently subsumed under the (absurdly inappropriate) label, "science fiction," from the origins of the specialty field to its present acceptance as a contemporary literary form.

Indeed, there is an intriguing parallel between the role Leiber has played inside the field, and the situation of science fiction in the literary world generally. The rigid compartmentalizing of American literature in the first half of the twentieth century which produced, among other things, the specialized category of fantasy called science fiction, continued to function within the field as it grew; and it is those writers whose names attach directly to one or another phase of that growth who have become identified with it in the great outside literary world: Heinlein, Asimov, Sturgeon, Bradbury, Simak, Clarke, Wyndham, Bloch; each carved out for himself a distinct and separate niche clearly visible to publishers, critics, and scholars. Leiber has been ubiquitous, seminal, influential, widely read—and, critically, virtually ignored.

It is customary to date the beginning of modern science fiction with the appearance of the first issue of Hugo Gernsback's *Amazing* in 1926. I think one must go farther back or nearer up: Gernsback initiated a publishing phenomenon, not a literature. For the history of the art rather than the sales, one must either begin with the diverse taproots of the 19th century, or go only as far back as the origins of the contemporary integrated form. In the first case, it is necessary to consider the "gothic" scientific romances and horror stories of Hawthorne, Mary Shelley, etc.; the Wonderful Inventions and Marvelous Voyages of Verne, Doyle, Kipling; the utopian, dystopian, and philosophic future visions of Wells, Chesterton, Bellamy; the symbolist, surrealist, and pataphysical beginnings with Jarry and the dadaists.

Between 1910 and 1940, roughly, these strains achieved a polarization unique in the history of literature, but entirely in keeping with that strange quarter-century of intellectual divisiveness and categorizing—and nowhere was the striation more complete and categorical than in America, where Realism and Fantasy were held to be common enemies, as were Enjoyment and Education, Intellect and Emotion, High and Low Brows, etc. When that much discussed first issue of *Amazing* appeared, the scientific world was still reeling under the impact of the twin heresies of Relativity and Uncertainty: the late nineteenth century (resistance to evolution?) insistence on regarding science as a body of knowledge to be sliced up between scholars and engineers, still ruled the popular mind—and many scientific ones.

Gernsback took these arbitrary divisions for granted, as did both the publishing world in general and the "Lovecraft Circle" which dominated *Weird Tales.* These two publications, then, marked the extreme points of the literary and intellectual polarity: "scientifiction"—the technocratic/predictive—on one end; "weird"—metaphysical/symbolic—on the other.

There had been some intimation of things to come in the work of H. G. Wells, where science, satire, sentiment, and the supernatural sat side by side, if not entwined, with philosophy, adventure, and romance. Actually, in Britain the polarization was never complete: or rather, the polar extremes were simply disregarded. Writers like Stapledon, Huxley, Orwell, Kersh followed Wells, Chesterton, Kipling, Doyle, et al., sustaining a comparatively "whole" literature of the imagination, both literarily respectable and philosophically respect-worthy. Only two ingredients of the current mixture were lacking—the technocratic and the transcendental. Jarry's reply to Wells's *Time Machine* was never absorbed, and mysticism was confined to the (Roman and Anglo-) Catholic, while most of the machines seemed more metaphysical than actual.

The first—abortive, but significant—attempt at true integration of the diverse elements must be attributed to John W. Campbell: first with his own fiction (as Don A. Stuart) in 1934, then as editor of *Astounding* in 1937, but most importantly as founder editor of *Unknown* in 1939. It was not until a decade later that the new magazines, *Fantasy and Science Fiction* and *Galaxy*, established the necessary conditions for cross-fertilization and hybridization of the new species. But for a short four-year period beginning with the fall of 1937, and concentrated in the summer of 1939, there was a dramatic emergence of new concepts and new talent.

This kind of conceptual/literary "quantum jump" has happened since then: most notably in the early years of *F&SF*, and in the past five years or so in the *New Worlds* group in England.

And much as the "new thing" or "new wave" in current s-f has spread from the dynamic center of *NW*, the excitement generated by the *Unknown* phenomenon affected the entire field. In his first two years, as editor, Campbell introduced the work of de Camp, del Rey, and Malcolm Jameson, and attracted Kuttner, Bloch, and Gold from the *Weird* camp, while Simak and Williamson, both old *Astounding* hands, began writing in an entirely new vein.

Asimov, Bester, Van Vogt, Leiber, Heinlein, and Sturgeon were all published for the first time in *Amazing*, *Thrilling Wonder*, *Astounding*, and *Unknown* during the first six months of the latter magazine's existence. In the same year, Ray Bradbury was publishing his first stories in American fan magazines, and Arthur C. Clarke's work began appearing in British semi-pro s-f publications. In the next two years, Anthony Boucher, Fredric Brown, Cleve Cartmill all began writing for *Unknown*, and a dozen new magazines sprang up, most of them short-lived but adequate training grounds for the next generation of writers.

All this may seem remote and unnecessarily detailed history, but it was these men who constructed the fabric of atomic-age space fiction and sociological prediction. In the fifties, new writers and new editors carried their innovations to a level of literary merit many of the "first generation" could not attain (and some could not even distinguish); but not until the sixties was there any basic change in the structure and content of the material.

Today, Sturgeon is in Hollywood, Asimov wins science awards, Bester works for *Holiday*, de Camp writes witty histories, Van Vogt is a lay psychiatrist, Brown writes for television, del Rey lectures, Williamson is an English professor. Cartmill, Jameson, Kuttner, and Boucher are dead.

Of them all, only three survive as regular writers of science fiction. Heinlein and Simak each produce a new novel almost every year, and they are usually good novels: thoughtful, provocative, entertaining, well written.

Leiber is swinging with the sixties.

I first met Fritz at a science-fiction convention in 1949. It would have been a memorable night anyhow: I met a lot of people either already legendary in that tight little world, or—like myself—novice myth-makers who would be friends and colleagues later: Poul Anderson, Randall Garrett, Joe Winter. We all wound up at a uniquely bemuraled restaurant called The Purple Cow (such as could only happen, I think, in Paris or the American Midwest). But that was later. At the beginning it was just a very crowded hotel room, and I was the almost-unknown author of two published stories, and I could not seem to find a single face I remembered meeting earlier in the day.

I was quite certain I had not met the man sitting on the window ledge, darkly handsome, remote…brooding? a bit amused? Our eyes met, and he began to stand up. (It took a while. Fritz is 6'4".) We both smiled tentatively.

"I'm Fritz Leiber," he said.

I said nothing. (Remember: this was a man I had been in love with for six years.) When I got my breath back I said, "I'm Judy Merril." And he said, "Judith Merril? You mean *you wrote…*?"

The next thing I remember clearly is that I was deep in conversation with Leiber (FRITZ LEIBER!—*who remembered my story*!) and that the room was even more crowded. (Eventually, we found talking air in a bathroom, and had a memorable discussion of, among other things, men's clothing.)

Nineteen years later, I sat talking to a bright young writer who was barely born on the Night of The Purple Cow. It was the first day of the Milford Science-Fiction Writers' Conference, and I mentioned that Fritz had just arrived. "Fritz *Leiber*?" he said, and I realized that glazed look must once have been my own. "FRITZ LEIBER?" Later, he came and told me, "Okay. I could even go home now, I mean, I met LEIBER."

Only one other name from the Great Old Days seems to evoke the same kind of response from the Bright Young People—Theodore Sturgeon—for much the same reasons.

Both men have been singularly uneven writers. Much of what they published was too hastily written, or too much limited by the narrowness of the specialty field they wrote for. But it is true of both of them that the *best* of what they wrote, at any time, remains as valid now as when it was written.

Science fiction is essentially a "literature of ideas," and the usual tidy scholarly/critical stance (from [Kinsgley] Amis to I. F. Clarke) exempts it from conventional "mainstream" standards of characterization and emotional values. The minimal requirements (of conceptual interest and simple literacy) imposed by this view are valid enough, I suppose, for consideration of science fiction *as genre*, a limited literary enclave. But the limitation is actually more descriptive of the criticism than of the literature, implying as it does a basic acceptance of the artistic validity of the "two-culture" system.

Certainly, this view applied to Gernsbackian "technifiction," and has continued to be true of many (particularly first-time) presentations of philosophic or sociological concepts in the science fiction of the last thirty years, where the characters exist not as real people, but as animated ideas. Just as certainly, there have been any number of individual works which have satisfied the limited definition, and transcended the limiting conditions.

This is not an easy thing to do. The dynamics involved are slightly more complex than those of the three-body problem; the writer must deal with *persons* and *peoples* at the same time, relating both the (e)motions of individuals and their shifting interpersonal relationships simultaneously to a *changed and still changing environment*. Historically, it took writers of the stature of Cervantes, Swift, and Tolstoy to accomplish this: but the idea of an environment-in-motion was in itself an innovation in the cultures out of which they wrote. In our self-synthesizing society, the only recognizable environmental constant is change itself; and the specific virtue of "science fiction," the quality (underlying campus fads and publishing figures) responsible for its re-emergence into the main body of contemporary literature (and art and music) is its capacity for its insistence on recognizing this dynamic.

Conversely, the specific qualification *for emergence* was the capacity to combine the old and new dynamics. The "real" environment of the Twentieth Century is as much conceptual as perceptual in character. Naturalism is no more realistic now than is a consideration of human behavior and emotion without regard for the environmental context. The ability to operate in (at least) three dimensions of experience is no longer the prerequisite of genius, but the prerequisite for communication.

Until very recently, the qualification was rarely met, but when it was, it was most often done in "science fiction"; Wells's *The Shape of Things to Come* and Kipling's *They* were early, sometimes clumsy, indicators; Huxley's *Brave New World*, Stapledon's *Odd John* and *Sirius*, Orwell's *1984* came closer; Stewart's *Earth Abides*, Miller's *A Canticle for Leibowitz*, Sturgeon's *More Than Human*, Vonnegut's *Sirens of Titan* are all works which deal with the human condition in a relative-and-quantal universe so effectively that the topical component of their idea-value is unlikely to limit their readability for the next generation any more than, for instance, Clarke and Kubrick's *2001* will be dated by the actual landing on the moon.

These titles are familiar to readers in and out of the genre. What is less commonly realized is that the novel has been the least successful science-fiction form, and that a large body of work existed before most of these books were published, in which the art of modern fiction had already begun to emerge. One thinks of Simak's "Desertion," Asimov's "Nightfall," Heinlein's "Universe," del Rey's "Nerves," Russell's "Metamorphosite," Bradbury's "The Veldt," Kuttner's "The Fairy Chessmen"—all written more than twenty years ago, all "dated" in that their scientific or technological ideas are too familiar now to provoke excitement—yet every bit as meaningful, moving, and provocative as when they first appeared, in their evocation of the dilemma of modern man at the interface with his self-made environment.

I cite these few titles, not as isolated instances, but as exceptional early examples of a success that became the (rarely-met) standard of accomplishment of the increasingly "literary" genre writers of the fifties. There were other writers in the forties, and many more in the fifties, who achieved this "merger"; but from the work of perhaps fifty or sixty such people in the two decades, one might be hard put to find more than two hundred qualifying stories—and of that number fully one quarter were probably written by either Sturgeon or Leiber.

The fact is, it was an almost impossible accomplishment: now, in the sixties, a few writers are beginning to develop new modes and forms of expression better suited to the three (and more) dimensional content of contemporary communication. When they succeed (as they must, if literature is to exist as a twenty-first century art form), the multi-dynamic approach will have its own conventions, to provide a footing for more enduring work. At the moment, the innovators must draw more upon the other arts than on literature for their examples and suggestions: their respectable literary genealogy goes back only to Borges and Joyce in the last generation, and (less respectable? less genealogical?) to Jarry and Apollinaire in the one before. But in the hit-and-miss history of the bastard line of the same blood—science fiction—they have inherited a whole library of demonstrably unworkable directions, failed experiments already recorded; a few volumes of false or premature starts in directions possibly worth investigation; and finally a few isolated successes or near-successful experiments of the fifties, from people like Aldiss, Ballard, Bester, Dick, Farmer, "Cordwainer Smith," Vonnegut, Sturgeon, and Leiber.

The innovators of the sixties are not necessarily genre writers: the explorations are going on in ground common to all of literature now. Even those whose background is in the specialty field, or who maintain one foot in its security while testing new ground with the other, actually think and write more as a part of the mainstream *avant garde* than as members of any specialized field. Most of them are very new, and very young, but a handful of "over-thirties" are still included. J. G. Ballard, of course, has been at the forefront of this movement all along; Brian Aldiss has recently come forward to keep the promise of such earlier work as "Nomansland" and "Hot House Planet." Kurt Vonnegut, one hopes, is resting between books rather than on his laurels. There are others less well known: Carol Emshwiller, Kit Reed, David Bunch....

And then there is Leiber. Erratically, inconsistently, sometimes clumsily (often, one feels, almost absent-mindedly), Leiber continues—astonishingly—to introduce and combine concepts, images, and techniques which have kept him not only abreast of the best in the field for thirty years, but—in his own best work—recurrently making his own quantum jumps that land him (sometimes unsalably) way out ahead of the rest again.

This is not simple virtuosity. It is a form of incurable, and enviable, immaturity. Most of us reach a point—say, somewhere between eighteen and thirty-five—at which we "settle down" intellectually; there comes a morning when one wakes to the realization that the question of "what to be when I grow up" has been answered. Even when the occupation is a chosen and cherished one, it ordinarily moves at that point from the design to the engineering phase, from burgeoning creativity into growing craftsmanship. Psychologists call it the "peaking of learning ability."

A few fortunate people of great vitality (and longevity) contrive to make a cycle of the process, repeating it several times during their lives (*vide:* Wells, Shaw, Russell). Leiber either never reached that peaking, or else it was marked by his recognition, some ten years ago, that for him, fiction was the best—indeed the only—way in which he could "vicariously at least, have all the lives I want to live."

This is an indefinitely self-renewing process—and a reiteratively self-destructive one. The nature of the continuing transaction is clearly visible, too, in the larger cycles which have marked his work—and his life—over the years. Thematically, also, the Love/Death dynamic has been central to his work, in all its aspects and guises, and he has carried his treatment of the theme to a degree of consciousness and symbolic clarity almost unknown in American letters. One thinks of Poe, Fitzgerald, Thomas Wolfe, Hart Crane—men for whom the death-each-time added up sooner, rather than later, to more than the renewals: it is a short-lived breed. What has saved Leiber, I think, is that he *is* a science-fiction writer, alive in what might almost be called a fictive-science time; that Realism is just as true for him—not more, not less—as Romance: that he lives as intensely with ideas as he does with emotions. Thus, every time he starts "another life," in another story, he also renews his intellectual adolescence (in much the same way Bertrand Russell describes the period of his shift from mathematics to philosophy).

Leiber's writing began, remember, under the sepulchral Lovecraft spell: his first efforts were all directed at the "weird" market—stories of necromancy, midnight, murder, and madness. But he had trouble selling to *Weird Tales* from the beginning: the reasons are apparent in "Smoke Ghost" (which eventually went to *Unknown*), and in one of the few titles that did appear in *Weird* (in 1942, as it began to move inward from its black pole), "The Hound." Here one of the characters speaks, apparently very much for the author:

> "'Meanwhile what's happening inside each one of us? I'll tell you. All sorts of inhibited emotions are accumulating. Fear is accumulating. Horror is accumulating. A new kind of awe of the mysteries of the universe is accumulating. A psychological environment is forming, along with the physical one. Wait, let me finish. Our culture becomes ripe for infection. From somewhere. It's just like a bacteriologist's culture—I didn't intend the pun—when it gets to the right temperature and consistency for supporting a colony of germs. Similarly, our culture suddenly spawns a horde of demons. And, like germs, they have a peculiar affinity for our culture. They're unique. They fit in. You wouldn't find the same kind any other time or place.
>
> "'...our fears would be their fodder. A parasite-host relationship. Supernatural symbiosis. Some of us—the sensitive ones—would notice them sooner than others.... Frighten and terrorize you, yes. But surprise, no. It would fit into the environment. Look as if it belonged in a city and smell the same. Because of the twisted emotions that would be its food, your emotions and mine. A matter of diet.'"

His first active writing period came to a climax in 1943 with the publication of *Conjure Wife* and *Gather, Darkness!* Although he continued to make extensive use of the symbolism and melodrama of the supernatural afterwards, those two novels were the last major pieces in which conventional horror images dominated; *Conjure Wife* was the last in which they were used in what could be called a conventional way. His first "dry spell" began shortly afterwards, while he was working at Douglas in 1944.

In the next five years, he wrote only a handful of stories, and sold only three. During this time, he was profoundly affected by events in the outside world: World War II and its holocaustic climax at Hiroshima; the ensuing atmosphere of anti-libertarian conformism, witch-hunts, and brainwashing in the heyday of Joe McCarthy; the not-yet-popular struggles of Negro-Americans for civil rights and full citizenship; the Mad Ave and PR explosion in the Wonderful Postwar World of television and "media"; the (sic) preverberations of the twin explosions of Western civilization into outer, and inner, space. Out of all these, in his own phoenix-like crucible he was "brewing his cultures," cultivating a knowledge of the new demons and modern horrors, learning new imageries, patterns, symbols. Two of the three stories of this time of silence pointed to where he was going. "Mr. Bauer and the Atoms" was in *Weird* in 1946:

> "Frank Bauer lived in a world where everything had been exploded. He scented confidence games, hoaxes, faddish self-deception, and especially (for it was his province) advertising-copy-exaggerations behind every faintly unusual event and every intimation of the unknown. He had the American's nose for leg-pulling, the German's contempt for the non-factual. Mention of such topics as telepathy, hypnotism or the occult—and his wife managed to mention them fairly often—sent him into a scoffing rage."

Then he learned about atoms:

> "…'See, we always thought everything was so solid. Money, automobiles, mines, dirt. We thought they were so solid that we could handle them, hold on to them, do things with them. And now we find they're just a lot of little bits of deadly electricity, whirling around at God knows what speed, by some miracle frozen for a moment.'"

The next story to see print was three years later. This is in part how Marshall McLuhan described it in *The Mechanical Bride:*

> "In a story called 'The Girl with the Hungry Eyes,' by Fritz Leiber, an ad photographer gives a job to a not too promising model. Soon, however, she is 'plastered all over the country' because she has the hungriest eyes in the world. 'Nothing vulgar, but just the same they're looking at you with a hunger that's all sex and something more than sex.' Something similar may be said of the legs on a pedestal. Abstracted from the body that gives them their ordinary meaning, they become 'something more than sex,' a metaphysical enticement, a cerebral itch, an abstract torment. Mr. Leiber's girl hypnotizes the country with her hungry eyes. . . ."

I resist, with difficulty, the desire to quote in full here the final statement of the story (as written by Leiber, not McLuhan). When you have found it and read (or re-read) it, think back twenty years, if you can—before Twiggy, Jane Fonda, *Barbarella*, before *Playboy*, Bardot, Monroe. "The Girl" was published in 1949, and McLuhan's book in 1951. They both had to wait for the audience to catch up.

When "The Girl" appeared, Leiber was in the middle of a new spurt of activity which began with the publication of a mimeographed magazine called *New Purposes*, and grew into such bittersweet prophetic "Love Generation" stories as "The Moon Is Green," "A Pail of Air," and "The Nice Girl with Five Husbands"; and (on the other side of a suddenly familiar coin) a strain of satire which emerged at its sharpest in the Spillane pastiche, "The Night He Cried," and at its most terrifyingly prophetic in "Coming Attraction," "Poor Superman," and finally the 1953 novel, *The Green Millennium*. These last three titles are part of a "future-history" satire system set in a world (circa 1990s) of "off-the-bosom" dresses and jeweled face masks, barbed auto-fenders and motorized sex/sadism, television brainwashing, automation redundancy, mystical cultism, violence-for-kicks, ocean-wide credibility gaps, and the sad dignity-in-defeat of the gentle "Dr. Opperly."

When they appeared, it was Joe McCarthy time. The science-fiction magazines were proud of being the last popular public arena for dissent and non-conformism—but one was not supposed to spell it out *too* clearly. It is not really surprising that editors began returning rueful notes about their readers' objections to certain stories—or that *The Green Millennium* had no magazine publication (at that time the main source of income from a genre novel)—*or* that "The Silence Game," a bitter story of the agonized-cool ultimate-dropout revolt, published at the time of the nationally televised

Oppenheimer hearings (1954), was the prophetic last word from Leiber for another three years.

Once again there were stories left over. By 1957, the field seemed to be ready for them. "The Big Trek" and "Friends and Enemies," both first-drafted in *New Purposes* (eight years earlier) were published and, again, demand seemed to stimulate supply, for a while—a short while, this time. The new stories of 1957-58 had two new themes, sometimes combined: time-travel and the hip (not-yet hippy) beat scene, *The Big Time*, the first of the Change-war "Snakes" vs. "Spiders" stories, won the annual Hugo award for 1958—but stories like "Rump-Titty-Titty-Tum-TAH-Tee" and "A Deskful of Girls" once again upset and irritated more readers than they delighted. And "Little Old Miss MacBeth," by far the most advanced piece of symbolic writing Leiber had done, as well as his first really effective use of Shakespearean background, went almost unnoticed.

To what extent the financial and critical discouragement that accompanied each of his most fertile periods of literary growth were factors in the cyclical work stoppages is hard to determine: certainly, he never seemed to stop producing when his work was actively in demand; just as certainly, each time he would eventually outstrip the demand. And each time, there were other factors as well. Surveying the titles of 1957-1958, one thinks again of Poe, Fitzgerald, and the rest: "Damnation Morning," "Pipe Dream," "Tranquility or Else," "Try and Change the Past." Leiber, at this point, was literally fighting for his life. His job at *Science Digest* had ended in 1956, when alcoholism and blood-poisoning incapacitated him in the hospital. For the next three years, his production was erratic: it was something of a victory headline when *Fantastic*'s cover shouted LEIBER IS BACK! in November 1959, at the end of the last really silent spell he was to have. It marked the time of Leiber's highly specialized kind of "settling down."

The cycles of surge and discouragement did not stop there. But when the really new 1960 stories like "The Inner Circles" and "The Secret Songs" took too long to sell, he stopped writing—*that* kind of story—and did some continuity for the *Buck Rogers* comic strip. Or, when his 1964 novel, *The Wanderer*, took another Hugo but failed to pay for the time it took (again, no magazine sale), he accepted the novelization assignment for *Tarzan and the Valley of Gold* (the only Tarzan book ever authorized by the Burroughs family for publication under another byline). Last year, *A Specter Is Haunt-*

ing Texas sold immediately to *Galaxy*, but had trouble for some time finding book publication. (Book publication now pays more than serialization in most cases: book editors have become accordingly more cautious. But the Ballantine/Walker joint publication should, I think, finally be on sale by the time this article appears.) While *Specter* haunted the editorial offices, Leiber went back to Fafhrd and the Mouser, finishing off a third volume for paperback publication. And when "Gonna Roll the Bones," a gamble-with-the-Devil modern horror story (a Dangerous Vision straight out of the *Unknown* period), won SFWA's Nebula Award for the best novelette of 1967, he was spending most of his time on critical writing: reviews for *Fantastic*, and renewed work on what must by now be a monumental volume on *The Modern Fantasy Novel* (commissioned by the University of Southern Illinois Press).

One way and another, Leiber keeps sorting out the elements of his many "lives," using Shakespeare, sex, chess, science and the supernatural, politics and pacifism, alcohol, Hollywood, Academe, Church, Stage, and the publishing world, to cultivate his cunningly fashioned demons and daemons of the world of today, using them in new modes when he can, in old ones when he must. And in both veins, the young as well as the old continue to listen, with pleasure.

Some of the reasons why a man who will be sixty in the seventies communicates so clearly across the Gap to the youth-oriented audience of the sixties are clear by now. But the most important factor is not so much innovation as empathy. What journalists like to call the New Morality is nothing of the sort: it is the New Romance; and make no mistake, it is a new *kind* of romance, based on an altogether modern, hard-headed, hardwared interpretation of the age-old romantic creed: What man can dream, man can do!

But Romance it is. And that suits Fritz, and he suits it.

The Night of The Purple Cow, I said, we found space in the bathroom to talk about men's clothes. Those were grey days in America; but in that gleaming tile-white we dreamed up trunks and ballrooms full of swirling cloaks and cloth-of-metal, scarlet and gold, tunics and tights, swirlings and swords and plumes—not too different from what you might see, in parts and combinations, at either a high-style party or a light-show freak-out today.

At the freak-outs, they wear badges on the cloaks and cocked hats, and one of them says REALITY IS A CRUTCH. They do not mean to repudiate "reality"—only to acknowledge the concept as an aid, a prosthetic indeed, to sustain life in the search for truth. These New Romantics know that the crutch of "reality" is neither immutable nor divine, that today's "reality" was yesterday's "magic" as surely as tomorrow's is today's—or as yesterday's "reality" is today's "superstition." They simply lay claim to all levels of "reality" to use in the construction of their world in the same way that the engineers have learned to pick and choose among alternate scientific theories to select the most appropriate orientation for their day-to-day business of turning dreams into hardware.

Romantic Realism has been the essential message of science fiction, but few of its practitioners have understood it as Leiber has. Call him the Harlequin-Kierkegaard of the Flower People: a great deal of what they are came out of him. And remember that the Flower Children are soul brothers of Black-is-Beautiful.

In 1940, Leiber's story, "The Automatic Pistol," began:

"Inky Kozacs never let anyone but himself handle his automatic pistol, or even touch it. It was inky-black...."

And the last spoken line in it is: "Two aces, Inky's little gun didn't protect him, you know. He didn't have a chance to use it. Clubs and spades. Black bullets, I win." After which the black gun inside the black suitcase fires at Inky's murderer and kills him.

There has been much learned discussion recently (and especially in reference to Vietnam) about the American refusal to acknowledge death. Well, death has come home to us now, and our young people, at least, understand fully that we can only live with death by looking on its face and recognizing it. We cannot turn from this black face any more than from the twenty-odd million living black faces among us. Not any more. We can conquer our fear the same way we can conquer our guilt. Our young people know this, and Leiber learned it in 1942—when he went from *Conjure Wife* to *Gather, Darkness!*

Black is Beautiful—*too.*

The hero of *A Specter Is Haunting Texas* is an animated skeleton (literally) known as *El Muerte* to the people of Texas (a country extending from Alaska to Acapulco, and from the Pacific Black Republic to the Black Florida Whosit). He is in love with two women: the pale Lady Death, and an earthly vital brunette; in the end he refuses to leave either one behind. And the lining of his hooded black cloak is a brilliant scarlet.

Author Biography

Judith Merril was a twentieth-century science fiction writer, editor, and critic from New York and Toronto. Much of her fiction appeared in the 1950s and '60s. She edited the "Year's Best" series of anthologies from 1956-70 and served as the book review editor for *The Magazine of Fantasy and Science Fiction* from 1965-69. She also edited a number of collections, including the influential *England Swings SF* in 1968. Shortly thereafter, she left the US and relocated in Toronto, where she focused on social and political activism. In Toronto, she helped found Rochdale College, and she donated her book collection to the Toronto Public Library. Her "spaced out" library became the Merril Collection of Science Fiction, Speculation, and Fantasy.

Editor Biography

Ritch Calvin is an Assistant Professor of Women's and Gender Studies at SUNY Stony Brook, New York. His research is in the field of science fiction and gender. He has published articles and reviews in *Extrapolation*, *Utopian Studies*, *Femspec*, *Science Fiction Studies*, and *Americana* on topics such as Joanna Russ's *The Female Man*, chicana feminist aesthetics and identity, and Philip K. Dick. He is a former president of the Science Fiction Research Association (SFRA) and won its Mary Kay Bray Award in 2010. He was also the media reviews editor for the *SFRA Review* from 2008-2014. He is a co-editor of *SF 101: A Guide to Teaching and Studying Science Fiction* (2014).

Aqueduct Press Heirloom Books

It Walks in Beauty: Selected prose of Chandler Davis
by Chandler Davis
edited and with an Introduction by Josh Lukin

> This scholarly volume...explores the work of Chandler Davis, who refused to cooperate with 1950s McCarthyism and was dismissed from the University of Michigan faculty, academically blacklisted, and briefly imprisoned. As Lukin writes in his extensive introduction, Davis's writings "remind us that nothing and no one is as immutable as the dominant order would have us believe." Five stories...are accompanied by numerous essays, a speech, and a lengthy interview, all of significant interest to any fan of political SF.
>
> —*Publishers Weekly*

New Amazonia: A Foretaste of the Future,
by Elizabeth Burgoyne Corbett
with an Introduction by Alexis Lothian

> When Elizabeth Burgoyne Corbett sat down in the late 1880s to imagine a world 500 years hence, she can little have imagined that her words would be pored over in another century, on another continent, in a community gathered around the kinds of imaginative engagement with gender that she was pioneering. L. Timmel Duchamp has described feminist science fiction as a "great conversation"; Corbett's speculations about New Amazonia are part of that conversation's prehistory, a fictional contribution to political debates with which the writer was intensively engaged. The book ... is a piece of utopian fiction, but it is just as much a feminist rant—entertaining, educational, and more than a little over the top.
>
> —from the Introduction

Dorothea Dreams,
by Suzy McKee Charnas

> In vivid, pungent scenes from a range of viewpoints, spiced with just a hint of the fantastic, Charnas reveals the confusion and splendor of humanity.
>
> — *Locus*, 1986